THE
Adventurist

THE
Adventurist

J. Bradford Hipps

ST. MARTIN'S PRESS ☙ NEW YORK

THE ADVENTURIST. Copyright © 2016 by J. Bradford Hipps. All rights reserved. Printed in the United States of America. For information, address St. Martin's Press, 175 Fifth Avenue, New York, N.Y. 10010.

www.stmartins.com

Designed by Anna Gorovoy

The Library of Congress Cataloging-in-Publication Data is available upon request.

ISBN 978-1-250-06223-9 (hardcover)
ISBN 978-1-4668-6812-0 (e-book)

Our books may be purchased in bulk for promotional, educational, or business use. Please contact your local bookseller or the Macmillan Corporate and Premium Sales Department at 1-800-221-7945, extension 5442, or by e-mail at MacmillanSpecialMarkets@macmillan.com.

First Edition: April 2016

10 9 8 7 6 5 4 3 2 1

FOR LAURA

Businessmen are our only metaphysicians . . .

—WALKER PERCY, *The Moviegoer*

THE
Adventurist

One

1

More and more I have been thinking: What this country needs is war.

Don't misunderstand. I'm not pining for another foreign adventure. I mean an honest reckoning, here on our own pilgrim dirt. One of the company's Finance men is forever reading military journals and wringing his hands over the Chinese, a billion-strong infantry or something, cinches for any war of attrition, etc. Whenever I bump into him, I make it a point to hear him out. "Chuck," I might say, "worst-case scenario: no way the People's Army makes it past Nevada." "Oh ho. You just keep thinking that. Here's a tidy little fact for you. Last year Chinese defense spending more than tripled the previous five years' total . . ."—this while I slide into dread anticipation like a warm bath. Mind you, I'm not winding him up. I want to be convinced. The more an old saber rattler like Chuck frets, the more I think: Let them come.

Later I am always ashamed. War is torture chambers, and fathers killed in front of sons, homes burned while children scream from the attics—what is the matter with me? But just moments ago I caught in the rearview mirror a glare from my fellow citizen. It was a look of such opprobrium, such astonished offense (I changed lanes too abruptly), that I would have the nerve, the *gall* to interrupt even for a moment her progress in the world, and back I am to thinking, Yes: tank treads and the tromp of boots, here on our courteous soil. It is the only remedy.

At last the Cyber tower rounds into view and I forget all about my military fantasies. This is a place anyone would be glad to work. A thirty-story functionalist construction, our building stands demurely aside from the steel sails and ribbons of the last boom—to say nothing of those glass three-stage rockets that sprang up across the Sunbelt in the futurist eighties. Its apartness is literal: the building is quite clearly removed from the skyline's huddle of commercial A-space. However, the difference is not more than a few blocks. The downtown district is scarcely big enough to get lost in. It would take some real trying, anyway. No, I do not deceive myself that this is a sprawling capital city. Ours is a first-rate building in a not quite first-rate town. I'm not complaining. The city is all the better for it. I have traveled to so-called world capitals and found the inhabitants only too aware of themselves as such—that is, as movers in a world capital.

The lobby is a cavernous glass place with a red granite floor. A gigantic Christmas tree still looms in the atrium entrance. People stride for the elevators in a billow of coattails and trailing scarves. The morning light comes in like snowfall. I am especially brisk of step this morning. Earlier I received a call from my manager's assistant. A summons at that hour, and from her, could mean only some wonderful or terrible bit of news. Except she gave nothing away. Her voice was colorless:

"Keith would like a word this morning."

"Of course," said I, just as soberly. We bid each other good-bye in tones gone positively funereal. Anyone listening would think what serious business this is, to be subpoenaed by the boss. Only not really. Keith and I are friendly.

Off the elevators and into a waking office. The floor plan is like an open range: elevators in the center, offices at the perimeter, desks among low divider walls everywhere else. Our eighteenth-story perch is generously windowed. Beyond the warren of cubicles is a bright winter sky. Small clouds stand in the blue like flak burst. Sunlight ricochets off downtown glass and beams upward through the windows. People attend the blinds, their heads looming like *moai* statues on the white drop ceiling. Others shuck jackets, greet neighbors, lift phones, punch buttons. Computers pop to life. It is a good bunch. Whatever stories we tell ourselves, it's the one about the American work ethic that is observably true. A rare instance of treasured impression borne out by facts. Some of the most satisfying days I've known have occurred inside these walls. Just yesterday while searching my computer for a document, I came upon an old slide whose bold-boxed message read, *Relentless focus to reduce waste, improve quality, and increase customer satisfaction.* Its font colors were a kind of Mediterranean blue. I was cast back years ago to the moment of creation: hunched with my cohorts in a conference room on a midafternoon in summer, the sun in the blinds and the smell of carpet fibers and fresh paint. Four centered youths, our brains keen and college-minted, eager to be of use.

This regard for work surprises some. My sister, for example. In her mythology a corporate job is a necessary evil, to be tolerated only until a person finds what he was Meant To Do. I once felt the same. I landed a job with Cyber Systems straight out of college, and no sooner had the hiring manager handed me a security badge and shown me to my computer than was my radar wheeling around for a destiny. What changed my mind was love. Of money. I am only partly joking. There may be satisfactions like a thick wallet, but you need a thick wallet to have them. It's no good avowing one's regard for money, I know. You set yourself up as a satirical creature. And in fact money was not the only thing: also my destiny never resolved itself. There's no lack of good to be done in the world, and as soon as any noble thing presented itself, it was replaced by another. To pick one and run is fine if there is nothing else. But when a person has already obtained a kind of momentum—it didn't take long to see that acquiring a skill, linking arms with others to fix problems, fulfilling one's duties with aplomb, all toward a commercial end, is its own kind of nobility. The nobility of no pretensions. Gretchen, my sister, works in Minneapolis for a charity shop whose wares are made by indigenous peoples guaranteed a living wage. It is a good mission. I must say, however, that her co-nonprofiteers are a fairly self-satisfied bunch. One of them, a Young Werther in East German frames, once told me that although his work might barely feed him, it would always sustain him. When I mentioned this later to Gretchen, she wasn't surprised. My sister is perfectly clear-eyed. She allowed that if he of the politburo (I don't recall his name) occasionally gave himself to stirring performances, it was all "positively directed." She guessed that Cyber Systems must have a similar type: heroes who stayed late, worked weekends, sure of a hallowed cause. This was no hypothetical, of course. I explained, not for the first time, that as an industry, internet security software was as dear to me as it was to her: not at all. The day I hold forth on digital security at a dinner party is the day I quit. What moves me to work is money's comforts, yes, and also a community of smart, mostly efficient people; the sense of place that a good office gives. If this sounds mundane, so much the better. Gretchen, in a dear little-sister way (she is thirty to my thirty-four), won't accept that I feel no tug to heroism. And in a way she is right. Only my heroes are the mundane sort: good managers, homeowners, taxpayers.

Keith is on the phone, frowning. His office is a corner one. Windows for walls; the city hustles beyond. I am motioned into a chair. His desk is a polymer thing with a vast black surface shaped like an apostrophe. It is bare but for computer and telephone.

"That's not the point," he says.

And then: "Right. Barry—I understand the algebra."

Ah. Barry is my counterpart in Sales. Sales is under tremendous pressure at the moment. Last quarter was horrendous, and this one has started no better. The responsibility for this ultimately lies with Keith. He has been General Manager a short half year, promoted from elsewhere to take over from the previous GM, who was shown the plank. I should explain that here "General Manager" retains its meaning. Cyber has so far avoided the usual arms race over position titles, the sort that ushers in dozens of "Chief" officers to the executive suite. Here each business unit is appointed one GM, and one only. They are the Mayors of the Palace. It's true that Keith is answerable to an opaque tier of masters installed somewhere in far-off Dallas. But locally there is no higher power. At Cyber it is simple: there is the

General Manager, there are the Directors, charged with running the various departments (I am one; Barry is another), and there is everyone else.

"Listen to me," he says into the phone. "I get it. Going to bat for your team is what good managers do. But only to a point. Because at the end of the day, *you* own the number. And if this guy isn't getting it done—"

There comes a tinny volley of apologetics. Barry is nothing if not persistent. Keith plants a heavy elbow on the table, laying his ear to the receiver. He is tall, big-bellied, broad-shouldered, broad-faced; heavy. Against the broadness of his face, the lips stand out. They are Cupid's-bow-like, and oddly sensual. Then there is the gaze. Perhaps if you were to pass him in an airport or hotel bar, you'd notice little more than his ample frame and draping oxford shirt, the lank black hair attached to thinning part: one more Southern salesman nearly gone to seed in discount brokering or life insurance. But he is no Babbitt. There is the gaze, and it moves over the devices of the world, and it does not forget.

Now he is nodding testily. "Look," says Keith. "My rule? Never carry a salesman longer than his mother did. You're profitable in nine months, or you're out." The receiver goes back into its cradle.

"How's the weekend."

I report the weekend was fine.

"Yep." The irritation of their back-and-forth has carried over into the room; he is not really listening. "Mine I spent doing honeydew chores. Not you, I know. No honey to tell you what to do."

"The chores were here."

"And? How turn the wheels of Engineering?"

"The team made some good progress over the weekend."

"No thanks to their Director." An absentminded jab. Really he is absorbed in his monitor.

"I'm single-handedly keeping this place afloat."

Harmless banter, but immediately I see it is a stupid thing to say, the worst possible rejoinder in light of the last quarter. He looks up.

"Aha." His eye goes past my shoulder. The door. "Shut that, will you?"

Now comes the first inkling that all is not well. At the doorway his assistant shoots me a curious glance. There is time only to offer an apologetic smile before the light of the wider office is sealed off.

"So," Keith says. "We're only as good as our last quarter. That's the cold hell of business. Let's start there."

I wait. When nothing else comes: "Meaning right now we're not very good."

He nods. "And another one like it . . ."

"The market doesn't forgive." I surprise myself. The market. What do I know about the market. I have a team to feed and care for, software to design, code, test. The market I leave to economists.

"No," Keith says. "The market forgives just fine. Nothing's got a shorter memory than the market. It's our bosses we need to watch out for."

I am silent. Do I imagine it, or is there not an echo of threat in this? Although he may be thinking of Barry. Or perhaps he means pressure being exerted from Dallas on him himself. Having been brought in at no small expense to turn revenues around, and with last quarter failing to show any upward signs, the noose around his own neck may be going tight.

He is distracted again by email. The only sound is the rasp of mouse on desk, the quiet click of its buttons. He swears under his breath.

"Anyway. It's what we get paid for. If there were only good quarters and better quarters, no need for managers. Now's when we earn our keep."

Though I have known Keith only these past six months, already he is the finest boss I've ever had. He uses only "us" and "our" and "we." In the mouths of past supervisors, this team-speak always sounded mealy and euphemistic. Why not with him? I think it is because his sovereignty doesn't frighten him. The worst managers speak of "us" in hopes of finding refuge among the masses. It is a bid to wish away the responsibilities of hierarchy. Keith has no qualms about the hierarchy or his place in it. We work at his pleasure, and he does us the courtesy of not pretending otherwise.

"To that end," he goes on, "I need to be sure I've got the full attention, the commitment, of certain folks."

"I see." I see.

"You do."

"I think I do."

"Tell me."

"The business is shaky right now. You want to be sure managers aren't poking around at other opportunities."

"I want to be sure *you're* not poking around."

"I'm not."

"I've seen to it."

Keith digs into his computer bag on the floor and withdraws a sheet of paper. He gives the page a frowning once-over, then sends it hissing across the desk: CS SALARY ADJUSTMENT FORM. The contents take a moment to register. My current pay is indicated at top; at bottom, the figure plus twenty percent.

"I'm counting on you. What happens in the next ten weeks will define us for a long time to come. Believe it."

I am at a loss. He pushes from his desk and heaves around. I rise to meet him. We shake hands firmly and formally. Keith smiles down on me, and there comes a feeling like a pressed knuckle at my throat. Ye lovely saints above. The joy of money is sharp as grief.

I was born and raised in Minnesota, went to college in Virginia, and chose the South to live. A proven decision, I think, not least for the mercy of Southern winters. Today at noon it is sixty degrees in the sun. I sit on a park bench a few blocks from the office, marking time before lunch. It is an attractive place, nearly ten brick-paved acres. Where once leaned tenement houses now are benches and green bandstands, potted conifers and towering obelisks of galvanized steel cut in the shape of torches. In summer, jets of water erupt from blowholes in the plaza's brick floor while children frolic like mental patients among the geysers. The bricks themselves are stamped each with a name or short message. A few are engraved in memoriam. Today I found another: WILLIAM C. DAWES 1982–1985. It reminds me of a trip I made last fall to see a friend in Charleston. The visit itself was nothing to speak of; what I remember is the drive home. The roads of the low country are tricky things. They wind through realms of gray marshes and haunted forests, and after dark they become especially tricky. In plainer terms, I got lost. Doubling back, I caught something strange in the headlights. I stopped. The forest ran right along the shoulder of the road, a thick flanking of elephant ears and draping limbs, but here there was a gap. It worked as an entrance, a vestibule of a few trunks' depth beyond which was a small clearing, opened among the trees like a bedroom. It was after midnight; the forest was quiet. No: in fact it was a riot of croakings and chirrings, but these were a solid pattern upon which the smallest exception could be heard. The engine ticked in the heat. Fireflies bobbed and winked their green signals. Soon I could make out the purpose of this place. Laid in a row were five cocoon-like mounds of bleached seashells, each glowing dully among the ferns.

What is my point? In the American South, Death won't be ignored. Slavery and revolution have soaked its clays red. Everywhere one bumps into history, tragedy, and failure. Bandstands on gravestones, but no amount of happy theater will change the facts. This is the South's great comfort, although, surveying the park, I am reminded it may not last. Across the plaza, a crowd of red-hatted tourists are admiring the two-story television marquee on the side of the city's new convention center. Some strange cartoon is showing. The South's major cities have, by tract house and conference center, begun to except themselves from their soil's bony history. No nation ever had less use for a graveyard, and Dixie's mayors know it better than anyone. Conventioneers have no chance at business with Death wheezing on their necks.

"I'm sorry sir: no sleeping on the park benches."

"Hm—? Oh. Hullo Barry."

"'Hello Barry.' Now that's—jeez, that's a funeral greeting. Let's try again."

Barry and I have worked together, not closely, though not by any means at odds, for almost two years. He has a decent, open face and reddish hair that is always neatly barbered. Today he wears gold-rimmed spectacles. I know this to be his academic look, the one he chooses when he is to be called upon to speak with fluency to numbers, as he will later today.

"Come on, Eeyore!" he cries. He really is waiting for me to try my greeting again. "What? Tough weekend? No, couldn't be. No honeydews for this guy!"

"Right. No, it was—" A punishing fatigue takes hold. It is all I can do to finish the thought. "—fine."

The lenses catch the sun and change his eyes to shining discs. Below the discs is a ferocious smile. I begin to fidget. Barry is straight as an arrow but this smile is the smile of a successful pornographer. Some time ago I discovered that certain faces give rise to an urge to smash them. This urge has little to do with personality; it is a reaction to pure physiognomy. With Barry's, there is the slight poppet bulge to the ears, a particular wetness around the lips . . . Understand, I don't wish any actual violence on anyone, and certainly not on Barry. Barry aches with good intention. But if I could have a model of his face done in Plasticine or frosted onto a cake, then I would smash it and be satisfied.

I ask after his weekend.

"It was very good. *Very* good. Say, let's have lunch. Seems I never see you anymore."

"It's busy for you these days."

Some of the wattage drains from his grin. It would not surprise me to learn I've ruined his day. Barry is possessed of an unpredictable wax-and-wane energy. He is not alone in this tendency; others of our coworkers show it too. Its characteristic is manic efficiency one day, ruefulness and exasperation the next. Yet Barry is a special case. When his batteries are charged, he'll hurl himself from meeting to meeting, bullhorning hellos at coworkers. I've seen him startle client prospects with his crazed friendliness, cutting to them across the blue of office carpet, his trouser creases sharp as the prow of a destroyer, hand extended like a cannon. But of late, particularly as sales have proven hard to come by, it feels to me precarious, a kind of supererogatory sweating. Eagerness, not confidence.

"Busy's good," says he. By glancing at his watch and searching out some far-off point behind him, he makes it known the lunch invitation is withdrawn. I am meeting someone in any case. There is a moment of awkward silence. Having nowhere to go with our eyes, we consider a nearby group of men huddled around a chess table. I cannot quite make out the players in their midst except to say that one of them is white, which is unusual. From time to time a spectator will step away from the huddle and silently bite his fist or point skyward. Even from a distance the game makes me uneasy.

"See you at the Management meeting," says Barry. He strides off, I fear bad-temperedly. Except when he reaches the chess match, he stops and takes perch among the spectators. His manner among these men, the sole white in audience to a game whose stakes surely involve the most delicate matters of tribal pride, is easy as you please. He watches the players. Now he shakes his head in marvel, confides some amusing thing to his neighbor, and is on his way.

We sit close as conspirators at our little bistro table. Jane studies the yellow plaster walls stuck with poster ads for bullfights, the cigar smoke and kitchen's stewy smells. She tells me about a restaurant from her holiday, a brasserie in the 7th arrondissement. Knowing little of the language and in abject terror of French waiters, she pointed to the first thing on the menu.

"And do you know what I got? I got a big ole bowl of fried sardines. Heads, tails, eyes, everything. I guess you were supposed to munch them like fries, but I never found out." Here she falls back and sets her face in profile. She squints abashedly at nothing. "Go ahead and say it."

"Say what?"

"What a rube I am."

"You're no rube."

"No?"

"No."

"Tell it to my in-laws."

Jane Brodel works in Marketing. She is very good at her job as best I can gather, though I know nothing about marketing. She shares a

similar bafflement where engineering is concerned. This mutual ignorance permits a friendship that is innocent of the usual office angling. Also she is married. Another simplifier.

She raises the menu for study, clucking her tongue softly, absently.
There is a smear of blood on her teeth.

"Jane, your mouth. It's bleeding."

"What?" She touches her lips. "Lipstick I think." She runs her
tongue over her teeth. "Gone?"

"Oh. Yes."

She nods. "Blech. You're nice to worry."

The food is very good. Roasted whole chicken, yellow rice, and
caramelized plantains. Parisian café life has suited her: she orders a
glass of chardonnay. A plank of winter sunlight lies across the table
and heavily, warmly, in our laps. There is nothing on my schedule until
two o'clock. It is pleasant to sit in silence, to slip a little ways forward
in time and think of nothing. Dessert is a kind of corn cake with jam.
I watch as she tends the jar: a little brutish, this grasping and turning, all arms and elbows. I am reminded of her slightly male slovenliness, a kind of athletic carelessness in her posture and the use of her
limbs. Holding the jar to her middle (its lid is stuck), the placket of
her shirt opens to show more than is perhaps strictly decent. But
there is nothing shameless here. It is simply her absorption in the task
at hand, her obliviousness of the body's own effects. The lid pops. One
of her knuckles comes away bearing a small blood-colored gem. Into
her mouth it goes, the finger sucked clean.

She asks, "What did I miss?"

"It's been quiet."

"Not good."

"No," I admit.

"People are worried. You don't see it until you go away. I met
Penny coming up the elevator this morning and she looked just aw-
ful. Who helps her if things go south? Is she sitting on a nest egg?
What do you suppose she makes?"

"I don't know."

"Twenty-eight thousand, if she's lucky. In *America*."

"Plus benefits."

The warning sign is in her eyes. They are a very deep brown. When she is angry the color stirs, tightens into itself until the eye's gleam is turned impervious, wholly reflective.

"Super. Something else she can't afford to lose."

Clearly I once loved her. And I very nearly made an ass of myself saying so. As near as last summer I was sure the feeling was mutual. What subtexts of longing I parsed from her emails! The most throw-away lunchroom chat crackled with double meaning. Even to pass in the halls, the mere swap of nods as we went about our business felt like some sly tradecraft. But in the end I couldn't budge the hard evidence of her marriage, the professional context of our relationship.

It is not strictly true to say it was love at first sight. I came upon her in a break room, bent over double with her hair down around her face. She was holding her side.

"Ooh," she said.

"Are you all right?"

She stood up straight. The blood had gathered in her face. "No. But it's self-inflicted. I'm a nut for iced tea. This is probably a kidney stone." From the counter she lifted an enormous Styrofoam cup and pulled a mouthful of dark liquid through the straw.

"And that's—?"

"Iced tea." She stuck out a hand. "Jane. I'm new." There followed the normal preliminaries, schools and roles and previous employers, a précis of our corporate existences. "Which department are you?" I wondered.

"Marketing."

"Ah."

"Marlene's group."

"Yes. Do you know Marlene?"

"Only from interviews."

"You report to her?"

"Doesn't everyone in Marketing?"

"I mean directly."

"Yes."

I nodded. She narrowed her eyes. "What?"

"Nothing. She's good, very smart."

"But . . . ?"

I weighed it.

"She eats her own."

A kind of glee came over her face. It confirmed my hunch. Here was a direct person, with no time for the usual corn syrup.

"Does she now! Well, well . . . Good tip. I'll watch myself."

Her color had returned so that it was possible to see her face. It occurred to me that she was one of those people whom you could not describe as pretty but who were nevertheless unusually beautiful. Her mouth was large, it was immodest, and her ears stood out. There was a faint asymmetry in her gaze, the left eye pointed slightly up and away. But you could not miss the gameness, the pulse of human intelligence; it came off her like a red aura, and together with her long-limbed ease, her natural male slovenliness, it was enough. It was plenty.

Jane seems to be waiting. In light of Penny's concerns, she wants my verdict on the business.

"I'm not really worried," I tell her truthfully.

"Sure. You can afford it. We both can."

This is true, especially in her case. I happen to know Jane's in-laws are what my sister would call pig rich.

"I mean I have faith in Keith."

Jane thinks on this. "All right. You know him better." She thinks further. "And Barry. I *like* Barry. He's done some good things for us, right? Recently I know it's been not so easy, but . . ." She peers at me narrowly. "No?"

I mention our conversation in the park, my theory of his highs and lows.

"You're saying, what? Never get excited?"

"This swinging from mountaintop to valley and back again—"

"It's undignified." She is indulging me.

"Sometimes I feel like I'm watching *The Passion of Barry*. That's not a dig at his religion." Barry is quite a loud Christian. "I mean he needs to fall so he can rise again in glory."

"Ah. Better detachment. Phone in what you have to, disconnect from the rest."

"Not phone in, no. It's not a vote for laziness. You can work hard without thinking the sun goes up or down on your effort."

"He's unabashed, and it bothers you."

I say nothing. It was a mistake to bring it up. I am not even quite sure what I mean. Jane smiles, shakes her head.

"Henry Hurt: my dear, repressed friend."

We laugh together, but I am stung.

The Monday Management meeting. There are five of us, department heads each: Sales, Marketing, Engineering, Operations, Finance. There is also Keith. We report to him; it is his meeting. I am aware that nothing conjures the tedium of business so much as a weekly meeting. And it is true we deliver our reports in the most nickel-plated of monotones. The worst you can do here is to insist: we are authoritative by our very bloodlessness. Yet the truth is I crave these sessions. Here commercial necessities are turned to concrete actions, with measurements and owners and due dates, and there is no pall to speak of.

Barry is last to present. He concludes his report by saying he remains pleased with the pipeline. Keith flips the few pages of the sales report with a sour look.

"You're pleased with the pipeline," he says finally. The pipeline is a list of sales prospects and dollar values, along with the percentage chance of our winning the deal. "Well. I *am* pleased you're pleased."

Barry shakes his head and gives the table a vaudevillian look. "I know I've said this for a couple of weeks, but if some of these don't hit next week . . ." Some chuckle supportively. Keith does not.

"Then what?"

"Sorry?"

"If some of these don't hit next week, then what?"

"Well . . ."

"Then I should look for a new head of Sales?"

"Ha. Ah—no."

Keith waits, an ear cocked in Barry's direction. In these meetings the role of listener also carries with it certain affectations: eyes narrowed, legs crossed, pen to lips, the occasional nod or frown. The corporate world's skeptical punctuation. None of which applies to Keith. Keith doesn't go for affectation.

"I feel excellent about these, Keith. Maybe not the ones listed at twenty percent probability, but these sixty-and-above ones, hoo boy—"

"That's two. Two opportunities at sixty percent. What's your revenue target?"

"Right at fifteen—"

"For the quarter."

"Four."

"Four million dollars. What's the total value of these two? Assuming we get them both, which I most certainly am not."

"One million."

"One million? It's not even that much, friend. Not according to this. You've got seven hundred fifty here. Five hundred thousand for Markitel, two fifty for Delta. Any deal north of a million is still sitting in sub-twenty probability, which means we have what? Two, three quarters of coaxing ahead of us for any of those? Best case?"

Barry's phone buzzes in its holster. He consults it seriously, hopefully.

"OK," Keith says. "All right. Let's take these one at a time, focus on the birds in hand. Markitel. It's the biggest of the sixty percent probabilities. You see them this week?"

"Thursday," Barry affirms.

"Talk to us about the strategy."

Having pressed him, Keith will back off. It is important that Barry leave on a note of confidence. Buyers can smell panic on a salesman.

"Well, I've got a new contact there. My old guy was bumped."

"Uh-oh," says Keith, but not without sympathy.

"No, it might could work in our favor. The G-2 I have on this new guy is that he's pretty respected. He could probably move things quick."

"What do we know about him?"

"Not a ton. He's from inside, I know that. I don't have to reeducate him on who we are."

"Good. No lost ground. He's from inside the company? What group?"

"Ah . . . Engineering I think. Ninety percent sure."

"A tech guy. OK. Take Henry with you."

Barry nods energetically, as though he were about to propose just this. But what he says is, "Yes, although I'm thinking on this one, since I haven't met this guy myself yet, I fly solo. Build the relationship. Then bring in a heavy hitter like Henry." He means he doesn't want to share credit if the deal closes. I don't blame him. It's not my desire to go along in any case. Business travel no longer suits me.

An ominous glow comes into Keith's face. Through sheer professional will, he appears to consider Barry's plan. Then he says, "No. No time. We need to hit this guy with everything we've got, and this week."

"Agree one hundred percent. My only thing is, I don't want to scare the guy off. You know? He hasn't even met me, and all of sudden I'm up there with an army of folks—"

"Not an army. One other person. Our Director of Engineering, which shows how much we value his time. We're sparing two of our Directors."

"Yup. The *only* other thing—"

"Because our situation, Barry?" Keith interrupts, his temper slipping again. "Our situation is this. It's January twelfth. We have about ten weeks to get to four million." He catches himself, nods, addresses the table: "And we'll do it. No question. But we don't have a lot of room. Markitel's key. Barry's done a great job priming them"—here Barry studies his lap modestly—"and the deal's worth a half million. So we'd be a good ways along."

"And I think we'll nail it," Barry adds, though he is distracted again by his phone and is tapping away even as he says this. This is too much. Keith sets a careful hand on the table.

"Barry? Next week I want to hear what you *know*. What you have made *happen*. Not what you fucking *think*." He slaps shut his portfolio and is first out of the room.

There is a brief, even apologetic, clearing of throats. People rise and file out. Barry touches a hand to my sleeve. He shuts the door behind the last person, ducking his head to scan the terrain through the room's low porthole windows. Satisfied the hall is free of spies, he faces me.

"That guy . . ."

"Keith."

"Keith, yes. I mean, sometimes he gets to you, you know?"

"He'll catch twice as much hell when he delivers his report."

"Oh, I know, I know," Barry replies quickly. He is silent for a moment, nodding his agreement while pacing a tight circle. He's tucked his hands in the pockets of his trousers so that the thumbs remain exposed. It is an unnatural stance; he has to stiffen at the elbows to hold it: a lawyer delivering impassioned closing to skeptical jury. The poor bastard.

"He might have waited to make his point though."

"Exactly! That's exactly it! I'm not saying he's wrong. I'm on the hook here, no two ways about it. But in front of everyone else? That's what gets me. That's all I'm saying. And then you get dragged along, which I'm sorry about that." He wags his head and sighs. "It just makes you wonder, you know? This place? Whether it's all worth it?"

Ah, but already he is recovering. I know that sigh. In it is captured the entire American romance of moving forward, moving on, a job well done, or not well done, or not done at all, never mind, turn the page, a blank sheet, a fresh start, and *this* time . . . Yes, Barry is a true wax-and-waner. Whatever his dejection now, it will not last the week. Sunday morning will come again.

Driving home I am reminded how the South in January boasts her own chilly glory. Denied the magisterial furs of snow perhaps, but the city is thick with woods. Everywhere the branches are wet with frost melt. Caught in the slashing beams of commuter headlights, the bark shines like sealskin.

My neighborhood is an older one, blue and yellow Craftsman bungalows plunked in modest yards, their wide porches within easy hailing distance of the sidewalks. Fences are uncommon. But do not get the wrong idea. I bought my home three years ago for an excellent price, and there are still deals to be had. Despite its antique houses set neighborly cheek by jowl, my neighborhood is not bucolic. The place two doors from mine is wrapped in red plastic chili peppers, string lights that at night lend half the block a bordello glow. Atop its perilously hammocked roof is a decorative mob of Santa Clauses and Uncle Sams and Easter bunnies. These characters hold their posts all year, never properly inflated and so sagging knock-kneed or doubled at the waist, pitched over the rain troughs as if to retch their holiday guts. The owner has lived in the neighborhood thirty years. Shortly after I moved in I asked him about its history, this to indulge his veteran credentials. I expected the usual newspaper phrases about a community tumbled into disrepair and then reborn, etc., but instead it was explained to me that "the niggers swarmed in, shat everywhichwhere like they do, then skedaddled back over the tracks, praise Christ." He said he never once thought of selling. In fact there leans in his yard a sign, hand-lettered on a plywood sheet: NOT! 4 SALE. The normal reaction to such a neighbor is to resent his effect on property values. But I am glad to have him. He is all the proof I need that I live somewhere actual.

The dash registers an old familiar music. I know this song: it's the one about the rains down in Africa. A soaring chorus that practically begs to be howled along with. And thus howling and driving it happens: scene details snap together in the best possible confederacy, the workday's end and home within reach, a faded winter sky, the glossiness of Southern woods in winter, African rain . . .

The evening blooms in possibility.

Only a lousy thing happens. Glimpsing the rearview mirror, I find there a woman in exactly the same pose. Her face is locked in a grimace of rapture. A terrible likeness. She notices our duet before I can look away. At a traffic light, she pulls alongside and lowers her window. Despairing, I do the same.

"Toto fan?" She smiles, eyebrows hiked ironically. "Don't tell me: only when no one's looking, right?"

Often in even small conversations with strangers I can feel the heat of klieg lights, sense direction being listened for. This can't end well. Having caught each other singing, we are like performers made aware that an identical act is going on one grandstand over—a reminder that there is no audience, only stages, one performer each, each flouncing proudly to his own orchestra. What is left is to applaud our own gestures as weighty, original, and that is an absurdity I will die rather than join.

On a business trip to Manhattan months ago, I had lunch with a colleague at a small restaurant just off the park. He asked our waitress for a recommendation, and when she'd told him, he leaned over his corner of the table and said to her: "Well, if *you* recommend it, it *must* be good." It was mock suggestive, deliberately boorish. A joke on the businessmen who might actually behave this way toward young, pretty waitresses. And she got it. She laughed, blushed (knowing that even the joke-on-the-joke proceeded from real admiration), and said we'd be surprised how many of those types she gets. When she left, my colleague raised his menu and pretended to absorb himself, tongue pushed into cheek, his pleasure spelled out like a lunch special. Here we were, two men of means, alive and flying in sunny Manhattan.

"Henry," he said, still in faux boor character, "I've always had a way with the ladies."

But there'd been something in her face, a fatigue around the eyes, that made me too depressed to eat. What settled like ash was the thought that this joke-on-the-joke, and even the end joke on the joke-on-the-joke, had been said, done, billions of times already and was, at very nearly that moment, being said in the same smirking sardonic way in a thousand restaurants across the country.

I smile to the woman, nod, say nothing. The light turns, and she is gone.

2

Thursday morning, underground, waiting for the train to terminal B.

Markitel is headquartered in Minneapolis, which means time with my family. It is something of a relief. I no longer have any appetite for business travel. Although once upon a time it was everything my heart

desired—those sacrificial days of late alarms and flying taxis, charging down concourse halls, the tyranny of luggage adjustments and
great sighs of defeat at the check-in lines . . . And there was the cast
of handlers: drivers, concierges, flight attendants, waiters, each at the
beck and call of an expense account. Even our clients received me like
an honored guest, the software seer.

However. After a few years in planes and hotel rooms high over
strange cities, an unsettling thing began to happen. My importance
evaporated. In small measure this would have been no more than
expected, youth's solipsism yielding finally to facts. But this was no
small measure. It was total. I became a Stranger: rootless, anonymous,
another well-meaning face to be passed from cab to gate agent to door-
man to reception to temporary cubicle and on again when the job
was done. The nights turned paralyzing. I would awake to find myself shrouded in cold hotel sheets in rooms as dark as caves. Staring
into the black, I could see only the pure impossibility of being so much
as a pinhole in the wide world. In this blind, wide-eyed state, I began
to mistake myself. No longer Henry Hurt, tireless engineer and
beloved brother and son, but *mammal*—a biological happenstance
as meaningful and inspirited as the shrew. On my worst night, a
fog-bound horror show on the tenth floor of a San Francisco Hilton,
with the buzz of the ventilation system pouring into my head, I cried
out. No, not quite a cry. I wasn't raving. It was more of a *pip*, a quick
yelp to pierce the buzz and reassert myself in scene: a businessman
in a fine hotel in a fine city who was having trouble sleeping.

And yet in the morning, showered and caffeinated and looking at
a day of binary computer riddles, the previous night would be revealed
as so much silliness. Hadn't I read somewhere this affliction was the
price of modern living, our streaming, borderless, disaggregated whatnot? And sure enough, the moment I was back on turf where I had
history, I slept like a lamb.

Barry is seated at the departure gate, nodding into his phone by
way of finishing. Spying me, he comes leaping over, grinning and popping his fingers.

"That was my guy at Delta. He's ready to ink the contract. Next week. I can feel it!" He hunches and brings up his fists, swaying in the manner of a prizefighter. I am delivered a roundhouse tap on the biceps. "Look out! I'm back!" Nearby passengers watch with amusement. I give Barry his due. Sometimes his buoyancy is contagious.

"Say . . ." He is still swaying, alternating slow motion taps to my biceps. "That little powwow in the conference room. That's just between us girls, right?" He squints and bites his lips together in mock effort. *Tap.*

"What powwow?"

He grins. *Tap. Tap.* "I appreciate it, amigo."

The call comes for first class. Barry winks and disappears into the gangway. Only then do I realize what he's talking about.

The sales call is a disaster from top to bottom. For starters, there is the weather. A warm front has heaved north from the Gulf and rolled the landscape under fathoms of advection fog. In the gloom we miss an exit and carry on for a full twenty minutes before realizing our mistake. When finally we arrive at the Markitel offices, Barry is in a state. He leaps from the rental car and is nearly across the parking lot before remembering his portfolio. I wait by the entrance. The building is part of a newly tilled office park near the Mall of America. A long, two-story brick affair, its architecture is as square and utilitarian as boxcars. There is little to inspire in these office parks, yet the companies they house are usually as stolid and profitable as banks, sponges for every bit of available local talent and run by top graduates of the state's best public university. Some of the most frank, rooted people I've met, people who've never in their lives coveted a more epic context, go gladly to work each day in these anonymous pillboxes. I envy them.

Barry returns with portfolio. He is wired, even by his own electric standard. "Let's hit it!"

Our contact is waiting at the security desk. His wide face burns with cheeriness. "You're the Cyber guys?" He extends a hand. "Mike Cottrell. I'm the new sheriff, I guess."

Barry clasps his arm and snaps it like a well pump. "Glad to put a face to the name! This is my associate Henry. He directs our Engineering group. We brought all the big guns!"

Mike is perhaps forty. He carries a sort of pregnant girth in his belt, slung over a pair of creaseless trousers. His loafers are stained with road salt. I am tempted to read in this mild sloppiness a genial spirit—but there is a beady-eyedness that puts me on my guard.

"Mike, I'm sorry about the time," Barry says. "The usual travel hiccups I'm afraid."

Our host lets drop my hand and turns to face Barry directly. His movements are oddly sedate.

"Hard stop at eleven."

"Oh. I thought . . . Could've sworn we booked through lunch."

"Eleven." His tone is mild, even benevolent. "You guys were any later I would've canceled."

We follow Mike to a conference room on the second floor. It is a narrow, hall-like chamber, featureless but for a bank of slatted windows. The carpet is gray. An immense oval table commands the floor. This is a room built to vet vendors, I know; solemnity is its point. But someone has made a mistake. The screws have been turned a little too tight. With its mass slab table and grim colors, its narrow dimensions and hyperbaric air, the seriousness of the room is in danger of turning over on itself. It is very nearly hilarious.

Four other men are clustered at one end. Each is introduced somberly as one kind of specialist or another. When we are acquainted and seated, Mike nods to Barry. Barry hops from his seat to begin.

"My apologies all around for the delay. We'll get straight in because I know our time's limited. Can we skip all the song-and-dance on Cyber's background and standing as a company? Everyone's nodding yes. All right. So. We'll start with the technical portion, my colleague Henry's portion. We can circle back for any more general questions. So, I'll just dim the lights . . . and the switch is . . . where? Here! Yes. Henry?"

It is a part of the job. A day out to help Sales make pitches of a certain type, often to large, cynical prospects who want to see and hear from the person whose team will make sure the software behaves.

And once the oddness of arrival and introduction is passed, I find it's a job I can do. I like to explain our technologies. Even the idioms of our science appeal to me. Wedding cakes. Fish bones. Bit rot. And usually among other engineers I'll encounter a shared interest—an appreciation, at the least—for the decisions we've made, for the strategies we studied and rejected, and the reasons for their dismissal.

Only today what I find is silence. Mike studies the table. The others regard my slides with the waxen look of actors feigning death. I can see nothing to do but press on. Barry, however, is itchy. After several slides he begins to hear interjections in every cleared throat.

"Mark, you had a question?"

Our host looks up from the table. There is a moment's confusion. He folds his arms and squints at Barry.

"Are you speaking to me?"

"Yes."

"*Mike.*"

"Mike—forgive me. You had a question?"

"No."

"I thought you looked like you did."

"You'll know if I have a question."

"Of course."

The best sales pitch I ever heard about was made by a Cyber competitor. It was told to me by the salesman himself, whom I met one evening at a conference in Washington. He told me about a sale he'd once made to the Central Intelligence Agency, as jaded and bored an audience as you could ever hope to find—there is nothing but nothing a mere salesman could tell the CIA about security—but who became suddenly inclined to buy when it was revealed that the salesman's analyst, pounding away on a keyboard at the back of the room, had contrived to deface the agency website in the time it took to pass around the coffee. (THE WORK OF A NATION. THE CENTER OF INTULLIGENCE.) But here there are only mannequin faces in the gloom. The minutes drip. When I am finished, Barry stands and raises the lights. He smacks his hands together, rubbing them and making a slight bow to our host. Mike remains as he has throughout, absorbed by the area of table before him.

"So, *Mark*," Barry prompts. "Now what are your questions?"

We are lost.

This emphasis on name is meant to show he's taken special care to get it right. Except because he has fumbled the name again, the effect is opposite. It seems he's making some bizarre point of defiance. Mike says nothing. He stares at the table, his arms crossed heavily over belly. A forelock of hair drops onto his eyebrow. He smooths it into place with his ring and pinky fingers. The gesture is ominously dainty, bottled.

Barry sees his mistake. "*Mike!* Mike! What is wrong with me today?"

Our host picks microscopic lint from his trousers. "I don't know. What *is* wrong with you today?" The question is posed offhandedly, almost kindly. It is possible to imagine he's as curious in the answer as Barry.

"It's the cold!" Barry cries. "Us Southerners don't do well in the snow. Our brains freeze—"

Mike leaps from his chair and thrusts out a hand. "I want to thank you." He is grinning, shaking Barry's arm. "A revealing presentation. Guys? Am I wrong?"

His team swaps private glances. Mike calls to one of them: "Tom! What was your favorite part?"

Silence.

Mike leers at the group. His eyes pop with good-willed expectancy. One of the men clears his throat.

"Tim, I think you mean."

"Tim! Yes!" He throws back his head in marvel. "How stupid of me! Goddamn brainless. You're critical to our business here, so to not get your name right . . . I feel like a turd." Tim smiles uncomfortably. Mike paces to the window. There he stands, nodding, tapping his lip. "I wouldn't be surprised, Tim, if you wanted to walk right out of here, never talk to me again. Wouldn't blame you a bit. Quality in everything, that's what we preach. So the least you'd expect is that I could remember your name. No?"

"Yes."

"Absolutely right."

He turns to Barry, whose face has gone bland and waxy.

"Safe travels, friend."

In the stairwell, Barry pulls off his spectacles and digs at his eyes with thumb and forefinger. Really his face has never looked more fiercely smashable.

"Barry, the man is certifiable. Forget it."

"No." Barry replaces his frames, blinking at me through glass. "We don't talk about customers that way."

So this is how he will have it. His dignity will be restored by lesson giving. As engineer I misunderstand the dynamics of selling. It falls to him to show how the licking just received is in fact small sacrifice for fealty to the high cause of customer service. It's no small alchemy, to turn a humiliating episode into a business lesson, with Barry as a master of subtleties that my poor nuts-and-bolts brain has missed. Having been condescended to, Barry would condescend. And if I were a bigger person, I might allow him his pose of sensei, might sit as apprentice while Barry lectures himself back to level. A smart thing where Cyber is concerned, because a salesman with doubts is like a prostitute with inhibitions. Only—

"Getting their names wrong. That's how we speak about our customers."

He glares. "By the way? Thanks for the assist. Really tremendous. Just sit there while I get"—even when he's angry, cursing comes hard to Barry—"screwed up the rear. Big help. Your problem, Henry, if you want to know, is you always think discretion is the better part of valor."

Nothing useful can come of this. When at last we part company, I am glad to be rid of him.

3

The fog has cleared. Revealed is the north state I remember, a land that in January is bright and cold as the moon. It's cold all right. Outside is the razor edge of ancient winter. The barest sliver of open flesh and *sffit!*—right down to the bone. But in here all is well. The Pontiac's heater roars like a firebox.

Before me is the family house. Idling at the curb, I consider it. A
boxed two-story of white aluminum siding and black shutters with
a single chimney, a style of dwelling as fundamental to suburban
Minnesota, and maybe the entire Middle West, as sod homes were to
the prairie. No one is expecting me. I was home only a few weeks ago
for Christmas and a return so soon is not such a big deal. It is my idea
that I would make a kind of drop-in surprise. Except now I am not so
sure. For one thing there is the matter of the foyer. The foyer alone is
enough to defeat reentry. There one is set upon immediately and without warning by the ancient smells, of firewood, of dog fur, the very
smells of a childhood yet closeted away in the secret dusty places of
the house. On the road I nearly drowned in anonymity, but in there
history pads the rooms like satin in a coffin. The closet shelf in my
old bedroom is lined with hockey trophies. On a lone hanger is a purple high school letter jacket. Propped on various surfaces are pictures
of a boy named Henry. He stands in a wading pool with his toddler's
potbelly; he waves from a tree branch; he smiles competently from
under his mortarboard. Too much history, too much affection for one's
own history, is also a possibility I think. There cannot be any charge
toward the future. Nostalgia cloys; it gums the gears. Who knows,
maybe it can even kill you.

It is as quiet as any winter night. Up and down the street the lawns
smolder. Their smooth white capes emit a purple radiation in the dark.
At last I shut the ignition and climb the driveway. Too much red meat
for a psychologist, to come this far without going in. My sister answers
the door.

"HH!"

We exchange a hug across the threshold. "What on earth? My God!
Come in, come in!" Past her shoulder at the end of the front hall, I
can see an edge of the kitchen cabinetry where our mother painted
roosting hens and nests of hay, all of it in country-French style. In the
evenings I used to study right there at that table. When the math assignments turned surreal, which was always (a train leaves an inscru-
tably named station with its windows open; if the amplitude of cricket
song something something but *not less than* the velocity of the first
apple, how far is it to the moon?), I would reduce myself and burrow

into the sweet-smelling hay and lie down with the eggs. Fare thee well, ye variables and sines and cosines! I am off to the chicken coop, whose x/y coordinates you don't have a chance in hell of solving. Only the scene's painter knew where and how to retrieve her son—but enough.

We stand apart now, Gretchen and I, inspecting each other in our overt fashion. She is white-blond. Not unusual in these parts, but exotic to the Hurt bloodline. Once there was a time when she renounced her blondness; in college her hair was black with violet streaks. But it has been its old color now for years, and for years worn like this, in cropped layers at the neck and with the front lengths tucked behind an ear. Under the chained light of the foyer her face is full of shadows. She tugs and wraps the corner ends of her long blue cardigan around her middle, holding them at her waist with arms crossed. Actually she holds together the ends and the waistband of her flannel pajama bottoms, which is soft and stretched and in danger of giving up the ghost. She is very good looking, my sister. Blond and hazel-irised and finely drawn. But tonight with these coal shadows around eye and cheek, the bedtime attire pinned up about her thin body by her hands, she looks a little postoperative.

"You look good," I tell her. "Thin, maybe."

"Makes one of us."

"The spoils of commerce. In fact I picked up a raise this week."

"Sickening."

"The more to spend at the Village."

"Right answer."

The Village is where Gretchen works. We have an arrangement, she and I, that whenever I am in town I will shop generously there. It pleases me to support my sister's work, and it pleases her to have that income go to good mission—and also, I believe, to have an older brother with the means to spend.

"Where's Dad?"

She puts a finger to her lips. "Asleep."

"With this racket?" The voice comes from the dark at the top of the stairs. He makes his way down, the light of the foyer rising on him as he comes: slippered feet, white shins, green tartan robe. The musculature of his long pilgrim face is drawn and droopy; he was deep under, but his mind is awake. "What ho! What brings you to town?" I explain the circumstances of the visit. At the mention of a customer meeting, he is keen for status. "And?"

"Not so hot."

My father is consoling. "You folks will figure it out. Those are some sharp minds you're working with." A retired schoolteacher himself, my father has an abiding respect for the machinery of enterprise. More than once have I been assured that a good businessman has "a brain like a saw blade." (True, where Keith is concerned. Barry's must be nearer an eggbeater.) He nods, settling the matter. "As long as they're not counting on you. That would really spell disaster." This is of a piece with the ancient paternal ribbing, but he speaks with such grave deadpan that it is hard not to laugh. Now he pockets his hands, not yet fully descended but stalled on the third step and of two minds, whether to join the bright land below or return to the night country above. At seventy-three, he does not look to me as old as he is. He is clear of eye and straight of spine, and his hair is thick and white. He might easily pass for the ageless New England stalwart, a Unitarian minister perhaps, though our stock is Scotch-Irish and our brand lapsed Presbyterianism.

I become aware of the silence. Not awkwardness, quite. More a new family habit of testing the air, the three of us parsing what is to be spoken of when; where, emotionally speaking, to next place our feet.

At last he says:

"Are you with us for the weekend?"

"Afraid so."

"You're not going to spend it talking technology, are you?"

"I'm glad you asked. I hoped we could speak about the challenges caching introduces to password management."

He yawns, shaking his head. Family footing reestablished, he is free to return to sleep. "I'll leave this one with you, Gretchen."

We fall in at the kitchen table. Beyond the foyer and the kitchen, the house is dark.

"Early nights for the Hurts," I observe.

"Winter hibernation. There's no other way through."

"How're things at work?"

She considers it. "You know, it's good. We found some crafts-people in Kenya who make the most beautiful carved giraffes, Masai giraffes, about this big. They're made of jacaranda wood, which is fast growing, very sustainable. And they paint them in the most extraordinary sort of berry red . . ." My sister trails off in mild reverie. She is not lost in her own do-goodism. Rather it is the beauty of the objects. To wander the shelves where she works is to be struck by sheer human ingenuity, found materials shaped into essential forms by hands that know. Software has its own symmetries, but software doesn't root you in the world in the way of simple, well-made things. In this atoms are superior to bits, I admit it. Although the pay is garbage.

"What about you?" she wants to know. "How's Cyber? You said it wasn't a good day?"

"No."

"And today was important?"

"It's all important these days. Jesus, our head of Sales. Everything that happens, good or bad, hits this guy right in the chest."

"He's alive, sounds like."

"Yes, well, the business counts on him being able to put aside his feelings from time to time and actually sell something." My sister is nobody's fool and I love her, but sometimes her instinct for the soft focus is too much. "I don't pretend to be a salesman, but you've got to be able to read people without being read yourself. Keith compares it to a relief pitcher—"

"Ugh. Is Keith big on sports metaphors? That's how I picture your world. Everyone talking about touchdowns and slam dunks. Or, I don't know, *paradigms.*"

This is not a tangent that interests me. To say business-speak is shot through with cliché is itself a cliché. And besides, I trust our clichés. They're dead, and everyone, or nearly everyone, knows it. To use them is a sort of code of modesty, a signal that none of us have figured it out on our own.

When I mention this to her, Gretchen is dubious.

"Seems like it'd be the opposite. A lot of making the obvious sound profound."

"No. The clichés come with a wink. It's a shorthand. Our clichés say that everything there is to say has been said already."

She says nothing, only traces the grain of the table with a thumb.

"This is all generally speaking, of course. Some people use the clichés earnestly, but they're understood to be ridiculous."

Nothing.

"There at the Village, you've thrown off the shackles of cliché."

"Somehow I don't think there's the same need to make a lot of guessing sound like science."

"It must be wonderful."

She puts her arms straight out on the table and lets go a long whispering sigh in which the only audible phrase is "robotic and god-awful."

A pause, lest things escalate. Not twenty minutes in and ready to lock horns. It's a foreign state for us, historically speaking. For most of our lives we've been especially close. In fact our mother used to complain about it, this in her put-upon and faux fatalistic way, a conveyance purely of tone that said her loving rule had produced only conspirators against it, and the monarch who expected different was kidding herself. But of course it pleased her. It pleased us too. Not just to be so bonded, but to have adults marvel at the privilege. Our closeness became something of a watchword around the neighborhood. Say anything enough and lo, you make it true. Recently, however, I've noticed our talks have begun to labor under the old superlative. We might be speaking of everyday things in the everyday manner, and one of us—or more often both—will be seized by worry that here finally is the conversation that sounds the depth of our partnership. We never name this trouble, of course. It is marked by a grasping that intrudes upon the talk, a fumbling for the confessional. "God, I wouldn't tell this to anyone else," she will say, before turning our idle chat about some movie into a revelation: she connects more deeply with *certain films* than with *most people.* Or perhaps in the course of talking about not much, I will theorize that an unmarried man feels whole only because *he doesn't see the half he's missing.* I know. But to our ears it's the way near-dear people are to speak. And although I'm as eager as she to pretend solidarity when the real thing isn't forthcoming, it is a slippery slope. Petty arguments I can manage, but the bigger worry is that we are becoming like everyone else: one more pair of happy fakers.

Even now the worry presents itself. Neither of us will resort to cheeriness or small talk, it would be too horrible a proof, and so the silence prevails. The small sounds of the house are not so small. Each drip from kitchen faucet hits the basin's enamel with a plashy *pap*. Heated air murmurs in the ducts. But when I hitch my chair to fetch a drink, the shriek of the linoleum spooks the other noises to silence.

"Where's the whiskey?" The cupboards above the stove reliably hold a bottle of rye. Tonight I can find only cooking sherry.

"Gone," says she, without further comment.

The sherry is not much for taste, but the esophageal burn is a comfort. I take my seat. We settle ourselves, two people perfectly at ease and not at all oppressed by the silence.

Pap goes the sink.

"Do you remember the Deep Devil?" she wonders.

"I haven't thought of that in years."

"You used to scare the hell out of me with that."

"I scared myself."

"How did it go again?"

"Let's see . . . It started with the old chandelier in the living room."

"Hardly a chandelier."

"Whatever you call it. A hanging light with arms. It was kind of a spidery little thing with brass arms, and plastic candlesticks with flame bulbs."

"And there were heavy curtains on the front window then so you could black out the room."

"Yes, right. And I'd turn down the rheostat to the barest current, so the filaments in the bulbs were only just glowing—"

Gretchen shakes her head. "First you'd say, 'He's coming!'"

"Did I?"

"Yes. Oh my God, the fright."

"All right, yes. Because the trick was to hide. You had to be hidden before the rheostat got down to where you couldn't even see the flame bulbs, only the red of the filaments . . ."

"Yes. Yes! And they made a kind of satanic circle, these strange wormy things just floating together. I don't know why but it was awful, how small they were. Like evil little spirochetes buzzing over your head. Also, I remember they made a dark orange stain on the ceiling. It was a popcorn ceiling, and in the stain it looked like old skin. Ugh . . ." She reaches for the glass. "That's when I first understood what the word 'nightmare' meant."

Gretchen touches a hand to her breastbone as she drinks, a kind of ward for the naked vulnerability of her throat. I feel toward her a very old tenderness. The Deep Devil. Who else knows this about her, about me? No one. Not another soul on earth. Even now she smiles. Between us there are no bad memories, not really. Never are we closer than when we revivify time like this.

"Do you remember at bedtime—"

"I was just thinking of that!" she cries. "Mom's game with the lights?"

"She'd call bedtime, and start snapping off the lights behind us as we raced upstairs, and if we weren't in our beds . . ."

"Yes, but that was a much safer affair. She never once let us get caught in the dark."

"True."

We take a moment, remembering, nodding professionally. The small sounds of the house come up around us. She gives me a look reserved for such times as these, when the wing shadow of grief passes over and we become aware of ourselves as Somber Survivors. It is not quite a year since our mother died. Leukemia. A bolt from the clear blue. She was ten years younger than our father and on track to outlast us all. Gretchen moved home to help with our mother's care; she has remained here since. There is nothing more to say about it.

Yet here we sit, and the pressure is on to Say Something. Whatever is said, it must be something that pierces to the heart of things. Yes. The trouble is that my mind is blank. She too struggles for it. Together we are practically sweating. Dear God, if ever a brother and sister were to affirm their bond, now would be the time . . .

Pap.

On Friday my sister goes to work and so do I. For me it goes poorly. Seated at my childhood desk with laptop open and the glow of email before me, I feel the mockery of time. The old spindle-legged chair is for a schoolboy, and in it the wide bottom of an adult feels obscene. Even as I type

> without a better measure of our accumulated technical debt, we cannot make a case for code refactoring

there is a strong sense of playing dress-up.

Lunch is a solitary affair. I have come down late, and my father is a committed taker of afternoon naps. (Also he is careful to leave his working son wide berth. All morning I have been aware of his method for going by the bedroom door: softly, almost on tiptoe, so not to interrupt commercial genius at work.) Outside is a low ceiling of winter cloud. The day pours down its gray light. Something is still not right. I notice it again in the act of chewing, which becomes labored because it is absurd. This dead-eyed jaw rolling, like a beast of the field. At once I am aware of the need to act naturally. Put down the sandwich, wipe your chin. The audience must be reassured! But—it is no small matter, acting naturally. What does the normal person do next? It comes to me: he moves on to the living room, and there selects an issue of *The Economist* from the coffee table. Yes. He settles into the couch, legs crossed and fingers propped on temple, etc.

The house is silent. The news of the world is old: checking the magazine's publication date, I discover it is from last year. The others too. Even the *TV Guide* is from before Christmas. On its cover a handsome actor I do not recognize gives a frozen cry of pleasure. A girl in a green velvet dress and white stockings is fitting his head with a band of reindeer antlers. The gray afternoon light is in the wide front window. It lies on the glossy covers. The images blanch, their old eagerness sepulchered in a fine layer of dust.

It is somehow unspeakable.

There is no telling what comes next. Then it is here: an episode from last summer. One night while flipping television channels before bed, I happened on a scene from an old film. A man stood in the doorway of a parlor, fedora in hand, fingering its brim nervously. An old woman in a shirtwaist dress and lace apron invited him to sit, then disappeared. The man looked around the room. His eyes settled on something. The camera cut to a staring black Chihuahua. A phonographic score, lilting and scratchy, played just beneath the surface of the scene. The dog darted; the camera cut back to the man with the animal now bouncing on hind legs around his knees and yelping. On the stairs, the old woman reappeared with a pretty young woman. They beheld the man's plight, then turned to each other and smiled. The man looked up sheepishly, holding off the dog with his hat. The final shot was a close-up of the Chihuahua perched in the younger woman's lap and eyeing the camera bulbously. I turned off the television and went to bed. It was then that something began to trouble me. The dog was dead. *Dead as a doornail.* The antique phrase ran on a loop. And yet here was the creature, fixed in monochrome, to be re-presented endlessly in its antic prancing, fateless and unaware.

Now, as then, a dim anxiety rises. There is an old trick of sound. Tiny noises are put right up against and made painful in the ears.

Concentrate on other things.

But what?

The heart beats its answer: An-y-thing, an-y-thing, any-old-thing.

When I was young and did not have a name for it, I called it boredom. It is not boredom. To watch on television a whispered round of golf, knowing that there is nothing in the fridge for lunch: that is boredom. But to sit on a childhood couch and wait in the gray afternoon while motes of fur from dogs long dead, the dust of trodden carpet, and smells of ancient dinners swirl the room like spirits—that is to feel the pall. It is a far more complex and desperate thing. Boredom's solutions are easy because boredom is no match for the immediate. But the pall is not so easily thwarted. When it settles, the body is irreversibly diminished. You become a speck of sand in the howling Sahara. Distractions of the sort that work against boredom only reinforce this sense. No, what comes is the need to be recentered in the world. And what follows, if a person lets it, is the imagining of great deeds. This is the danger. You make for yourself a mission, a struggle. The pall may be natural, even inevitable, but it is not innocent. The trick is to accept one's minor plot without despair, or the invention of grander narratives.

The remedy is obvious: to the laptop. Metaphysical dislocation is no match for a to-do list. Upstairs again and seated at the desk I feel stirrings of relief. When I open the machine, there comes the familiar glow. I wait for the pall to lift.

Only today it doesn't work. I don't know why. The light of afternoon is no different from the computer's screen. A few uncomprehending minutes and I am on the bed, rigid as the dead, heart thumping like a wound.

"Catatonic," my father pronounces with a yawn, coming into the living room. "Out like a light." He consults the bookshelf clock. It is after five. He shakes his head, then is distracted by one of the spines. "Know this one?" He draws out the book and holds it up: *Eastern Approaches*.

"No."

He is glad for the chance to explain it. There follow several minutes of description and keen judgment both. It is stoked by his capacity for recall, the canonical antecedents right at his fingertips: a knack for memory and catalog such as only the self-educated possess. When he was seventeen his own father contracted tuberculosis and was sent away to a sanatorium, so my father dropped out of school to support his mother and sister. His aborted education made him a fiend for generalized knowledge. He tutored himself in the classical, liberal, self-made sense, a program of encyclopedias and Great Books and primary sources. Even today there remains something a little Rosicrucian in his fervor for self-taught revelation. Except that my father has no use whatever for secret societies or everything-is-connected symmetries—nor, for that matter, God Himself. Luckily, among the public schools there was no prejudice toward a noncredentialed expert. In fact he was a board favorite, able to fill for every subject but the foreign languages. Upon his retirement he was presented with a medallion embossed with the Vitruvian man. Each of the circle positions touched by the figure bears the name of a subject taught by my father. It pleased him very much.

". . . I mean the only doggone thing Byron has on this guy is that he swam the Hellespont!" He pauses, watching me. "Anyone home?"

I am still reeling a little from the afternoon. He comes to the wing chair and puts a hand on my head. A testing squeeze. "Thinking great thoughts. My God. Just feel the heat." I have to smile. Long has my father accorded deep thinking to these fugue states. His hand remains, testing. The pall recedes.

"I know what . . ." He disappears into the kitchen. There is the knocking of cabinet doors. After a moment the noise stops. "That's strange. The whiskey seems to have wandered off."

"Yes. I noticed."

"I wonder if Gretchen knows something about it."

"Why? Have you been doing the Irish proud?"

Ha-ha, says he, not quite answering. "She can be an aggressive minder, your sister."

This is true. My sister is a born caregiver. She is drawn, moth to flame, to the damaged, the confused, the rib-kicked, the well-meaning but self-sabotaging. And while she is a born caregiver, under no circumstance will she be cared for. She's left cold the men who failed to understand this.

My father returns with the sherry bottle and two glasses. "Best we can do." He has an idea and goes into the kitchen again, there fetching a lemon and the red-handled peeler. Perched on the couch's edge, he hunches over with the peeler braced in his spotted hands. He turns the fruit under the blade, and off comes a waxen yellow coil, one for each glass. When we have fortified ourselves a little, he says, "How are you getting on?"

"Fine. Business could be better, but I'm confident—"

"I meant in matters regarding your mother."

"Oh."

It is a curious circumlocution. Usually on this subject he is never less than precise. No quaint constructions for him. She has not passed on; she did not leave us. She is dead.

I tell him I am managing. "You?"

"It's difficult. I can't say whether better or worse." Now he sets down his glass, clapping hands to knees. The casualness of it means:

on to trivial matters. "Tell you what. I've got to get the blood flowing again. The firewood bin's empty . . ."

A half cord is arranged against the gardener's shed in the trees behind the house. The moonlight makes things mysterious. The tree line is very dark. No more than a stand of pine and maple, but there is about it a proximate, slightly minatory presence. My father pays no mind to any of this, of course. He is enjoying this march across the property. He thrusts along like a general; I must scramble to keep up.

"Why not just move the firewood against the house?" say I, panting.

"Not on your life. A woodpile's a hotel for mice."

Yes, but also it pleases him to be tested by heavy cold and hard labor. In profile he is a portrait of Midwestern resolve: ear tucked in wool watch cap, eye sharp to the task, straight Hurt nose steaming like a freight.

At the shed he instructs, "Crook your arms. I'll load you up." He selects the pieces two at a time, drawing them slowly from beneath the blue plastic tarp so as not to buck its roof of snow. He claps the wood, then sets the pieces across my arms. At the house the storm door looks to swing open of its own accord: Gretchen, home from work. "Brr," says she, holding off the door. The stack hits the bin with coppery, clanging thunder. My father is close behind, red-faced, a pile hooked under one arm and a single piece in the other.

Out again. The snow squeaks like Styrofoam underfoot. Not the crunching sound of milder temperatures, but an actual squeal. How well I remember this setting, our walking measurements of the property and the world. Although never in this cold. Always it was at the turn of fall, when the entire Northern Hemisphere becomes wistful and contemplative and everyone girds himself for five months of life as a root vegetable. Then we would venture out, under leaves gone to rust, the frosted grass crunching underfoot. What did we talk about? Nothing less than the histories and adventures of the species— revolutions, market capitalism, Maginot Lines, the catastrophes of '42 . . . all of these things unpacked and laid out on the table, piece parts accorded their genera, then put properly away. The rationalist-humanist father and his whiz kid son.

My father too must be thinking of the old talks, for now he says:

"It's a funny thing, Nietzsche talking about there being no facts in this world, only interpretations."

"Mm-hm," say I (but sagely, sagely).

"I don't know if he was syphilitic by then and just raving, or what. But it's the damnedest observation." He points at the moon. "That body is about four and a half billion years old, which we know by the decay of chemical isotopes. There's a fact, Herr Friedrich. Those white pines are the tallest tree we've got east of the Mississippi. Another fact."

"We're a few miles west of the Mississippi."

"Wise guy . . . No facts, my foot. You don't build bridges based on interpretations."

"Not systems either," say I, thinking on it. "Computers aren't interpretative machines. The machine only knows what you give it; it won't make any educated guesses on your behalf. In programming we call it GIGO—garbage in, garbage out." I am not sure this is quite to the point, but he is generous with me.

"Exactly. We're only as good as our facts. And heaven help us if at every uncertainty we were to throw up our hands. Anything can be sorted. It only takes patience and a little elbow grease."

"You've got to get inside the clockworks."

"You've got to get inside the clockworks!" A favored classroom phrase. He's pleased I remember. "How's that for a codger's metaphor? Straight from before the Great War."

The frozen wood is heavy as iron. I stagger home. Inside, he deems our collection sufficient. Gretchen begs for a fire. My father grumbles that in these temperatures an open chimney is murder on the thermostat, but he is secretly glad to oblige. He builds a pyramid of logs on the fire grate: a nimble, practiced assembly, his fleshy ears red with pleasure. Watching him, I think perhaps it is not so difficult after all to work out one's place, to be in the world simply and as oneself, without recourse to grandiosity or despair. The flue draws beautifully. Orange flames spring from the wood and flap like tatters. The day's confusions fade like memories of a bad dream. We stand at the brick hearth, abridged as a clan it's true, but no mere remnant, and all of us with enough sense not to jinx our gladness by naming it.

4

Monday morning. At last check my email queue showed 117 unread messages. Most of my team are programmers, for whom direct communication is a thing to be avoided at all costs. This means some desperate and time-sensitive decision—say, whether there is wiggle room on an imminent deadline—is almost certainly ticking away inside my inbox as we speak. I've lectured them, but my engineers are like the British soldiers I have seen in war films. Short of a German wire breach, it is impolite to ring the brigadier. Still, today I prefer to watch the city while passing idle semicircles on the oiled swivel of my chair.

Now there comes a rap at the door and Barry's wet-brushed head.

"Got a minute, chief?" He strides in and closes the door. "Look. I owe you an apology. I had no right to lose my temper with you."

This again. I make some noises of absolution and develop a frowning interest in the papers on my desk.

"You'd only taken time out of your busy schedule to try to help." To *try* to help. This qualifier is the only sign that any resentment lingers. Otherwise his apology is genuine. The problem is that before finishing, he will ask my forgiveness. I know because each of our past disagreements has ended this way, with a door closed and Barry eager to humble himself.

"Henry?" He sets his palms on the desk, leaning over them. Here it comes. "Will you forgive me?"

Now the solemn wait. I hate being made to feel that I would withhold something so dear to him, but neither do I want a part in his asinine morality play. These acts of contrition are, I imagine, tied up in his religiosity. They are the same each time. For one thing, he is formal to the point of belligerence. Always: "Henry, I have something I need to say to you . . ." Also he leaves these sessions irritatingly buoyant. I don't care to be part of his penances. They leave me feeling somehow one-upped.

"It's not as bad as that, is it?"

He only looks at me from under his brow. There is something a little predatory in his supplication. This goddamn beseeching—

"Yes! Yes. You are forgiven."

"Thank you. I mean that. I'll let you get back to it."

Back, wearily, to email.

124 . . .

123 . . .

122 . . .

Pecking, pecking.

120 . . .

119 . . .

The world will end in tedium.

118 . . .

117 . . .

Four new messages arrive. 121 . . .

120 . . .

Another email pings in. 121 . . . And another. 122.

Peck, peck. 120.

Ping, ping, ping. 123.

Go for coffee.

Returning, I am stopped dead by a vision. It is Jane framed in a conference room's windowed door. She sits sideways in a black Eames chair, as easy and elongate as a lioness draped in the afternoon branches. Her eyes are directed at some unseen speaker, lips faintly parted: a moment of rapt concentration. One bare foot is tucked beneath her thigh; the other traces figure eights on the carpet with a crimson toe. Desire strikes. A bolt like holy retribution. There comes a riot of spots in my periphery and a strangled sound. Suddenly her eye catches mine. It is all I can do to fix my face in nonchalance—a little raise of eyebrows, a sip of coffee (bitter, bitter): *So?* She gives a grin and broad wink, then returns attention to the speaker.

Only the speaker has noticed. Jane's eyes widen in innocence. She laughs, makes some soundless protest, gestures to me. Her inquisitor looms into frame.

Keith.

He opens the door a crack and says good-naturedly, "Beat it. We're working."

Laughter as the door shuts.

5

Today I forgo the Management meeting for my own with Engineering. These departmental gatherings are not my idea. Human Resources has asked that all Directors "take the pulse" of their teams monthly. They mean for us to find out what people might be unhappy about and feed this information back to HR for remedy. It is a recent policy and might be a fine strategy if it weren't obvious what people are unhappy about: our terrible quarters.

After having done my bit to reassure the organization I return to my office, only to discover my fine assurances are too little, too late. Working the email queue, I find this, sent Saturday:

Henry,

In advance of the meeting Monday, I want to share some concerns I have hear from people on the floor:

• If another bad quarter, are cuts planned?
• If so, would Eng. be at risk or only elsewhere?
• What is Sales doing?

I think good to address head-on. Rumors are flourishing.

thank you,
RAHIM

Rahim is the head of my Development team. Beneath his message there is one from Cory Freer, who heads Architecture. His reads:

H-
Some caterwauling among the troops. "Last quarter sucked,
now look at this one" etc. Have told them: less hand-
wringing, more coding. Think you should too.
-C

I summon both leads to my office. Cory arrives first. He sits heavily
opposite my desk. A bearish head with stiff copper hair brushed back
in waves. Thirty degrees this morning but he is in a short-sleeved
polo, impervious.

"This 'bout my email?"

"Yes."

"Storm in a teacup."

I have trouble imagining what it would take to worry Cory. Only
twenty-nine, he carries himself as an old son of the soil. He is an
unironic follower of stock car racing, and proud brewer of a dande-
lion whiskey he calls GatorByte. He is also quite probably a genius.
In his senior year at some godforsaken public high school in middle
Georgia, he wrote a program that forecast, with an accuracy near
eighty percent, the selections in the National Football League's annual draft. It earned him a partial scholarship to the Massachusetts
Institute of Technology, which he turned down in favor of the University of Florida. He did this not because Florida offered better
money (they did), but because "MIT's sports are for shit."

And now Rahim. Rahim has a good, fierce face, with a wide
squashed nose and a black strap of beard that holds his chin like a
stirrup. Except today he looks chastened. Unusual to be summoned
to my office.

I put the matter to them directly:

"Is there panic on deck?"

A pause.

Cory says, "What we've got is a bunch of Henny Pennys." Seeing
Rahim frown, he explains: "Hen gets knocked on her head by an acorn,
thinks the sky is falling."

"Ah." Rahim nods. "People like to predict disaster." He considers it. Rahim is a gifted programmer and, inasmuch as I understand these things, a devout Muslim. Once, racing to a meeting on 16, I nearly fell over him in the stairwell. He was crouched on the landing with his forehead flush to the carpet, abjuring this world in a rather beautiful tenor voice. "But . . ." says he, "is there not more than an acorn?"

Cory slides his bulk low in the chair and props his head on its back. "It's the L-word people are worried about."

" 'People'?" I ask.

He lifts his head. "Not including myself. But—"

"I am," Rahim confesses. I remember Rahim is a family man. As breadwinner, he experiences the usual dark rumors with a different weight.

Very well. One of the first managerial tricks I learned is how to shore up employee faith. Convincing a group is much harder than convincing people one or two at a time. To speak to a group is to perform. Your audience becomes aware of themselves as such, and everyone fights not to be taken in. But to speak in intimate numbers is to confide. If a manager approaches his team piecemeal, if he is known to be fair and human, allergic to hyperbole, very often his employees will assign him something like omniscience. It helps too that businesspeople, though rational to their very marrows, are natural believers. In the American corporation, optimism brims like laughing gas.

So it is that I fix Cory and Rahim with a solemn look. They steel themselves accordingly, sitting upright or leaning forward: the seriousness of entering their manager's confidence. What follows is a frank but encouraging appraisal. I am careful to emphasize "Keith's plans" because I know even an old cynic like Cory respects him.

"Now here is what we'll do," say I, still solemn as an eagle. "I'll send a note to the department, summarizing what we've talked about. To call the team together again for purposes of encouragement would be too suspicious. It'll only worry them more. But I want you guys to talk with your folks. One-on-one—that's important. Let them know we're in good shape."

Cory and Rahim take their leave, exchanging serious, knowing looks.

Team-

I've realized there are some concerns about company performance I meant to address more directly in this morning's meeting. A few points to bear in mind:

1) It is January 19. We have until the end of March to meet first quarter revenue targets.

2) We are but one business unit in the wide Cyber Systems universe. Even if we were to have another down quarter, CS isn't going anywhere.

3) In the catastrophe scenario—layoffs—Engineering is very well positioned. We are a software company. Our department is at the heart of business strategy.

4) It won't come to 3.

As usual, if you still have concerns, please do not hesitate to share these with your managers.

Thanks,
Henry

A sound email, I think. Direct, transparent, calm. How quickly the stage is regained.

Cory reappears. "Just sent the email," I tell him.

"Yup, OK."

He says nothing more, only stands with bunched fists, curling his wrists and studying the play of tendons.

"What is it."

"Hm? Oh. About next Friday."

"Your day off."

"Cracker Barrel 500." He speaks of a major stock car race.

"Good. Don't kill yourself on booze."

"Want to come? One of my guys backed out. Track's not but an hour from here."

I am surprised. Between Cory and me, the relationship is pure corporate: arch, even playful, but not especially close.

"I can't take Friday off."

"Don't have to. The race isn't till Sunday. Friday's to get a start on the tailgate."

I have never been to a stock car race.

"You're on. It'll be a good education."

"Yankee, you got naw idear." He says this in the droll way between us, wherein he will sometimes crank up his Southern saltiness and I my Northerner naïf, these mechanisms looser and less brittle than our employee-employer roles.

Now he stretches, fitting his knuckles to the points of his hips. He looks around the room as though he's misplaced something. There is more.

"Mebbe I'm just an ignorant Reb—" He catches himself. When he speaks again, it is not as the salty Southerner.

"As straight as you can give it: We on track here?"

"We are."

"Because I don't like to think what happens. We got people who've given about all there is. We can talk about difficult quarters, but that's the world from fifty thousand feet. On the ground it's folks with families to feed and but two weeks' severance."

"I know. Don't worry."

Cory pushes out his lips, bobbing his large head. Whether because he feels better or because he knows it's the only answer I can give, it is impossible to say.

6

The drive home is slow. I mark my way by checking off billboards.

This one asks, GOT SALVATION?—a churchy play on another campaign sponsored by the Dairy Association.

And a few minutes later: OUR GIRLS STOP TRAFFIC. Beneath, a woman in a bikini and white gloves blows lusciously on a whistle.

Gradually another Christ-themed one, WHO LOVES YA, BABY?, signed JESUS. Then we are under the leaden eyes of the buxom giants of TIGER LILIES.

It occurs to me that certain people I know (none better than myself of ten years ago) would be tempted to read into this back-and-forth a very easy kind of irony about the South. And it is true these signs aim for the same audience. It is the man who Friday night rollicks in a champagne bath in one of these club's private rooms, but who Sunday morning can be found muscling in on the front pew. Yet despite appearances, hypocrisy doesn't enter into it. This man is not a hypocrite for he never pretends to have another self. He embraces the strip club or sanctuary, each in its moment, as honestly and fervently as a convert; the other he forsakes with all his heart. It is only that his abandonment doesn't last. After some time—a night, a month, a year—he sees the error of his way and returns to the other, shaking his head, rueful-joyful. Why? Because he has convinced himself the other is purer, truer? No. They are both traps. He knows this, without being quite aware of it. What rescues him is the switch. He lives by the thrill of changing course, of putting it all behind him, of starting again. Only by tacking and jibing does he keep full the sails of his existence. It is quite a serious business. He must court the liminal to survive.

Ah, but the rational mind rejects the switch. The rational mind is not distracted. It works out the secret of itself by diligence and study. My father is right. Our place in the world may derive from mysterious cosmic programs, but the code is not indecipherable. If a person is patient and watchful enough, if he observes quietly enough and resists the exaggerations of the liminal, lo and behold what comes?

The wits to pick the lock.

7

"Tell me about Markitel."

Keith is not given to abruptness. I proceed carefully.

"Not great."

Silence. My phone emits a low seashell roar.

"Where are you?" he wants to know.

"Home. Just walked in the door."

Another pause.

"Early, isn't it?"

I cannot think of an answer.

"Where were you today?" He means the Management meeting. I explain about my department session. There is some muttering, then:

"I need you back here."

"On my way."

A mile out, he calls again. "You eaten?"

"No."

"Meet me at Cirelli's."

This is a happy turn. Cirelli's is a very good trattoria. A dinner invitation confirms that whatever the day's disasters, I am not to blame.

The restaurant is midtown's last standing wood structure, a converted four-bedroom bungalow. It is flanked on three sides by the soaring glass obelisks that dominate this quarter of skyline, a plucky last-century artifact, happily, stubbornly lousing up the city's cool steel march. Inside I find Keith already installed.

"I took the liberty of ordering us some plates," he says. He splashes wine into my glass. "Good visit with the family?"

"Fine, thanks."

We are seated between bar and fireplace, in what was once a living room. It is early; Cirelli's is not crowded. He sweeps the room's few faces, attending each a second or less. It strikes me we have been catalogued, confirmed in a role (Laugher, Smoker, Young Beauty, Lonely Old Man, Loyal Lieutenant), and will be held to account.

"So. What happened?"

With the matter suddenly at hand, I am not quite at ease. "What did Barry say?"

"I'll tell you exactly what he said. Then you'll do me the courtesy of not being coy." There is no heat in this. It is a simple statement of contract. "Barry said the new guy at Markitel is a tough customer but he was cautiously optimistic that we could turn him our way. Now, there was a lot of hemming and hawing while he said it. But Barry's not much of a liar, and when I pressed him he didn't budge. I wanted you there to check his story, but never mind. 'Cautiously optimistic.' That was his mantra. You don't feel the same. Let's hear it."

I comprehend two things at once. First, Keith's irritation on the phone was exaggerated. He only suspected catastrophe; my reaction confirmed it. Second, this change from office to restaurant is to remind me of our bond. Last week's generous raise, tonight's fine meal: flattery for a trusted deputy. I am not a little in awe. Here is a boss who need never shout or bully. His guile is more than enough.

While I summarize the Markitel adventure, Keith only listens impassively. I can detect not a single change in his face.

"And?"

"We were kicked out, more or less."

He sips, says nothing. The silence makes me nervous.

"I'm not sure they were much interested in any case. There wasn't a single question in the technical portion. And the new contact, Mike. This guy might be a little unhinged—" But I have put my foot wrong. Keith comes to life:

"I don't care if he's Charlie goddamn Manson! The man has budget! And I'll tell you something else. Barry's been working on this for six months—*six*. If he'd closed already, he wouldn't be sweating this new character. Disinterest is leverage, every fool knows that. The guy was prepared to meet with us. He's a serious buyer."

The waitress arrives, balancing a line of oval dishes. She refills our glasses and slips away. More silence now, punctured only by the screech of knife on plate. "I had no idea you were so forgiving," he says, chewing. "You've always struck me as a guy whose tolerance for bullshit is nil. But what I'm hearing is . . ." Keith pauses, mopping his mouth with his napkin. "I'm hearing if you'd been sitting in the meeting today and you'd heard Barry report that he's 'cautiously opti-mistic' about our chances at Markitel, you'd have agreed?"

"I don't know."

"You don't know."

"I'm not sure."

Keith sets down knife and fork, and jerks his chair as if to have a better look. "Well, this I should hear. I'm certainly paying you enough. Why might you have agreed?"

It occurs that Keith aims to convince himself of something by first convincing me. And the longer this takes, the worse my standing. But I am stuck now and must make a case, if not for Barry's sake then for my own. So I point to Barry's natural optimism, his honest belief, per-haps, that the sale is still salvageable. There is also the matter of the holiday slow period—

"What do you mean, 'the holiday slow period'?"

"I mean the, ah, whatever we call it. The slowdown in corporate buying around the holidays."

"Henry, you worry me. Don't confuse what we tell the employees for Management's expectations. If I tell the staff our struggles are part of a normal slow period around the holidays, that's lipstick on a pig. We don't need people quitting in droves because they think the place is going under. But you imagine I go to my bosses and say we're going to be short on revenue because of *Hanukkah*? Think. Any seasonal slough-off is part of the forecast. When Barry and I sat down to plan out the quarterly numbers, those were the ones he agreed to. We *expected* fewer dollars this quarter. And Barry hasn't even hit *that*."

Now I do feel foolish.

"I see."

"Good. Then you understand there's not much to be done."

It's not clear to me where we've arrived. But I am not interested in embarrassing myself again. "I suppose that's true."

Keith is happy to find agreement. "At last. He sees the light." Up comes the bottle, its neck steadied above my glass, then his own. The bottle is turned upside down and given a shake. He slumps back, throwing his arm up to signal for another. Not his first serving tonight. "Wish it were different," he says. "You know?"

"Sure, sure."

He eyes me significantly. "Aw, hell!"

When the new bottle comes, he adds to our glasses. The waitress clears our plates. He admires her backside as it disappears into the kitchen. Seeing my eye, he fixes me with a wolfish grin.

"What about we finish this bottle, then see if we can't take in the ballet?"

This is said conspiratorially, the favor of favors. I am the good soldier reenlisted. Yet my heart sinks. "Now that *is* an idea," say I. Enthusiasm without commitment. But this seals it. He slaps the table.

"Drink up!"

The water-stained marquee locates this as the home of "Big Blondie," she of the eighty-eight-inch chest measurement. The marvel of it is signaled by a heraldry of exclamation points. Also, naturally: GOD BLESS OUR TROOPS.

An overpass thunders above. We are in a nether region somewhere near the airport. Only under extraordinary social pressure will I go to these places. This has nothing to do with prudishness. It is simply a policy of avoiding misery. Patrons of these clubs the world over labor under the same mandate: that in their happy welcoming of tits and asses and fetishistic getups and grinding drum dances, in their whooping embrace of the uproarious naughtiness, they corroborate for all mankind what a bite of the real life looks like. I've seen adult men seized by their ties and led to private rooms by women dressed as kittens, and to a man their behavior is the same: a broad, backward glance at his woofing cohorts, the headshake of faux resignation, and then a wild little shimmy at his escort's back. Keith goes into the gloom ahead readily and with the sap rising. But already the show is over; already the subject waits, stripped and laid bare. There's only one thing ever truly naked in these places, and its name is Despair.

I am not mistaken. Inside the club there isn't a dancer in sight. It is dark but for a catwalk whose margins are traced by a glowing plastic tube. I can make out perhaps ten other men. Each sits with chin on chest, stirring some radioactive concoction from the bar, looking caved-in and alone. They have come straight from their orphanages. This is worse than imagined. A strip joint too seedy and sad even for the tyranny of high times. We fall into one of the tables at a remove from the stage. Keith casts an arm at a passing shadow. Some form appears at our table with a wooden rack of test tubes. Their liquids glow like fissile material. A voice says: "Watermelon, raspberry, banana . . ." Keith hands me two tubes and takes two himself. His are finished in short order.

"Those aren't made for sipping, you know. Down the hatch."

The flavors are indescribable.

"My policy?" Keith shouts, apropos of nothing. "Don't. Over. Think it." A jab at each period. His gestures have become broad and lunging, like a thespian who must signal the action for the balconies. "We want to come here? Done. And I love my wife, it's not that."

I nod. It is the first tactic of active listening. One nods, and pays no mind to the jungle narcotics spidering along one's brainstem.

". . . But some people, they never get there. Everything goes under the microscope, nothing gets decided. Too many possibilities. Or— You can stop nodding."

"Sorry."

"Or they get to a decision but"—he flops his hand over and back—"second-guess it every time the wind blows."

"Ha. Yes."

"Either way will sink you."

"Yes." Though I am not so sure of myself. Have I made a poor showing at dinner?

"You go on what you know. Think of a guy who's decided his best bet is to stand stock-still, hoping to see any one thing"—here he makes a little framing device with his hands, squinting through it—"right square as it is. Nobody's opinions, not even his own, to block the view. What happens to him?"

"What?"

"He's dead of old age before he's done it!"

"Oh."

Keith leans over. There comes a hard, avuncular squeeze on my shoulder. It activates a quivering resonance in the speakers. The curtains part in a hissing jet of fog. A spotlight blinks to life on the floor and goes racing for the stage. He falls back.

"Ho now . . ."

Some black-clad creature, an assemblage of knee boots and cinched leather, separates from the fog and comes prowling along the walk. There is not a single whistle, only a scraping and scurrying as men drag their chairs to sit at her feet. Ah, but not so fast. First we must endure her choreography. It is a rodeo pantomime. Some galloping in place, an arm whirled loosely above her head, etc. I study my watch. Twelve minutes of this. Only by degrees does she oblige the room: a long undoing of bodice strings, the slow-motion spilling of her marquee gifts . . . The audience remains transfixed throughout. These poor souls. When I see them lined along the catwalk, gazing up with open mouths, there enters my head a blasphemous image of Communion takers at the altar rail.

Keith is clawing his face. "You lucky devil."

"Me?"

"You!"

"Why?"

"Why. Only one free man at this table."

Under no circumstances will I be going home with an exotic dancer.

"Ah, but you *could*. Hundred bucks plus cab fare, maybe."

"You know."

He gives a sidelong squint. "I wasn't always married."

"Baloney."

"Believe what you like."

The dancer steps down from her platform to go among the men. Here and there she stops, choosing. She reaches out and grasps her man by the head, then buries his face in her bosoms. Truly "buries" is the word: the men go in up to their ears. They remain as docile as sheep, the chosen ones in particular. There is no hooting or hollering. Each one looks up gravely from his chair, nods, and bends his neck.

"I can think of someone I'd like to give me that treatment," says Keith.

"Who?"

He turns sly.

"If you could pick one person from the office, who would it be?"

I am surprised. Sober, Keith doesn't engage the usual locker-room amusements.

"I don't know," I tell him.

"Let's have it."

"I'd need to give it some thought."

His cheeriness begins to slip. "It's not an essay question." I am on thin ice. Wrecked as he is, his antennae for angles remains keen. There is no question of his disclosing anything personal, not even in drunken jest, without me going first.

"What's-her-face. Sixteenth-floor reception."

Keith is gratified. "Ho! All right. I know the very one. You like 'em young."

"Well—"

"I'll remember that!"

"Yes."

"So OK, my turn."

I regard him dutifully.

"Jane Brodel."

"Aha."

"Marketing."

"Yes."

"Now: she's not the only one. I'm not saying that. But she's right up there."

"She's married I think."

Keith, who has been keeping a weather eye on the dancer's performance, shifts it to me. "What?"

I am a fool. He screws up his face. "Jesus Christ," says he, baffled to the point of irritation. "What, I'm going to torpedo everything to run away with her? Am I that guy?"

"No, no."

"We're just bullshitting."

"I know that."

Still I am under watch. Why did I open my mouth? He is drunk, but not so drunk as to miss the scent of jealousy. It doesn't help that I can feel my spine stiffening of its own accord. The mere mention of her name, in this place, in another man's mouth . . . I have an idiotic yen for chivalry. It rose up in boyhood and never left. I blame my sister. What pride I used to take in chaperoning her past imaginary neighborhood dangers, a role that occasioned one of our mother's friends to remark, "He's such a gentleman, your son," thereby ruining me for good. I have been conscious of my standing as a gentleman ever since, and it is Gretchen's fault.

Keith watches, but to my relief when he speaks again it is as the office scold: "And don't you get any ideas about that receptionist."

"Absolutely not."

"I'm serious."

"I know."

"Bad for business. Find someone you're not going to see in the elevator the next day."

This settles it. He tips out of his chair and lumbers upright; I am bid to hold tight, smaller bills are on the way. Like that, we are comrades again. The fog machine pumps its sweet-sick smoke into piles on the stage. Our dancer fades to apparition, and soon we are all subsumed in the gas.

8

Early the next morning I am awakened by the phone. The bedcovers sit like a lead apron, but hearing the voice I am instantly bolt upright.

"What is it?"

Gretchen is slow to answer. "It's probably a simple mistake."

"Tell me."

"Last night . . ." A small ticking comes over the line, the sound of her nail on a tooth. "It started with one of those awful dreams where what's actually happening goes into the dream. I dreamt a winter branch reached its arm in through my bedroom window and was rubbing at my shin. It was the strangest thing. The rubbing was like a slow torture."

Her objective tone is enough to raise hackles. Whatever this is, she has the narrator's bird's-eye advantage. But for the listener it is pure agony.

"Finally it was too much, I woke up: it was Dad. 'Gretchen, I'm concerned.' Scared me half to death. He had a look on his face like, I don't know. I mean it was clear he'd just woken up, but he didn't look confused." The line is quiet for a moment. "He sits down on the edge of the bed and says, plain as this: 'I simply cannot think where your mother might be.'"

I become aware of a pain in my hand. I have the receiver in a kind of death grip. Changing hands, it is difficult to straighten the fingers.

"I said, 'No, Dad: she's gone, remember?' And he said"—there is a small harrumphing noise as she bears down—"'Remind me where.'"

"What did you say?"

"What could I? 'I mean she's dead.' But all of sudden he was fine. He just sort of popped to. 'That's right, that's right. What the hell's the matter with my brain.'" She makes another clearing sound in her throat. "He asked that I not say anything to you."

"I won't mention it."

"How worried are we?"

I tell myself there is no cause for alarm. Likely he was not fully awake himself. In those twilight states anything is possible. As I interpret it for Gretchen, it seems he proceeded by old memory, and finding her asleep in the house no doubt worsened his confusion: Here is my daughter, in her bed as she should be. Where then is my wife?

"I feel better for calling," she says. "I wasn't sure."

"I'm glad you did."

"OK."

"Absolutely."

Silence. With the urgency past, we are at something of a loss.

"What's the weather like?"

This I actually say, so excruciating are these dead spaces of social protocol. She laughs, then is embarrassed and makes a kind of midair adjustment: "Well, it's . . . cold. I mean, it's winter. You remember."

"Ah yes. Winter. Cold you say." It's no use. Not even irony can save me. "You should come visit," I tell her, now well and truly desperate, although in the instant after I see what a good idea this is. "Really. It's at least sixty degrees warmer here. Take a long weekend."

"Hm. Tempting."

"I'll pay. It's a no-brainer."

" 'No-brainer.' What a gross expression." She is prickly in the face of charity, especially her brother's charity. Her caregiver pride is roused. But not to the point of refusing. "Maybe I'll look into dates."

We are at the cusp of disconnecting when something else occurs to me—"Gretchen?"

"Yes?"

"The whiskey bottle, the one over the stove."

"What about it."

I am silent.

She says, "I'm trying to be—how would it go in your world? 'Proactive'?"

"Is it connected to this sleepwalking episode?"

"No. This was a first. But he's better off without it."

I am a little fearful of asking what she means. We leave it at that.

Awake now but with no inclination to get up. A bar of sunlight materializes on the ceiling. Gradually it descends the far wall, at last settling on a small family picture above the dresser. The Hurts at a scenic overlook in Arizona. Gretchen stands with hands in pockets, blond as can be, foal-legged in her canary short-shorts. A middle-aged edition of my father gazes into the lens with a faraway look. My mother is to the side, behind me, with her hands on my shoulders. She wears turquoise earrings and a turquoise bracelet and a red-fringed serape. (This was during her Southwestern phase.) Her eyes and teeth are alight in the flashbulb or settling sun. Mine also. This flushed grinning is a mystery—perhaps we have just switched places, a little firedrilling before the shutter's click.

A parent dying is no world-historic event—I know this. One of the aims of the grief literature, I discovered, is to remind you that you're in good company, that legions die every day, and in any case dying is as natural as birth: we are all leaves in a stream or stars in the firmament or raindrops on a something. Yes, true. But it is also true that when we sat together school nights at the kitchen table, she with her crossword and I with my story problems, and after I'd given up hope and climbed into the cabinetry's painted hay (become "lost in a brown study" in her phrasing, an expression that provoked its own images and wanderings), I would be summoned back to place by her voice—*What's transpiring in that brain of yours?* And if I remembered I would tell her what it was I'd been thinking, easily and forthrightly, never mind how stray or odd, because when she asked you something she meant to hear the truth. Her curiosity wasn't rhetorical. The miracle was that a truthful answer seemed possible. There opened a space for two people to speak, however fleetingly, without the talcum of safe sentiments that powders everything.

The alarm sounds. I rise and busy myself at the dresser. Yes, yes, lay thee thy garments out and never mind the picture. She smiles as ever, I know. I know every inch of that photo, having searched it many times for the filament, the fine thread that attaches the here and now to the there and then. Once found it can be followed, back to this snapshot eternity where she lives, in perpetual coincidence with her family, just as was agreed.

The truth is I understand my father's confusion. It never occurred to me she would die.

Two

1

Good news: On Wednesday Delta agrees to sign for two hundred and fifty thousand, just as Barry predicted. The little victory is buoying. For a day or two the office is chipper as a Disney village. Barry of course is the embodiment of this cheer. He sails around the hallways with a friendly word for everyone. I am glad for him, and for the company, and also not a little energized myself. What a pleasure it is to work among smart people, to have at one's reserve the brainy and eager, to instruct a team member that the SWOT analysis from last quarter be rethought in light of a competitor's newest product release, and to know it will be done and done well.

The weather too is on our side. By Thursday the air has turned damp and carries a smell of earth. Come evening, I stand on my wide veranda in the warm dark, stretching calves against the porch rail and sucking in great drafts blown direct from the tropics. It is a little before nine. A pared moon is mounted cockeyed in the heavens. I am no health nut, but a run is just the thing: a matter of throwing oneself into the waiting dark and seeing what happens.

When I set off into the night, there rises an agreeable sense of prelude. It manifests as a color, the purple of the evening, and a kind of resonance, a distant kettledrum roll in the atmosphere. Ordinary things are invested with relevance. Yes, it is a hovering awareness that the most throwaway detail (this aureole of street light, that darkened Buick) is placed with intent. The sense is of being tracked in frame. What precedes the frame has not yet come into being; what passes its trailing edge is gone for good. Only within the frame is there instantiation, consequence. Everything in the frame is a harbinger of the great thing to come. Probably nothing will happen, of course. But you never know. Perhaps the great thing is a chance encounter with Jane! Not really, I know. Her neighborhood is a long way off.

Once I did in fact encounter Jane on a run. (It was she who was doing the running.) Driving home from a movie I came upon her, plodding up a midtown street. What now, I wondered. Tap the horn? Leave her alone? But she settled it. Spying me, she let out a cry. I stopped. She heaved open the door and fell in.

"Oh God. Thank you, thank you." Panting, elbow on the windowsill, her eyes under her hand. "Oh Lord . . . That was absolutely too much." She wore a man's polo shirt over Umbro shorts, and tennis shoes instead of running shoes—an improvisational outfit. Her bare arms and bare legs emerged from its drapes in a way that pleased me.

"Where to?"

"Home. Could you?"

"Of course."

"Gah. You really are a saint."

Between pants she issued directions. It wasn't far. We drove along, she at her ease and me in that travesty of ease where even the smallest shift in posture yelps mirrors and rehearsal.

"I'm sweating all over your seats."

"Sweat away."

Sweat away. What a Casanova. My language center was fried. It had blown a circuit. It was the shock of her arrival, the nakedness of her limbs—the absolute reality of her presence, damp and panting in the seat beside me.

Jane's house turned out to be a substantial Colonial Revival in the city's second-richest neighborhood. I was impressed. In the roundabout under the shadows of the porch columns, we said our goodnights. She didn't leave. Her fingers engaged the handle, but she stayed put, eyeing the house. She sighed. There was wine on her breath.

"You know . . ."

Nothing. With a shake of her head she was out and up the brick steps, and that was that.

After a mile the neighborhood is suddenly full of hills and I decide that is enough prelude for one night. At the top of a rise ahead is a bungalow whose yard lights are much brighter than its neighbors'. It becomes my marker, a place to touch before turning for home. Lumbering toward it, I spy someone I know on its porch. Not that I know her quite. Someone I recognize. We frequent the same dry cleaner and Blockbuster and have only ever traded certifying nods. She is a beauty with a cape of dark blond hair and yellow eyes. Yes, I know her as well you can know someone whom you have never said a word to. Her style is one of rolled jeans and Roman sandals and blouses with flute sleeves, a grad-student chic whose easy riding I prefer to find convincing. She sits on a porch swing, straight-backed with hands tucked under her rump, lost to a book in her lap. You are thinking: an Arabian moon, an evening whose odd wet warmth is plainly sensual, and now a familiar beauty alone on a bright porch? Come off it. But she is real enough. I hear as she clears her throat.

As I near, it occurs to me I might climb the porch steps and make an introduction. In the worst case she is married or otherwise settled. So a quick pivot, a friendly wave, and off into the night. Any humiliation is left there on the doorstep. In a moment she'll hear my plodding steps and look up. I plot my face, its stages: grimaced exertion, an incurious glance upward, then recognition, surprise. She must understand my intentions so that when I slow and turn through the gate, she doesn't race for the door.

But there is a problem even if I gain the stage. Namely, my awareness of it. I would stand before her as who? The Gentleman Caller? A Man on the Make? Not that it is easier for her. Interested or no, she must assemble her response and fit it to a character that suits mine.

```
                    HIM
          [planting a hand casually on
          porch strut] Don't I know you?


                    HER
          Oh—yes [friendly, wary] . . .
          Blockbuster's, right?
```

Etc.

To hell with it. I pump my arms and sprint past her perch. She does not look up.

2

On Monday evening I screw up my courage and try again.

Atop the hill, the light. She sits reading. But in my adrenalized state I am too fast. Before I know it I have gone past, at a loss for strategy except perhaps a second lap or to leave it for another night. Then a lucky thing happens. Past her bright lawn all is darkness. Some broken sidewalk lump presents itself and down I go. In a blink she is off the swing and through the gate.

"My God! Are you all right?" She kneels at my side. "Can you stand?"

"I think so."

She holds my elbow. Her fingers are cold and firm on the soft underside of my arm. I have an impulse to flex the tendons there. "Does it hurt?"

"Quite a bit."

"Come over here where there's light." We step gingerly to her gate. "Oh God," she breathes. "Come up to the porch."

My knees have been scalped. At the bench swing she lifts and settles my legs along the wooden slats without a trace of self-consciousness. Intimacy is possible thanks to the shock of my spill. It has knocked out our compasses. Each action now is catch-as-catch-can. We can look only to the other for clues and together feel our way along. For the moment our standing is thus: she is the kind, competent tender; I the broken, grimacing tended.

"I'll be right back," she declares briskly, and disappears into the house.

She returns with a folding chair and white tin box. From the kit comes an ominous brown plastic bottle.

"Bourbon?"

"Ha. Iodine, I'm afraid." She makes a fist on the cap. Her index finger bears a jade stone the size of an almond. One bracelet looks to be an ordinary table fork bent around her wrist. She gives the cap a sharp twist, and the seal cracks.

But before she can pour—

"Wait," I say.

She stays the bottle above my knees.

"This will hurt, you think?"

"I imagine this will burn like fury." She speaks to my wounds, determined.

"Your honesty is appreciated."

"Are you ready?"

"*Do* you have any bourbon? I'm pushing my imposition here, I know."

She pulls the bottle to her lap and regards me sympathetically. "I don't drink. I could make some chamomile tea. Or, well, I also have a little marijuana."

Herbal tea, not booze; marijuana. Her book is *Eat, Pray, Love.* Yes, I have her coordinates. On paper they do not interest me. But here in the blond and breathing flesh . . .

"Never mind. Thank you. Fire when ready."

She raises again to pour.

"Wait."

Now she smiles gamely. "Yes?"

"May I ask your name?"

"Madison."

"I'm Henry. Not as pretty. Henry Hurt, in fact."

"Hurt is your last name?"

"Yes."

"Oo." She signals with the bottle. "Now?"

"All right. Are the neighbors heavy sleepers?"

The pain is breathtaking.

Madison McClendon is twenty-seven. She is an artist—a painter and also a sculptor. She grew up in South Boston, Virginia, and attended Agnes Scott. Her parents now live in Tampa. She has a younger sister, Martha, who lives in New York and works for Goldman Sachs, and who last year made more money than their father had in his final years as an engineer for ConocoPhillips, a fact that gave rise to something like screwball comedy at the Thanksgiving table as Dad tried to calibrate between pride and outrage. Madison's own means are vague. "Painter" is the only answer she gave to the work question, and while my ignorance of art is equal to hers of business, I thought a person couldn't make a living from paintings unless hers were of cozy snowbound cottages, or cats, or Jesus, which Madison's are not. Hers (she's kindly brought her portfolio to the porch) are of filled-in circles of varying circumference, entirely monochromatic to my eye, though she's explained the difficulty in getting the shades so closely matched and yet different. Still, her paintings are unusual in a way that interests me.

She presents her work from the folding chair, portfolio splayed on her knees. Because she sits opposite me, her view of the portfolio is upside down. Sometimes she will pause and rotate the book, the better to scrutinize some sample. I try to pay attention and remember to ask questions, though the real intrigue is the play of her hands. She will indicate a certain detail by swirling above it with her little finger, or she will explain proportion by making blocking motions with her thumb. In these moments I lose the painting altogether.

When we reach the end she claps shut the portfolio and hunches over it, pressing its cover with her forearms. There is a small show of back stretching. The evening's first forced gesture. It is time to go.

"Impressive," I tell her.

"Don't know about that. But thank you."

I drop an eye to my watch. "Is it ten thirty?"

"Did I bore you?" (But already she is standing.) We face each other. Bandaged, my cuts do not hurt so much as itch. "How do you feel?" she asks.

"Fine, actually. I'm grateful."

Now we cast about the porch. She tucks portfolio to chest, chewing a corner of her lip. (Is she too much the bashful schoolgirl?) I trace my hand through a hanging chime. The hour's oddness is dying. Beyond the fence is a green Southern darkness as thick as murk. It is not the pall, I tell myself. This is no grand melancholy, only the little oboe note of subsidiary endings.

"You have a lovely porch to bleed on. Thank you again."

"You're not walking!"

"It's not far."

"Oh no, come on. I'll drive you. Wait here."

She reappears on the driveway in a yellow VW soft-top, a car whose chirpy free-spiritedness rather depresses me. I'd placed her in something functional and trend-bucking, an old station wagon maybe, the better for transporting canvases.

We wind along in unforced silence. The streets are dark and lush. A soft, wheedling croon can be heard. Madison is nodding gently, tapping the wheel. "Do you like Dylan?" she wonders.

I consider it. We have skirted pained courtesies and managed to speak as actual people.

"Not really."

It is in this same spirit of truth telling that, when we have reached my house, I ask if she would join me in an experiment.

"Sounds mysterious," says she.

"Hopefully not. I want to ask about seeing you again."

"Oh—"

"But under these terms. That you answer exactly as you feel, without any sugarcoating."

Madison holds her chin to throat, appraising me from beneath her brow. Surely I am being cute. But when nothing more comes:

"OK. So have you asked me?"

"No. Now I will: I wondered if you'd like to go to a NASCAR race this Sunday."

She is tickled. "You're a sneak! That buildup. It was starting to sound like a marriage proposal."

"But I'm serious about the experiment."

"All right. So now, what again?"

"Your honest answer."

"Right. My honest answer is I'd like to see you again, but I'm not exactly a NASCAR girl. How's that?"

"It's very good. I ask because I'm not a NASCAR guy either. It would be a first for both of us, and I think it might work if we go into it together."

This is as near as I want to get to naming my idea. If she and I are to hold our reality, the best chance is to again find some odd context. Were I to invite her to drinks and dinner, or dinner and a movie, or whatever the blueprint, I might not have a word to say to her.

She ducks to regard the sky through the windshield. This silent studying of the cosmos makes me a little uneasy. It is not for fear of rejection. Rather I worry she is making too much of my idea, that I've spoken too mystically, and that now she will seek to meet me, contorted and operatic, and queer the whole thing.

But no.

"What the hey. Sure."

3

At the edge of downtown cars are hemmed in like beef cattle. I can't remember a worse morning drive. Tap gas, stamp brake. A maroon flower blooms on my right knee.

In the lobby I bump into Jane. It is a slightly awkward meeting. Only yesterday she sent an email:

How was your trip home? How was the sales call? Where
ARE you? I have the oddest sense I'm being ducked.
Paranoia?

I have been avoiding her, to tell the truth. It is from fear of another wallop of desire. But here we are. We shift around, exchanging pleasantries. She spies the blood on my knee.

"What on earth is that? Henry, Jesus! Come with me right now." A fierce sympathy. It recalls a time when I could bring to my mother a pinched finger or wasp sting, and feel the injuring world shrink in fear.

Upstairs she retrieves a first aid kit from the supply room. I am led to an empty conference room and instructed to sit on the table. She wheels a chair opposite.

"So. Let me see."

Gingerly, I roll up the pant cuff. She bends to investigate. Our arrangement is such that it is possible to lean forward undetected and inhale her clean soap smell.

"Henry—!" she scolds.

I jump and tip back. But no: it is only her shock at the wound. She takes hold of my calf, pressing fingers gently, while her other hand negotiates the knee. Her breath falls light and warm. Sweet Mother Mary.

"Hold still."

She aligns a fresh bandage. An act of great concentration. Her tongue curls to feel at a canine, pressing the tooth's point.

"Sorry—did I hurt you?"

"What? Not at all."

"You moaned."

"Did I?"

"I know you," she says, smoothing tape. "If someone doesn't doctor this for you, you'll just bleed in silence." This is ridiculous of course. She says it only for something to say. Has she too sensed the charge? "Did you even disinfect it? Next time, hydrogen peroxide."

"Yes. I'll remember."

Jane clips shut the kit and stands. She leans against the table, propping one foot on the other. I busy myself fixing the pant cuff. There passes a decidedly strange instant. It is something like postcoital shyness.

"So. I think that's pretty royal treatment for a guy who's been avoiding me."

"I haven't been avoiding you."

"I know. I'm kidding!"

"Oh."

"So. Everything OK? Otherwise, I mean?"

"Can't complain."

"Good."

"You?"

"Yes."

"Good."

"Yup."

"Thank you for this."

Jane bounces her palm lightly on the table's edge. She looks to the
windows, though the view is mainly of the warehouses and rail yards
at the city's southwest edge. How little I really know her. For all the
scene space she has occupied in my head, I have not much to show in
the way of actual familiarity. Office friendships are strange beasts.

Early on, I felt I had her number. She was quick to laugh and liked
to be entertained. I discovered that a brand of scorched-earth humor
worked best. Not cruel: sharp-tongued. Despairing of human foibles.
And nothing was better than a well-placed curse. A heartfelt obscen-
ity, deployed just so, activated her pleasure centers like a neon sign.
I used to work myself into a lather over some political matter or piece
of bureaucratic office nonsense, something I wouldn't otherwise
have given a second thought, just to have a store of material for
coarse, comic rants. Yet no sooner had I perfected this act than was
I brought up short. One day driving with her for lunch, I spied a fat
woman seated in the shelter of a bus stop. To my eye, trained as it was
for human absurdities and the opportunity for comic rant, this woman
was wearing a stupid expression. "What do you guess she's thinking
about?" said I to Jane, in the old knowing voice. But Jane missed
her cue.

"I don't know," she said, considering it. "Maybe she's thinking about
the work she has to do today, or she could be thinking about her
mother . . ."

There was a sense of having put my foot into empty space. Our standing was not at all as I'd imagined. Jane was the grown-up, she knew what empathy was, it came to her without thinking. At best, I was one to watch. There was hope, but you couldn't say how I might turn out as an adult. It was too far off to tell.

Now Jane turns from the window. Her mouth is drawn tight. We nod mutely at each other, a meaningless gesture. She pulls at her watch. "Oh! I've got a meeting with the boss man."

"Oh?"

"That's right. Jealous?"

"Very."

"Better not keep him waiting."

"No." What an ugly turn. She collects the first aid kit. "So long!"

I study the empty room, feeling spurned somehow. The whiteboard is blank but for a half-erased note in its corner, *Please Do Not.*

"Barry? It's Henry. Any lunch plans? That's right . . . No, no agenda. The agenda is food."

The agenda is to broach the subject of my dinner with Keith. I am thinking in business terms. It is not a confession. Not quite. Keith wanted to know about Markitel; I told him more or less what I believed he already knew.

At ten of twelve, I seek Barry out. His cubicle is the largest in a line of three-sided alcoves along the building's western side. He used to have a proper office on 17, but he was moved upstairs when Keith arrived. This was so that he, Keith, would have all of his direct reports on one floor. I happen to know it is also because Keith did not want anyone in Sales to have a comfortable home nest. "There's only one place you want a sales guy to feel at home," he explained to me. "The buyer's office."

Barry is standing at his window, studying clouds. An impressive mackerel sky is organizing at the city's southern edge. Steel filing cabinets rise like a privacy hedge above the cube's shared three-quarters wall. On top of these is a miscellany of corporate trophies, small glass obelisks with marble bases and tiny plaques proclaiming one or another sales goal achieved.

"As a kid I used to do this for hours," he says, not turning around. "We moved *constantly.* I'm talking Missouri, California, Texas, Florida, Maryland . . . I'm a military brat, so. When we landed in a new place, it was new schools, different neighborhood, new friends, the works. My trick was whenever I was feeling out of sorts, I'd go out in the yard and look up." He looks up now. There is no back wall to his cubicle, only the immense floor-to-ceiling panes. He cuts a dark figure against the soaring light. "Do you know what I saw there?"

I am on guard. He sounds to be gathering sticks for a religious metaphor. But he surprises me: "I saw the same sky from where we lived before."

I cast a wary eye over the cubicle's shared wall. No one speaks like this. Not in this office. Naked humanity is at odds with the very furniture. This is not as cold as it sounds, only that workplace decorum means attending the Now, not fishing memories from childhoods long dead.

At last Barry turns. He paces the cubicle. At the cabinets he touches a finger to each trophy point. "Can you believe this weather? Maybe seventy tomorrow! Have to get in a little . . ." He faces me, hunches his shoulders slightly, folds his hands together at his crotch. The small pendulum motion and a conspiratorial wink. Barry has remembered his place.

It is a fine day, diamond bright. Lunch is a ten-minute walk. It occurs to me the best strategy is to raise the issue now, offhandedly, out here in the gleaming hope of a Southern winter day.

"Had a good meal with Keith last week."

"Oh?" Barry is smiling, nodding to people as we pass.

"Cirelli's."

"Makes for a nice lunch!"

"Dinner, in fact."

"Well, well. Thanks for the invitation."

"Very last-minute. Keith wanted to talk through some things."

"I'm kidding!" Barry crows. He is in high spirits. I note him glancing at his figure in shop windows, touching his belt or running thumb under waistband to smooth the tuck of his shirt. I am uneasy and fall silent.

We move along the city's main boulevard. Once this was a grubby alley of stores hawking booze and stereo equipment. Now it is strung with sidewalk tables and umbrellas. Often there is live music, a middle-aged guitarist in a Hawaiian shirt who sings of beaches and parrots. This makeover was hailed as another coordinate on the city's upward trajectory. It pleased me no less than it did my coworkers, all of us glad to see blight pushed from the downtown business districts. Only now I confess to a certain jitteriness when I come this way. The street's vitality has turned despotic. I detect in the patrons' chatter, their barking good times, a kind of parlousness. Five minutes here and my shirt is soaked through.

Barry says, "Keith wanted to talk about what things?"

"Markitel."

He stops short.

"Ho: wait one second. We already talked that out. At the Monday meeting."

"He was under the impression the trip wasn't so hot."

"He said that? Because I sure as heck never said that. No, sir."

"No?"

"Heck no! Why would I? The name thing? That's *nothing*. That's a *hiccup*. For what Markitel needs, our stuff's perfect. Keith doesn't need the gory details. He just needs whether I think it's still a solid prospect. I do; it is." He regards me suspiciously. "You didn't tell him . . ."

Above us pigeons leer from nooks in the windows of the MetLife building. Its white stone cornice is crowded with eager peeping heads.

"Look, Keith called asking what the hell happened in Minneapolis. So I agreed it wasn't great—" Barry has stalked ahead. He pivots, glaring.

"'What the hell happened'? The answer to that is 'Why? What did Barry say?' But by this point he had you at the dinner table, am I right? 'Have some wine, Henry . . .'"

"For chrissake."

"Don't brush it off!"

We are drawing attention: a small audience of diners at a nearby table. Even the panhandler by the MetLife's entrance goes bug-eyed and tiptoes away in fearful burlesque. Barry wanders ahead, sunk in his own council. We move along in silence. The silence doesn't last.

"God. You—you fucked me." He seizes his skull and actually wheels in a circle. "You fucked me!"

Above the city spires, clouds plumb the sky like zeppelins. Barry turns in his circles; I watch the sky. What I wouldn't give to be up there. He halts his turning and storms off the way we've come, descending the boulevard's gentle north-south slope, a sad spectacle shrinking against the landscape of forking streets and traffic lights and flanking towers.

Then he is gone, absorbed by the world at work.

4

Old Glory and NASCAR and WINSTON SERIES and two I can't yet make out . . . Madison thinks they read CASTROL MOTOR OIL and POW/MIA. The flags writhe and crack with the morning clouds behind them. Between sections of concrete amphitheater come glimpses of the wide gray track and an infield of cars whose bright-painted sponsorships would shame coral fish. A ridge of mast lights circles the stadium. Their standards are stark black against a low orange sky. Something in the silhouette quality of the stadium and these lights suggests a fortress under siege, the poles standing like the lances of a patient cavalry. Morning at the Bank of America Motor Speedway is an imperial spectacle.

Less so the scene in the fields. The speedway is flanked by acres of dirt parking lots and scrub lawn, the greater part taken over by tailgaters in their third or fourth day of revelry. Trucks, vans, campers, and RVs, rows on rows of hoods and fenders, so that, turning from Richard Petty Boulevard into this midway, I begin to despair of ever

finding Cory. And what then? Park and sit emptily with Madison until the race begins? Already she is nervous. She does not regret coming, not yet, but the jerseyed hordes, the smoking grills with their
gamey smells, the tribal cheers and bellowing country anthems . . .
From either side of the lot's alleys we are watched by the gleeful, the
entrenched, the inalienably belonging. They regard our blundering
passage, then huddle at their keg barrels and cooking stoves. What
conspiratorial smiles! No matter how liberal a person's sentiments, how
tolerant and unprejudiced his cardinal humors, he is glad to see the
outcast, to know conclusively it is not him.

". . . you're sweating."

"Sorry?"

"I said, are you feeling all right?" She is concerned.

"Of course! I'm looking forward to this."

"Me too!"

Silence. My plan to elude the horrors of the first date, the aching
self-consciousness and flights into role-playing, has boomeranged. She
pats at her upswept hair. For our excursion today she has massed her
hair on top of her head, a woolly burl speared through with a black
chopstick. It does not escape my attention that the jade ring and bent-
fork bracelet have been left behind.

"We're on the stadium's proper side, in the right section. Cory said
they'd be impossible to miss. And we can always call." Except in this
ocean he can't guide us anywhere, the idiot.

On cue my phone buzzes:

"We're looking for you, boss."

"Likewise."

"Yall're here? Which way you pointed?"

"We're on the western side of the stadium, probably a hundred
yards out."

"Right. Hold on."

"How do you plan to—"

"Look left, 'bout fifty yards up."

Lifting from the sea of glinting hoods is a long, segmented pole.
The pole tips drunkenly, then wiggles upright. It is still for a moment,
thinking. Then a swirling motion takes hold. Gyrations climb its

wobbly body; a bolt of black cloth unwinds at the tip. Another pause. The pole falls left, rises, pitches right, up again, left: sluggish arcs that set the pennant flying.

A Jolly Roger, in sunglasses and missing a front tooth, flutters above the crowds.

We park and pick our way between two long rows of pickups, vans, SUVs. The grassy corridor between, still wet in shadow, has a jostling, hemmed intimacy. Grill smoke, tin-can stereo music, sputtering keg hoses: the thick cheer of the communal drunk. Cory sits deep in a folding chair beneath the raised gate of a monstrous four-wheel drive. Spying us, he tugs his hat brim, pitches forward and pulls himself upright. He stands with spine arched, one hand pressed daintily to the small of his back; the other tips a beer can above his throat. In two swallows it is finished. The can lands on a glittering stack in a nearby yellow barrel.

"You believe I work for this guy?" he says to Madison by way of introduction.

"Why not?"

"Look at him! He's a disgrace!" Now he extends a hand. "Cory Freer."

"I'm Madison."

"Glad to meet you, Madison." He raises his cap with half-ironic gentility. White splotches ornament the bill. The front reads GODDAMN SEAGULLS. "Now Madison, pardon me for saying, but you look familiar. Where'd you go to school?"

"Agnes Scott."

"Angry Twat!"

I shift uneasily. "All right now."

"An Angry Twat grad! I don't believe it! You're a long way from home here. But these are good people. We'll look after you."

He actually drops an arm around Madison and squeezes. Far from looking put out, she smiles and lays her head on his shoulder in good sisterly fashion. He turns with her to face the milling crowd behind him. "Fellas? Hey! Everyone? This is Madison." The crowd calls its welcome. "It's her first race—am I right, Madison? I thought so. And she's here with this guy. He signs my tiny paychecks." Jovial booing. How easy they are in his company. Even Madison—not five minutes in and already she too is smitten. She attends closely while he points to one person or another and confides some zinger by way of introduction: "Guy with that goddamn Frisbee and the floodwater pants, that's Teddy Zendler. Teddy met his wife on the innernet and probably's trying for kids the same way. By the grill in the cowboy hat is Samantha Willis, she'd have it 'Sam'—a lesbian I believe; she's twice turned me down," etc. His is a discerning shtick of which the Southerner is king: wicked-sounding but affectionate, droll, imperturbable above all.

"And *this* guy." Cory wheels with Madison and points to me. "Well. You know all about him."

"I don't," she says. "Tell me!" I am heartened by her mood. It is Cory's centrality, his self-sureness. He has not wrecked the strangeness but merely parted it, shown us in.

"Sanest guy I've ever met," he replies solemnly.

"Safest?"

"Sanest."

"Oh! Good. Sane is good. Safe is boring."

"Mostly," I say, "I'm thirsty."

Here Cory collects us, Madison and me, a heavy hand falling on each of our shoulders. "I'll tell yall something, boy. I am well-oiled. Well. Oiled." *Wail. Awled.* His drawl has seized him. Madison asks if there's anything to drink besides beer. "I hope not," he says. When I explain she doesn't drink, Cory frowns. "Jesus Christ, what a tragedy. Why?"

"It's a toxin," she says primly.

"Sister, you said it. Kills boredom and the blues. I guess there might be some ginger ale for the bourbon drinkers, but . . ." He is distracted by something behind us. A group of seven or eight men is passing along the corridor. I can see nothing to distinguish them from the midway crowd. They are cheery, early middle-aged, faintly grizzled. Except as they near I observe their hats, each embroidered with a number 24 and dyed in rainbow colors. Cory is muttering something.

"Gordon is a faggot!" he bellows. Madison and I jump. The men stop.

"That so?" says one. He stands astride, sizing Cory. "Well, that faggot's got four Cup championships."

"Four!"

"Four."

Cory ponders this. "Yall come on in," waving them into camp. "Have a beer with us before yall watch that faggot lap the field." He ushers them away to one of the kegs. Madison grips my arm excitedly. "What was that all about?"

"I have no idea."

They are filling cups, introducing themselves. "Does he *know* them?"

"I don't think so."

"I thought they were going to kill each other!"

The morning's orange ripeness has lifted into a clear, aching light. Above the pandemonium of hoods, the light and sky bring to mind my mother's old luminist prints of English countryside in summer. Clouds, lumbering and inviolate as bulls, graze in a field of blue. Nearer the stadium they are harassed by kites darting and swimming against their white hides like tsetse. From behind the walls comes a bass growl, tremendous and brooding. The sharp morning air carries a taste of fuel. I fetch two drinks and wait with Madison. We stand almost hip to hip, our affections rushing to life. The sun-warmed denim of her thigh brushes mine. I take a pious sip of ginger ale, thinking I might cry for love of her. How helpless are the goliaths of Past and Future against this instant. Lovely, sweet Madison; lovely, sweet life!

Soon the food is set out. Quilts are draped over lowered truck gates and spread with steaming foil platters. Brunswick stew, corn bread, white-and-purple slaw, brown sugar baked beans, half-moon cuts of salted potato, heaps of barbecued chicken and pork, and even grilled black bean patties. An impressive buffet, pioneer ample. To my surprise, Madison plunges into the barbecue. "Mostly I'm vegetarian," she explains. "But good pulled pork . . ." She groans and takes another reddening mouthful of sandwich.

The men in numbered hats have moved on. Yet there remain two new strangers among us, a man and woman perhaps in their fifties. They are bent over one of the tailgate tables, eagerly forking provisions onto sagging paper plates. Each stands stooped and thick-waisted in loose jeans and white tennis shoes. They have the settled, vaguely bowlegged carriage of British retirees. He is all business, parsing the food with eagle eye and quickly picking the choicest bits. She follows, straightening the platters as she goes. The man looks up. Noting my attention, he nods amiably.

"Good chow, beautiful day. I mean, what more could a guy want?"

"Are you a friend of Cory?" I ask politely.

"Oh, we're old pals."

The woman nudges him. "We only met your friend today," she says. "He invited us over. Such a gentleman!"

"That's our bus," says the man. He indicates a yellow school bus parked nearby. It is the blunter, wider sort built to accommodate the wheelchairs of disabled children. The rear gate shows a patchwork of stickers, like destination labels on a steamer trunk. Madison squints at the messages. "Bought it at government auction," he explains. "Tricked it out like you wouldn't believe. Come on, I'll show you." I make a motion to beg off, but Madison interrupts:

"Is that a Marfa sticker?"

"You bet."

"Have you been to the art colony?"

"Sweetheart, we go to the Chinati Open House almost every year."

"I don't believe it!" She falls into step with the man, who is already on his way to the bus. There is nothing to do but trail along.

"Do you know Marfa?" the woman asks me. I do not. She explains it to me. The explanation is rich in encyclopedia nouns (Dostoyevsky, Fyodor; Judd, Donald; minimalism . . .) This casual fluency, her manner of tossing out erudite signifiers like candy at a parade—I sense an invitation, nearly a challenge, to match wits. Probably she is a polymath. Such people like to sound the depth of their knowledge off others. In this she reminds me of my father. "I'm Karen, by the way." She nods ahead. "That's my husband, Paul." He and Madison are bent in conversation.

Entrance to the bus proves difficult. Its accordion door is jammed at the middle hinge. We must turn sideways and shove past. "Sorry!" Paul cries. "Not by design, obviously. Don't worry—it's easier to get out than in."

The interior is oddly spacious. It seems impossible the exterior dimensions are enough to contain it. In an instant I understand why: the bus has been emptied of its benches. There is a couch and an easy chair and even an old legged kitchen stove. But the strange cavernous feel is not only the missing seats. There is something more. Beneath the steel sashes each window has been painted over in midnight blue, leaving only the top panes clear. Lancing sunlight illuminates the bus like a cathedral.

Paul rattles off his initiatives to outfit the bus—the tearing out of seats, the particular challenges of the stove, carted in piecemeal and assembled in place. It's an animated telling. He jumps spryly about in pantomime of his efforts. Karen sits reared back in the easy chair, watching her husband fondly. From time to time, as when he recalls that the stove's placement blocked the sleeper bed in a previous couch, he shoots her a beleaguered glance, and in her wince is summed the entire episode.

"Why are the windows painted?" Madison wants to know.

"Privacy of course!" He hops to the stove and swings down the oven door. An itching, bitter smell pours out. It is like the smell of a garden hose that has been lying in the sun.

"Paul . . ." Karen warns.

Reaching inside, he withdraws a plump freezer bag whose ash-green content is cannabis or nothing.

"Paul!"

He throws out his arms, innocence crucified. "Their friend was good enough to host us." Karen squeezes at the bridge of her nose. Paul busies himself at the stove.

Madison tiptoes over to me with a gleeful, conspiratorial look. I should be glad for her eagerness. The trouble is I haven't touched the drug since college, and then only twice. Its effects are hilarity or fear. Hilarity *and* fear. These are lunacy's ingredients.

Very softly she asks: "Are you going to . . . ?"

"Are you?"

"Not alone."

"You certainly won't be alone."

"You know what I mean."

So. The choice is smoke or stand as the killjoy whose very posture is iron with disapproval. This after all my shamanism about putting ourselves in the way of the unexpected. Madison waits to see if I have the courage of my convictions.

"Why not."

She grips my elbow, a quick squeeze. Karen speaks from the far end of the bus, eyes still closed. "Paul," she says wearily, "it may not be something they want to do." Paul doesn't budge. "It's a free country." Now Karen eyes us. "I'm sorry. When this one gets an idea . . ."

"We'll try a little if it's all right," Madison says.

Paul turns from the stove. The cigarette is a miniature white-rolled bat. "A little is right! We brought this stuff back from Vancouver. Potent like you don't know."

A match flares. Madison puts the bat to her lips and gives a modest suck. She waits with eyes closed, contented as a maharaja, then releases a luxuriant white sigh. The bat is passed to me. In one acrid draw, my fears are shown to be absurd. It is a pleasant molten procession, like bourbon in the esophagus, though it traces the blood's total course, pumping wine-warm into even the tiniest vessels of the fingertips. Madison stands on her toes and whispers to me. Her message is lost to effect, a buzzy effervescent murmur like a flute of champagne raised to the ear. Gravity, in both senses, lets go. My balloon floats like a skull. Switch that. The bus's arched steel ceiling looks to be propped on heavy beams of sun. Each storms with bright particles. I sink with Madison into the couch.

For some time no one speaks. Karen is upright in the chair, eyes closed; Paul holds trance at the stove. Madison studies the weave of her afghan. The outside world is silent, esteeming our sacramental hush. Above us the purpled windows. Yet even the high clear panes show nothing, not a kite or contour of cloud, only the mute blue-blank sky. It seems possible we are soaring. Yes—camped in the belly of an unmoored dirigible, bound for infinity. I have the dizzying sense that to look over the painted glass is to see the parking lot falling away, shrinking to nonexistence against a great continental swath that runs to the planet's edge . . . I rise from the couch to check.

"Still there?"

Somehow it is natural that Karen should know my suspicion.

"Yes."

"Mm-hm. It makes me think . . . Do you know Laing's theory of the crying child?"

"Remind me."

"A child wakes in the night and cries out 'Mama! Mama!' and waits in fear until she comes. What is it about her arrival that comforts him?"

"Proof she hasn't left."

"It seems so. The child cries, the mother comes, and only when she comes does he stop. Only Laing said something else. It's not the mother's presence the child wants confirmed."

There comes a pricking of dread, like a spur in the stomach. "Whose then?" Karen wipes her fingers on a napkin.

"His own."

Madison's eyelids sit at half-mast. She raises her chin, the better to watch Karen. "What does that mean?"

"Oh, I think it's one of the old worries. That the world we know might tip away like stage walls—*flump!* With nothing behind."

Madison watches Karen with a look of stoned skepticism. When she opens her mouth to speak, it enters my head that she will embarrass herself. She will thwart this sharp possibility with some ramshackle cross. Aromatherapy. The I Ching. But in fact she says nothing, instead taking up the joint.

Karen waits.

"That doesn't bother you," she says finally.

"I've never thought about it, to be honest."

"And now?"

Madison shrugs. "No. It's too different from how I feel when I paint."

"You're an artist?"

"Yes—oh, it's Paul I was telling, wasn't it." Paul is propped against the stove. He looks to be asleep on his feet. "Yes, I am."

I ask what she feels when she paints. Madison sets down the cigarette. "Wowza . . ." She gives several quick blinks. Her eyes are pure
iris. In this light and up close, they are not so much yellow as the color
of wheat. "What did you say?"

I too have forgotten the question.

"Oh. When I paint, it's not . . . me." She pauses as though choosing her words. "I feel something brought into being, a person called
I, but who isn't really myself."

"Proust," says Karen.

Madison reddens. "Is that who? I didn't know. I heard it once and
that was the way I'd always wanted to put it."

What on earth are we talking about? One puff and everyone scatters into secret languages.

"And you, Henry?" Karen wonders. "Does it bother you?"

"Which part?"

"The idea that we can't take for granted anything we see or seem
to know. That it might be just a veil we've drawn over oblivion, or the
unexplainable."

God in heaven, remove me from this dorm room.

"Nope."

"No?"

"As my father would say: Show me the data."

Karen makes as if to ponder.

"Yes, though you may find there comes a day when some certain-
ties become a little less—certain! I shouldn't presume, but when you're
younger, things like . . ."

"Death."

"For example. Yes. The end remains . . . abstract."

In this she is not wrong. Even after my mother died, there remained a problem of abstraction. I found myself in a kind of rarefied
grief that was not grief at all but instead a survey of a person grieving.
What does the bereaved do? What is his appetite? How does he speak
to his sister at the breakfast table three days after? My family was no
better off. We wandered the house like ghosts, not knowing what to say
to one another, how to sit, where to put our hands. So it went for days,
each of us adrift in the high thin air of the notional, more observers

than subjects. Then one afternoon while rummaging a kitchen drawer I came upon her crossword pencil. A newish Ticonderoga No. 2. So suddenly alive was I to place and time, so wrenched and hollowed—it was like the panic of a sleepwalker slapped to consciousness. Standing in the kitchen of my childhood at two in the afternoon on a Wednesday six days after my mother's burial. It was as astounding as the moment of her death. More so. There in the present instant was the first proof. Her pencil, the markings of her teeth tight in my hand, even as history was bearing her away.

Again in her uncanny way, Karen picks up the thread:

"I'm the oldest in my family, and after my mother died—my father died five years before her—so after she died I remember thinking, Well, if it's a line . . . Put it this way: I felt I'd been presented suddenly with a new fact, however obvious. It reminds me of Kierkegaard's summation of Hegel, that single, damning—"

"Hopping Jesus!" Paul leaps from the stove. He dances in place, holding his wrist. "The goddamned burner!" He whirls on the appliance, crouching as if it might lunge, then shoots out an arm to snap off the offending dial.

Karen is out of the chair. "Darling? Let me see." He brings her his wrist. "Whooch! Baking soda!"

In the ensuing medicals, I signal Madison we should go. We push from the couch and offer Paul our sympathies. His wrist is not so bad. Madison thanks our hosts for longer than seems necessary. In truth I am anxious to be out of this goddamn machine. So it is that I beat her to the exit, and in clumsy fashion leave her to hold back the jammed door while I push and heave, half tumbling, blinded but thankful, into the glaring sunlit present.

5

Standing for the national anthem. A hundred thousand lean over the track and moan together. Next to me Cory is red-faced but somber as a judge, bird-shit hat touched to patriot heart. Madison screws an eye against the trumpeting notes. (She climbed to our perch with the look of a child lost in an airport, measuring the stadium with wonder and terror.) On "brave" there comes a high turbine shriek. Three jet fighters, tremendous in silhouette, flash overhead—then only the colored trails: red, white, blue. There is barely time to cheer before a metallic voice exhorts the drivers to start their engines. Ignition is like detonation, a thundering heard, then felt.

The start is not as I'd imagined. There is no dropped flag or searing wheel-spin. Instead the cars lumber forward together. They stalk the pace car as a pack, a kind of growling phalanx. Each holds place among his starting neighbors, but impatiently—zigzagging tightly or gunning forward before falling back. Soon the pace car defers. A column of bulb lights climbs to green. Cory bites his thumb and finger and gives a piercing whistle. The crowd, already standing, stomps and wails. The pack rounds the near corner. As cars gain the straightaway, drivers stand on the gas. The phalanx dissolves. They pour down the long track, shearing the deafening absolute, their roaring engines pushing and flattening to high harmonized drone. Each passes us as a humming blip, a blurred dart, traceable to the eye again only when past and sweeping into the parabolic arc of the far turn.

"That's how she's done!" Cory leans forward to look across at Madison. "Madison?" he shouts. "Madison! You look like a fawn that wandered onto a bombing range!"

"What?" she shouts to me.

"He asked if you're OK!"

"I'm OK!"

"What'd she say?"

"She's OK!" I lean to her, waiting as the race recedes to the far length. "Are you?"

"Yes, but I'd like to sit down."

Through the standing thicket of spectators I watch the second pass, a sequence of whip-snap streaks. It is impossible not to flinch. Soon the crowd settles in. Cory drops to the bench, fishing beneath it and coming up with a brown plastic flask. He offers it to Madison, but she sits now with head in hands. Cory points the flask at me.

"Is that GatorByte?"

"No. I'm experimenting with ingredients. Don't have a name for this one yet."

"Pass."

"You'll wait for FDA approval."

"I'll wait for a label that's more than a strip of tape with three *X*'s in ballpoint."

"It's so I don't mistake it."

"What else do you have lying around in brown flasks?"

He snaps a pull from the flask, then squints into the neck while working the sample around in his mouth. "I forget. That's the trouble."

The race proves to have a mesmeric rhythm. There is the plummeting, pitched-whine velocity on the near length, then a fading . . . the quieter skimming of the far side, cars moving like cutters across a bay . . . then around again, big and screaming. But I discover the rhythm is more than loud reiteration. For among the crowd, people are variously leaning to pound their knees or rearing back with hands on hats, thrilling to some well-wrought deke or feint among the racers, or a driver's sacrificial gesture to advance his team. (The drivers race in teams, I learn.) Cory watches it all keenly, pitching about in fits of body English. Now he leaps to his feet, shouting, "Ma *boy!*" Several spectators shake their heads, their driver gone down to defeat in some meticulous skirmish for wheel space.

Madison excuses herself.

I watch the track without a thought to speak of, gently stunned by winter sun and track noise and buzzing hash afterglow. Presently Cory makes some remark that goes missing under an avalanche of noise. I am of a mind to leave it, except his sidelong glance says he is waiting for a reaction.

"Come again?"

"I said, there's a rumor going round."

"Isn't there always."

"This time mebbe more serious." He says nothing more but instead falls into an absent study of his hearing, placing a cupped hand over one ear, then the other. He's a canny drunk, I think. Perhaps not even drunk. Cory can drink like the English.

"OK: What about?"

"Barry." He watches me.

"And?"

"You really don't know?"

"Enough. Say it or don't."

"I hear he got shit-canned."

It is my turn to watch him. "I'd think I'd have heard."

"Me too. But there's more. Enough to make me think this one's real."

"It's a resourceful rumor mill," I say dryly. "What else?"

He hoists the flask, then hunches over, resting on his thighs and worrying the cap with deliberate twists.

"Goddamn it, man. *You* brought it up."

Now he smiles. "What I hear is—" The wall of sound rises and crashes down again. Cory tracks the line as it rounds into the turn. "I hear Keith's already got his new guy. Somebody he worked with before. A ringer."

"Is that right."

"What I heard."

I consider the matter calmly. The rumor is almost certainly true. More than elaborate, it makes business sense. But Barry—! Not that we were great comrades. No, in the final analysis it is a sound commercial decision. More proof Keith has the company in hand.

(So why this strange screw-turning in the belly?)

"Tough break for Barry," Cory says. "This mean things are worse than we think?"

" 'We'?"

"I'm in a capacity as employee spokesman here."

Regarding him, I have to laugh. He's wedged the flask in a back pocket, where it juts precariously, riding up his shirttail to bare a white handle of flesh. His novelty hat sits on his head as though balanced. "Is this how you happened on extra race tickets? Get me drunk and ply me for information?"

"Get you drunk? You won't even wet your lips! No, this is fresh news, captain."

"It would only mean Barry's 'moved on to explore other opportunities.' I'd have no doubt we would find 'an experienced and high-caliber professional—'"

"*Software* professional."

"'An experienced and high-caliber software professional to pick up the great work Barry has done for Cyber Systems . . .'"

"'We wish Barry all the best in his future endeavors.'" Cory makes a hawking noise but does not spit. He raises and resettles the hat so that it slants sharply on his forehead. His eyes disappear under the bill. "But *do* you?"

"Wish him the best?"

"Yep."

"Why not?"

"No reason."

"You think he was fired, and you think I had something to do with it."

"It's better for the company. If I'm honest I'd say I'm relieved. Other people too."

"Glad to hear it, but you're reassuring the wrong person."

"OK, captain."

"I mean it. That's Keith's decision."

"The captain has spoken."

"This is serious. And don't call me captain."

Madison returns, threading her way along the bleacher. Cory stands and waits until she's taken her seat before settling in again. (I am forever being outflanked by Southern manners.) The blond strands at her temple shine darkly. "I just needed some water on my face. It's hot." She squints over the track. "Who's winning?"

"God knows."

The field makes another earsplitting pass, and now there is some noise from the crowd. A car in blaring orange sponsor colors has swept from the pack's middle to an outside edge. The driver finds a corridor perilously close to the wall, then accelerates.

"Not on the *turn!*" Cory cries.

As the leading three cars lift into the banked curve, the orange challenger moves parallel to a fourth, a green-bodied vehicle whose

emerald sheen I've observed making patient progress over the last ten
or so laps, sliding up the colored race stream. Orange and green hit
the turn together. "Won't happen. Inside advantage." Cory is resigned.
He is for the challenger. Yet even as he says this, the crowd is rising,
howling. The orange car has yielded nothing. It holds between the
green and the turn's high embankment, coursing the bend as though
on a rail. From our vantage the two cars appear at the shallowest of
angles, almost a single profile, green with an orange trim. But watching, the profile shifts. Orange creeps ahead, machine revealing from
behind its green twin: a blunt snout, now the furious front wheel. Cory
seizes his hat in a fist and commences lashing his thigh. "COME ON,
YOU BEAST! YOU BASTARD! COME ON!"

Suddenly the challenger jerks backward. He has touched the embankment. Whether from green aggression or orange mistake is impossible to say. Green fires ahead; the orange car goes sawing through
his wake. Their bumpers miss by a razor. Orange veers crosswise over
the track, a sideways plummet like a fighter plane peeling from its
echelon. So abrupt and sure is the move that it looks almost an inten-
tional feint, except the tires scream for purchase and the chassis erupts
in smoke, tracing the course in a billowing screen. The trailing cars
are blinded. They go careening one into the other, banging and clattering like steel trash cans tossed in an alleyway. Debris scatters:
bounding tires, sheared body panels, orphaned bumpers whirling like
hatchets, the bits and pieces churning down the raceway as though
in pursuit of the cars that shed them. The orange car passes nearly
the full width of the track before being struck. It is rammed from
behind, an angling blow that lifts the rear wheels and sends the back
swinging around. The car lands lengthwise to the course, then wrenches
upward. It twists violently in midair and crashes door down on the
track's shoulder to go rolling into the grass infield, kicking great
earthen lumps as it tumbles. Men in white coveralls race the field with
extinguishers. The tumbling slows; the car pitches over a final time
and jounces to rest. Its body is stripped to the roll cage. The driver is
pulling himself through the window as the rescue crew arrives. He is
merely angry.

The track looks like a beach after a heavy storm. The slowest cars negotiate the wreckage and join the leaders, now corralled by the pace car. A thin blue vapor drifts from the course into the stands. There is a smell like burnt trash. The crowd shifts in reined excitement, hoping for news that none of the injuries are serious, awaiting license to dig in on disaster.

Cory is grim.

"Dumb. Just plain unnecessary. And Parkson was making a show for it. Goddamn it."

"He and Sharper been going at it since Bristol," says a woman nearby.

"That's what personal rivalry gets you: hotheaded thinking and a crash."

I look to Madison's reaction. She is curled in her seat, holding her arms against her stomach.

"Ooh."

"What is it?"

"I think I'm going to be sick!" Alarmed, I bend to help her. Too late. She keels forward, places a hand to her throat, and retches. Below us a man leaps as if bitten. "God*damn* it!" He yanks off his protective headphones and turns on us. Feeling his backside, the man fixes our bench with a malevolent stare. But when he sees Madison's bent and forlorn figure, he softens instantly.

"OK now. That's alright, sweetheart."

"I'm so sorry," she cries quietly.

"Nope. You're all right. I been puked on before, none of them near as lovely." He eyes me. "Rockefeller, now you help her."

6

We drive back in the high glare of afternoon. Madison sits with her cheek to the window, drawing coolness from the glass. It is nothing serious, she says, a mix of stiff cannabis and track fumes. I am relieved because in fact she looks quite sick, gray-green and wet across her brow and neck. I am also a little put out, to tell the truth. It was she who was so eager to smoke, and now here we are, bound for home, the race not nearly finished. Madison pushes at her hairline with the heel of her palm. She resettles against the window, shutting her eyes against the afternoon light.

But I kid myself. It's not leaving early that rankles. No. It's the closing off of carnal hope. Whatever might have been, now I will only walk her to the door and wish her a speedy recovery.

Miles south of the city, the highway is wide and empty. There is little contour to the land here, fewer trees and more scrub, the state sinking toward swamp and southern panhandle. An open, pounded space made flatter by the light. Without doubt it is a perfect culture for the pall.

But how? you wonder. A warm weekend day, not ten minutes removed from friends and the excitement of the race? Madison's lovely form, however slumped? The trouble is this. Now, when the adventure should be moving toward its loveliest mystery, all is decided. This is the sorrow. Not thwarted sex after all but knowing, absolutely, how the day will end. (And if I'd known absolutely the other way? Had Madison pulled me around the neck to whisper hoarsely in an ear, *Get us home, old boy* . . . ? Yes, the same hollowing. Though not till afterward.) I am reminded that our mystery can't last. She cannot remain what she was last week, or even an hour ago. Already I am casting ahead: I will discover how she votes, her favorite food, tics in her speech; I will learn her first pet's name and how it died . . . possibilities lopped like branches, the secret wood reduced to suburban hedge.

Do not misunderstand. It is not my aim to belittle Madison's life. On the contrary, I would have her remain inscrutable. I would never arrive at that moment a month or year hence when, watching her fuss over one of her eccentricities (she dislikes the color palette assigned to traffic lights, say), I catch myself thinking, Now that's Madison for you! Thinking this and knowing too she is not truly fussing, that it is a hamming kind of fussing, distracted and fluttering—is in fact a code for us to celebrate our odd-couple pairing, the mercantile rationalist and artistic neurotic; cue for me to sigh and tell her to let it go. It isn't much of this before a person finds himself fitted to persona, all promise extinguished, all mysteries solved, his "style" set down as surely as an epitaph.

Madison shifts again, setting one ankle across the other. On the swell of bone above her sandal is a red streak of paint. A leather strap is run beneath her heel. I am seized by an image of Madison in a white studio, wearing only a man's dress shirt and these trodden sandals, standing long-legged before an easel . . . There is no understanding it. That a man should be so set upon, so defeated by the inevitable, the world emptied but for him and his misery, and still be pricked by that old thrill, that trusty phoenix: the hope of a good screw.

I put a hand to her knee. Not lasciviously, mind you. A simple presence she may take as she likes. Perhaps I have nothing in mind but her well-being. She puts a hand on mine and squeezes once. Hope withers. The gesture is as practiced and sexless as an old nurse.

Still my hand lingers . . .

She waits a polite moment, then recrosses her legs so her knee falls out of reach.

FEBRUARY

Three

1

I arrive at the office Monday to find Jane in my chair. An industry periodical hides her face.

"Well, well," she says into the paper. "Good weekend?" She folds the paper and places it on the desk. Both hands settle on the packet; she taps dryly with her fingers. "Let me rephrase: Better weekend than Barry's?"

I say nothing. So it's true. She watches me blackly. The tapping pauses. I see that her hands are trembling. It dawns on me that she is furious.

"I am going to ask you a question. And on penalty of our friendship: Did you have a hand in it?"

"Why do people think this is my doing?"

"Do they now? How *interesting*."

I am tired of this. "Barry doesn't—didn't—work for me. He worked for Keith. *Keith*." She gives a peremptory nod. This is no more than she expected. Now I am well and truly irritated. "May I have my desk?"

"You may." She brushes stiffly past me and out of the office.

But in a moment she is back. She stands inside the door, smoothing an eyebrow with her nails.

"No, look. It's only . . . I came in early this morning and happened by his cubicle. I hadn't heard, but there was no mistaking it. It was just so *empty*. Those little prints in the dust where his trophies were, like he'd been drawn up or vanished . . . And then—suddenly there was a terrible noise, this *guffawing*, from Keith's office. 'Har, har, har!' I had a mind, I swear I did, to throw open his door and scream. Well, before I could do anything stupid, out steps Keith. He sees me and calls out, 'Jane!' he calls. Like that, hale and hearty. 'Jane, come down here and meet someone.' Along I go, dutiful as a schoolgirl—amazing how a simple command from the boss banishes all other thought. And who do you suppose he introduces me to? Barry's replacement! He's *here*. 'Jane, this is Ian. He's going to be helping us in Sales. Ian, this is Jane, an absolute ace marketer. You two are going to be attached at the hip, aha-ha.' The entire time we're shaking hands I can think only, You *vulture*. Which isn't fair, he didn't have anything to do with it. So then I came in here and seethed." She lifts her eyes to the ceiling. "So. I'm sorry." Her apology is curt. The explanation has made her angry all over again.

"That's all right."

"Good."

"Ian is it?"

"Ian."

"What's he like?"

Wrong question. We are grieving Barry, not gossiping about his replacement.

"What's he like? Oh, he's tall and well-groomed and smells nice. A real catch! Keith seems pleased, so he must be *very* good." Acidly, Jane adds: "You two will be thick as thieves, I imagine. Only I would be exceedingly careful if I were you."

"Why?"

But she will not tell me. She frowns at her watch and disappears.

Ian is not in fact tall or well-groomed. He is stout and casually rumpled. The rich purple knot of his tie hangs beneath an open collar. His sleeves are pushed to the elbow in wide rolled cuffs (though it is

an expensive shirt: its buttons are thick and give an iridescent shine).
He has a broad face and black hair that comes across his forehead in
a wave. When he smiles—as he now does, recalling his introduction
to Keith a decade ago—it is the delighted grin of a sadist. He is handsome in the way of a person who knows himself and does not try too
hard. I like him immediately.

". . . I said to him, 'Well, take whatever the last guy quoted and see
if our number isn't better by half.'" He nods to Keith, who is looking
on fondly. "And what'd you say?"

"That it was a federal contract."

Ian smacks his forehead. "Here I am with a hundred subcontrac-
tors in Mumbai, trying to pitch our services to the prime. And who's
the client? Uncle Sam. Only U.S. citizens on U.S. soil need apply."

"What did you do?" I am a sucker for tales of stranded salesmen.
It is the engineer's schadenfreude.

"In my defense, let me say the whole thing was a rookie mistake.
Don't think now I'd ever go without my homework done. So . . ." He
runs a thumb under the heavy lay of bangs, looking to Keith with a
humorous expression. Keith picks up the story.

"He said to me—now I can't do the impression, but he said it in a
proper Hindi accent—'It's not a problem. The team is in Mumbai,
Ohio!'"

Ian pinches his eyes. "This guy knew my pitch before I'd even
made it," he tells me. "I hadn't so much as hinted how we were going
to undercut the competition, but he filled in the blanks like *that*. Then
got right to the point: federal contract. Well, thank you very much."
He looks to Keith. "And now? Here we are."

"Here we are."

Some silent understanding passes between them. Ian shoots out a
hand. "Henry? I'm going to put some time on your calendar, get a
proper education on what it is I'm selling, warts and all. Look forward
to working together."

He leaves us, closing the office door softly behind him. Keith
watches me from across the black expanse of his desk. He is pleased.

"You know how much that guy sold for SSC last quarter?"

"No."

"Guess."

"I don't know. Three million."

"Three!" He makes a face. "At their prices?"

"Five?"

His thumbs come up, pumping: higher.

"Six."

Still the thumbs.

"Eight?"

"*Nine.*"

"In a *quarter?*"

"He admitted to a couple bluebirds. But the rest was all him."

I am dumbstruck. Nine million in three months!

"Think how hard SSC fought to keep him. I wasn't even sure we could make it happen. I put out a feeler a month or two back, there was interest, but when we finally started moving—it took through Friday to get him signed. Otherwise you'd have known."

"Sure."

"Don't think anything was held back."

I have the agreeable sense of being tended to. In fact he does not owe me even this explanation. "I understand."

"You're going to like this guy."

"I believe you."

"We've turned a corner here. Just watch."

2

Shortly before two I wander in the direction of the weekly Management meeting. I say "wander" because along the way I stop at various desks to see how it goes with my team. This is not unusual, but today I have a special purpose. Keith has made official the open secret of Barry's firing, and I want to measure the reaction of my engineers. It is possible I also want to see whether they too harbor suspicion that I pushed Barry out the door.

My investigation yields nothing out of the ordinary. People are sorry for Barry but understand the decision. Some are a little too quick to understand. The younger employees especially. Listening to them leaves an uneasy feeling.

"Sales is binary; you're making your numbers or you aren't."

"It's too bad, but CS isn't a charity."

"Management has to look out for the greater good."

All true. But where do they pick up these phrases? Their corporate fluency is a little unnerving. It's a faith owing less, I think, to any particular confidence in who was let go or who will replace him than to a shining-eyed belief in sacrifice. They trust the right god has been fed.

I am late to the meeting. Taking my seat, I am surprised to find opposite me not Marlene Bartel, Director of Marketing, but Jane. Keith is saying something in an unfamiliar tone and every face at the table attends him seriously.

". . . plenty of news, some good, some not so. Bad news first. Most of you have been here long enough to know about Marlene's knockdown a few years ago. Well. I'm sorry to report it's back."

There are murmurs of dismay. Marlene's "knockdown" was breast cancer.

"She called me an hour ago—from the hospital if you can believe it. Of course if you know her, you don't have any trouble believing it. Routine visit, and some test threw the wrong marker. I don't have all the details, but . . ." Keith swallows, changes course. "I'll tell you what she said. She said, save your cards and flowers. Because she's coming back. That's right. The only thing she wants from us, her words, is a good quarter." His face has gone red. He minds his portfolio, squaring it with the table's edge. The room sits for a moment under pained hush. Keith's concern for his own is enough to raise lumps in throats, whatever our true feelings toward Marlene, who to tell the truth is something of a cannibal. "Now, it seems to me that's the least we can do. And I for one don't plan to disappoint her. I expect you feel the same."

Vigorous nods, everyone. How he manages this, an unloved

woman's bad luck now the emblem of duty, and without a shred of gaucheness: it is beyond me. I am instantly so joined to these people, so full on pride of place, there comes a piercing urge to urinate.

"So, what does this mean for us? The main thing is that Jane here is going to take over Marketing. Only until Marlene is back. Let me say two more things on the subject. First, no one at this table is more upset than Jane by what's happened. Second, we couldn't ask for a steadier hand on the wheel in Marlene's place. We're not going to miss a beat. Jane, is there anything you want to add?"

His speech, and now this deference—Jane is no less affected. Her gaze is wet-eyed but fiery, her bearing like a newly sceptered heiress. She looks magnificent. I would like nothing better than to clamber over the table and kiss her smack on the mouth. "Thank you, Keith," she says. "No."

"All right. On to other things. The other new face at the table today is this guy's." News of the dismissal is managed politely, directly. Marlene's illness serves Keith well. Next to it Barry's firing seems picayune, an unfortunate but necessary bit of corporate house-keeping. "The upshot is, whatever the causes, I couldn't be happier with the team now assembled here. So. Let's start with Operations . . ."

Like that, we are past it. Marlene, Barry: both are swept to the rearview. Now to a practical seriousness, the seriousness of business. There is nothing dreary about it. Set against the morning's emotion, our work is shot through with new significance: the good feeling of carrying on. I could swear the room's fluorescence actually jumps a notch brighter.

When the meeting is finished, Keith asks Ian and me to stay behind. He waits for the room to clear, then launches in:

"It's going to work for us. It's a jolt, these changes, but the right kind of jolt. It'll energize folks."

"Including buyers." Ian nods. "If we manage it right."

"Ian's got a thought for Markitel," Keith explains to me. "He thinks we can spin Barry's firing as a direct result of getting what's-his-face's name wrong."

"Mike."

"Ian, tell him your idea."

He shrugs modestly. "It's what you've said, really. I go to Mike with an apology, tell him we've built our reputation on getting the details right—the buyer's name constitutes an important detail—and the fact that I'm there instead of Barry is proof. I won't say that second part, of course. Better that Mike draw his own conclusion. And he will."

Keith watches me. "What do you think?"

Ian is also watching. His expression is politely bland, but I detect a certain blinking impatience. "It might work," I say so as not to disoblige him. The truth is I think any return visit can only end badly. Keith nods.

"Good. I need both of you up there this week."

"Both of us?"

"We need Mike to see you're still on the right side of the law. He's buying the product your team builds. Also, I want someone to chaperone this thief. New sales guys always need chaperones. They're liable to give away the store trying to make their first deal."

Ian takes on a look of very great umbrage. "I can assure you, good sirs, I've never given away so much as a penny."

"Delta signed for two fifty," says Keith. "We secure Markitel this week or next it's another five hundred. Puts us at seven fifty against four million." He holds up three fingers. "Nexus, Digitex, Billico. Ian?"

"One, one point five, and seven fifty."

"Four million, on the decimal. Time to quarter's end?"

"There's some wiggle room in when we sign the contract versus when we account for the revenue of course, but—"

"No." Keith shakes his head. "Don't talk to me about accounting wiggle room. We're not going to Finance to bail us out. Champs don't go begging to the referees for help."

"I didn't mean—"

"I know you didn't."

"Eight weeks."

Keith stands and walks to a corner of the room; he returns at the same measured pace.

"What I'm about to say stays in this room. The other Directors know the situation is serious. I want you to understand how serious." We are watched from a great height. My scalp tightens agreeably.

"The first point is relatively minor: missing this quarter's number will mean I'm out. The Board gave me two quarters to turn around the business unit. One to sort the problems, one to prove the unit's still viable. Now my dismissal, however heartbreaking it might be, is not our motivation. Our motivation is out there." He holds up an arm, pointing to the door. "A hundred and ninety-plus people, bang out of work."

The weight of this presses all air from the room.

"I'm sorry to say it. I'd be the second GM to fail. The Board won't trouble with a third. Neither would I." Keith sits with us. Having delivered the blow, he joins us now as a comrade-in-arms.

"I'm confident with your own jobs on the line—never mind the jobs of coworkers you hold dear, and the employees who've trusted you—I'm confident you're perfectly motivated. Nothing more is necessary, I'm sure. But I'll give you something anyway. Ego. As part of this company's management team, your first responsibility is this: Make. The shareholders. Money. And to do that? You get the authority of kings. Whatever the chaos out there"—Keith makes a gesture with his hand, taking in not just the office but the world—"in here is control. If you can't make our shareholders rich with all you've been given? Then who are you? The hell's your purpose?" He studies us now, each in turn. "So?"

Ian clears his throat.

"You know, it's just occurred to me I might've left one or two stones unturned in the course of my interview . . ."

Keith leans into the table past where I can see his face. For a moment I can't tell he is laughing. But now he tilts to Ian, wheezing and pressing him as though he might join. Ian gives a rueful smile. To his credit, he does not seem much put out.

"Yes." Ian is nodding. "Another lesson learned, as they say. But I'm wondering—to state the obvious, it's not the amount so much as the time we have to get it. I mean, it's just south of a half million a week."

"And?"

"And . . . yes. And. Hm. What can I say? I'm cautiously optimistic?"

Keith slaps the table. "It will happen!" He is grinning. His pleasure is not only Ian's late realization, I think, but also an appreciation of his own performance. This capacity to be in on the joke and deadly serious is a part of his gift. Having reminded us our fearsome obligation, the signal now is to relish it. We are joined as surely as crusaders for the great work ahead. "I'll leave you guys to it."

When he is gone, Ian and I share a look.

"Welcome aboard."

He consults his watch. "Shortest honeymoon on record."

3

The following workday passes quickly. Seldom have I worked with such focus. Not that it will help. Everything rests on Sales. Still, to speak with any of my team strikes a pang. Without this place, what would become of them? I encounter Rahim, bent at the monitor of an eager young programmer, coaching her through some riddle, and the only moral thing is to race back to my desk, all efforts redoubled. A hopeful sweat over a trivial penance, because there is nothing else.

At nine o'clock Tuesday night I step from my office to stretch. The wider floor is gloomy. Desks and computer shapes lurk in the darkness. The objects are suspiciously still. An ambient glow pushes a row of cube walls into blue shadows on the carpet. The city gleams in the north windows.

Ah, old lonesomeness.

It comes howling down the aisles like an autumn gale. Yes: precisely the cold, soughing ones of Midwestern memory, which thrummed storm panes and sent invisible stampeding herds over uncut lawns, and which carried a scent of wet bark and leaf rot: the very smell of desolation! Now, as then, the ache is almost pleasurable. Once I used to indulge this feeling. It was my habit to wait until the office had emptied, and only then begin the ceremony of departure, neatening papers and squaring my chair, one more businessman preparing for the day to come. In fact I was teasing myself with a fantasy of solitude. *They are all gone. And here I am, left behind . . .* What sweet melancholy. Really I wanted for nothing so much as a train whistle to keen somewhere in the distance. Nothing certifies a person like the sad-solitary. Nowhere does he feel more authentically himself than alone on a beach, contemplating the gunmetal horizon while a stiff Atlantic breeze tears at his shirt. Except the sad-solitary works only when its spell can be easily broken. The man on the beach knows that beyond the dunes is his vacation house, a family snug in their beds, his faithful hound snoring on the porch. Now when I finish and find the office empty, I can't get out fast enough.

I am startled by a plastic tub-thumping sound, someone emptying a wastebasket. Peering across the open floor, I see a small light at the far end. It is Jane. She sits at her desk with head in hands, enclosed in her monitor's ghostly ray. Behind her the skyline looms like a jeweled mountain range.

I approach softly.

"Henry! Jesus, you scared me. Don't just appear out of the dark like that."

"Sorry. Hullo, the camp."

"Why're you still here?"

"I was going to ask you the same."

She nods at the screen. "Keith wants this by tomorrow, part of Ian's education. So here I am. The spoils of a promotion."

"I meant to congratulate you."

"Don't. It's too gruesome. And temporary besides."

"Stop it. It's well deserved."

Jane makes a small demurring motion with her hand. The light makes it impossible to tell if she is blushing. It enters my head that her promotion occasions a drink.

"Now?"

"Sure."

"Tempting. However—" She signals her computer, the papers on her desk. "Another time?"

"Of course."

We bid each other good night. I turn to collect my things. At mind's periphery (not quite thought of, but present enough to require a conscious holding off) sits my open front door and the earthen evening gloom inside, the dusty television and silent unlit lamps.

Happily, she surprises me at the elevators. "I've changed my mind. It's a woman's prerogative."

We take the city in brisk strides. Lamps curl overhead and make floodlight circles on the sidewalk cement. Stepping from one circle to the next sends our shadows winding around like clock hands. The sky is deep and dark. It is a good night to come out of and into a small warm place, a glow of light on wood and the bite of a neatly mixed drink. Except downtown has none of these places. Little in the city is open past sundown. The streets are ghostly. It occurs to me I have never actually gone for a drink downtown except at happy hour. The best we can do is a soulless-looking place whose name is scripted on brick in the half-dark above the door: THE *something* ROOM. Inside is a narrow room of redbrick walls and a lacquered cement floor. The bar is a long counter of panel steel with welded edges. Jane drums on it impatiently. "Find us a table."

"This is mine, remember."

"You get next round."

Next round?

The bar is not crowded. I secure a table and wait. I've never set foot inside, yet I know this place well. The city is chock-full of them now: old depositories that have been gutted and polished and turned into microbreweries or "speakeasies." These buildings were better off as forgotten places. At their broken panes you might catch the boarded-up, sawdust scent of Americana. Now their moldered wood smells have become museum quality. Inside you find history reduced to a sequence of antic old doings, the past alphabetized like dishes in a Crate & Barrel.

Jane comes back with two dripping, thick-bottomed glasses. "I forgot to ask, so I guessed. Gin and tonic."

"Perfect. And yours?"

"With soda. Quinine makes me ill."

"To Directorship." We touch glasses—*clip.*

"And to Barry, and Marlene."

"To them."

"And also I'm sorry about yesterday."

"Can we drink now?"

The gin and tonic is very good. Crisp and pine-bitter, icy in the throat. Jane gasps and sets down her glass.

"God, that's good. It's been a long week already. A *strange* week."

"True."

"And on top of it all, guess who's coming for a visit."

"Who?"

"Michael's parents."

Michael, Jane's husband, is from a patrician Connecticut family. There is no love lost between Jane and her in-laws. This is because Jane is from "the wrong Lexington," as she puts it, meaning Kentucky.

Very innocently, I ask if Michael's grandfather wasn't a senator.

"Why yes, Henry. He was."

"And someone else was big in sugar . . ."

"His great-grandfather. What a memory you have!"

"It's just with a lineage that impressive—"

"Oh, it's impressive all right. That family goes all the way back to the apes."

We finish our drinks. I fetch two more. She takes a deep sip, then remembers something. "Mm—I meant to say. We're having a brunch while their highnesses are in town. Promise me you'll come."

"But I don't know them."

"Doesn't matter. It's not really for them; they only need to think it is. Oh, please, Henry. You can bring a date!" This last is said brightly. (Too brightly?) She does not look at me but instead takes another long drink.

"When is it?"

"Weekend after next."

"All right then. My sister will be my date."

"Oh, good! I'll finally meet the famous Gretchen. And you can meet Michael."

"Actually we've met."

"Have you?"

"At the Christmas party."

"Of course. I forgot. I was a *tad* overserved. Speaking of which—" She slides from her stool and makes for the bar.

Is she pretending?

Michael was leading Jane from the ballroom of the Omni. He had one hand firmly on her elbow. With her free arm, Jane was giving flailing good-byes to each person they passed. When I came upon them, she jerked loose and fell around my neck.

"Henry! Henry, where have you been?" She buried her nose in my chest, pressing her head and rocking slowly. "Don't let him take me!"

"For the love of Christ." Michael hooked her around the middle. When she refused to let go, he tried lifting. Jane went limp. "Fine," he said to her back. "Stay. I'm leaving."

Wordlessly and without looking, Jane reached out an arm and found his. She transferred like a sleeping child, head bowed, passing droopily from my chest to his. Michael stood with his fists at his side, peering stonily at the exit. Wet-combed strands made neat arcs over the pink flesh of his head. "Now? Can we go in peace?" Jane turned her ear to his chest and looked dreamily at nothing. Her lips parceled out something I couldn't hear.

"What? Yes, all right." Michael put out his hand. "Hello, Henry. Michael. I'm married to this one. For my sins."

"Good to meet you, Michael."

"You here with anyone?"

"Oh no," Jane said, drawing herself off her husband. "Not Henry. Henry wouldn't be so pedestrian as to bring a *date*." She was suddenly reanimated. "Do you know why? It's quite complex, but I've figured it out. The last thing *Henry* wants is some woman having him act in all the little predictable . . ." She waved her hand around vaguely, then noticed Michael, who was sighing through puffed cheeks and studying the ballroom chandelier. "You have no idea what I mean, do you."

"Neither of us do," he said. "Good night, Henry."

"Good night."

With this, he swung around and headed for the exit. Jane poked my lapel, her eyes narrow. "I'm on to you, buddy boy." Then she followed trippingly after her husband.

Now she reappears with fresh drinks. She eyes my glass. "S . . . l . . . o . . . w. I'll drink these for both of us, shall I?"

"You know, speaking of the party, you said something—"

"I won't discuss any more things said or done at the Christmas party." This is said mock severely, but she means it.

"Bad?"

"Don't ask." Her tone conjures a morning after loud with spousal negotiation, the kitchen court's verdicts and sentences. Whatever the judgment, it still rankles. Because now she says rather irritably, "Would you care to hear how *I* met Michael?"

"All right."

"It was at the museum. My mother was in town, and there was a show on American impressionism. It was awfully dull. Anyway, Mom was taken by one of the pieces and went to share her rapture with the woman next to her. You know, just spilling over. That woman, as it happens, was a frigid Connecticut bitch. But her son couldn't have been nicer. He listened as Mom went on and on—I mean, people were having to move around them to get a look at the piece.

"We went on two dates. I liked him, and we got along well enough, but nothing jumped out as being any great shakes. A week or two after the second date, what comes looming up on the calendar but Valentine's Day. Terrible when you've just met someone, to be faced with that pink monstrosity. But Michael calls and says very nonchalantly how he sees Valentine's Day is around the corner, and how it happens to fall while he's away on business in San Francisco, and oh, by the way, would I like to come. Like that. Two dates, here's Valentine's—why don't we make a trip out of it? That takes some courage, don't you think?"

Jane peers into her drink, then rattles back the half remainder. She is silent, trading the glass between hands. "It was awkward, as you can imagine. We barely know each other, and here we are tooling around a city drenched in romance. Neither of us could so much as belch without the other nodding and grinning and generally making a scene about how wonderful it all was. Awkward? It was *oppressive*. Worse, for Valentine's, the actual day, he's booked us up north in wine country. I mean, my God, we barely know what to do with ourselves in town, and now we're going to strike out alone into the countryside?

"He'd rented a convertible. A red Mustang. So up the coast we go, our hair flying and the gorgeous lolling hills and the red Mustang, two young things straight out of a gum commercial. Oh my God, but it is *gorgeous*. Have you been to wine country? It might be Italy—not even Italy but a dream of Italy. The hills look soft as velvet, green velvet humps, and the sky blue and cheerful and entirely too close, like in a child's drawing. And the scent . . . the scent! If nostalgia has a smell, it's that. I'd never been to the wine country, but somehow the smell of grapes was as old and familiar as autumn. Now, I doubt very much what I was feeling was love. Not yet. But it was a pretty good simulacrum. And you know, it all might easily have been too much. When things are that lovely, that perfect, it only takes one false move. You smile a little too widely, or you're moved to some hope-less remark—*Oh, how glorious!*—and that's the end. It becomes ridiculous."

"True."

"So I avoided his eye. And we didn't blow it. We were saved—by rain clouds. They came racing in from the Pacific, and I mean racing. Big black things, suddenly hunched over us like buzzards. Michael pulled the car over so we could put the top up. Only we couldn't find the switch! It was the damnedest thing. We checked *everywhere*. We're not idiots; it's not the same as the switch to open it. And there's no owner's manual. So we're stuck. Truly stuck. The clouds are get-ting darker, pushing lower. We're both ducked down, bracing for the deluge. It may sound funny now, but it wasn't. I was wearing a white linen shirt, and I remember panic. How humiliated I'd be soaked to nothing but bra and skin with this . . . this *person* I barely knew. In fact, I was quite angry. I mean, the goddamned convertible was his idea." She sounds angry but isn't. This brusqueness is in imitation of herself, a way of holding up for mockery not Michael but her old fury. "Anyway, what happened was we came upon a factory. A factory! Actually a chicken-packaging plant, right there smack among the hills. And lo and behold, someone there had some mechanical sense. It's under the parking brake."

"The switch."

"The switch. It's a safety feature or something, tucking it under the brake like that. So you don't try to close the top while barreling down the highway. God save us from engineers."

"Easy now—"

"Not five minutes later, the skies open up. I mean sheets and sheets of rain. But now it's a different story. We're snug in our little canvas cocoon, safe and dry, with that heavy drumming just overhead. I felt wonderful. More even than when we'd been sailing along without a care in the world. God, it was all so strange. A glorious afternoon, and then suddenly the desperation, and then just as suddenly salvation—by a chicken-packaging factory smack in the middle of wine country . . ." A bartender circulates the room with a tray of votives, distributing them to the tables. Jane reaches absently for the candle, cupping its flame as though for warmth. Her fingers turn red and spectral. "I would say it this way. The sheer loveliness of the day, of our arrangement, a neat little couple in a neat little convertible passing through the most romantic of all places: it was *fraught*. So to have things upset—not wrecked, mind you, which it would've been had it rained on us—but just thwarted a little, and only then to arrive at that wonderful place, cocooned from a heavy storm and with the pleasure of thinking about a cozy hotel just up the way . . ." She blinks wetly at the candlelight. Shadows leap and shrink about her face. She might be a Gypsy soothsayer hunkered at her crystal.

"It gave me enough breathing room to fall in love and believe it."

Having said it, a small tremor seizes her lip. She takes a mouthful of ice and chews fiercely. But her eyes won't settle. She watches the flame, the comings and goings at the bar, the floor.

"You know," she remarks flatly, "I might just be drunk enough to sob." Her jaw is struck out to suggest the absurdity of it all. I study my hands and try not to look hopeful. It is not nostalgia that afflicts her but regret. I am convinced of it.

Now she arches her neck, stretching. "Ah, Henry. What a comfort you are."

"I was only trying to think of something that wouldn't sound idiotic."

"No, I know. I'm a terrible ingrate." She lays a hand on mine.

I freeze.

What is announced, with the clarity of a trumpet flourish, is a be-

ginning. By rights I should fall to a conspiracy of nerves, either taking her hand in clumsy equivalence (only to scare the wits out of her)
or jumping back and leaving us both embarrassed. Yet my spine holds.
I am the model of cool.

"Well, mister!" Jane cries, suddenly breezy and faraway. "Tell you
what I could use. A certain mix of juniper berry." She is worried things
have become a little too serious. It is enough soul melding for one
night, thank you. And she is right. I eye the bar uncertainly.

"Would gin work?"

Jane squeezes my hand good-naturedly and with not a little relief,
free to let go.

"Get the drinks, you jackass."

4

My father lets me in.

"Cage it! See what it eats!"

We embrace. His neck smells faintly of bay rum. How well I remember this smell, the shower-and-shave bustle of adult preparations
for the adult day while the dauphin lounged, invincible in his privilege of cereal in the den. "Your sister is out," he says. "She asked us not
to wait up."

"I'll see her next week."

"Yes—she's paying you a visit. I'd nearly forgotten. No chance you
might take a few days with us poor kinfolk up here?"

In fact so quick is the trip that I was not planning a stop at home
at all. Yesterday I changed my mind, for reasons that only now am I
pressed to recall. I want to take the pulse of my father's mental state.

I explain that tomorrow Ian and I meet with Markitel; then it is
straight back. My father is sympathetic as ever to commercial de-
mands, though in truth my larger reason for getting back is Jane. At
last the adventure is begun, and where am I? Dispatched on a miserable sales call. Already I fear a cooling of those first lovely sparks. Earlier, while giving my email a final once-over in the airport, this:

H.

You're a sweetheart for listening to an old drunk. Stop by whenever free. I have something for you.

J.

My stomach fairly heaved.

We settle in the living room. Where his mental state is concerned, I detect nothing out of the ordinary. He is rereading *The Gathering Storm* and recalls for me Churchill's description of blitzkrieg war, "an avalanche of steel and fire." This reminds him of something. He excuses himself and disappears. When he returns he puts into my hands a photograph, a picture of a boy, my mother's father.

"Gretchen found this with some of your mother's things."

The boy stands before the mouth of a large stone fireplace in full Scotch regalia: kilt and sporran, the squared-off Argyll jacket, cutlass slung to hip. By propping a hand coolly on its ornate basket guard, he manages to keep the blade levered by his side. The frame's velvet backing gives way to a faint-scripted caption: *William S. McCord, 1925*.

"How old is he here?"

"Let's see. That was 1925 . . ." My father whispers calculations. "He would've been six or seven."

The young face is fashioned in the period's stoic, self-possessed mold. A boy in itching kilt, impatient for the photographer to finish, dying to pull sword from scabbard and mow down like corn Balliol's hordes of the Disinherited. But already I am aware of it, the uneasy tenor of certain old photographs. Something in the grainy black-and-white suggests a fabric shot through with the dead particles of history. To stare at the boy's face is to lose him. The years layer darkly as burlap.

"Do you know," my father says, eyeing the rug and slipping into reverie, "that your grandfather saw Hitler? The Führer himself!"

"I remember."

"He'd gone to Berlin in '36. Part of a student cultural program organized for the Olympics. The Nazis were eager to show off the greater glory of the Reich. All student groups were bunked with the

Hitler-Jugend." He pronounces it with relish, as if to take a great jaw-breaking bite of the epoch. "So there were your grandfather and the other Canadians, loose in Europe, getting tight on Bavarian suds and barely able to rouse themselves for the day tours. Meanwhile their hosts were up at the crack of dawn, beds made and boots polished, marching in the yards and serenading the Fatherland.

"The first day Owens won, your grandfather was there. He watched Hitler storm from the box before the medal ceremony. Imagine: all that preparation, the parades and careful scripting, and here come those damn Yanks—*black* Yanks, *Gott in Himmel*—to shoot it all to hell! So much for Aryan supremacy . . ."

"Right."

Wrong. I don't mean his facts; if anything, the facts are too straight. In his version, everything fits tidily to newsreel. The happy-go-lucky Americans succeed without really trying, making their peevish hosts look ridiculous in the process. I can visualize nothing of the race, only the brassy clip:

```
SCENE: EXTERIOR, THE OLYMPIASTADION

              ANNOUNCER
      (pitched and nasal) Berlin,
      nine-teen . . . thirty-six!

Runners at their marks; starter's pistol
fires; runners windmilling around; OWENS
atop medal stand.

              ANNOUNCER
      Owens cops gold for Uncle Sam
      in track and field events!

(Near shot) unsmiling Führer . . .

              ANNOUNCER
      Hey! What's the matter, Adolf?
```

. . . stalking from balcony.

ANNOUNCER
Now there goes one sour Kraut!

To tell the truth, I liked my grandfather's version better. Do not get the wrong idea. His wasn't gravelly and wise, a sagacious morsel from the grandfather in the oatmeal commercial. When it came to Hitler's leaving, he would rise from his chair and enact the führer's stiff shuffle. "They've taught you about Hitler?" "Yes, sir." "But like this." And there would be Germany's chancellor: not the character or history's devil but the flesh-and-blood being, a frustrated little man struggling in his jodhpurs past the seat backs. In my grandfather's telling, what happened was returned as odd and unparsed, as felt, as the present. Of course I have heard it said that so-and-so or such-and-such *brings history to life*. That is not what I mean. History wasn't a place of corpses needing resurrection. This was the mystery. At his knee, past and present let slip the secret of their coexistence.

My father is still away in the era. "Do you know what your grand-father did the day he got home?"

"He enlisted."

"He said to his parents, 'There's going to be another war.' And he went straight out and joined the army. He knew. These kids, all of six-teen or seventeen years old, parading in uniform, disdaining the Brits and Canadians for their sloppy ways. He knew."

Try as I might, I cannot transfigure events as my father does. In this perhaps his mind works a little too well. His recollection sets my grandfather squarely amid the century's larger schemes, schemes that in hindsight snap together as neatly as a model track. (This is another solution, of course. If history is dead, so much the better. A person discovers the tidy satisfactions of autopsy.) One glance and my father can summon up the boy and the man, the entire cause-and-effect of the Second World War. But how? I stare at the picture. There is no reconciling the prim child here with the carousing teenager in Nazi Berlin, let alone the sobered adult who returned—and certainly not

with my grandfather. Sword still, kilt frozen, eyes glassed: a taxidermy
that precludes the man. Never will he join the artillery battalion that
survives Monte Cassino; never will he come home, marry, settle into
law practice, beget my mother. This boy is locked away for good.

A moaning rises at the front bay window. The panes quiver like
notes. Ice crystals sweep against the glass: *tic, tic-tic*. It is not new
snowfall but skiff blown from the yard. My father goes to the window. He studies a woolen, plum-colored sky.

"You may be here for the weekend after all." Every Midwesterner
is a practiced weatherman, especially in winter. "Tell you what. The
cupboards are a little bare. How does Denison's strike you? We'd be
around the corner from Bell Lake . . ."

"You're on."

Not two hours later we have taken up our positions at lake's edge. A
pigeon rises and goes chasing into the sky. The boom sounds; the sau-
cer is split to pieces. My father is showing off a little. He waits for the
bird to break instead of loosing great roaring volleys on the ascension
(the habit of a certain son). Also he is using a .410 bore. The 12 gauge,
a true scattergun, was passed to me with a sort of baronial charity.

"Pull."

The trap flops; another pigeon is sent whirring into the night. He
waits, fires, has the breech snapped and smoking shells ejected
before the fragments have come down. Two birds, two barrels, two
shots. His marksmanship tonight makes him crisply tutorial. I am
directed to stand in his footprints, shoulders squared to the ice.

"I've done this before, you may remember."

"Let's see it then."

". . . Pull."

Out goes the bird, a Day-Glo disc ablaze under the landing's stark
floodlights. The barrel marks its trajectory and erupts. The bird continues its journey.

"You're leading too much."

"Pull."

Another vibrant disc appears. It levitates over the banded darkness of the piney far shore. A powdering of crystals comes down from the boughs overhead.

"You're behind it."

"How can you see where the bead's lining up?"

"Take another."

He is right.

We swap places. My father hunkers into his shooting stance. Peering over the barrel he says:

"I brought your mother out once, did I tell you?"

"To shoot?"

"Not long after the news. I had an idea that waving around a gun and shooting things out of the sky might be a help."

"I don't remember her being angry."

"No. In my mind it had to do with giving her a sense of power. Maybe I was interested in making my own show of force to the gods— that we weren't just flies to wanton boys, that sort of thing. Christ, the fantasies that come over you. Pull." He clips the pigeon, not cleanly; its broken remnant goes careening into the drifts at shore's edge. "Shit."

"Was she any good?"

"She was not. Too afraid of the gun."

Yes, I see her. An amateur marked by her improvised shooting outfit, cinched flannel and rolled jeans; the tentative, vaguely fetal posture, elbows tight to the ribs with the long gun propped uncertainly, braced for the mule kick. Another "good sport" wife. No, she was not herself. She had become a somnambulist. She traipsed into our desperate notions without cynicism or faith. We should hold a family reunion! We should paint the bedrooms! What ever happened to our Sunday drives? We should see Rome! So would she have entered into my father's shooting party: bemused, pliable, arranged on this hillside with the gun pointed according to his instruction, another good sport wife, freshly possessed of her death sentence.

It is quiet. Bell Lake has few cabins and none are winterized. The pines are stock-still. The fish are deep asleep. The sky is a raven dome ten billion light-years across and better not thought of. Pull, says my father. His voice is over the hills and far away. The gun pops; the smothering cotton silence swells up again thick as ever.

"Your mother could be an odd bird. She was as rational as the day is long, except when she wasn't. And there was very little filter. Whatever she was thinking, she wasn't one to keep you in suspense." He evacuates the breech, rubs away particles of snow from the receiver. Its bluing shows an etching of mallards rising among Western curlicues. "I asked her why she was so spooked of shooting. Once you get the first kick out of the way, there's nothing to it. And she said the damnedest thing. She said, 'Samuel, when I hold this gun I have visions of how badly things could go.' I thought she was talking about the precariousness of life or something. So I said, very gently, 'What do you mean, dear?' She said, 'I keep thinking: What if something happened, I slipped or pointed in the wrong direction, and blew your head off!'" He laughs at the queerness of it. "And she was no nervous Nellie, your mother. So go explain it because I can't."

But I myself have experienced precisely this habit of the brain. It will seize upon some idyll and, out of sheer boredom or perversity, pull the scene threads into wildly incongruous, even fiendish shapes. (Certain Sunday lulls in my boyhood were frequented by a recurrent dandy of my peeing in Jesus's ear.) I understand perfectly. The gun was too suggestive a prop. Her imagination couldn't but indulge a kind of sweet tooth for calamity: the hair trigger, his cranium opened like a burst pomegranate, red and steaming in the drifts. Not that there is any explaining this to my father. These are not things that signify.

"Well. I miss her very much," my father says. "I'll say that. I miss you, you peculiar old girl."

The road home is straight through white fields. Beneath the crust, sleeping crops dream of resurrection. A wire fence races in leaps and bounds alongside the Wagoneer. My father studies the upper sky in the windshield.

"The Rhino has his hands full tonight." As a child, I heard "Orion's Belt" as "A Rhino's Belt," a misunderstanding the family adopted. He traces a finger on the glass. A cloud front is moving like a dark tide against the constellation. "Rigel's already gone under, but up in the clear somewhere is Betelgeuse . . . yes, there. Now, when she goes

into supernova? That will be something to see." There follows a ruminative sort of address, astronomy and astrology both, ranging and
directionless ("In Spain they call the Belt 'The Three Marys' you probably know, which I've always liked. The Dutch used to call it 'The
Three Kings,' not quite as imaginative to my mind . . ."). Absurd to suspect his brain as anything less than a loyal steward. I listen intently
and with a taste of the old thrill. Another vast solar system, but
gradually there is revealed, clear as day, the whir and click of its
mechanisms. Proof it can be done.

In Sauk Falls we stop for gas. My father climbs out to stand with
me while I fill the tank. He is energized by the night and its stars and
in no mood for a lull. He leans on the Jeep, casting about for new top-
ics. Our breaths erupt in billows and go ghosting up into the sodium
light of the canopy. He says:

"I once brought your mother out shooting, did I tell you?"

5

It is over almost before it begins. Mike receives us in his office, shaking hands from behind his desk, where he remains, shuffling papers
and frowning, a man too busy even for introductions. He would as-
sume the aggrieved party with no time for us. But Ian heads him off:
it is *we* who are short of time. The apology is quick and dignified. Ian
doesn't grovel or self-deprecate; he does not dwell. He leaves Mike
no chance to lever himself onto the martyr's perch. The best our host
can do is a small gibe about having expected better, to which Ian
replies, warmly, that he's glad to hear it, that it means Mike's got
exactly the right expectations of Cyber. Now Mike is at a loss. He's
expected a pair of sheepish envoys, sent for a lecture on matters of
respect and basic professionalism. But to grandstand now, in the face
of such swift and gracious apology—the balance would tilt against
him. He'd look like a jerk.

With the main matter put to rest, there's nothing left but to fulfill
the duties of host. We are offered seats.

"So. Ah, what happened to the other fella, then?" Mike wonders. Ian is briskly matter-of-fact: "He's not with the company anymore." Mike's eyes round, then go blinking rapidly. "Now I hope, I mean, I didn't want—"

Ian is rummaging in his laptop bag, but here stops to look at Mike.

"This is an important account. Maybe the most important we could have. What happened isn't acceptable. Not to you, not to us. When our GM told me the situation and asked us to get up here and make amends, do you know what I said? No way." He shrugs and reengages his bag. "Not because it wasn't important or the right thing, but because I don't take kindly to fool's errands. I just couldn't see how after a crazy screwup like that you could be expected to hear me out. 'Ian, we're the industry leader, bar none,' our GM said. 'That's what every independent study says, not to mention more than half of the Fortune 500 . . . Our software's never been hacked—except by our own audit guys, who work twenty-four seven to find and fix trouble before the real hackers can . . . Some corporate insurers actually give price breaks to accounts using Cyber software, it's that good.' You know the story." Not once does Ian look up from his search. He speaks in the offhand manner of someone who reckons his listener isn't interested, who understands he is probably talking to himself, and though humble to these facts is bound to say his piece. The pattering style, his absorption in the bag, all of it suggests a man with no brain space left over for guile or showmanship. This can be nothing less than a frank, candid confession. "Still, you come blundering into a world-class operation like Markitel, and you can't even get the customer's *name* right? What do you *expect* them to do? Give a serious listen the second time around? I don't think so."

Now he stops riffling to again look at our host.

"But Mike? I have to say. You've been more gracious than we had a right to expect. And whatever happens, I appreciate it. Frankly, Cyber Systems appreciates it."

Mike permits himself a small, clement shrug. Before the compliment can hang too long in the air, Ian is distracted again by his search. "Well, damn it. And after all this I may not be doing much better myself. I left my portfolio at the coffee place across the street! Henry, I hate to ask: I wonder if you'd mind grabbing it?"

Something is afoot. His portfolio is in the bag. I've watched him thumb over it twice. Nonetheless, I rise agreeably and leave them.

When I come back, Mike and Ian are standing in the hall outside his office, shaking hands and chortling like henchmen. Seeing me, Ian holds up the portfolio. "Sorry!" he calls. "Found it." Our host gives me a warm, high wave and disappears into his office.

Outside, snowflakes have begun pouring from a low, leaden sky.

"We make a good team, Henry. I mean that."

"I hardly said a word."

"Right! You didn't bat an eye on the portfolio bit."

"You knew where it was."

"Sure. But it was important I talk to the customer without my chaperone present."

"Your chaperone—come off it."

"Oh, Keith was serious. Make no mistake."

"Well, I sure as hell don't see it as my job to chaperone you."

"I don't doubt it. Although our boss is something of a genius when it comes to getting what he needs from a person, whether the person knows it or not. Jesus, don't think I'm complaining! I love the man! We'll learn plenty from him."

The snow falls in curtains. Snow piles his shoulders in woolly epaulets. His hair is whitened; flakes cling whitely to his brows. We stand like two hoary generals in the aftermath.

"Why was it important to talk without a chaperone?"

"This feels like serious weather. Is this serious? Let's get to the airport, see if we can jump earlier flights. I don't want to get stranded. We'll get our travel sorted and find a bar, I'll give you the full download."

O'Stewart's is a low-ceilinged place, tucked like an arbor off the C terminal's concourse hallway. A rear wall of windows is brilliant with gray storm. In the distance two snow-capped planes trudge a runway, looking as stolid and long-suffering as pachyderms. I sip my coffee and listen to the bartender comfort a traveler:

"Here the airport alone's got more snowplows than the whole *city* of Boston! You ask any road warrior, they'll tell you. In winter, hub through the Twin Cities. We know how to clear a runway and get a plane up, don't you worry about that!"

A voice behind me mutters, "Christ, let him be right." Ian comes around the table and drops his bag on the chair opposite. "The hell's this—coffee?"

"It's not even eleven."

"Use your imagination."

When he returns from the bar, it is with a whiskey and a packet of cigarettes. One of the bar's televisions scrolls market news. Ian studies the ticker while unfastening the middle button of his dress shirt. He tucks his tie fastidiously away. (Again I have the impression his rumpled bearing is practiced and expensive.) So buttressed, he raps the Marlboro box on the table like a card deck. He snaps the lid and shoots a cigarette expertly from the pack.

"So. Where were we? Why get rid of the chaperone to talk to the customer?"

"Yes, but setting aside the chaperone crap for a minute—"

"We disagree on it being crap—"

"Fine, but my question is: Why do it in such an underhanded way?"

Frowning, he sets the cigarette on his lip. "*Under*handed?" The cigarette bobs wildly. He straightens his leg to fish a pocket.

"You knew where the portfolio was."

"Yup, and I admitted as much to Mike as soon as you were out of the room."

"What?"

Out comes a matchbook. Ian peels off a match and strikes it to flame. "Sure." He touches fire to cigarette, then blows out the match with a smoky huff. "Yanked it out as soon as you'd left."

He sets his hand atop the table, cigarette pinched erectly between the fore and middle fingers. We regard each other through spooling curlicues of smoke. He takes a sip of whiskey, enjoying this drawing out of the mystery. We both are: Ian is a very fine master of ceremonies. He trades whiskey for cigarette with aristocratic grace, each gesture of such casual perfection that I can only watch fixedly, waiting, a little anxiously, for the next.

"You're wondering why fake the matter at all? Why not just, 'Henry, could you excuse us'?" A plume of lung smoke goes hissing up and floats colorfully in the televisions' digital light. He might be that old shamus, unpacking the plot in good Socratic style for his dim-witted assistant. "Because if I do it that way, Mike and me aren't in cahoots."

"Cahoots?"

"The minute you left, it was my chance to talk numbers. Frankly, given circumstances, I couldn't see any other way to do it. Not without handing the advantage right back to Mike." He brushes a whisper of ash from his belly. "So you became our pivot."

"I don't follow."

"Look, there's an ancient sales play where the salesman becomes the customer's partner in crime. Ever had a car salesman say he's got to check some price demand of yours with his boss? Then come back and tell you that, against every odd imaginable, he's managed to pull it off? Only if he's any good, he says 'we'—you and he—managed to pull it off. But whatever the deal, it's possible only if you'll agree to buy window tints, or a longer warranty . . . OK. That's the play in its crudest form. Suddenly the two of you are sharing a foxhole against a common enemy: management. He helps you, you help him; that's what comrades do. So when you stepped out, I confided the situation to Mike: that you'd been sent along because you're our ace technical guy, yes, but also as the boss's mole. To make sure that I, as the new guy, didn't cut some ruinous deal just to claim the sale. And if we wanted to talk the best possible pricing, now was our chance."

I consider this.

"I'm the bad guy."

"Not the bad guy. As far as Mike's concerned, you can be the guy just doing his duty for the man who pays him. Anyway, it's me he needs to like. And shit, Henry." He speaks side-mouthed now, in a cornpone sort of whisper. "This ain't exactly the time for hurt feelings, y'know?

Without these deals—what was it Keith said? Something about the collapse of the business unit . . . ?"

"So by leading Mike to believe—"

"Hold it. I didn't 'lead him to believe' anything. Say it that way and it sounds like I'm some slick door-to-door man bilking housewives. I didn't tell a single untruth in there. If he assumed Barry got it in the neck solely for the sake of Markitel, that's what it is: his assumption. OK, fine. I might've let on as being more reluctant to make the call than I was. But that's only to prove to Mike how serious I considered the screwup. It *was* serious. And that's as far as it went. The rest were plain facts. I can't help how he assembles them."

He takes a long draw on the cigarette, burning it nearly to filter. The remainder is stubbed hissing in his glass. Ian is quiet. He watches the storm, letting go the smoke in an even sigh.

"Remember, Henry. It was *you* we were putting one over on. Not him."

I am not sure quite what to make of this. "Well? Did it work? Are we back in good graces?"

Ian comes to. "He'll sign, but not for five hundred." His face darkens. "Exactly what kind of moron was this Barry guy? He didn't leave a cent of wiggle room for negotiation! What Markitel got was our target number, not a reach number Barry could come down off of. Which means I'll have to give some up. No customer in the history of corporate software ever paid what he thought was list price. Goddamn it."

"Wait a minute. He's ready to *sign*? You think—"

"Four hundred thou, best case. Mike'll calculate the whole name fuckup is worth at least twenty percent."

Four hundred thousand from a client who kicked us out not three weeks ago! I am exultant. Ian is not.

"At least someone's happy," he says.

"Are you kidding? Keith will give you the key to the city!"

He looks morosely into the bottom of his glass. "Seems fair to say you don't know Keith like I do."

The worst of the blitz is over. Wide white flakes sail thinly out of the sky, tumbling the windowsill like spent moths. Across the runways come the plows, hulking things on tank treads, to pave dark, clean rows in the snow.

"It makes me appreciate the decision, though. Where Barry's concerned, I mean." Ian draws another cigarette, lights it, and waves the burning end around meditatively. "Sales is a tough business. I'm sympathetic. Never eager to see a fellow salesman fail, not unless it's the competition. But with this deal here, I'm starting to understand. Even the most rudimentary things, like the price quote. Totally ham-fisted. I never met the guy, but he was real friendly. A real palsy-walsy type, I imagine. Going over his tickler notes, they're full of favors to customers, birthdays to remember, all sorts of overhead that has nothing to do with closing. The Santa Claus act only works in commodity sales. You're hoofing pens or paper rolls, fine. Maybe you smile wide, wider than the other guy, and that's the only difference. But in software—" Ian consults his watch. He tucks the cigarette in a corner of his mouth and pats down his pockets. We are leaving. "Anyway, a hard decision. But no one should feel badly about it, is my point. Absolutely not. Just the opposite in fact."

"Sure."

We step from the bar to a bright and busy concourse hall. The blue scheduling monitors show only short delays, no cancellations. Ian's flight leaves before mine. We shake hands and part as teammates from a well-played match. Bound for my gate, I am reminded how good it is to be swept along with the charging hordes, bag in hand and the satisfaction of places to be and a schedule to keep. Only when I am settled at my gate, a leftover sports page in hand and nosing through the Vikings' plans for free agency—only then does a vague unease present itself.

Ian too thinks the firing was my idea.

Four

1

Friday and Jane is nowhere to be found. Keith has dispatched her on a market fact-finding mission, something to do with site visits and focus groups. I don't dare ask many questions. I've known men smitten by a coworker, some beauty off-limits for one reason or another, and no matter how subtle their inquiries, how practiced their disinterest, each wore his hope like a sandwich board. Her absence makes the day dreary. The feeling is entirely at odds with the facts. It is week's end; yesterday was an impossible success; the weather is so clear and bright that my office glimmers like the bottom of a pool. Yet when Cory drops by and mentions Small Al's Smokehouse for barbecue, as ideal a place for languid Friday lunch as the South has, I tell him no, I am too busy, and instead pick through a box of raisins at my desk.

There is, however, a compensation.

This morning I found an envelope standing in my keyboard. I've left off opening it. The envelope waits, tucked in a plain manila folder on my desk, one corner revealed in a way that only I can see. At three o'clock I give in. The card is a pale crisp square with a gold border.

For Henry—as good a confidant I know. (Better than any bartender!)
God knows what I said, but thank you for listening . . .

Then a small crosshatched heart and her looping initial.

Tamer than one might've hoped, really. But there is more. At the bottom of the card, in neatly printed capitals:

THE BEARER OF THIS CARD IS ENTITLED TO ONE KVETCH-FREE DINNER

Because my office door is open, and because it is not the nineteenth century, I do not put the card to my nose, snuffling for trace scent. Neither am I guilty of standing at the window with fists in pockets, nodding out onto the city and thinking, By God, yes. No. But I do feel toward these gestures a new forgivingness.

I jot my reply on the back—*Mr. Hurt will attend*—and steal across the office to settle the card beneath her keyboard. Is it too grade school, this volley of notes? Yet there is joy to match, a memory of those earliest games of infatuation and detection, the hopeful inquiries couriered by trusted go-betweens, a bit of folded paper handed from warm palm to warm palm and blooming finally to show (with luck!) the right box checked.

"Her birthday?"

"Hm? Oh—" I am startled. Ian is standing at the adjacent cubicle's half wall, blowing over a steaming Styrofoam cup. "Not her birthday, no. This is a, what-do-you-call-it. A thank-you note."

"Ah. Just wondered if I should wish my neighbor many happy returns."

Is the card showing? None. Very little. How dry my mouth. "So! Is this where we've got you situated?"

He makes an expansive gesture. "This is it." I stand with him at the wall. His cubicle is as plain as any.

"Nice." A sly-sardonic dig. The trick is to hit upon the note that sounds one's ease.

"Don't you think? Even a chair."

"No expense spared."

"You office guys, shitting on us little people."

"I'm commiserating. You're welcome to spend as much time in my office as you like."

"Prick."

And so on, the de rigueur little ironies and jabs, surest proof nothing is out of the ordinary.

2

I have mostly given up television. Not because I am fed up. Far from it. There are still good programs to be found. But I can no longer bear the endings. An ending is a very sad thing. Minutes before it arrives there comes the sweet-but-terrible awareness, and then—the final darkening. Watching the credits scroll, I am rewarded with a sense of shared exhaustion. We have made a good team, they and I. But now our work is over and they are gone . . . Only sometimes I wonder if the characters don't carry on merrily without me. In fact I would not mind so much if it were they who were ended until next week. This while I went on my own rich way, welcoming them back at the scheduled time. But it is almost certainly the reverse. The program ends, the darkness rises, and the strings play elegy for me, not them. There is nothing left but to stab the remote and sit in the awful quiet.

One of the programs I used to watch concerned a team of trauma surgeons. I liked the beginnings best. Each episode started the same way, with little half-glimpsed scenes of nurses and doctors flirting and cracking wise, EMT personnel bustling the corridors, receptionists hunkered in their bay desks—everyone loose and easy, the workplace at its most banal. Of course the trick was that in this setting, disaster threatened at any moment. This was the secret thrill: knowing that their breeziness, their routine ministrations, would soon be punctured by some wailing and bloodied catastrophe. Over it all hung a sense of significance.

There was pleasure too in waiting for the change. For when the emergencies came, all were instantly transformed—their jovial camaraderie put aside for the suffering patient, the ironic looks gone, traded for brows knit in steely competence. How easily the characters shed their blasé skins to reveal their true colors: serious, able, courageous. It is not an exaggeration to say they made me glad for humanity. What affected me most was their American good-heartedness. Here was as smart and handsome a band as you could ask for, every door open to them, and what was their chosen work? To mend the poor (their hospital serviced a rough neighborhood), to take science in hand and put hope in hearts. And how lightly sat the mantle of their nobility! Each week I watched with a mixture of marvel and disbelief. That among such coinciding beings could intrude some howling wreck, not to be stood up in a mop closet but tended, as gently as a gosling. (It made me even a little envious. A man could do worse than to be carried bleeding into this hospital.) But more I liked to imagine joining them. For I too know how to leave off the jokes and petty rivalries when the Real Thing arrives, and also how to pick up again when the crisis is dispatched—how to sit massaging my neck, sobered but still with the old twinkle, wiser, not gloomier, ready for whatever life wheels in next.

Then the end. TV snapped off, my den a shrunken little mockery in the glass. And seated in the center of this collapse? Where moved just an instant ago those bright, friendly faces? This poor pale ghost tapping the chair's wooden arm as if to test his corporeality . . .

Knowing this and still tonight the mistake. The Movie of the Week concerns a mentally challenged man struggling to raise his daughter. Whatever his disability, they are a good match. They make pancakes together; they sing karaoke. The state, however, feels differently. An officious social worker seizes the girl. The father is left to devise a plan. His only help is a gang of oddball friends who are themselves variously (and, it would seem, comically) impaired. The plan, it turns out, is to hire a lawyer. She is a spitfire in stiletto heels who over the course of an ambitious career has lost touch with her son. Gradually we learn that whatever the difference in mental faculty between client and council, he is the surer parent. But in a pivotal courtroom scene, he is made to look hopeless by a hardheaded prosecutor. The father slouches in the witness stand. It is over. The prosecutor returns to his table with a smug look; the spitfire lady attorney cannot meet her client's eye. Then, something happens:

"What I THINK?" the father cries in his halting, screeching fashion. "I think LOVE? Is ENOUGH!" The judge pounds his gavel. But no matter. "It *has* to be. IT HAS TO BE!" His lawyer, stricken by her own familial failings, can only look on, eyes wet, her iron composure slipping finally, mouthing, *Yes, yes.*

It is not a little moving. In fact, my throat is full to bursting with tenderness. The lawyer I am not so worried about; she is gorgeous and loaded. But the man and his daughter—! Were it up to me, I would bring them home to be doted on like pets. Visions of securing the father work as a janitor at Cyber, perhaps teaching him some elementary grooming skills . . . The lump in my throat swells. I cannot help but be touched by this generosity. So it is that I miss how the girl is returned to him, and why. (As a practical matter, I am on the state's side. The man is an incompetent.) The last scene sees the father charging around a soccer field with his daughter swept up in his arms and a flock of children chasing them, the great aerial camera shot pulling ever higher to show the entire sunny park, the entire sunny world—!

Off goes the television.

A static charge crackles on the glass. The sound is made somehow disquieting by its very smallness. A feverish sizzling of particles in the corner, dread counterpoint to the roaring silence of the house.

An awareness comes.

Of what?

Of the need to be aware.

I collect three empty beer bottles from the foot of my chair. They clink loudly, piercingly, the only sound for miles. My palms break out in sweat. The silence is malignant. It is not to be riled. Think of a hushed theater, late to your seat, the extraordinary loudness of small noises and a thousand angry stares, the terrible calling of attention to yourself—*you*, for Christ's sake.

The bedroom is no better. My old and sturdy bed, yet still the silence plays tricks. Infinitesimal sounds fall loud against the ear. The filament in the ceiling fixture buzzes like a hive. The light of the room has a strange, boiled quality. Colors seem parched and wrung out.

Later I am rigid in the dark, whispering the old devotion:

I think, therefore I am.

When all is malevolence, a return to first things. This is the way sometimes. You must go to the worst, a universe of no-thing, and start over. Take nothing as given. Not work or Jane, not mother or father or sister, not the bed or the house, not city or country, not the natural world or anything seen or heard or touched—*not even myself.* It is all a figment of some master creature's devious mind. I've been told a story and taken it for truth; I have been tricked utterly.

But. How can I be deceived unless I exist to be deceived? This is the loophole I slip through. It allows for me, even if nothing else. *Cogito, ergo sum.* Better than any prayer.

3

I wake to a horrible trilling.

Hello?

It is my mother calling about my father, who is dead. She is exasperated. It seems he entered a relay race ("At his age!" cries she). He was carrying the baton across a vast frozen lake. The ice broke, and he was eaten by a great white shark.

"Oh, Samuel," my mother clucks. Her tone is sympathetic, mildly scolding. It is as though my father has spilled soup in his lap. I become aware of the extreme inappropriateness of crying out. Everything depends on my matching her nonchalance. The only trouble is my lungs, which have stopped working. My heart thrashes in terror. God, what a hammering! Now the trilling again. The summons is too wrenching to bear—

Awake.

The phone is in fact ringing.

"Henry!"

"What?" I am breathing hard, braced for catastrophe.

"Henry!"

"Who is this?"

"Can you hear me?"

"Jane?"

Music and laughter, the clattering of glasses.

"*Henry!*"

"Jane, yes, I can hear you."

"You'll never—(Is that tonic or soda? All right.) Are you there? You'll never guess!"

"What?"

"Where I'm stuck: in Denver!" She exclaims this as though here finally is the news we've been waiting for. I gather my wits. Denver, Denver . . . What does Denver have to do with anything? "There're storms there, so no more flights tonight."

"Oh. But . . . there's no storm here."

"*No.* In *Dallas.*"

"Ah."

"So I thought: Hey, two hours' advantage, I'll just see what ole Henry is up to."

"Yes, good. Only—"

"What *are* you doing? You sound strange."

"Actually, the time difference is the other way around."

"It's . . . Oh my God."

"That's all right."

"No! Is it . . . Oh *no.* It's nearly two there! I am *so* sorry."

"I was up anyway."

"No, you weren't. You were deep under. I probably scared you to death. Oh Lord . . ." She sips, swallows, no longer minding really. "Now I'm going to have to think of something important to say. Hum. Well, here it is: Denver has mountains! *Mountains!*" She slaps hard on something, a table or bar counter. This is followed by a frantic off-phone apology. "Sorry! God. I'll get that. Another for her, whatever that was. I'm truly sorry." Now to me, in a loud whisper: "I? Am a *train* wreck. If I get kicked out of here . . . Are you coming to my brunch? You did promise, I think."

"What? Yes. I did, I am."

"Sunday. Not the day after tomorrow. *Next* Sunday."

"I remember."

"I invited other work people," she informs me, defensively it seems. "You won't be stuck in a corner with some *person.*"

"Very good. I wasn't worried."

Now Jane sighs. I can't tell whether in dread of her in-laws or the small sorrows of an airport bar, a hotel bar, in the middle of the night.

"Is everything OK?" I wonder.

"Peachy."

The line is quiet. After a moment there comes the hollow rustling of her cheek or shoulder against the mouthpiece.

"Jane?"

"Did you get my card?"

"Of course! Yes. I absolutely did. Thank you." I am aiming for a casual, offhanded enthusiasm. "Dinner would be . . . fun." Good God.

"Maybe I'll cook!" Jane cries, cheery all over again. "No, no, that's a terrible idea. I can only make waffles. Really even those aren't very good. Then of course there's Michael. I can already hear what *he* would say."

I experience a sharp thrill. Though I'm not sure what she means. Michael would not like his wife dining with a man he barely knows? Michael is included and simply dislikes her cooking? Only now does it occur to me that I don't know what we are up to, or if we are up to anything at all. "Tell me about the trip," say I quickly, fearing she will clarify things.

"The trip? Well. I'm gathering product testimonials from customers acquired within the last year. That's the published reason. But actually I'm trying to generate new leads." A recitative note in her voice says she is not really listening. "Keith's idea is that these customers might resent having new services pushed on them so soon, but if we get them started just by talking about themselves and their experiences with the product, there will naturally be opportunities . . . Want to know something?"

"Sure."

"Here it is whatever time, I'm stuck in Denver, and it didn't even occur to me to call Michael."

"He might be worried."

"Do you know how I know he isn't?"

"No."

"Because it hasn't occurred to him to call *me*."

"I see."

Again a silence.

"Jesus. Sometimes I hear myself—" Her throat catches. "I hear myself and I swear it makes me *sick*." She exhales slowly. "I wonder, Where did this person come from? Thirty-six. I'm thirty-six! Did you ever think you'd be sailing headlong into midlife and still be without a genuine bone in your body? Still playacting through little dramas like an adolescent?"

I wait. The noise of the bar is gone.

"I'll tell you my theory," she goes on. "Somewhere along the way we lose ourselves. No, I won't hide. I'm not alone in this, but we're talking about me: *I* lost myself. Who knows when. I only know because every now and then I catch myself. Hm, I'll think. Whose life is this? Whose ambitions are these? Remember college? God, what a time! It's the last time I felt my attitudes weren't something I'd received from somewhere, or picked off a menu. I don't pretend I had it all figured out. I had very little figured out. But I knew it, and I was honest with myself, and the effort was *mine*. What happens? You're so hell-bent on independence and self-discovery, but then slowly, surely . . . Why does the seriousness of that struggle get painted over as 'youthful idealism'? Why do adults take such an amused and condescending view of that time? It's a gallows humor if you ask me."

"It may be." To tell the truth, the only person I knew in college who used words like "self-discovery" was a theater major who wore glitter on her eyelids. She was famous for leading unsuspecting freshmen to wardrobe, where she would clamber into a costume and then present herself to give head. She was later institutionalized.

"When I was twenty-two, do you know what I very nearly did? Joined a dance troupe. They were headed for Guadalajara to start touring on the Day of the Dead! And why didn't I? Because I knew I could never explain it, career-wise. How's that for courage? I still haven't seen Mexico City."

Ah. But I know this one. I have entertained similar notions myself. If only the right place could be found, the right place with the right rewarding profession to be shared with the right person. The only trouble is that, having aligned the stars, you're still obliged to get out of bed the next day, to plant your feet on the cold floor, to assemble breakfast and rinse the dishes, to scour your teeth and pull on clothes and go forth to face the hours . . .

"The last time I was stranded in an airport was in Chicago," I tell her.

"Oh, I *beg* your pardon," says she. "I didn't mean to interrupt." But beneath the irony there is a knowing camaraderie. This abrupt change of subject is for her proof we understand each other.

"I was twelve. My family was flying home from a funeral. A cousin I didn't know, a boy about my age. He'd been playing Kill the Carrier, and when on his turn he was finally tackled, all the other kids piled on as a joke because he'd been so hard to bring down. It was innocent, but under the pile he'd had some sort of seizure and that was that. There were tornado warnings in Minneapolis, so no flights were going in. Gretchen and my father had gone to another terminal to watch takeoffs. She was crazy about airplanes. I was hungry, so I'd gone with my mother to get something to eat. This was before airports had turned into malls. We sat at some gray counter and I ate a hot dog and it was the best hot dog I ever had in my life. My mother was upset but hiding it. I knew because she kept putting a hand on my head. Each time she'd catch herself and pretend to be brushing down my hair. Was I OK? she wanted to know, over and over. It's sad, I would tell her. Really I wanted to finish my hot dog. Finally she said, 'Tell me the truth.' Whenever she said this, she meant it. She wanted to hear what was going on in your head, propriety be damned."

"Which was?"

"I was happy. Here we were stranded together, the whole family, in O'Hare, which for a kid is a huge, exciting place. It was an adventure. I was bellied up to the counter like one of the grizzled truckers from *Convoy*, eating a very good hot dog, with all the time in the world. The airport seemed unbelievably big and just waiting to be explored. I wasn't glad he was dead of course; I was only glad it wasn't me. They'd inched him into the ground with ropes. Glad—I was *elated*. It was a shock of relief. To be there, at that counter, with her, with my mouth full, and not in a box, going under the summer grass in a cemetery in Chicago."

The line is silent.

"Hello?"

"Is that really what you said?"

"More or less."

"Elated." There is something like marvel in her voice. "Cold, cold, *cold . . .*"

But the truth is, she sounds better.

4

Gretchen's choices for nightlife are not mine, but it is her holiday. The Sun & Moon Bar is sunk at the bottom of a half flight of narrow concrete steps in an alley of a neighborhood I normally avoid. A darkened place with rock walls and red vinyl booths. The air smells powerfully of cork. In fact, this space once served as a wine cave for a good French restaurant on the floor above. The restaurant closed when the neighboring streets were given over to poets, runaways, the homeless. Gretchen gets the history of the place from the bartender. He is a gaunt, bearded boy in a red Western shirt and battered jeans. The history of the neighborhood I fill in for myself.

We are here for music. The Sun & Moon Bar has some reputation for it. A black plywood stage sits at a right angle to the bar. The stage is cramped by a simple drum kit and a magnificent broad-shouldered standing bass. Behind the instruments is a wall of gold lamé curtains. The curtains are of a piece with the bar's décor. On a line of wall shelves is a collection of trophies from bowling and fishing tournaments; their brass plates confirm them as sardonic relics of the long-gone seventies. By the entrance is a recessed glass immurement the size of an orange crate. A velvet portrait of Elvis Presley is propped inside, framed in a black toilet seat. Spread before the picture is a decade's worth of Presley marketing: record sleeves from old seven-inches, refrigerator magnets, postcards, souvenir dolls, novelty jewelry . . . There is a slot in the glass. Coins and bills are mixed with the iconography. Gretchen absorbs the scene from our booth.

"I like this place."

"Good."

"You don't."

"Sure I do." The ashtray between us is the old Hamm's bear done up in yellow ceramic. It takes only a little imagination to see the creature rise up and give a tremendous cartoon wink. A girl in white knee socks and saddle shoes wriggles at a Flash Gordon pinball machine in the corner. She is wearing a coonskin cap.

"I like it," Gretchen affirms. She taps the neck of her beer bottle to mine and drinks hungrily.

I am relieved to find the musicians are no joke. This is not plain at first. They appear from behind the curtain, three of them in dark suits and shirts and white string ties. There is some tittering from the crowd: each wears a beige nylon over his face. One smooths a laminate sign over the face of the bass drum—HOMMES D'OMBRES. More titters. My heart sinks. Yet their bearing is exactly right. They go about their absurdity with consummate seriousness. I am wrong to say they are no joke; the joke is total. It is a matter of integrity. So given are they to their gag, so direct and unsmirking in manner, that what would be otherwise risible becomes something interesting. Also they can play. Having arranged themselves at their instruments, they stand stiff-backed and silent. A featureless gaze. The bar quiets. The suspense lasts one

two

three—! They leap to action and sound. It is jangling, furiously paced. The front man turns his back, strumming hard, then wheels and makes a languid move to the microphone. His is a pastiche of old Vegas balladeers, but arriving he smashes his lips to the mic's wire ball (*pap!*) and looses a high hollering. The note is a difficult one. He throws his legs wide and pinches in his toes, holding the guitar for dear life. The guitar is a beautiful old dreadnought with dark enamel. Flares move on its caramel veneer. The bassist drapes his arms around his instrument's wide shoulders. His fingers pluck nimbly at its chest. Now something happens to the singer's yelp. A tunefulness creeps in. With this the bassist is transformed. He lets out a cry and hops to one side of the bass, where he goes into a fit of high standing leaps, tugging strings as he goes. They play for a long time without stopping. I wait for one to pause finally, to push up the nylon and mop his eyes with a sleeve, to let slip his self-regard with an exhausted wink. But no. They are good Dadaists.

For the final number, the drummer stands and produces a disc sander and what looks to be a length of exhaust pipe. He waits at his kit, the disc racing, while the noise of guitar and bass rise around him. When a crescendo is reached, he applies disc to pipe. It kicks off the metal with a bright shriek and gust of sparks. A joyful noise comes up from the crowd. The drummer waits with arms outstretched. When another crescendo comes, he again brings disc and pipe together— *zzzSCRICH!* Sparks leap and fall away.

Faster now: more crescendos, more touches, more spark bursts like water chucked from a pail. At the very end, the bassist leaping again and the singer huddled with an amplifier (the better to wring cries from his guitar), the drummer brings his tools together for a last diabolic clap. Only this time he holds contact. A burning rooster tail erupts. He holds: arms trembling, chest reared back, face canted down and away. Smoke now, soap white against the brilliant yellow burning, and an acrid foundry smell. The crowd goes into ecstasies. This finale is so sensational and exaggerated, so purple, that the flushed pleasure it yields is easily mistaken for embarrassment—*is* embarrassment, in fact. I become a little uneasy. The musicians are lucky. When it's over they'll duck off behind the curtain. But the rest of us, seized by spectacle and having made their childish abandon our own, will be left in silence, the lights coming up, naked in our euphoria. Gretchen experiences it too, this shameful-joyful plenitude, this afflicted glee. Our booth is such that she must sit sidesaddle to watch the stage. Her ear and neck are scarlet with it.

Soon the band is finished and we are left in loud silence and the lights coming up and everyone squinting around, trying to repossess himself. It is just as I suspected. Rapture is a lousy public emotion. Gretchen turns around, eyes cast down and brows raised, picking at the label on her beer bottle. To speak now will only deepen our embarrassment.

Only I am mistaken. Hers is not embarrassment at all.

"I've been thinking. What is it, in another month or so . . ." She glances up, then lets her eyes fall again to the work of her fingers on the label.

"Less."

"Less, yes."

"Eleven months last week."

Now she eyes me. "I know."

"Better we don't pretend."

"What I wanted to say is that it would be good if you were home."

"It's a Monday."

"Work? HH, be serious."

"I am serious. Next month's the end of quarter. We may be in trouble. Days count. The appearance of taking it seriously—which I do—also counts. And I'm not clear—"

"No ceremonies. Is that it? I don't have anything in mind except to be together, for Dad's sake if not ours." She is being disingenuous. What my sister has in mind is a proper family catharsis. I know too well her caregiving ways.

"Let's play it by ear."

"Henry."

"Drink?"

"Henry."

"I can't promise. But I'll do my best."

She touches my hand, wise enough not to push it. Although the matter is not altogether finished.

"'Better we don't pretend,'" she muses. "That's a good, fatherly way of putting it."

"Fatherly?"

"I mean our father. Dr. Rational."

"Ah."

"Dr. Rational and Son."

"Guilty."

"Do you ever get bored, keeping it together like that? Where there's no mystery anywhere, and everything's got a system?"

"No. Just the opposite. It's trying to sort the patterns, the 'systems,' as you say, that keeps life interesting."

She is picking again at her beer label. "You know, I've got news for you. You're much, much stranger than you let on. You've got a Walter Mitty side. Placid on the surface, but . . ."

"Full of dreams and secret adventures?"

"Yup."

"No ma'am. If there's anything my immune system is conditioned against, it's that."

"Famous last words."

"You see me wandering around in a fog, imagining I'm a fighter pilot?"

"No, you're not crazed. Let me see if I can say what I mean." She collects herself, searching the tin tile ceiling. "You're very good and very focused about your job. But I refuse to believe you don't see any grander possibilities for your life, whether you want to admit it or not. And I suspect—I *strongly* suspect—that Focused Corporate Guy is a mechanism for avoiding thinking about the bigger things you might be doing."

Now I understand. This is old ground for us. It has to do with Gretchen's belief that I am meant to advance the cause of humanity somehow, and that my day job keeps me in a state of denial. "And the longer you go around," she is saying, "in this, I don't know . . . nose-to-the-grindstone *coma*, the more you're liable to take some crazy leap one day."

"A grand gesture."

"A grand gesture . . ." She is wary, sensing some trap. "What does that mean."

"It means that a quiet, so-called unremarkable life is intolerable, and the only way out is to go charging at windmills."

She thinks on it. "I don't know about the windmill part. But I think there's more to life than making money—is that what you mean by the quiet life?"

"Making money, paying bills, doing your job . . . Yes."

"Then yes, I'm agreeing with you. More is needed. It's not sustainable. And if you pretend it is, then one day you just pop."

"How do millions of people do it."

This succeeds in irritating her. "I'm not so sure they do. Anyway, you're not millions of people. You're you." Gretchen is blinking, and the flush is on her neck. "You may fool yourself, but you don't fool me. You're smart, and like a scientist you put everything under the microscope for cool appraisal. But you haven't figured out half as much as you think you have. Dad comes by his rationalism honestly. But yours? Yours is a kind of stopper—"

We are interrupted by a loud voice from the bar.

"BUD? DON'T YOU NUT UP AGAINST ME. DRIVE A MAN FUCKING CRAZY."

For a moment it is difficult to tell who has spoken. But then young patrons are peeling from the counter. They are studies in nonchalance, though I notice they wander off with or without their drink orders. In the clearing a figure sits unmoved on a bar stool. A formidable hump of shoulders beneath dark T-shirt. In his hunkered posture he looks as guarded of himself and his drink as a lone seaman in a strange port.

The young, duded-up bartender arrives as peacemaker. "Getcha another?"

Silence.

The boy worries a phantom spot with his rag. Now the man tips back his drink. He escorts the empty glass across the counter with a heavy thumb and forefinger. Before I know it, Gretchen is standing.

"It's my round, isn't it."

She walks over and sets up shop near the man. Oh Lord, I think. Don't involve yourself. But already she has said something to him. Really she astounds me. Her instinct for engaging the lost, the furious, the ill-fitted-to-their-own-skins—he drops his head and smiles! They speak for a few moments and soon I am waved over. The man has a padded, well-worn face with a humped Gallic nose pressed down against his upper lip. It's the face of broken-nosed thugs in old comics. Plainly he has no interest in my joining the party, but he softens when Gretchen explains our relation.

"Now that I wouldn't've guessed," he says.

"I got the brains and left her the looks," say I on cue.

"Afraid yes, you did."

"Oh, now . . ." Gretchen pats my hand consolingly. "Really he didn't get much brains-wise either."

Gradually we find ourselves arranged in a loose hemisphere of bar stool fellowship. Actually it is Gretchen and I who arrange ourselves; the man only opens his shoulders a little to include us. His name is John-Paul. ("My folks couldn't settle on whether John or whether Paul.") I judge him to be at least two decades older than anyone else in the place. John-Paul is Louisiana-born, New Orleans but raised in Baton Rouge, where he still lives. For a time he was a bosun in the merchant marine, like his father. Eventually, however, life on the open water began to unnerve him. He tells a riveting story of a ship's engineer who, overcome with fever, mistook the ocean for a meadow and demanded to be let off the boat to feel the grass under his feet. Now he is a driver for Allied. It is his fourth trip to our city but only the first overnight. His family is down to an older half brother who lives in New Orleans. "A hom'sexual," John-Paul allows, only a little defeated. It dawns on me why the other patrons were nervous. It was not merely the flash of temper. In this place, teeming as it is with ironists and seekers, his mere presence is a rebuke. He is estranged from these people and their place—this ersatz honky-tonk with its walls and shelves of cleverly signifying decorations, objects to provoke not nostalgia but "nostalgia" (God knows nostalgia is perilous enough; it doesn't do to taunt its effects), a stretch of decades here reduced to episodes of vulgar hobbies and bad taste, these years he lived through, with all the phrase evokes: a time of affections and forfeiture and happiness and endurance, now gone for good, ceded to this hour, this counter, this bar stool, these trinkets, this Pyrrhic arrival. I don't envy him.

Gretchen's questions are steady but not prying. She has a natural marveling curiosity, and gradually John-Paul yields to the role of interviewee; he asks not a single question of us. This suits me fine. I am content to drink my beer and listen. And for a time it really does seem our campfire is equal to it, his terrible awareness. No easy thing, to duck into an unfamiliar bar with hopes of sloughing, however briefly, the lug of one's existence, only to find yourself in a place where people wear theirs trippingly, mere featherweights. For a time we are but well-met strangers, sharing good plain conversation with no thought for other things. But we are not true comrades. A true comrade would, by his presence, substantiate lost time. In that department we are little more use to him than these flea market mockeries of history and place.

A lull. We sip our drinks.

Gretchen asks John-Paul how he liked the show. His face changes. "Boys with panty hose onner heads?"

"Well—"

He tugs a wallet from his pocket, tossing out money enough for all our drinks. The gesture strikes a pang. It shows a cutting of losses. He stands and angles for the toilets.

Gretchen is stricken. "Do you think he's all right?" She is keen for a better ending—that we find a way, each to hand the other on, crediting ourselves some restoration by this chance meeting, sojourners warmed by a passing solidarity.

"Yes. Let's go."

My sister doesn't like it one bit. "God, you're a cold fish."

I say nothing. Earlier I was the analysand; now it is John-Paul's turn. (And he has the nerve to leave!) Gretchen has always been tuned to the frailties of others, but lately her fever for nursemaiding is like nothing I remember. There is a kind of selflessness that isn't selflessness at all, the sort embodied by the doctors on my hospital dramas, specimens so besotted with their own goodwill that the world around them ceases to exist. But this is not her trouble; rather it is the opposite. I fear she is becoming "selfless" in a very literal sense. Always the mirror is turned outward. Always the aim is others, others, others, the better to annihilate any thought of herself.

As it happens, we do run into John-Paul again, outside at the edge of the parking lot in the half-dark. He is hunched over with hands to knees, searching. Gretchen is heartened. "Lose something?" she calls out to him. He inclines an ear to her voice and seems to nod. We are on our way over to join the hunt (comrades after all!) when he spies the object of his search. He makes a sudden shambling move into deeper shadow and there, with surprisingly plaintive cry, empties his guts into the sweetshrub.

5

Jane declines a passing tray of mimosas.

"Here I am doing my level best not to . . . What was it? *Overre-fresh* myself." She casts the word in Michael's direction. His back is to us, at the entrance to the living room. He entertains a small circle of guests, my sister foremost. Only when he gives no sign of having heard can I breathe again.

The brunch is a crowded affair in their impressive house, this stalwart Colonial Revival with wings added left and right. The day is cold and glaring. How good it felt to step into the warm house, a place buzzing with the Sunday cheer of Baptists and Presbyterians, freshly sanctified and hungry as devils. From somewhere comes the chemical-plum scent of Sterno. It is a smell forever promissory (at least to the traveled businessman) of hotel banquet breakfasts, heaps of eggs and hot bacon, and stainless flagons whose black boiling coffee streams from profligate valves.

"God, your sister is gorgeous." Jane is peering at her husband's circle. We stand together in a shallow alcove beneath the stairs, a space adjoining and yet excepted from the gleaming parquet foyer. "Truly a knockout. Who does she take after?"

"No one, really. Well, she's direct. Our mother was direct."

"If she were my daughter, I'd plant myself at the mirror and will a resemblance." (But unless I mistake it, her dryness has another target. It is Michael's special attending of my sister that has really drawn her eye.)

Ian and Keith are among the guests, deeper in the living room, an upholstered, curtained space of thick Oriental rugs and gilded chair legs that brings to mind an Arab tent. They are huddled together, Ian and Keith, though for the moment Keith's attention is elsewhere. Ian is looking directly at Jane and me. Spying me spying him, he raises a glass, then turns away.

"Oh!" Jane waves down a passing couple. "Philip, Cynthia: meet a friend from work. This is Henry." These are Jane's in-laws—I see it before the introduction. She wears a fine-ribbed turtleneck matched to an auburn head. Her hair is cut short as a boy's and worn in a wide brushed part. The lines at her eyes and mouth are mild, artful. "A handsome woman," as the Sunday magazines would have it. He stands with hands in his trouser pockets, roughing the hem of his blazer. A tall figure, New England lean, with a blessing of hair turned presidential gray. His manner is as attentive, as easy in its competence as a colonial doctor hearing out the natives' superstitions.

"What is it you do for Cyber Systems?" Cynthia's gaze is heavy-lidded, even seductive. "Yes," echoes Jane. "What *do* you do?" When I have explained myself, Cynthia says: "How *interesting*. You're a technical person."

Philip wants to know if I have an MBA. I do not. "You might think about it," he says. "No need to stop your career. There are some very good executive programs. And someone with technical expertise *and* a business degree? In this economy, you could write your own ticket."

"Philip went to Wharton," Cynthia says, less as a boast than to explain her husband's fervor for business school.

"I'm just a boring finance man," he deflects. "I don't know any more about computers than I do refrigerator repair. But I'll tell you, an MBA was the best, most rewarding decision of my life—after marriage, of course!"

Jane tells me she has been getting the same pitch. Philip corrects her. "Your case is different. You're a marketer. So what you need, what an MBA brings, is hard skills. Finance, accounting, et cetera. For someone like Henry, he's done the difficult bits; what he's after is the broader business perspective. Classic New Economy CEO."

I like the sound of this very much. We exchange a glance, Philip and I, in which is contained the full recognition of our mutual exceptionalism. Between us is the wisdom of his decisions, the warm promise of my future. And what a future! Consider its ambassadors, Philip and Cynthia both: modeled, serene, galvanized against decrepitude, full of the peculiar fitness of their breed, a lasting stock reared in cold climes on hard currency. The twilight approaches, yet here they stand with clear eyes and consciences, as erect and self-possessed as German shepherds, rounded on the homestretch with no thought for anything but career strategies and New Economies and—

"Aspirin: Jane dear, do you have any? I've rummaged the upstairs cabinets with no luck whatsoever." (Cynthia's question is harmless enough, but I can't help hearing it with Jane's ears: *Is the house not yours to keep? Is a basic medicine chest too much to ask?*)

"Oh, sorry. We're a bit bare around here. Crazy days at work." (*Ah, if only my life consisted of bridge and golf and managing the help.*) "Michael might have some in his travel kit. Michael?"

At his name Michael turns, then begs off from his circle with a sideways remark that provokes snorts.

"Your mother needs an aspirin. I wondered about your travel kit."

Michael falls into a frowning study of the floor. "Hum. Aspirin— or hair of the dog?" He proffers his mimosa. Cynthia is affectionately scandalized. "It's not a hangover, you brat!"

"Of course not."

"Smart guy. Just you watch it."

"Luckily, aspirin is all I travel with. My kit has *only* aspirin. Well, and"—he goes coughing into a fist—"prophylactics!" Now his mother really is scandalized. "Oh all right, enough." Philip bobs and keels in silent mirth. Jane stifles a yawn (poorly). For my part, I am free to watch. Summoned for an errand, Michael is not really joining us. The rules do not call for our reintroduction. It strikes me what a different character he is from the night of the Christmas party. Then he was stony and sour. Now he is buoyant, centered, the very soul of hospitality. And why not? It is his court.

When he goes for his kit, I excuse myself.

Gretchen is at the fireplace in the living room. Its high white mantel is crowded with vivid yellow nesting dolls. She peers at these, her elbow cradled in her palm with the arm straight up, ticking away at a tooth.

"His collection," she tells me.

"Whose?"

"The host. Michael."

"He collects dolls?"

"I don't get it either." She moves in for a closer look. "He told a long story about buying his first one on a business trip to Kiev. There was an old woman from one of those market stalls where the wretched sell their last possessions for bread money. Apparently she threw herself on him and begged him to buy the doll, and after she'd made enough of a scene he relented, and then later, passing a long line of people waiting for God knows what staple, weevily flour, tentacled potatoes, he happened on her again, waving and bowing like a good serf. And so *ever after*"—she invokes the moral phrase with savage irony—"he's felt a special attachment."

"For dolls."

"Don't try to parse the logic. It's all bourgeois tenderheartedness and crocodile tears and retarded emotionality." I brace for it. When cross, Gretchen is a bomb thrower. "Not to mention it stinks of the sort of antic hobby the rich affect so that people will say about them, 'Now *there* goes an original . . .' And I'll tell you something else. I'd bet anything—" But to my relief, her judgment is cut short. Ian interrupts us.

"Morning, Henry. Ah, hello: Ian." He extends a hand that my sister, choked off, takes numbly. "You're Gretchen?" She nods, blinking, righting herself. "I'd say Henry's told us all about you, only he hasn't."

"How surprising."

"Better for you. None of us trust your brother any further than we could throw him." To me he says, "Keith and I have got a table. Make a run through the buffet and join us. We're over, ah, thataway. Through the archway, and then around, and around again." Signaling these directions he becomes distracted by the dimensions of the room. He appraises its coffered ceiling, the soaring sash windows hung like museum paintings. "Must be nice."

We find them bent low over their plates. Keith is quick to stand, giving Gretchen space to set down her food before introducing himself. Ian buses a cluster of empty champagne flutes to make room. "Yours?" I wonder. He feigns shock, pointing to himself and Keith. "*Ours*."

"Baloney." Keith turns to Gretchen. "Let me tell you about this guy. Few years ago I ran into him at a wedding reception for a friend of ours. Now, this reception was in a dry county, which we've still got here in the South. The only booze around was a little champagne they'd brought in for the toasts. When Ian gets his three-quarter-glass ration, he waits for the toasts to finish and then hightails it out to the garden. This was a summer wedding, Union, Georgia. Blazing hot. He stands out there, dark suit, tie knotted right to his throat, in direct sun, for—how long?'"

"Not long enough."

"Thirty, forty minutes. When I find him he's a mess of sweat, red as a tomato. 'Ian, you all right?' 'Sure, Keith.' 'Can I ask what you're doing?' 'Oh, I'm just dehydrating enough to feel faint, then I aim to swig this champagne and hope for the best.'"

"I'm a problem solver," Ian says primly to the laughter. Gretchen is genuinely tickled. It pleases me they would open the circle so quickly. Three minutes in, and already she is part of the gang.

As we eat, they fall to questioning her. Keith wants to know what it is she does. Because her work bears no relation to profits, I think it will not interest him. I am mistaken. He wants to know how the Village identifies its suppliers, whether this is done directly or through middlemen, and how sales proceeds are shared with people who lack bank accounts. He asks if the Village has thought of branching into microcredit. Gretchen is surprised. "You know about microcredit?" "Very little." Still, he remarks how the Village, having done the hard work to find natural entrepreneurs, might offer them not only distribution but also the capital to take proper advantage. Ian regards him with an amused, admiring look.

"Now that we've sorted that, tell us something about this guy." He motions me with a thrust of his knife. "He's a mystery and I don't like mysteries. I'm looking for a little ammunition."

"Aha!" Gretchen smiles evilly. "Let's see, what secret could I spill . . ." But eyeing me, her face changes. A look of tenderness comes over her. So abrupt is the emotion that for a moment she appears to struggle. "Actually—he's great. He's great." She claps a hand on my shoulder, a horsey sort of gesture meant to restore things to the trite and easy. "I'm a big fan."

Ian is put out. "Boring."

My sister smiles at this, but she's struck a vein of sentimental memory. The gush is not so easily stopped. "In our high school there was a girl, Audrey, who was mentally disabled. You can imagine the kind of fun all the jocks and other apes had with her. They called her 'Grubber,' those assholes. And the big fun was tailing her around the hallways, imitating the way she walked. It's the only time I ever wished I was a boy, so I could punch someone and make it count." She gives my shoulder a shake. "But who finally put a stop to it? This guy. My brother."

Ian perks up. "Did he now?"

"Yup. Stepped right in and smacked one of the ringleaders in the face, knocked out his tooth. That was the end of that."

"Whoa, Nelly!" cries Ian.

My sister is coloring the memory somewhat. A good deal, in fact. It was much more a case of leaping before I looked. I said an angry word to one of the boys, not quite realizing he was one from the wrestling team, the last bunch on earth you wanted to cross. In a flash my role changed from chivalrous interposer to cornered rat. I fought like a man drowning. It's true my opponent ended up with a loose tooth, but not through any real doing of mine. He was working my arms into some iron hold when an elbow caught him in the mouth.

Gretchen is regarding me now with a look of pride. Ian too. Not with pride, of course; his is a look of puzzlement. "Who knew? He seems like such a quiet SOB."

"They're the ones you have to watch." She winks at me and excuses herself for more coffee.

When she is gone, Ian says, "Henry, Henry . . ." He is stretched out in his seat, a gratified eye on the ceiling. I wait for some wisecrack, but in fact his mind is elsewhere. "Your sister: forgive me, but your sister is not of this world." Now he jumps upright, making as if to ward me off. "Whoa! You really *are* a protector, aren't you. A real guard dog. See that, Keith? One loose word on her and there's murder in his eyes!"

"Watch your teeth." In fact Keith doesn't show much interest in the game. He is busy working the last of his eggs onto a fork.

Ian is swept by his own momentum and misses the signal. "That's right!" He claps his hands over his mouth. In a muffled voice he says, "Henry, let me ask you: You got any Arab blood?"

"Settle down," Keith tells him. Ian goes limp, hands contrite in his lap. When Keith ignores this, Ian really does settle himself.

"I'm being an asshole. I'll shut up."

Our table sits in a windowed bay that projects over a back terrace. The terrace is a floor below, an expanse of brick spread like a plateau atop three sides of sloping lawn. So green is the grass it seems untouched by winter, a rich, even carpet that falls away into a roil of kudzu and vine-saddled hardwoods. Some guests have wandered outside to smoke or stand in the sun. They cradle glasses of coffee against the day's briskness. Directly below, under the dust-colored limbs of a hawthorn, two women trade puffs on a cigarette. Not until their faces appear in a wider aperture of branch do I see that the women are Gretchen and Jane. A hot star blooms high in my chest. It is like bringing home the person you aim to marry, and watching as she finds quick common cause with your family, and they with her, and seeing in these mirrored affections a reflected glory.

Ian tolls his champagne flute.

"Gentlemen? I've had an idea."

Perhaps fearing he has played too much the boozy fool, he regards us now with a candid business seriousness. "First, a restatement of the problem. The challenge is not the amount of money remaining but the time we have to get it, yes? Namely about six weeks. Six weeks to land a little more than three and a quarter million."

Keith interrupts him. "A little more?" He is the picture of friendly innocence. Ian drops his eyes.

"One hundred thousand more."

"Aha. Why?"

"I inherited the situation at Markitel. Per our discussion, four hundred thousand is an absolute best case—"

Keith lays a broad hand on Ian's shoulder. He feels at the bones. "Three point three-five-zero. This is our number." His tone is neither fatherly nor cautionary but a stabbing register between. My heart practically quails for Ian. It is the spur, and the millstone, of presumed success—this in a trial whose outcome means only everything.

Keith falls back in his chair, plucking a stray grape from the edge of his plate and popping it in his mouth. "Go on."

"A road show."

"A road . . . show . . ." Keith turns it over, chewing. He nods. "A road show."

Ian looks to my reaction. Finding blankness, he says, "This guy's in the dark. OK: when a company wants to go public, it'll pile all its key execs onto a plane and go on a sort of barnstorming tour of institutional investors, analysts, major I-banks, et cetera. It's an intense campaign, maybe five, six weeks, to drum up interest in the stock right before the offering. You get every key decision maker in the company right there in front of the target buyers so they—the buyers, I mean—can get every possible question answered in one fell swoop.

"Now the other thing that happens is you get all your execs singing off the same song sheet. I've never been on one personally, but what I've heard is that you wind up with a close-knit, trench warfare mentality. By the last couple pitches, everyone knows exactly his points to hit. So now you got your audiences elbowing each other aside to drink the Kool-Aid.

"But look at it: this is us. Not a public offering, no, but everything else. What do we have? A small group of critical buyers, a short window of time, and so one chance with each to hit them with everything we've got. And, might as well say it"—he drops his voice—"the future of the business riding on it."

Keith has swept aside his plate. He taps his forehead with clasped hands.

"You can push the similarities even further. We'll explain that after quarter's end the prices are only going up. Just like an IPO: here's your chance to buy in on the ground floor." He lifts his head. "Who do we need?"

Ian counts fingers: "Three of us, plus Operations and Finance."

"Not Operations. Hendersen's a big brain, but he's no good on his feet. Henry can cover if there're Operations questions. Why Finance?"

"Wait—no, you're right. I got lost in my own analogy. We're not talking to bankers; we don't need Finance. So three. Three's better. Smaller, tighter, focused."

"Marketing. We need Marketing."

Ian thinks for a moment. "Of course."

"Jane should hear this." Keith stands, rapping knuckles on a spot near Ian. "Well done, old man. I might just forget that extra hundred grand we've got to find." Ian watches him go. He tips back the dregs of his mimosa.

"Sure. I'll hold my breath."

In fact he wears his heroism well. He sits in a mild left-to-right slouch, fist to thigh and elbow propped at angle, staring out the window, oblivious of his halo. For this is what surrounds him now, a holy light of corporate ingenuity. When I offer my congratulations, Ian receives it abstractedly, eyes lost in the window. "All this means is our chances go from zero to some fraction you need a microscope to see."

A clatter erupts from the kitchen, a tray banging its stone floor. It is an enormous showcase kitchen, all mahogany and polished steel, separated by a broad slab island from the room where our table sits. Through a far double-hinged door comes Michael's inquiring head. The head takes inventory of an unseen mess below it and presents the staff with some quick words. Then, spying me, Michael emerges fully and makes his way over.

"This must be the Cyber table!"

Now I do reintroduce myself. ("Sure, Henry, I remember!") "Michael, this is Ian, our new head of Sales."

Ian is a head shorter and must not look like much to him, for the next thing Michael says is: "Where's Keith?" So here is the real reason for his warm approach. To buttonhole the boss.

"Not sure where he got off to," says Ian. He too is on to Michael. He maneuvers him to new subjects: "Lemme ask you a question. How do you keep your lawn so damn green?" Michael lifts his chin to rub there with a thumb. The chin is cleft and ample. Freed of sullenness, it is a handsome face.

"Easy. I water it every night with the blood of virgins."

"That right?" Ian squints onto the backyard. "Would've thought that's a recipe for drought, this being the New South." The reply pleases Michael. It identifies Ian as a kindred wit. Our host searches for the finishing stroke; his blue eyes actually work in their sockets as he casts about. Nothing comes.

"Ha. Good point," he says finally.

On the terrace directly below, Keith explains the plan to Jane. She stands like a diver, shoulders back and arms at her sides, giving pert schoolgirl nods. This morning she wears a gray pencil skirt and a tawny suede jacket cinched like a safari coat. Here all is tidy and smart: a neat, tailored competence. With each nod, dark lengths of hair become tucked against her neck, now to be gathered together in a single hand like a sheaf and laid again outside the collar. (The smallest of unremembered gestures, but what dry-mouthed longing it provokes!) Keith stands with feet apart and hands deep in his pockets. His lips move measuredly but without hesitation, eyes gone dark and serious. In manner he is like the agent of some dire piece of news. But now the picture changes: Jane rocks forward, righting herself with a quick clap. She throws back her head and gives a shout of laughter. Keith is unmoved, deadpan. A twitching at his mouth betrays him.

Michael is talking. He flatters Ian and me with a confiding look, prelude to some admission.

". . . so I had my guy paint it."

I've lost the thread. "The lawn?"

"Like Augusta," says Ian.

Michael points at him. "Bingo. Same idea exactly."

"Isn't that wild." Ian has a salesman's genius for looking utterly bowled over by fascination. "How long does it last?"

"My guy says about four weeks. Up to six depending on rain."

"Incredible."

"It's quite a process. Have to tape off the patio, cover up the back windows. Still, they put down a coat and I took one look and said huh-uh. That's not going to do it. Give me two."

"What is it, rollers, or some sort of sprayer . . . ?" Ian stands with arms crossed, surveying the lawn, almost certainly thinking of anything but.

"Sprayers. Rollers'd mat down the grass."

"Sure, sure."

"Got a fair-sized yard here, so they wheeled in a couple of tanks, two hoses each. They started back at the wood line, which is tricky. The thing is you can't get it on the plants back there because the green won't match. Have to spray the whole forest to get it matched back up! Anyway, what happens is once they get a perimeter track—"

Ian jabs the windowpane. "Oh, say, there's Keith now."

"Hm—?" Michael shuffles around the table to see. "I'll be damned. Fella looks to be making time with my wife! Gentlemen, if you'll excuse me . . ."

In a moment he appears below us, touching Keith on the elbow and pumping his hand. He looks every inch the game show emcee to Keith's contestant, regaling him with some chuckling anecdote. Except that Keith has the advantage in height. Our host is fastened under a downward stare, and just as quickly his standing changes.

"I'd like to be there to hear that," Ian remarks. He is grooming his thumbnail with a toothpick left over from the canapés. "Keith'll have that dope in two pieces before the poor fucker even feels the cut."

6

"I can see why you like working for Keith," Gretchen tells me. "He seems decent and engaging and sharp, sharp, sharp. Honest to God, he knows more about my work than I do."

We drive along a winding gray lane flanked by thickets of swamp maple and dogwood. Substantial houses are nestled well back from the road, glimpsed only as white flashes atop tall drives of crushed cinder. "I'd expected . . . I don't know what. Somebody much more boxed up and dull."

The sun at its winter angle and the play of tree shadows on the road, a filtering light that stirs archaic memories. Yellowed shafts beheld from the green deeps of summer lakes. Great attic fans wheeling among wooden beams segmenting the golden rays of ancient afternoons . . . Gretchen yawns mightily. Shadows deepen. Sunday afternoons, above all Sunday afternoons in winter: loss in a minor key.

"Ian, I'm not so sure about. He's harder to read. He's a little— What was Mom's word for it . . . ?" She pulls a blond lock straight before her nose, parsing the strands for dry ends. The investigation leaves her mildly cross-eyed. "Oh, come on. This is going to kill me. What she said about Kevin, my date for Snow Daze senior year? Impish! Ian's a little impish. You know?"

"Not really."

"Yes. He's a bit sneaky and knows it and knows you know it. Fun at parties, but I'd hate to be on his bad side. He's got guile to spare, I bet."

"He may have saved my job. Mine, his, everyone's."

Gretchen hears nothing ominous in this. "You'll pull through. I have faith." Her lack of concern is afforded by a belief that in the world of commerce, there can never be much at stake. Were I to lose my job, she would be only passingly sorry. Perhaps not even that much. Cyber Systems is the main culprit for my unrealized contributions to the world, as I have mentioned. For my part I am reminded of what lies ahead, our new adventure to save the company, Jane and me together. A helium tingle comes into my groin. The small suffering of Sunday afternoons blows away like smoke.

Corresponding to this change, the neighborhood comes to an end. Its trees and shadows give way to a strip of good honest American retail. Gretchen pulls a stockinged foot into her lap and sets about popping the joints of her toes. Thus limbered, she wedges the foot beneath her thigh. I wait for her impression of Jane.

"Is that a giant pig on top of that mall?"

"The Pink Pig. It's an amusement ride Macy's puts up at Christmas."

"Oh! Did I tell you I was in the Holidazzle Parade this year?"

"No."

"The Village had an entry. Three Men in a Tub. We wore nude suits and a big tin tub on suspenders. I was in the lead. We couldn't quite stay coordinated in our march, so the tub kept swinging out and coming back right into my shins. You wouldn't believe the bruises. But so fun!"

"Did you talk to Jane?"

Gretchen holds her palms to the dash vents, then dials down the heat. "Not like you did. My God, I thought I was going to need the Jaws of Life to pry you two apart."

I ignore this. "I thought I saw you chatting on the patio."

"She saw me smoking and wanted to know if she could sneak a drag. Something about not wanting her in-laws to catch her."

"And?"

"The usual small talk." She is seized by another lion's yawn, coming through with eyes watering. "Whew. Nap time. She likes you, of course."

"Is that right."

"Of course. What's she going to say? 'That brother of yours, now *there's* a guy who should be castrated.' I asked about her job, she asked about mine. It got a little tedious, to be honest. Can we open the sunroof?"

"It's too cold. How do you mean, tedious?"

She opens the sunroof. The seal releases with a sucking sound; cold whistling air comes pouring in. "You forget how strange it is to ride in an open car in February."

"Tedious how?"

"Oh, just that when I told her what I did, it got her playing quite a sad violin about wanting to involve herself more, to give back, et cetera. Which reminds me. Another thing about Keith is he didn't feel obliged to sing his admiration for the great nonprofit workers of the world."

"She might very well mean it."

"She might. For all I know, she does. On some days anyway. Still, she reminds me of all the finance majors I knew in college. People barely out of their teens who'd gotten it from somewhere that money was The End, and just went chasing along after it like pigs. From time to time some of them do what she does, lift their heads from the trough and pause in midchew to think it over. But always there's the shrug, the plunge right back in."

This is too much.

"Who're we talking about?"

Gretchen turns from the window. She eyes me for a careful moment.

"Jane."

"Really. All this from a five-minute conversation."

"I know the type. Not what you'd call a rare specimen, I'm sorry to say. Sensitive, are we?"

"Only to veiled little passive-aggressive—"

"Passive-aggressive! Hardly. Not this gal, not the passive part."

"Then say what you want to say to me. Don't bounce your criticisms off her."

"Ohhh." Gretchen struggles to hold the O of her mouth, but it goes curling away in the pleasure of her discovery. "*Aha*. My oh my. Henry Hurt."

"Enough."

"And she's married!"

"We're *friends*."

Gretchen is thrust back against the headrest, smiling but with her eyes held shut. "Well. What can I say? I only hope there's no pedestal involved. Because if there is, and her foot were to slip so much as an inch . . ."

"The hell are we talking about now?" I am annoyed by her misreading of Jane, annoyed at being so easily discovered.

Gretchen sets her elbow on the door's armrest, turning her face to the sinking light. Her nail beats time on a tooth. I fear more questioning, but in fact her mind is elsewhere.

"Look at that." She indicates a billboard advertising mobile phone service. A man in heavy black glasses offers his hand to the viewer. Behind him is a V of fellow subscribers, their numbers stretched to the vanishing point. A red sash at the corner reads: 8 MILLION PEOPLE CAN'T BE WRONG! "I'd like to put that banner over one of those photos of the Nuremberg rallies." She turns serious. "Dad watches all the TV ads now. He used to be so good about muting them; now he asks me to turn them up. Not all of them. The sappy ones. Or zany. Zany or sappy. Which *is* all of them, come to think of it. He watches them as closely as the shows. The one for Puppy Chow. The little fuzzball Labrador in the tall grass? Charging and falling, with the folk guitar strumming along in the background? That's the one these days. The other night it was so bad he actually reached for my hand."

"He what?"

"Yep." She speaks in the old, tough-minded stoic voice our mother called upon when troubled by something. "There we were, father and daughter holding hands while that mutt gobbled dry pellets from a bowl." This is as peculiar as it sounds. Our father is not unaffectionate, but he doesn't have a sentimental bone in his body. "I meant to ask: How did he seem when you were home last week?"

"Fine. Better than fine. Sharp as ever. We went shooting. He couldn't miss." I do not think his near repetition of the story about our mother worth mentioning.

Gretchen accepts this without comment. In the brooding silence that follows I am reminded how much the true solitary she is. Gretchen is a person of good looks and good brains and would easily have moved among our high school's gentry were it not for her distrust of charismatics and winners, and her preference for kicked dogs. Once when she was eight I found her alone on a swing on the school's playground, drawing with a sneaker in the trough of dirt worn by a thousand kickoffs, and softly singing a triumphalist ditty then popular among the neighborhood kids:

> *Who likes the Ayatollah*
> *Kho-mei-ni?*
> *It ain't me!*
> *It ain't me!*

Except in her rendering it sounded impossibly forlorn, a kind of dirge for our better angels.

At last she says: "You have to come home next month. You *will*. Tell me."

"I said I'd do my best."

She lifts her chin and goes scratching at her throat. Her nails leave tracks in the sudden redness. "Sorry, I don't get it. I really don't. You'll have to explain it again."

"Will you listen to an answer?"

"I'll listen."

"I wasn't kidding about things being touch-and-go. We're talking hundreds of people, a good many of whom I like and trust, and who in turn like me—or at least trust me to help keep them employed.

Now we've got some kind of barnstorming sales trip in the works. This thing is truly last-ditch. I can't just say, *Sorry, folks, I've got to pop out for a few days, you're on your own."*

"Better you say it to your family."

Ah. Now here is a dramatic way of putting it. Here is another dissonant note in the old harmony. I mean that my sister is thirty and lives at home and works a retail floor, all of it by choice, all toward nobler ends. Meanwhile her comrade-in-arms is in this faraway capital, hooting it up with the charismatics and winners.

"I need to tell you something," she says. Her tone is different. There comes the hollowing feeling of imminent bad news. "A few days ago I was tidying up in his study. I found a Post-it under his desk. There were notes on it about us. I mean the simplest things—*Gretchen, daughter. Henry, son.* Like that. Our names, a line on what each of us does for a living."

I feel sick to my stomach. It is like a kind of stage fright. The consequential thing has arrived: account for yourself.

"Why didn't you tell me?"

"I'm telling you now!" She has turned her face well away; she peers out her window with a newly fierce regard for the landscape. (It is all tanning salons and gas stations.) "Also, I didn't want it to be true."

With this at least I am in perfect sympathy. It dawns on me she is not the only one hiding things. I confess to her his quick memory lapse after our evening of shooting.

"You weren't drinking . . ."

"No. Oh—the whiskey bottle."

She nods, warming to the practicalities. "Better if it isn't lying around. Ethanol's a memory killer. Even one glass and he starts to repeat himself."

"When did you hide it?"

"A few days after Christmas."

"What made you?"

Here my sister closes her eyes and falls back against the headrest. "I don't know if it was the holiday or what. But for days after Christmas, he kept referring to Mom in the present tense. 'Your mother isn't going to like this.' 'Just don't tell your mother.' That kind of thing. The first time I thought he was making some sort of ghoulish joke."

The last of the sun wavers in the pink glass of a low office building. It is an ugly, vault-like thing, with wraparound mirror glass and hidden entrances. I curse it silently. Nobody cares about your damned secrets.

Gretchen makes a quick swipe at her eyes, then pushes on matter-of-factly. "I wasn't about to corner him on it. So I've done what I can around the edges. No more whiskey. I put some ginkgo supplements in his pill organizer."

"What about a doctor? Some kind of test?"

She swings her head around, looking at me from beneath her brow. "No, you're right."

"We're talking about his *mind.*"

"You're right, you're right. It would take a crisis."

"And even then . . ." Now her tone makes another curious shift. "If you ask me, there's at least some aspect of denial."

"Denial?"

"These little trip-ups with verb tense. I think those are honest-to-goodness Freudian slips."

My heart sinks. We are not unified in the problem after all.

"He looked like he grieved plenty to me."

"I know. But some of the books I've been reading suggest a person can cycle back through the stages. This is why it's crucial we're together for the anniversary. Who knows what it could trigger? Maybe nothing. But if something: familiar, supportive faces to see him through to whatever stage crops up next."

Stages. Hm. Here is another problem with her role as caregiver. It encourages this therapeutic mode. She becomes invincible in her diagnoses and prescriptions. (In this, at least, our mother's leukemia was a boon. Gretchen became a dervish of macrobiotic cooking and amateur reflexology and herbal supplements.) Whenever this therapist appears, my impulse is to say, *Yes, thank you, Doctor. Now: Would you please put my sister on the line?*

Gretchen returns to pressing her case, albeit more gently. "I'm not making light of your work, you know that. But surely your company will see this is a special situation."

"It's not a matter of anyone seeing anything. It's a matter of there not being enough money to convince the Board to keep the lights on." But I no longer have much heart for the argument.

"And without you on this trip they couldn't possibly manage."

"They need me, yes."

The words leave an echo. She says nothing; better I am left to stew. To my irritation, it works.

"I'll plan to be there. It's the best I can do."

"I understand. It's not like it'd be the sort of thing you'd regret."

Whether because of these new depressing facts, or because the argument is pointless and lost, I am now good and irritated. "Wonderful."

"Oh God, H. Don't be so dismissive. That's not you. Don't be one of these robots who're always trading in their families for work without a second thought."

"I'll try not to."

"Thank you."

"Just out of curiosity: What's the trade value?"

"Ha. I'll tell you, since you ask. You get that." She turns in her seat, pointing back in the direction we've come. She means: that house, those rituals. "God. I took a bit of time to wander around that place. Call it morbid curiosity. Do you know what I found in one of the rooms? They had a television, one of these silly flat panel monsters you hang on the wall—they had it in a *frame*. A *gilt* frame. That's where all these grand sacrifices lead: to framed TVs and smart Sunday brunches and imported little wooden dolls. It's beyond crass. It's *deranged*. Now, none of that's you, I know. Not yet anyway. But you see the danger."

"The danger?"

"That you turn into a cynic where there's no grander calling to anything, life's just acquisitiveness and utilitarianism and hardheadedness. It's a death sentence."

I squeeze the wheel enough that its leather creaks. We are making brands of each other. This is the agony above all agonies. She is the dutiful-daughter-cum-therapist-truth-seeker, I the benumbed gray flannel man. The gray flannel man has but a single narrative. One day he sees the light, kicks to the curb his life of quiet desperation, and goes leaping renewed into the world. (But what are the characteristics of this renewal? In the narrative it is quite simple: a desk job swapped for boycotts and picket lines, a tender and meaningful relationship with a pretty veterinarian, life on an apple farm.) Somehow, someway, we have misplaced our old confidences and sympathies. And these goddamned brands are rising to fill the vacuum.

Well, better nothing at all than these brands. Recently I've begun to nurture the idea that what Gretchen and I need is a proper battle royal, an argument so severe, so wounding, as to leave us not angry but exhausted. More: *shamed*. Such that in the aftermath our choice is stark: to survey the smoldering grounds and know there is nothing left, to rejoin hands and pick our way out of ruin and toward some new country—or to never speak again.

Five

1

Keith explains the plan at the Monday management meeting. It is received with the small, stony nods of a people who have heard their last best chance. All are humble and serious before the facts, but also secretly thrilled that it has come to something as grave and special as a mission.

Immediately following the meeting, we—Keith, Ian, Jane, and I—assemble a war room. A whiteboard wall is quickly covered with bullet lists running beneath headers like *Value Propositions* and *Known Issues*. It is mostly Ian's show. He holds court before the eye of the projector, charts and figures ballooning on the ivory cloth of his dress shirt. Though technically a management secret, word of our mission (if not quite the full consequence of its failure) has spread. From time to time someone looks in the glassed door and, seeing our grim determination, will himself stand a little straighter, carrying on to his desk with new purpose. Such is the honor an office grants its champions. And for the first hour I am positively drugged by this admiration. For the first hour I am catapulted by the role of champion . . . until the tasks of sorting the messages, of manufacturing the slides and deciding our weaknesses, speaking about what we will say and how we will say it—the dreary, daunting particulars—bring home its actuality, its urgency. It is then that I sit, still nodding, still voicing mature and reasonable-sounding opinions, my mouth run dry and a terrible pit in my stomach.

During a break I encounter Cory in the Xerox room. Something is wrong with the machine. He works the machine's buttons in a caricature of patience.

"Looks promising."

He ignores this, only mashing buttons with a fist. Then:

"You know Rahim's H-1."

"H-1?"

"No job, no visa."

I had forgotten. There are at least two others on my team in the same boat.

"The captain is speechless," Cory observes.

"We're going to be just fine."

"Uh-huh." He gives a hard kick to the base of the machine, then reasserts his grip.

The room is humidly warm, a gray-tiled cell under fluorescent panels, sealed off by industrial double doors. Bottles of toner give off an earthy purple smell, a carbon-and-carrot fragrance that summons fall days and classroom desks in the old battle formation, surprise quizzes warm from the press (and held mindfully by the edges), the cadence of instruction, take one and pass it back. How sweet that bygone anxiety now feels! But sweet to the point of sorrow. Homesickness for a lost country.

Cory tries a violent shake of the machine. The copier doesn't budge. He lays down his cheek, folding his arms around his head. "Also she's pregnant."

"She?"

"Rahim's wife."

God Almighty. "Speaking seriously, I'm optimistic."

"You're optimistic."

"I am. It's a little early to panic."

Only when I have turned to leave does he answer. "If you say so."

I wait, one hand on the door.

"Pregnant, no health, COBRA five times the price, never mind deportation . . ." His head in his arms, a weary voice.

"No one's losing his job."

"Naw."

"No. The plan is good. Ian is on to something—"

"Don't much care to hear it."

We leave it at that.

2

In the afternoon rehearsal I move through my slide portion competently, if not quite dynamically. When I am finished Keith turns in his chair for the group's verdict.

"Not bad." Ian nods, staring at nothing. "Only—"

"We could lose them," says Jane.

"Yep." Ian nods more vigorously. "Exactly my worry."

"How do you mean?" I am annoyed by their little private agreement. Jane makes a placative sound in her throat.

"No, not you. What I mean—"

But Ian has no time for niceties: "What you've got is all fine for what it is, a description of the nuts and bolts of our software. But senior buyers aren't looking at the technology, not really. Technology is a commodity. No offense, that's just how they'll see it. What they're really going to be looking at, after our market share, is *us*. I mean they need to like and trust the folks behind the product. Jane: you were saying something."

"I *was*, wasn't I." Her irises have gone dark. "I mean there's a basic marketing problem with us having our little rehearsed portion of slides. Everything gets a bit too determinedly rah-rah. If we four come marching in and proceed to launch forth one by one, the customer will do the math and have us tuned out by the second speaker."

"It's a good point," Keith says. "We need to vary the pitch."

Ian pushes from the wall where he has been standing and comes striding to the front whiteboard. "So here's what we do." He executes a series of quick, squeaking strokes. Keith watches in frowning amusement.

"The hell is that?"

"Seating chart." Ian touches three X's at the top of a large oval: "You, me, Jane. This X down here at the other end, that's Henry. In every pitch, he's part of the audience. No slides, no formal speaking. I'm serious now. This isn't a knock. What you are is the consultant."

I have no idea what this means, but Keith doesn't like it. "They're going to need to hear something about our technology."

"They will, they will. But from a guy who's on their side, one of them, and not up with us, bragging in front of a bunch of complicated diagrams."

Jane raises a hand. "Am I the only one lost?"

Keith gives her his full attention. "The idea is Henry becomes an expert presence, sitting with our audience. He asks the 'probing' questions—all softballs—and lets the speaker highlight whatever it is we mean to highlight."

"Talk to them too," Ian says to me. "Draw them out, get them talking about themselves, their business, their problems. Hell, cut us off to do it! Show you're more interested in their struggles than our presentations. 'Consultant'—maybe's the wrong word. What you are is the moderator. You're a neutral, knowledgeable, reliable third party, just trying to make sure everyone gets his money's worth."

It is not clear why this role-playing should fall to me. Ian shrugs. "People trust engineers. Those harmless propeller-heads, et cetera. Anyway, they'll trust you a lot more than the sales guy or the marketer or the fucking GM."

Sometime later during a break, Jane seeks me out in a small bay off one of the hallways. It is a little standing area with fridge and Coke machine and cabinet sink. She absorbs herself with the machine's selection, running a finger down the column of illuminated panel buttons.

"So? What do you make of it all?"

She would seem purely absent and unconcerned, except she keeps a sidelong eye on my reaction. The hallway fluorescents are motion-activated. At present the corridor is dark. Its gloom is held back only by a small sconce above the sink. This, and the furnace glow of the Coca-Cola logo. The dim light gives our space a safe, bunkered quality, low-beamed and torch-lit.

"It's coming along I think."

She turns, putting her back to the machine and nodding, now rolling her neck from shoulder to shoulder. There is perhaps, in these little exertions on the way to unwinding, a hint of ceremony. They point to humble self-sacrifice, a minor martyrdom too modest to be named.

Something occurs to me.

"I'm impressed. You've got a knack for this."

"Oh, please." But the color is on her cheeks. I am right. She is exhilarated by our work. And it is true: she has been impressive. On three different occasions this afternoon Keith has complimented her for one suggestion or another, and each time Jane's body language—a modest nod of thanks, a lighting-up from within—spoke of realization, even astonishment. (Not that it has all been happy. When Keith dismissed an idea she'd had about pro rata discounts, Jane retreated as if into a shell, not venturing another opinion for nearly an hour.)

The hall lights shudder and blaze to life. Ian rounds the corner.

"Uhp! Pardon. Just here for my sugar fix. Didn't mean to interrupt you lovebirds."

"Lovebirds!" I cry—much too loud. There is the briefest of unfilled silences. Ian holds a finger to his temple.

"Let me guess: 'Can you believe what an asshole this Ian guy is?'—and I've interrupted."

"Don't be silly," Jane assures him. "We were finished."

He nods appreciatively. Feeding a bill into the Coke machine, he says: "In all seriousness, boss"—meaning me—"don't think I was crapping on your stuff in there. When I get antsy my etiquette goes to hell. What you've got is good. Jesus, you make software architecture sound like poetry! But I agree with this lady here. A big part of our pitch comes down to how it all spills out. So the only thing we do, we package how you say it a little differently." A brief whirring, a hollow tumbling—*thunk*. Ian fishes out the can, pops the tab, and raises a brief toast. He tips back.

"Anyway. Just punch me if I get out of line." He smiles winningly, even sheepishly, at both of us. Then with two vigorous pulls, his Coke is finished and he is off down the hallway, shoulders held high, smacking one fist on the other.

Jane gazes after him.

"I wish you would punch him."

"What?"

"'Technology is a commodity'! That takes nerve. So desperate to have all the big ideas, be the center of everything . . . You don't think?"

"I don't know. He's got a full plate. Keith's been pretty tough about the numbers."

"Well, he's getting under *my* skin. Why do I have the feeling he wouldn't hesitate to throw either of us under the bus? Watch his face the next time one of us makes a point Keith likes. I swear he looks practically panicked."

Panicked? In Ian's shoes, I'd be scared to death.

Shortly after seven PM, Keith pronounces the day finished. We are to go home, rest up, and not think about any of this until tomorrow. He decrees our progress good. Nods all around.

I close up office. Passing the conference room on my way to the elevators, I see that Keith has ignored his own advice. He remains at the whiteboard, putting down ideas for tomorrow's session.

"Don't stay too late."

"Ah—Henry. Just the guy I wanted to see. Got a minute?"

"Of course."

"Have a seat."

This I dutifully do while he finishes a thought. He takes a half step back from the board to survey his work. "This thing you're going to do, this moderator bit, you're comfortable with it?" With his thumb, he rubs out the word *Achievable*. In its place he writes *Winnable*.

"I think so."

"I need something stronger than that."

"I'm comfortable, yes."

"It's not anything you rehearse. You just commit to the mode and stick with it. Show a decisive enough lead—the Knowledgeable Fellow at the Back of the Room, that sort of thing—and they'll follow. Never mind that they're the buyers and we're the ones with hat in hand. Play it right and everyone forgets." He scans the bottom half of the board, sighting along an outstretched hand. "For one thing, they'll have their own internal rivalries and political grudges. These big pitches are never as simple as vendor versus buyer, thank God. It's always us versus them versus themselves." The hand pauses. He leans in. *National* is smeared to oblivion; *Global* fills the space. "But you're not part of them and you won't quite be one of us. You'll be a bit removed, neither fish nor fowl. That's a golden opportunity. Suddenly you're the only trustworthy voice in the room."

Ian is right. There is a great deal to be learned from this man.

"Just don't overdo it. You're not a guru on a mountaintop. You're a sensible guy trying to get to the bottom of things: what problem does Client X need to solve, and how does Cyber do it?"

Trends is deemed insufficient. It becomes *Facts*. Satisfied, Keith caps the marker and sets it on the rail. He brushes off his hands.

"Not that I worry about you overdoing it. But if you go weak-kneed . . ." He wanders across the room and closes the door. This is done without a shred of import, yet my heart takes note. "If you go weak-kneed, they'll see it. In a minute. Any doubt, any stutter on our part, gets added to certainty on theirs. Damn it man, you look nervous already!"

"I'm not nervous."

"There. Good."

"I've passed the audition."

"Flying colors. One other thing." Here he parks himself on the table. "Look. We've worked together not even a year. So understand that when it comes to motivational technique, my habit can be . . . Call it too much stick, too little carrot." He is careful not to look at me, for to lock eyes would be too much. Instead his gaze is downcast, fixed on the spot where his fist presses the table. I know well this trick of the heart-to-heart. It is the same I use with members of my team when needing to motivate one especially. But knowing the trick is not the same as being immune to its effect. "It's true things are serious right now. Damned serious. The business unit's at risk, and as a Director your job is to see us through. But there's opportunity here too. We pull out of this nosedive, there'll be credit aplenty to share. And if I get bumped up, you better believe my key folks come with me. As a matter of simple fact—"

There comes a respectful knocking on the door's pane glass. Ian is there in dark overcoat, his bag at his feet. Keith cranes around and, finding the source of the interruption, waves him off. "Go home!" he calls. He will not have the spell of the heart-to-heart broken. Ian shoots me a comically wounded look.

Keith resumes, impatient not to lose the confiding charge between us. Ian remains in the door pane, watching. Finding my eye, he makes an invitation by raising a thumb to his lip and tossing back a cup.

"But my point here," Keith is saying, "isn't some cheap vagueness about opportunity. Let me be specific. If I move up, the General Manager slot comes open. Now. There'll be more than one candidate, and final say belongs to the Board. But nobody knows Cyber's product better than you. You're a smart manager, with a proven tenure; your folks like you. This quarter comes out the way we need it—" He catches himself. "Never mind the jinx. Just know you're well positioned."

A slightly uneasy silence falls on the room.

"Thank you," I say. "Certainly the regard, if that's the word, is more than mutual."

What is the matter with me? His words are everything a professional's heart could desire. Yet my immediate feeling is one of adolescent awkwardness. Keith now seems embarrassed too. We are like young sweethearts who have declared their love to each other for the first time and only in the echo after discover the seriousness, the vulnerability, of their new standing.

But the awkwardness is short-lived. He buffets the table lightly with his fist; his wedding band raps out a suitable punctuation. We are restored to plain standings, superior and subordinate, and no promises on anything until we've hoed the hard row ahead.

3

With Ian there is no stumbling around the city after dark in search of a suitable watering hole. He has a tab at the lobby bar of the Four Seasons hotel in midtown. I did not think bars were still in the habit of carrying tabs for patrons, and yet it isn't hard to see how he has negotiated his credit. He and the concierge exchange whispers; the maître d' steps away from his post to say hello. Upon arriving at the bar there is already waiting for him a glass lowball, three fingers of neat whiskey molded at its bottom like a thick amber disc.

"So! You and Mr. Keith looked to be having quite the little confab."

"Not really."

"Sure, what do I know. I was on the wrong side of the glass."

"I think I was being bucked up."

"Bucked up? No. He's not much of a bucker-upper. Trust me." He sighs hollowly into his glass. "No, that Mr. Keith is one tough hombre to please." He makes a quick pelican jerk of the neck, throwing back his drink. "Never mind all that. Like the man said, let's clear our heads, come at it fresh tomorrow."

The bar is a private, geometrically pleasing space on the hotel's mezzanine. What is pleasing is its parallelism, a square room with a low-pile square rug, a large square table fenced by blockish sofas. Every surface is polished to an obsidian shine. We set down on a sofa each, met at a right angle. A black-haired boy in a maroon coat sweeps up molecules at the entrance; a maid burnishes the counter's brass foot rail. Yes, here is a room finally in which it is possible to *think*—one of those clever assignments of square footage a person comes into, out of the tempest of his day, to feel the world snapped to ranks around him. The table gleams like a scientific principle.

We talk about not much, recent poor trades in sports and stocks, the ridiculousness of Cyber's competitors. Ian is wicked in his judgments. After each point scored, up comes the glass, a cubic centimeter of whiskey dispensed into the neat eversion of his lips. Behind his eyes the mists blow in. Soon we are entered into that fast friendship of men whose shoulders have been put to the same heavy wheel, the bond of shared labor as high-minded and ironclad as that of any fraternal order. Ian talks of his upbringing in Tallahassee, where his father owned a series of bars, a rugged business that made the family rich. With the telling comes a memory of a fight he witnessed between one of his father's bouncers and a local drunk.

"Now this ole boy was something, big black sombitch who'd been one of State's star recruits. Only what does he do? In his freshman year, no less? Puts his motorcycle in a ditch. Sammy Sproles. Good-bye knee, good-bye career. Ever since he'd been a charity case for Tallahassee's bartenders. On this day I'm at the bar helping the busboys. I used to do that after school. Not that my father gave me a dime for it, the cheap SOB. But I snuck plenty of inventory. Anyway: What happens is, Sammy comes up to the door with this dog, an old Lab gimping along about as bad as Sammy himself. He says to Rojo—one of Dad's bouncers, tough, tough Indian cat—he says, 'Dis heah guy coming in wid me.' He had an idea the dog would sit with him at the bar or something. Ole Rojo doesn't even look at him. 'Ah naw, he ain't.' 'Oh yea, he *is*'—Sammy is not sober, to put it mildly. Not Rojo either I wouldn't imagine. So right away it's: You don't like me, I don't like you, let's fight. And man, I mean this is one *fight*." Ian sets down his drink to better tell it. "These two gorillas just sawing away at each other, Sammy's dog gone berserk, snapping and barking its head off. I'm maybe fourteen, standing there waiting for someone to yell cut. Then"—he smacks the meat of his palm—"POW! Rojo lands a haymaker square on the temple. Pops Sammy's eyeball out."

A helping of gin reverses course in my throat.

"Yep. Just erupts that sucker right from the socket, leaves it swinging on red muscle."

"Jesus Christ."

"I know, I know. Crazy stuff." Ian does not in fact look much affected. My own reaction is a surprise to him. But it is an awful story. The brutality is enough to turn the stomach. Sensing some misstep, Ian recalibrates. "No, terrible. Absolutely. Gave me nightmares, I'll tell you what. Lordy Lord . . ." He hunches forward, rolling his glass in his palms. What is wanted is a philosophical landing place. "Cruel hunk of rock we live on."

Soon he has forgotten all about it. The bartender, out of cordiality or boredom (the bar is nearly empty), brings two drinks without being asked. He is a tall, monk-bald man in a white coat. Ian calls him Rory. The name seems a joke between them. Being tended revives Ian's sense of place. He sips and sighs, settling his head on a cushion. The glass is cradled to his stomach.

"Your turn. Let's hear something."

"Like what?"

"How long you and Miss Jane known each other?"

I affect to do the math. "A year?"

"Not exactly a couple of old souls."

"No."

"Seems like a nice girl."

"She is."

"And not too hard on the eyes, if you don't mind me saying."

"Nope."

Something in his eye has gone keen and searching. But he turns to other matters.

"What're your folks do?"

"My father's retired. He was a teacher. My mother was a home-maker."

"Was?"

"She's no longer living."

"Sorry. What did your dad teach?"

"Little of everything."

"A thinking man. Professor Hurt." His eyes are nearly shut. Only a thin gleam at the lashes reveals him.

"Not professor, but yes."

"Who're you more like?"

Behind him is a bank of tremendous pane windows. A new office tower is going up across the street. Through its frank steel bones the lower buildings of midtown can be seen, now dark and empty.

It is a bland enough matter until a parent dies, and then you are in stranger waters. Not long ago it was precisely these sorts of questions (set in gallant, orotund words: "Inheritance," "Identity," "Allegiance") that I set out to answer. Really, my idea was that if grief was to be turned to productive ends, a rigorous program of self-investigation was needed. So I did what the conscientious griever does: I went to a bookstore. Mine was not only a harvest of how-to-grieve books. There were also titles on practical psychology ("Acceptance may require multiple cycles through the preceding stages before becoming a proper end-state"), philosophy (". . . it is this transmutation from Subject to Not-subject that gives form to the central conundrum of the Not . . ."), life coaching ("Tonight cry your eyes out. Don't be ashamed! But tomorrow when you wake up, say to yourself, Today I resolve to live *mindfully, gratefully, purposefully.*"). I even seized upon a novel called *What the Saints Dream* whose dust jacket described "an unsparing story of loss, but no less an unashamed celebration of the mystery of renewal." I read these dutifully, marked their margins, and passed them along to my father or sister with recommendation. (Not the novel. Its solemn sincerity was death itself.) But mostly what I discovered is that I am a person with not much attention span. I could never remember quite what it was I had learned. There were my notes, yes. But there was also, for example, the index card that fell out of one of my mother's Agatha Christies. It was an old recipe for meat loaf. A mysterious artifact; I studied it as closely as my books. Here in ballpoint was a fossil record of the hand I remembered, the birthday cards and college letters, the fond notes tucked inside packed school lunches, embarrassing and babyish and marvelous and lost. A recipe for meat loaf, which swept before it all my recorded epiphanies and arrivals and solutions.

Now Ian puts a clumsy hand to his face. "Jesus. 'Who're you more like.' That's a womanish question, isn't it. Next I'll be asking about your ideal husband. Then we'll slip into our sorority pj's and have a pillow fight. Rory? Another round if you please." Rory tends the mixtures. When the drinks have materialized, Ian picks up the thread. "I see it that I'm my father's son. Except I worry more. My father's never lost a wink of sleep in his life. Marines, Vietnam, three tours."

"Tough."

"A man with high expectations, put it that way." He lifts and resettles his leg on the table, grimacing like a sore athlete. Now he casts an eye over the fall of his clothes. A pant leg is tugged to bring the crease in line. "I remember one time he took me to a park to practice fielding grounders. I'm probably nine. He's up there at home plate, smacking ball after ball my way, when all of sudden he decides I'm not showing enough hustle. Doesn't say a word. Just storms the infield, jerks the glove off my hand, the hat off my head, marches over to a Dumpster and drops it all in. Bat, glove, hat—bye-bye!"

It is difficult to say what seriousness Ian assigns this memory. For one thing he is distracted. Three women in scaled cocktail dresses have arrived at the bar counter. They hold low conversation with Rory; Ian speaks to them, not me. He works a hand along his chin and throat, measuring the scrupulousness of his razor.

Now he returns his attention. "No, look. Dad's not one of these old-school bores who practically have a fetish for toughness. You meet him now, he looks about like any other suburban father on the far side of money. I tell myself I've got a nose for the buck. But my father—! Six months ago we're talking about various projects he's pursuing, car washes, an import-export business, and out of the blue he tells me one of the ventures he's backing. You'll love this."

"What?"

"It's an expedition. Guess what they're looking for."

"I don't know."

"No, but guess."

"Sunken treasure."

"Bigfoot!"

"Bigfoot . . ." I wait for a punch line. "I don't follow."

"These are big game hunters up in Alaska or somewhere. One of them was in Dad's platoon. Their idea is they get a group of investors to back this expedition, with a share of all the merchandising and marketing rights if they find the thing. You find the Sasquatch, you write your own ticket."

I cannot make head or tail of this.

"It's a scam?"

"A scam? No. No, this deal is deadly serious. They see real money in finding Bigfoot."

Rory holds out a packet of cigarettes. A tea candle is passed around, its pinpoint flame alighting among three shades of acrylic nails. The smell of burnt cloves haunts our squared-off space. It sneaks up the nostrils and down the throat, not so much a scent as a tang on the tongue—the very taste of occultism and carnival confusion. There is nothing to do but nod politely and grip the armrest for dear life.

"Unusual," say I, hedging. I still cannot be sure he is entirely serious. He is grinning, but I think in delight of the enterprise.

"The best ideas are!"

What is unusual—what is baffling in fact, what accounts, perhaps, for this sudden unmooring, this seasick sense—is how fluently he moves from tragedy to confession to absurdity. He glides over experience as if on a skin. There is nothing, it seems, that can't be covered over, smoothed out, and made to match, the serious and the unserious, the devout and the glancing. All that is wanted is a ready, crazy-world shrug. But how does the method come to him? Does he meet sadness, strangeness, as would a crusader: eye to eye, keenly seeing the world as it is but refusing to be budged from his own pilgrim's progress? Or is he as inattentive to the puzzle, the dissonance, as one thumbing channels (. . . poker, Bogart, beer ad, massacre . . .) before dropping off to sleep?

"Bigfoot!" he cries again, clapping, lost for a moment in the marvel of it. And here a delicate thing happens. The women at the counter are near enough his sphere of good humor to become infected. One volunteers herself with a small laugh. Ian whips around as if accused.

"Not a joke!" He fixes the group with a stern glare, mock severe.

"Oh, I'm sure not," says the one who laughed, mock conciliatory herself. It is doubtful any of them has heard a single word of our conversation, but she is pleased to be noticed, pleased to have thrown a line from her raft to ours. She and Ian eye each other in their impromptu roles, a spry little game between strangers. A small freeze comes over my heart. None of them is pretty enough to play the game out. How now to disengage without seeming cruel?

"You don't believe me!" Ian protests. Except that he is in retreat as he says it, turning to me—"She doesn't believe me!"—seizing the mantle of spurned party, even as he squares our circle. The woman and her friends are restored to scenery, but in a way that doesn't cut her dead, the game ended without disobliging her play. It is extraordinary. The entire matter is as nothing to him: she and her friends engaged, sussed, found wanting, and sent along without coldness, handed gently on their way, all in less time than it takes to tell it.

Already he is on to another story.

4

Strange dreams at thirty thousand feet.

In one I am lying in the middle of an English heath. The sky is storm green. There is no end to the country, a continent of long grass running away in all directions. The scene is accompanied by a piping sound, the high sweet piping of Mouret's trumpets. Ah: my parents are watching *Masterpiece Theatre* in the den. Overhead steep white clouds trek from one horizon to the other. Really they are extraordinarily high-peaked. Each is carved from the others by plummeting crevices, their depths long lost in shadow. A squirming arises in my lower bowel. It is the kind of vertiginous anxiety that comes when peering into a canyon. Now a breeze starts in the distance. Blossoms shiver; acres of blades of grass are rolled over, pressed pale, then restored to green vigor. The squirming rages. Oh, this old piping music and the drenching rural gorgeousness! It is enough to suffocate the senses, the kind of saturated experience that comes only in art and dreams and that leaves a body past all nostalgia, bereft and voided and practically soul-sick.

When I wake it is with eyes on the very clouds that gave rise to the dream. I take up my magazine, a *Businessweek* profile of A. G. Lafley, CEO of Procter & Gamble.

> "I'm in the business of studying people, how they work, how they relax, where their needs are and how P&G can meet those needs better than the next guy." Lafley pokes at a spear of asparagus. He is rarely out of

the office for lunch. "I've stood at the base of Machu Pic-
chu and talked with Andean peasants about the dyes
they use to make blankets. I've navigated rice paddies to
speak with Vietnamese washerwomen about their laun-
dry challenges."

It is no use. The uneasiness will not be shrugged off. Of my coworkers, only Ian is in sight. He taps away at his phone, some missive
for immediate dispatch upon landing. Jane is in the back. The other
passengers are curiously still and straight-backed. All seem to be staring at the same fixed point. I marvel at their composure. Here we sit
in our little pressurized tube, cannoned skyward on trajectory for
Miami, dead to the lunacy of it. Only tonight I am not so easily reconciled as they. Home behind and the dark shoulder of the Atlantic
ahead, this whiplash swap of the familiar for the strange . . . We speed
along between darkening layers of cloud. The sun has given up, slunk
off to other hemispheres. There in the impossible distance is the rim
of the world, an ember-orange curvature that marks finally and forever the end of safe havens and solid ground.

A. G. Lafley is unperturbed.

The man who oversees such brands as Cheer, Always,
and Pantene spends "three-quarters" of his life on the
road. But he uses the time productively. His new book,
The Game-Changer, was written almost entirely in airports and hotels as he crisscrossed the globe meeting
with customers. When I marvel at his efficiency, Lafley
shrugs modestly. "That is who I am."

Down comes the moon. An electric orb emerging from under its
black brow of cloud, half lidded and sleepy, but watchful, watchful.

Six

1

"And I'll tell yall something else, frankly. I'm having trouble seeing a dime's worth of difference between your product and whosit's who was down here last week."

He would put us on our heels, this man. If my assignment is knowledgeable bystander, his is junkyard dog. His coworkers, six in all, regard our side of the table with bluff expressions.

"I don't think that's unreasonable, Dan."

I fashion the words from the same modulated, not quite honeyed materials I have used since arrival. Even to my ear the voice is polite, reasoned, thoughtful, amenable to correction. The very music of Presbyterian temperance. We are late in the conversation and this tone comes now unrehearsed, wholly natural. I say "conversation" for this is how I've come to think of it. Not "sales pitch," no, not even "negotiation." It is as though I am here by accident. I imagine it thusly: Going about my daily concerns, I happened upon this conference room of well-met minds poring over a business problem. And after a moment's polite listening, I decided to stay. But the sum of my ambition is to be of service. Do not look to me to judge or score points. No, I am merely a friendly stranger, a steward of consensus and mutual reward.

In this spirit, I describe for Dan how our competitor's architecture is brittle, which is to say harder to change, and so bound to increase Digitex's total cost of ownership. There is not so much as a solitary note of triumph in this. If anything, I am saddened. Our competitors are good people who mean well but despite their efforts, etc. Dan, it's true, is dismissive. He is not so easily bought. But his cohorts are not as immune to reason, to reasonableness. While I speak, several jot notes; one even nods before catching herself. In any event the victory is won. Dan himself has handed it to us. In seeking to belittle he has let slip an important detail: our competition was here only last week. As a buyer, Digitex has a sore need. Perhaps they are even desperate. Ian maneuvers for the killing stroke.

"If I hear you right, you're getting knocked around pretty bad in production. We catch those security holes before your applications go live . . ." He hangs fire, allowing for a reverie on the virtues of Cyber's software. "I see your investment returned in twelve months—eighteen months at the outside."

Dan snorts. "Where've I heard that one?" But he speaks to himself, the diminishing voice of the odd man out.

"From every vendor who's been through here," says Ian. "But you haven't heard this: Cyber will back that return. If in eighteen months our software isn't saving you money, we'll pay back . . . Call it another ten percent discount on license."

I am surprised. What Ian proposes is actually quite sophisticated. It's a convincing price strategy, one I didn't know we had in our bag of tricks. Their procurement man is quick on the trigger.

"Can we get that in writing?"

"I wouldn't say it otherwise. But the end of quarter is near. This is a today-only offer."

Ian looks as relaxed as I've seen him since we got here. There are final figures to be agreed upon, but doubtless he sees what I see: Digitex's fat green logo taking its alphabetical place in that proud catalogue of buyers, that august register of forward-thinking companies, the Cyber client directory.

So ends the first pitch of the road show.

Miami at dusk. The taxi's window shows a fading cityscape: storefronts and sidewalk tables, blurred columns of palmetto trunk. Here and there comes a squirt of neon, the blazing scripts passing too quickly to be unscrambled. Jane sits in darkening profile by my side. She thinks of nothing; her eye on the landscape is still and staring. It pleases me to steal glances of it, this eye, a dark shining vessel in which is captured the bolting colors of the city.

But now I am startled: she jerks upright and slaps the armrest. "I am so *proud* of you!"

Keith and Ian have remained behind, a matter of follow-up questions about Cyber's financials, and almost certainly to discuss contract. They saw us off at the elevators, Keith standing away, signaling me with an approbative nod. Ian leaned into the compartment, holding off the doors with outstretched arms, a touch of theater there, Samson and the temple pillars, so to give dramatic weight to his whispered ruling:

"Bull's-eye."

The truth is I feel very good. It is Wednesday, three days before month's end. If Digitex signs, we will have caught the largest of our quarry before March. That leaves a month. One month to bring to heel two significant prospects. Not easy, no. But an upgrade from impossible to improbable.

Jane is absorbed again by the scene in the window. She says:

"I haven't forgotten our dinner, by the way."

What a streak. Cast down your palm fronds, Miamians: in this taxi rides a king.

But dinner, our dinner, is not to be. I scarcely have time to change clothes before being summoned by Keith. He and Ian are in the lobby restaurant. On my way down I think their quick return is either a very good sign or a very bad one.

The answer is not immediately apparent. I find them with eyes in their menus and barely a nod for me. Whatever the news, it will wait until Jane arrives. We sit in silence. When Jane comes, she approaches with the same cautious uncertainty. She takes her seat without a word. Pinned above her ear is a barrette, a little blue-jeweled damselfly. A black stripe of bang comes in a swoop past her cheekbone, into the insect's clutches. Her face is freshly scrubbed. I clear my throat gruffly. This damned unconscious wholesomeness, the girlish barrette and dutiful washing up before dinner, a strike keen enough that all other considerations—family and revenues and quarter's end, the impending news, even appetite—fall down dead. The emotion is not altogether explainable. On the one hand I feel toward her a great tenderness, a fierce protectiveness. On the other, there is about her something of the coquette: the way she lifts her tablet menu with both hands to make study of it, furrowed brow and bitten lip, a certain calculated obliviousness of her own nubile allure, holy in white innocence. I am nearly angry for want of her.

Ian is first to speak. He snaps out his napkin with a flourish.

"Signed!"

We collapse in relief. Water glasses are raised, heads shaken over the immensity of our fortune and accomplishment—although to my eye, Keith's participation is curt. He shares our toasts but is first back to his menu.

As hotel restaurants go it is not a bad place. The dining room is built in the spirit of a French brasserie, booths and brass railings, an amber parquet floor, bright bulbs overhead. There is a modesty of wine. It is as though the very swiftness and generosity of victory has instilled in us an abstemious spirit, a fear of lording it over the gods of good work and good luck. Over the salad course we speak of what went well and what might have gone better, each of us clear-eyed now, matter-of-fact, as disassociated from our achievement as clinicians at a postmortem. In matters of personal improvement, the American businessman is without rival. No confessor ever showed more wringing devotion to self-betterment, more hardened hostility to what is past. Progress, advancement, these are the sciences perfected in the laboratory of the corporation. Yet there is superstition here too. By moderate tones and rigorous self-review, by sticking humbly to adage and cliché (that we are only at the fifty-yard line, that chickens are not to be counted), we cross ourselves against every ironic lesson of pride and fall.

So prompt is our change from celebrants to penitents that a casual observer might wonder what catastrophe had befallen our table. Ian himself seems to wonder. A salesman and new to our company, he is slow to the idea that success is best received in chastened arms. He attends the shift closely, aping it as best he can. But the style doesn't suit him. Soon Ian is itchy in his hair shirt.

"Hell of a day though. That needs saying again."

Jane and I look to Keith for a ruling. He saws a corner of steak and daubs it with mustard.

"I've seen worse."

Ian goes into a little seizure of disbelieving merriment. He drops his head, pounding a soft fist by his plate. Keith carves off another bleeding morsel.

"Ah me . . ." Ian recovers himself. "Fantastic." He takes up his fork, jabbing clumps of lettuce and munching fiercely.

To focus us on the work ahead, or perhaps for the simple martial pleasure of moving troop pins around a campaign map, Keith undertakes a review of our itinerary. We leave Miami for Houston tomorrow. Two working days in Houston, Friday and Monday, where we also will spend the weekend. (Returning home would be costly, and not in keeping with the victory-or-bust spirit of the road show.) From Houston we head north to Kansas City. He is on to the particulars of our meetings there when Ian interrupts him: "Remind me. What would a *good* day look like?"

And because Keith shows little surprise, because he answers offhandedly with scarcely a break in stride—

"No discount."

—I am confirmed in my suspicion that what nags Ian is an earlier disagreement between them.

"Ten percent back, eighteen months from now, *maybe*," says Ian. "*If* our stuff doesn't do what we say it can. And in return we get the license deal now, *today*. Bird in hand. Beg pardon, I thought that was the point of this trip, this quarter above all quarters." Keith seems not to hear him. He carries on a methodical dissection of his steak, cutting and daubing, chewing thoughtfully.

"What did I say about playing accounting games?" he says after a bite or two.

Ian slumps in place, broken-backed. To Jane and me he is dark-eyed and imploring. But in this, his plan to replay their argument before a sympathetic jury, Ian is bound for disappointment. I would no more stick in my oar than I would tell Keith how to run the company. As for Jane, though she keeps her eyes down, spooning up her soup with the circumspection of a wallflower, I know she is enjoying this humbling.

"It's the thing I've never understood about sales—" Ian sighs to no one. "Makes me feel like I know what it's like to be a soldier. You've got field marshals conspiring with bureaucrats, setting up the rules of engagement, and then you've got infantry in the field, up to their elbows in muck, going knife to knife with the enemy. And while they're at it, you want them to be mindful of the dos and don'ts?" His tone is not defiant but mournful. Allies evaporated, the cause lost, all a man has left is to state his principles. "Out here at the tip of the spear you need a little entrepreneurial wiggle room, that's all I'll say."

Keith sets down his knife and fork, touching their handles to align them with the plate. He takes up his napkin, drawing it over the corners of his mouth. There is in these movements a discipline of restraint. Indeed, when he speaks it is without heat. Without heat—but with finality. His tone as much as says that this public airing of their private dispute is excusable and will be forgiven—but do not press your luck.

"Our customers see each other at conferences. They do business together. They talk to each other, they compare notes. And one of the things they talk about is the great deals they squeezed from their vendors. So. You volunteer a discount, you set a precedent. I don't want that precedent circulating in front of prospects we've still got to close, never mind our current book of customers, all of whom are paying full freight and might start to wonder why." His knife and fork are found to be not quite parallel. A correction is made. "Now. Maybe this discount is a fine idea. There are umpteen variables to it, none of them in our control, all of which've got us by the throat. The math alone will require a goddamn Cray. But if—*if*—something like this is a good idea, you talk it over with me first. We get Henry and his guys to work out the return scenarios. We run it by Finance, we run it by Legal. What you don't do. Under any circumstance. Is wildcat some idea that touches our bottom line and then spring it in the middle of a pitch." Keith pauses, again touching knife and fork, this bother of their geometry ever more like a taunt, a pigheadedness on the part of the utensils. "One other point: it wasn't necessary. Henry had them eating out of his hand. But here you come, waving the white flag, just as the war is won."

This last stings Ian worst. He shoots me an evil look. To be victim of such a reversal, having plotted the company's one possible course out of trouble, only now to be cast as the scheme's goat—it would be enough to send me to the ledge. But Ian is made of sterner mettle.

"My experience is there's a big gap between a softened customer and a signed contract. Easy to be nice, much harder to turn around and get someone to cough up the green. But point taken. No more deal making without approval. I get it."

Jane drinks her soup, tidy motions of wrist and spoon, the broth ladled away and up and into her lips with no drop lost. Her table manners are exquisite and she knows it. By careful etiquette and humble reserve she is the model child whose conduct gleams all the more brightly beside her scolded sibling. And like that child, she is practically fizzing with delight.

2

Dismay in Houston. Billico, our prospect there, has done a clever thing. They have thrown out the agreed agenda. Now our two days with them are to be divided between the technical and the financial. This means Friday's session is purely a nuts-and-bolts review of our software. All efforts to raise matters of price and value, of seat counts for licenses, are waved off: "Monday, Monday." This partitioning is sensible enough, and the time it requires speaks to their seriousness. What is clever is their coyness of purpose. The extra day was presented to us as purely a matter of contingency, an overflow should it be necessary. It marks them as savvy buyers. They know how to wrong-foot the seller. The surprise agenda means our careful allotment of roles is shot to hell. Friday there are no bosses for Keith to impress, no strategists for Jane to amaze with market data, no purse holders for Ian to seduce. There are only beady-eyed engineers. My cohorts are sent backstage while I am shoved from the wings, unrehearsed, to stand before the staring mob. My audience wants diagrams and details, and I must sweat to create them, struggling with a battered flip-chart and drying pen, all the while galloping hither and yon in search of suitable temperament. A sorry performance.

Later the four of us march along a tile-floored tunnel back to the hotel.

"It's good, it's fine," Ian is saying. "The propeller-heads got what they wanted, next we get exec buy-in. Frankly I prefer it this way. Monday we go straight to the money. Now, what I want to do is start Monday's session with a quick recap of today's. Show 'em we appreciate the chance to focus on the caliber of our technology, et cetera." His concern is unmistakable. He speaks to me, but his eyes are on Keith, several paces ahead. "Could you work up a slide that summarizes the discussion? Main questions, our responses, and make sure to thread in all our tech differentiation. I want to have the last word on whatever their engineers might report over the weekend."

"Sure," say I, gloomy that the day's damage, my damage, should need control.

Jane falls into step beside me. She carries her valise behind her, hands clasped to handle, the bag's trim leather heft bouncing softly against the backs of her knees. She bumps me with her shoulder but says nothing.

"Tunnel" is not quite the word for our surroundings. It is an underground thoroughfare, complete with shops and directional signs. (A labyrinth of these connect Houston's downtown buildings. I am informed that in summer the entire urban workforce moves around below earth, so great is the heat.) Even here below the city there is no want of good commercial cheer. The walkways are clean, well-lighted places full of yogurt shops and nail salons. Only the longer we are down here, the greater are my sympathies for the claustrophobe. I am reminded of winter weekend afternoons at the Southdale mall, my sister and I young and carless and seeking distraction. After some hours of wandering, Gretchen would complain of "mall head," her denomination for the hazy, headachy feeling that comes after you have parsed every magazine stand and gift shop, after you have consumed a giant kiosk pretzel and drunk your Styrofoam holdings of an Orange Julius and have reached the point in the afternoon where every exploration is at an end; there have been no chance meetings with friends, no surprise finds, nothing to dress your plain sense of self (*Good heavens, not at these prices!* in the dreary commercial-speak of Midwestern mothers), and you stand before a crashing fountain under a gaping skylight pouring down the gray afternoon, musing and slipping a little, reproached by the woolly green pennies spread like leprosy over the basin's floor.

But . . . if this is mall head, it is an unusually malignant strain.

Keith halts. "Where the hell is the hotel?" All of us look around inquiringly. One path looks very much like another. Two flights beneath the city, we are deprived of landmarks. "The last goddamn sign said Hyatt this way."

Jane winces. "Aren't we at the Hilton?"

Momentary confusion while we fish for our room cards. She is right. Keith says nothing. We are herded around back in the direction we've come, more quickly now.

Soon we are on our way, to the foot of the right escalator, and up and out. As we rise into the open Hilton lobby, Keith lifts his eyes to its atrium ceiling. A rainstorm works a splattering fury.

"Clusterfuck," he remarks.

With matters so ordained, he leaves us for the elevators. Ian watches him go. "Guy's getting jumpy in his old age."

"He has a right to be," says Jane.

"Oh, listen. Where the deal is concerned, that man is a stone-cold killer. I'll tell you a little story. Once upon a time there was a group of underperforming sales managers. So one day Keith calls them all together, and without any warm-up says, 'The only person in this room with a guaranteed job is *me*.' Everyone sort of—" Ian rears back, blinking as if slapped. "Then he says, 'First guy to close a million-dollar deal this year gets two-*x* commission and bumped up to Senior Sales Manager.' Like that, the managers are back on his side. Two-*x* commission on a million! This is ages ago, that's real money. Only then he says, 'Last guy to do it goes to work for the first guy.' End of meeting. And no word on what happened if you didn't land a million-er at all. Everyone was going to close a deal that size, that year, period. You have to admire the clarity."

"Let me guess," says Jane. "We're looking at the first guy."

"Well, you're not looking at the last!"

"And the demoted man never filed a complaint, and HR and Legal never got involved."

"Believe what you like. Charlie Bastion, and I was good to him. He never missed quota again. Made himself a pile of money. Now who needs a drink?"

Jane squints at her wrist. "I've got some calls to make."

"Of course," says Ian. He makes the slightest of bows, a defunct little gesture of polite leave-taking. Whether solicitous or sarcastic is impossible to tell. "Henry?"

Three quick drinks on an empty stomach and I am all nerve endings. What are these calls that are so important she couldn't join us for one lousy drink?

Ian eyes me over the huddle of empty glasses. "You seem to me one of those guys whose booze tends to get on top and hold him down."

"I haven't had that much."

"You haven't had nearly enough."

Moments ago he fetched a packet of cigarettes from the vending machine. Now the box lies facedown before him with a single cigarette on top, held in place by a red Bic. "Working my way up to quitting," he explains. "Marshaling willpower. When I'm going about crazy, I'll smoke that one and toss the rest. Part of the discipline. Knowing it's at your fingertips but still you can't have it."

This doesn't sound good at all. "Let's get another drink."

"You're not still mooning over today."

"Not good, was it."

"What annoys me is that it's these idiot buyers who suffer. You want to play games, keep the agenda a secret, fine. Only don't be surprised if we can't give you the answers you're looking for." He hears the wound and moves to restate. "Not that we didn't give them answers. All things considered you did a pretty solid job . . ."

"I was a mess."

"Never mind. The perfect sales pitch is a rare bird. And still deals get done."

"But Miami was close?"

"Miami *was*, forget what Keith said. We got what we came for, and we got it quick. Anyway, whatever happens, it's my neck on the block, not yours." This last comes out a touch bitterly.

"Nobody's blaming you."

"Thanks a million! Did I say they were?" He pinches his eyes. "No, you're right of course. Matter of fact, Keith pulled me aside right after the session. 'Ian,' he says, 'if I'm going to own the victories in this thing, I'm also going to own the mistakes.'"

"Did he?" I am surprised. To my eye there was nothing benevolent in Keith's mood.

"You bet he did."

Now Ian gives in to his craving. Cigarette in hand, he stretches out as best one can in a low club chair, watching rain batter the glass overhead. Periodically he touches his fingers to his lips as if to blow the ceiling a kiss. His cheeks hollow, the cigarette comes to life, and beneath it his face—glowing like the devil.

"'Course with Keith you know how it goes," he continues dreamily. "It's when he's being reassuring that I get worried."

Soon thereafter my empty stomach sounds the end of the charms of a few drinks after a long day. I perceive the bar for what it is: a chilly, exposed space. In fact it is little more than a set-aside in the wider Hilton lobby, an exception described by a sorry perimeter of low wood-paneled barrier walls and some potted greenery. Hotel guests file past silently on either side. One has the feeling of being peered down upon, like animals in a pen. The high atrium glass keeps us dry but not sheltered. It all but welcomes in the elements, gray light and pelting rain. The latter's savagery is everywhere, on the carpet and table-tops, on our suit jackets and hands and faces, a peppering of shadows to match the exploding drops overhead. Ian is in a motionless sprawl, slouched and lax in wrist. The cigarette sends up a fine blue tendril.

"Anyhow," he remarks, "my spider sense tells me there're other things on his mind, if you know what I mean."

It takes me a long moment to reorient. Still I come up blank.

"I have no idea what you mean."

He drops his gaze from the ceiling to meet mine.

"Aha." He stands. The cigarette is stabbed out.

"You're off?"

"I'm off." Ian makes a mysterious miming gesture, a quick little device of cupping his palms about his face and head, then claps my shoulder on his way past. "You're my favorite monkey," he says, leaving me to puzzle out the performance.

3

There comes a quick knock at my room door. I am happy to find Jane, bearing aloft several airplane bottles of gin. She makes a dramatic step-stomp over the threshold, flamenco style, chiming the bottles in her fingers. "Have a drink with me. Then let's go explore!"

"It's pouring out."

"No, it's not!" She sweeps past me to the back of the room, where she throws aside the curtains. "Ta-da!" It's true; the rain has left off its clattering. Here and there a fat drop pecks the window, nothing more.

"Yes, all right. But I need to eat."

"So do I! And I owe you dinner, remember."

"You don't really."

"Don't you dare back out."

"You're on. I'll call the concierge."

"Oh God, no. The Hilton concierge? We'll be sent along to some restaurant with 'factory' in its name. No, I want us to find the place for ourselves. Let's make an adventure of it!" There is something of the mare in her eyes, rounded and dark and a little wild-roving. It dawns on me just how vaulted are her spirits. She is seized by the mysteries of evening, of wet streets in a strange city, the storm spent and now a doused landscape, washed and heavy-hushed—a purged territory whose blank-slatedness avails only the first venturesome souls to come into it again. Also she is plowed. She takes hold of the minibar door and gives a brute yank; the door comes away easily and nearly topples her. "Tonic, tonic . . . only tonic. No soda water." She makes a face. "Sprite it is." She snaps open a can and sets it on the credenza. For my drink she cracks a bottle of tonic. The tonic explodes. "Shit! Towel, towel!"

When I come from the bathroom, she is waiting with arms apart. Her hands are wet and dripping. It is left to me to dab her stomach and hip, even to press the towel lightly against her eye. "Thank you, m'dear," she says easily, and turns to fix our drinks.

"I had a little brainstorm," Jane says once we are settled with drinks in hand, I in an armchair by the window and she cross-legged on a corner of the bed. "I was in my bathroom having a drink of water. And when I went to put down the glass, I noticed that I had to take almost a full step forward to reach the sink. Look at me, I thought: the older I get, the farther I stand back from mirrors. I imagine that for every year since I turned thirty, I've moved back two inches. So now I have another way of dating myself. It's like counting tree rings."

"What was the brainstorm?" I am hungry and a little impatient.

"Oh. The brainstorm was, What am I doing here, trying to forget my crow's-feet? Out the front door of this hotel is a whole world I've never seen!"

"Yes. So we should go."

"Finish your drink."

This I promptly do. I stand and give a clap of hands to sound the charge. Jane buries her nose in her glass. "Hold your horses. I haven't finished mine." She eyes me darkly from the bed. I am motioned back into my chair. "Sit, sit. Christ, you're like Michael, always—" She snaps her fingers angrily.

What a fool I am. She has arrived in a rapturous state, and here I am threatening it with clumsy practicalities like when to leave and where to eat. The right way of course is to parlay the charge of prelude, to speak for a time under soft lamplight, our work clothes shed, growing pink on gin while the wide Gulf night beckons. I fix myself another drink. And when I have returned to my chair, with Jane smiling again from the bed, her legs crossed and her dark hair swept around her neck and placed over a shoulder, it becomes possible to see it as she does: suite 455 at the Houston Hilton (downtown) transformed into the very anteroom to adventure.

We descend to the lobby in matching spirits. No, not quite matched. Her exhilaration is pure and unlabored; I am still aware of a need to catch up or keep up. But the gap is closing. More and more I am inclined to the gin's persuasion of bliss. Only hunger reminds me of myself.

The step from chill hotel climate into open night is a shock. I am not prepared for the city's closeted, wet-warm heat. It is like stepping into a mouth. "Pah," Jane gasps. She peels off her sweater and cinches it around her waist. "Where to?" I ask her. She thrusts a bare arm straight in front of her, aiming across a square block of green space opposite the hotel. "Thataway." We proceed into a shelter of live oaks, a cement path under a dark billowing ceiling held up by tortuous beams. Grackles, yellow-eyed and imperious, peer down from the limbs. They scurry along in quick goose step to keep watch. Puddles shine like oil. I feel very good. It is nothing at all to reach out to my coworker and pluck a damp seed husk from her shoulder. The drenched air smells of riverbank and brewed coffee.

"Do you know what I would like?" says Jane. She makes a wide bowl of her arms. "A helping of gnocchi like this, and a salad, and a thumping big glass of red wine. Doesn't that sound good? Can we find proper Italian you think?" I tell her I'm sure we can. She nods, liking my sureness, becoming sure herself. "And we mustn't ask anyone." "No." "That would be cheating." "Yes." Such is our peculiar seeker's agreement that we are pleased but not surprised to find exactly the right place. It is along the sloping side of a large sandstone building that looks like a courthouse. What catches our eye, what practically spells out FINE ITALIAN, are its three bulbous maroon awnings with scallops edged in gold rope. The host leads us down a short flight of steps onto a sunken dining floor of wide dark planks. We are shown to a corner table. Directly overhead is a lofted, balcony-like area with more seating. It is a narrow space, too narrow for a server carrying a tray of dishes. Dumbwaiters have been rigged along the main floor to ferry meals to the diners above. At the back is an open kitchen. Flames erupt from saucepans while men in stained white jackets shout cautions and encouragements. The voices are Mediterranean—another good sign. Jane quizzes the waiter and is convinced of the gnocchi's excellence. With orders placed, she takes a moment to study our twilit surroundings, not in disbelief that we should find such a place but expectantly, verifying that it's as perfect as perfect. "Here we are . . ." she says softly.

"Here we are," I agree, hoping to break the trance. Her rapture makes me uneasy. "And am I ready to eat!"

"Finally. I've *owed* you."

"Dinner? I don't know why."

"Don't say that. You know why. That night we wandered the city and finally found a place to duck in, and you sat there while I prattled on and were an absolutely first-rate listener. I won't embarrass you, but you understood and I was grateful. I have to tell you . . . Oh, it was just a good night in my book. I mean actual conversation about real things. That sounds spacey. I don't know what I mean." She drops her eyes, worrying at her napkin. The waiter positions two stem glasses on the table. Jane forgets her thought long enough to approve the tasting.

Our glasses full, she begins again.

"I'm as practical as practical, I think. And good for me. But sometimes I get a feeling like I need to break through something, or break free . . . God, no, that's not it either." She pushes fingers through her hair, clasping the top of her head. Caught strands are sprung out comically. Now she drops her hands, ignoring the dishevelment. "It's like I'm here—" She carves a line in the tablecloth with the edge of her hand. "And from time to time I think, What was I like before? Say, back here?" She moves her hand an inch. "Oops, no, pure nonsense. How about here? Still nonsense. Here? Nonsense." Now she places her hand at the table's edge. "But *here*. Ah. Back here somewhere, who knows when exactly, is *me*. I imagine her like an abandoned little girl, or maybe a jilted young woman. She's in an empty train station for some reason. Yes, I know. But it's very vivid in my mind. Pigeons in the rafters, a sooty glass archway letting in that sort of sad museum light . . ." Jane shakes her head and goes muttering into her wineglass. "Anyway. Vivid. Probably something I saw on television." Seeing my uncertainty, she laughs. "Don't look so nervous! It's not some analogy about missed trains. I'm just telling you the quality of it, how it presents itself in my head. I've only been in a few train stations in my life, but what a hollow feeling. All those crowds racing around so sure of themselves, stopping at the timetables for a fluent little study of what they already know, then off again, striding right to where they need to be." Jane smooths down her hair. "Say something, damn you."

"It reminds me. There's a principle in engineering—it has to do with the problem of fidelity. We don't see it in software, but in analog reproduction, you start seeing imperfections even in the first copy. Very small ones. But each subsequent copy builds on the flaws of the previous, plus introduces its own. So that by the end—"

"Chinese whiskers."

"Whose whiskers?"

"Whispers. Chinese Whispers. You know. Someone starts with a phrase and whispers it to the person next to them, and that person repeats it as best they can to the next person, and so on, and the last person repeats a totally garbled version to the room?"

"We called it Telephone."

"But that's this same principle, isn't it."

"Maybe, yes."

Jane holds up a thumbnail, rubbing it in the candlelight. "God, why is it your gloomy directness is more reassuring than reassurances? But you've described the feeling. It makes me wonder. Maybe a certain engineer has felt it himself."

I consider it. "No."

"I see." She takes a mouthful of wine. "Henry the blank slate. Yes, you've done it right, haven't you. You're unencumbered. The idea of being settled, not just in the married sense, but in any sense—that must horrify you."

"Horrify? But I am settled. Going on fourteen years at Cyber. Just last week I bought a new lawnmower. I'm thinking of having the house painted."

"Ha. I'm not talking wanderlust or some idiot idea of the bachelor's life, and you know it. You live your quiet little life all right. It keeps the slate blank. But secretly you're waiting for the Big Thing. Admit it. And the trick is not to let anything get in the way of waiting. It's like preparing the house for guests. You tidy up and set out flowers and arrange the table, you turn down the lights and set the music. Then it's just you and your things, tidy in the half-dark, surrounded by expectancy. It is perfect and nothing must disturb it. And you wait. And the longer you wait, the sweeter the anticipation."

I drink my wine.

"I hope not."

"Why? What's wrong with it?"

"Because if nothing comes . . ."

"You keep waiting."

"Fine, and then?"

"Yes, exactly. And then, and then. Every one thing leads convincingly to the next. It's not just a sequence, it's an adding up. It seems to me it would be quite wonderful. Everything becomes a preparation. There's always the certainty in what's come before, and the looking forward with anticipation."

"But if one day there isn't."

"I don't know. You tell me."

"It would be bad."

"How bad?"

"Very. The worst. Now that person's a candidate for suicide."

Jane pinches the stem of her glass, washing circles on the tablecloth. The wine sweeps around the bowl and settles. Its coating melts into a hundred fine red legs that run down the glass like strings. "He might have company anyway," she says with not much humor, and drinks.

But there is no real glumness. In fact we are secretly pleased with ourselves. How easily the pressures of an apt follow-up to our drinks of three weeks ago, the rich mysteries of evening in a strange place and our long-postponed dinner finally arrived—how easily these might all have led us into forced gestures and bad faith. Instead we find ourselves in the right perfect place, easily arrived and communing without directive. We sit in our little candlelit space in the darkened lee of the balcony, tucking into fresh, complex dishes while overhead there is the small noise of shifting chairs and knives laid to plates, a muted set of chimes and creaks that puts me in mind of eating in the galley of a very old ship on roiling seas. "Divine," whispers Jane, the last word until our bowls are cleaned. Too soon the bottle is emptied, the bill paid. We watch the table's candle flame, full bellied and hypnotized, awaiting signal for the night's next movement. The flame sags, stands up, sags again, and disappears.

"Shall we go for a walk?" Jane wonders.

"Good idea."

Outside a breeze has picked up. It takes the sweating stillness out of the evening and makes breathing easier. A little way ahead is a maroon edifice that proves to be the opera house. The building is set at the back of a large brick plaza surrounded by big red globes mounted on granite plinths. The plaza beyond is broad enough that not until halfway across do we register the screaming. It comes from the far side. There, a stand of trees has been set upon by legions of starlings. More come pouring from the sky, a great whirling pillar that dissolves in the branches. The walk beneath is dark and deafening. An ammoniacal stench, the crappings of ten thousand birds, brings tears to my eyes. "God, how awful!" cries Jane, pressing her wrist to her nose and hurrying through. We come out onto a railed path at the edge of the city, overlooking a bayou. A curled, intestinal thing, black and gleaming. The water pushes between shallow banks covered thickly in reeds and yellow sweet flag. Above the far bank rises an electric-blue Ferris wheel of tremendous scale. White gondolas climb into one segment of night sky and fall out of another. The wheel's mirror image is sprawled below us.

The path descends, widening to promenade by the bank. Here the smell of river comes into the major. There is a taint of rot, but the reed and sweet flag are enough to defeat it. The air is mostly sugared and green. We meander along without a word spoken. I wonder if perhaps Jane is on to something after all, for the *and then?* tentativeness of things confers excitement and fear in equal measure. The promenade is attached to the far bank by an arching plank footbridge. Up we go, pausing halfway to look into the curls and muddied eddies fifteen feet below. Some ways down the bayou there is a disturbance, a small wake opening the surface like a zipper. The wake comes toward us, a rippling without discernible source until the head lifts from the water as if to sip the air. Jane grips my arm.

"Is that—?"

"Yes."

"It's *big*."

The snake swims beneath the bridge. We trade sides to follow its course. The black trowelish head is set at a fractional angle to the surface, just enough to keep the tongue and eyes clear. Down the bayou it goes, serene in purpose, aimed and going with the sort of chin-up purposefulness of a bird dog channeling back to her master's boat. It passes into the shadow of a willow and is gone. Jane lets go of my arm. She gives the sleeve a quick, grooming scrub.

"I don't care for snakes, but to see one coming out of the dark like that, in this strange place on a haunted sort of bayou—I mean to watch it, safe and snug from the bridge . . . it's rather wonderful! I get a feeling in my stomach like Halloween." She is possessed by a relieved shiver. "Now. Would it be too ridiculous for words if I said I wanted to try that thing?"

The Ferris wheel is on the grounds of a dubious-looking aquarium surrounded by palms. The aquarium is a three-story stucco cube, floodlit and painted with clownish murals of sea horses and dolphins and hammerhead sharks. We pay at the gate and follow a path around the building. Stage lights direct blue and green rays into the tree canopies. The path is tiger-striped in shadow.

There are but a few other couples waiting for the wheel to stop. I say "other couples," for a short time ago (it was on the bridge when she seized my arm), I began to think of us as such. You do not, on an evening such as this one, in a place like this, far from the familiar, and she and I unmoored from everything we know and sworn to sustain the intimacy of three weeks back, an intimacy then possible because it was unexpected and unsought—you do not take anything for granted. One false move. But we haven't jinxed ourselves yet. On the contrary, we've flitted from one perfection to another. And the older the night grows, the better our standing. We are storing up goodwill, an easiness in the other's presence.

Last in line, we clamber aboard our compact little gondola and settle on its hard plastic bench. The wheel groans; the gate and grounds sink from view. We rise out of the garishly lit fronds into open night. The skyline looms over the shriveled bayou, glassy and vivid and strange in scale, at once tremendous and close but also very far-off. It is like a clever drop curtain run across the opposite bank, painted full of depths. As we climb to summit, what comes into view behind the city is the Texas coastal country, flat and giant and unimaginable. It expands above and beyond the falling buildings like a sky, congested by hundreds of thousands of red and gold stars, the lights going up and away until diminishing to a sort of moth-eaten middle distance, and then to darkness. Not real darkness, surely. Only the end of what light the eye can see. But how much better to imagine it as a true end, the end of land and light and the commencement of the open Gulf, and there beyond the old, vast darkness of the sea.

"Oh my," whispers Jane.

Then down the far side, more swiftly than the climb (a swiftness felt keenly in the stomach and organs of the groin), down into the fronds and skimming across the pavement and up again. Jane holds her middle with both hands. "Maybe not the thing after a meal—but here we go! Oh me. When's the last time you saw anything like that?" She slumps back against the bench, conquered by beauty. "It takes your breath away!"

"Yes."

We sink in a slightly embarrassed silence. The city buildings grow up again and disappear above the palms. Jane is whispering crossly to herself.

"Look. Don't humor me. Say it."

"I'm not sure what you mean."

"Henry, Jesus." Jane takes hold of my jaw, turning my face to hers. "If you won't, who will." She blinks now, rather less sure of herself even with my jaw in hand. This brusque gesture of sisterly frankness is awkward. It bothers her almost as much as the shrill brightness of the cliché. I take her hand away, kneading it, tending her as you might someone recovering from a fainting spell.

"It's very simple," I explain, patting the hand softly and leaning on irony. "Next time around, you only need to keep your trap shut."

She hides her face in my shoulder. "Yes," bumping me with her head. "I know."

Penitence finished, Jane lifts her face and looks at me from under my chin. She is too close to see without undignified contortions. I gaze at the horizon like a stoic fool. Her hand is on my neck. We sit that way, awkwardly, for a moment when the obvious forces itself upon me and I put my lips to hers. There is an instant of terrible fright—if I have misread, it is the end of everything—but no: she replies with a pressing sort of hunger, smashing lips to teeth and hardly stopping.

Up into the cosmic Texan sky we go. Bless this centrifuge. Its forces are all the alibi we need to cleave furiously and carry on. In her animal warmth there is the pinning down of all mysteries a man could dream for himself, the cessation of every tortured second thought. The old thinkers and their earnest books scratched out in a fine sweat under somber brows—it was all a dodge. What ailed them wasn't Truth or Existence. It was want of warm nights and a woman's arms. The poor saps.

We come up for air. Jane's hands are clasped behind my neck. Her ear is pressed to my chest. My arm is heavy on her shoulders. I am aware of the limb as an entity, invested by a sort of lion's guardianship over the smallness of her bones. A magnificent arm and not to be trifled with. Ours is an easy silence. There is no commentary on what we've done, no impulse to stand aside and interpret and freeze ourselves out. There is only the groan of the axis far below, the pendulum sway of the cab, rubbing thigh on thigh and breast to chest, a compliant motion that endorses (insists upon!) carnal closeness. At summit the window shows things in their proper scale. The troubles out there are very far away and of no account. The night is deep and blue and the land sparkles and the water sparkles, and Jane's body is warm and convincing.

She lifts her head, peering from side to side.

"Will this thing ever stop?"

"Better it doesn't."

She resettles herself, nodding into my shirt. "Wouldn't that be wonderful."

"Mechanical failure. We can hope."

"Yes. How lovely to watch the sunrise from up here. But would we never get down?"

"We would, only it would be a big production. Crowds, emergency vehicles, flashing lights, a hook and ladder."

"Yes! Everyone craning their necks, all eyes on us. *My God, those poor people! How long have they been up there?*"

"Down into a hero's welcome."

"Would we be raced off to the hospital together?"

"To be on the safe side."

"Sirens and high speed, cars parting to make way and us laughing in the thick of it! Oh, I like it. Only . . ."

"What?"

"Well, I was only thinking of you. A little emasculating maybe, to be rescued like that? I mean, would the firemen carry you?"

"Probably. But I would tell everyone that I kept you from panicking."

"Aha. True enough. How?"

"I sang you songs from my childhood."

Jane pinches my side. "What would you say really?"

"I would say that when things looked really bleak, I told you not to worry: we can always jump."

She sits bolt upright and studies my face in the changing light. Then, smiling, she falls back into my arms. She holds on tight as ever.

But after some time and as if in mockery, it begins to seem the goddamn wheel will not in fact stop. And here I begin to sweat. You cannot sit forever in untended bliss. It ripens too quickly. Also I have to pee. We must move on and soon.

The mockery continues. We are hoisted to zenith, *the jeweled world spread at our feet* or some such thing, then down, and around, and up. And again. And again. Yes, yes, I think on the umpteenth turn of the wheel. The jeweled world. Noted. It is not very long before I am sick to death of the view, which has no jewels of any sort, only the taillights of gas-guzzlers and the porch-light wattages of their destinations. Jane experiences it too, of course. Her body is stiff in my arms. I am on the verge of some despairing wisecrack when the wheel slows. We descend in stages. After an eternity our gondola arrives at the bottom; the door opens and we are free.

As we go back along the bayou, there is some confusion of posture. Do we hold hands? Noodle along with heads together? Jane staggers over to a line of reeds. She bends at the waist, gathering her hair at her neck. Is she going to be sick? And yet how glad I would be if she were. It would give us a renewed surefootedness, a rooting in plain little problems to be tended, aspirin and water, home to the hotel and off to bed.

But no: she is only inhaling the fragrance of a clutch of purple flowers, the loam of the wet bank.

"My God. Now that's the smell of *life*."

Returning, she wraps her arms around my waist and plants a hard-lipped kiss. Then just as abruptly she pulls away, heading down the bank to another cluster of flowers. When I catch up to her, she jumps back. "Are you following me?" I am at a loss. She seizes my hand and goes racing onward. "Hurry! They're right behind us!" I trot along behind in the spirit of good sportsmanship, but not understanding and not much liking it either. We come to a long flight of brick steps, where she drops my hand and charges up. At the top she turns and waits, chest heaving. Above her is the open sky, light-polluted and gray. Shades of bats come in a ragged line from out of her head, passing over to hunt along the bayou. When I reach her, she holds me off with hands on my shoulders. Her head is down between her arms.

"Whew! Made it. We'll be. Safe here."

"All right."

She lifts her head and gazes out over the water, now a good thirty feet below. "Oh, look!" I am pivoted to face the same direction. A low moon has freed itself of the clouds. It holds fast over a network of high-way overpasses far away to the west. "Wouldn't it be wonderful to discover a little boat stashed in the reeds, and to row away toward the moon, to follow the water and find where it leads?"

"Well, yes. But I owe Ian some slides for Monday." This is met with more laughter than is warranted. She grips me firmly around the ribs and peers up into my face, suddenly quite serious.

"What an extraordinary night."

"Yes."

"What you expected?"

"I don't know."

"Nor I. I only know . . ." She trails off, still watching. I have some trouble meeting her eye.

"What?"

"Never mind." She gives me another squeeze, now hiding her face in my neck. "How *good* this all feels!"

For the first time tonight and with a falling away at the bottom of my stomach, I understand that her rapture is built on sand, and that she knows it, or she suspects it, and is by way of fearful compensation, and with a sort of buried fury, lashing her spirits higher and higher. In an instant I see my job is to join her on the trapeze, yes, but in the event our somersaults should fail—to man the net.

The worst is yet to come. At the hotel doors we pass from the private adventure of open night into a bland and fact-based locus. The lobby is bright and businesslike. It hums with the low energy of late arrivers, all of them tired and plane-rumpled, dutiful earners who know how to bear their exhaustion, checking in with irritable good manners, then piloting their luggage straight for the bar. Returned to our people, we are careful to go among them in the old ways. Even Jane, rapture or no rapture, becomes circumspect in her touches. We ride on opposite sides of the elevator car.

Because our rooms share a floor there is no hesitation about stepping off together. But moving along the hallway, I am positively sick with nerves. If we could have tumbled from the Ferris wheel straight into bed, that is one thing. Then you are in the realm of a crime of passion. But now, having passed through the lobby and waited for the elevator and begun our slow march down the hall, we are in the grip of the premeditated. The hall is dim and smells of the vacuum's bag. How small and shabby it all begins to feel, a little fling between cube mates. Strange to say I think of Ian, and with not a little envy. How easily and with what trivial good humor he would partake of this fruit of the business life, a romp in a hotel room on the corporate account, one more opportunity seized. The door numbers commence countdown: 465, 463, 461, 459 . . . Jane takes my hand. It is a stern grasp, not so much affection as defiance.

We stand facing at the door of my suite. A small bulb lights the recess. It casts us in ugly shadows, eye sockets turned black, necks gone to darkness. Two alien heads, waiting. We stand facing, not quite committed but certainly past any charade of first-date demureness, and standing there I am aware of what hangs in the balance, this most transcendent and special of all evenings come to this, bodies nearly touching in the dim light of a hotel doorway, and still I think of her marriage and the sheer tawdriness of what is at hand, however unhappy she or they may be—Christ, what horseshit. It isn't half so noble as this. What truly gives me pause is knowing the moment that will follow what is at hand, a terrible point past climax, past promise, when you must look upon that old familiar face for whom you'd harbored such high hopes, such faith, and find him revealed as but one more sorry schemer, given to easy pleasures the same as anyone else anywhere else—

Jane has pulled back and is eyeing me with a hard look. In a panic I lean forward, damn the torpedoes, hoping against hope. Too late! Her hand is swift and sharp. Humiliation comes in a red haze. She watches me fiercely, jaw set and nostrils flaring, then makes a face as if to sneeze. What follows is a burst of tears.

"Jane . . ." Her aim was poor; cicadas sing in my ear.

"Goddamn it," she whispers, tearfully but no less fierce. She crosses her arms tightly. "God*damn* it."

She shoulders past, holding herself and rigid in spine, and not once does she look back.

4

The next morning brings patches of blue sky, but only patches. Vaporous clouds blow gray and white across the sun, like smoke from a battlefield. It is an uneasy clearing.

Yet the morning sky bears along its old, reliable notions of new beginnings. It is Saturday after all. I throw off the covers and do fifty push-ups and fifty sit-ups. Rinsed of the night's disaster and with coffee in hand, there begins to pulse in my veins a caffeinated hope. Perhaps I haven't blown anything. I consider the matter squarely. We have not cheapened ourselves; it leaves the possibility for something of worth. There is even a certain pleasure in the difficulty. What remains is to step over the rubble of the past, to plan the how and where of restoration. I work efficiently, even gratefully, on slides for the Monday meeting. Yes: how clear the way forward seems. If yesterday was a day of mistake, today holds the promise to set all things right.

At noon I ring Jane's room without answer. It is the same at one, and one thirty. So there will be no explanations over lunch. I work until four thirty and then order a club sandwich to the room. On television a historical program explains the Battle of Midway. I award myself a twelve-dollar beer from the fridge and settle in to be educated.

How well the narrator tells the story! It is a marvelously graveled voice, roughened by experience and generous with tolerance and pity for the follies of men. (I am certain I recognize it from the pharmaceutical commercials.) Describing the run-up to Midway, the voice prophesies that "for the Americans, there will be no more Pearl Harbor surprises." A modest pause. "They have broken the Japanese naval code." My arms prickle in satisfaction. There is nothing American engineering cannot do.

Now the battle begins. One piece of colorized stock footage shows a seaman cringing, hands to ears, in the turret of his Bofors. Above him a great column of barrels pumps flak into a chaotic sky. The picture is silent but for the voice. It tells a dependable story of epic bravery joined to plain old Uncle Sam know-how. The seaman fumbles with a shell as long as his arm. He delivers it into the breech, then finds the fetal position. The man cowers; the voice reels off data on fleet coordinates, enemy missteps, hardware lost. What a comfort, I think dreamily, to imagine one's circumstances from thirty thousand feet and thirty years hence, hammered into shape and fit to purpose, but one more piece in a puzzle whose end form is triumph, as it was in the beginning is now and ever shall be.

Awake with a start. The room is dark. In a snap I am upright with feet on the floor, painting my hair into shape. I am ready! cries my brain. I haven't missed a trick! The television casts a jumping light on surfaces. There is a need to clear my throat peremptorily, to set the room at ease. Here is all watchful preparedness, you see. Gradually my heart calms itself. What time is it? After ten. I am out the door like a shot, down to the lobby bar and civilization.

The bar is nearly empty, but the kitchen is still open. At the counter I order fried shrimp and an olive martini. I am not overly fond of chitchat with bartenders, although tonight I would not mind so much. Except this bartender wants nothing to do with me. A dark-haired lurker in rolled sleeves, he delivers my order and then goes to the far end of the counter, where he hunches over his elbows and reads the paper. A sports program on the television behind the bar shows silent clips of basketball. Something is wrong with the closed captioning; nonsensical glyphs pile at the bottom of the screen. There is some hangover from the nap. It is a hazy bad sense of being left out, or left behind. Still, it is relief to put food in the stomach and a cold drink on the brain, and to be away from my room.

I think of Jane.

That is not quite right. I am not mooning away like an idle poet. Better to say I am alert—to vicinity and chance. It is a case for active waiting. I sit with spine straight and shoulders squared. After some time and as expected, there rises at the back of my neck an importuning presence. "Why Jane, here you are—" But turning, there is no one. Nothing is out of the ordinary. The odd guest at check-in, a few inside the bar's pen, one or two in armchairs on the lobby's wider floor, reading. The glass is black above us. The silence persists. It is of the sort that in Westerns heralds a terrific bloodbath, the brooding stillness that descends on noonday main streets and occasions one deputy to remark, "Sure is quiet," and the other, "Yep—too quiet." A man seated in the lobby holds up his newspaper to the lamp at his shoulder. The facing page shows two grinning tycoons, their hands clasped in a bond of new partnership. He turns a page, snapping the broadsheet crisply into place. It is then that the storm breaks. The lobby explodes in brilliance. Sound disappears under the crash. Everyone jumps. A close strike, it shakes every pane in the atrium. There is some nervous laughter; several cast a weather eye on the glass overhead. Now the lights fail. Silence again, but for the boulder roll of thunder moving away. The only illumination is a very dull light in the windows. It is like the light on a sea's horizon at dark. Exit signs gleam evilly.

A tremendous cascade of marbles begins to fall on the atrium ceiling and goes on falling—not hail but the sheer volume and violence of the drops. The world beyond the lobby is gone. There is only the curtain of rain, thick and white. In the darkness it is possible to see straight through the glass. A dark blob materializes in the white. It becomes a wavering length, then resolves into the shape of a man. He shoves through the revolving door and into the lobby, singing.

Draaap-kick me, Jesus, through the goalposts of life!
End over end, neither left nor to right—

The hotel's generators rouse themselves. Lights flash and come back up. In the vestibule is Ian, soaked to the bone. He looks around at his audience, shaking water off the ends of his hands. Spying me across the floor, he cries out. It seems he can't believe his good fortune. He makes his way over, a little heavy of tread, and plunks down on the stool next to mine, rapping a summons on the counter.

"One whiskey, and one whiskey. Whatever's at hand." Really he is soaked. His blue oxford clings to his chest. "How're things, Henry boy?"

"Fine. You've had a big night?" I am glad for the company.

"Have I! Some old friends, working here now in O and G. *Rich* friends, goddamn them. We're in the wrong line of work. Third most profitable industry on the globe, oil. First is small arms. Second, I forget." He thinks for a moment. "Not smut . . . Anyway. *Salut.*" We tap glasses and drink. "You're here all by your lonesome?"

"Just me."

"Where're our compatriots?"

"Haven't seen them."

"Not at all?"

"No. You?"

"Hide nor hair."

"I've been in my room all day."

"Ah. Not *working*?"

"I have those slides."

He presses together his lips, shaking his head.

"What's the matter?"

"Goddamn, Hurt. We need more men like you." His voice is strange. Full up as he is, I cannot read him. This may be sentimental tenderness; it may be acid irony.

Now he looks up at the rain on the glass, blowing out whiskey fumes. He pushes back his hair with both hands, wringing drops at his neck. "You know, if the women in this town could take a joke, you'd still be drinking by your lonesome."

"I'm sure."

He looks at me sideways. "Cocksucker. What sport is there, razzing a drunk?"

"I mean it."

"Sure you do."

"What sort of jokes can't they take?"

"It's an expression."

"Oh."

Ian fishes in a bowl of pretzels. He holds one up, sighting through it. "Some freshmen are sitting around a dorm room. They're planning the college clubs to join. One decides he'll go out for debate. The other fellows wish him well. But when he gets back, he's dejected. 'What's the matter?' they ask him. 'Didn't make the team?' The freshman shakes his head. 'No. They s-said I was t-t-too . . . *tall!*'"

"That's pretty good."

"Only clean joke I know."

He tells another about a blonde in pigtails, but I miss the punch line. The rain is a blitzkrieg.

"It's all big down here," Ian marvels, again watching the ceiling. "And more where we're going. This thing's raising hell all over the Midwest. Kansas City got hammered last night. Foot of snow in an hour or something—could that be right?"

"Could be. Hard to get flights in."

"We'll get in. We'll get in, and we'll take 'em for all they're worth, and we'll fly out fat and happy."

"You're sure."

"No bout adout it."

"And Monday?"

"Monday's nothing. Mopping-up exercise. Then onward to destiny." Up comes his glass. "To destiny!"

"To destiny!"

"To sunshine!"

"To sunshine!"

We drink at pace, speaking of this and that. There is no question of catching up to him; I do not even try. He is tapering in any case. Overhead the glass changes from black to white, black to white. In the breaking the lobby is transformed. What is lamplight and potted greenery, the Muzak-like patterning of bulk upholstery, becomes a moonscape shocked of color and familiarity. Dimensions go flat, pressed under blue atomic glare. In the corners violent shadows spring like flames. Gradually Ian falls silent. He slides his glass close to vest. For a time he peers down into the polished liquid, turning the heavy-bottomed base like a dial. His smile ebbs.

"Ah Lord . . . Here we are."

"Here we are."

"This is all right, isn't it? Good booze, the open road. Thrill of the hunt, and so on."

"The trip's a good idea."

"Thank you! Nice to hear it."

"It's the truth."

"You'll remind Keith of that, will you?"

"He knows."

"Remind him anyway."

"Sure."

"He listens to you. Mr. Favored Son."

"I don't know about that."

"You don't know much, do you? Neither of us do," he adds quickly. "When it comes down to it, we're hired muscle, you and me. Don't think. Only do as we say."

"'We'?"

He dips a finger in his drink and sucks it thoughtfully. "Forget it."

And after a moment: "You're a good company man, Henry. I can appreciate it."

"Cyber's been good to me."

"Yes, I believe it. I do *believe* it. To Cyber!"

"To Cyber." I oblige him and set down my glass. Ian is still slugging. "Jesus—"

Now he claps his down, empty. "Hahh!" He wipes his mouth with a sleeve. Lightning flares, and in the dazzling his wet dishevelment gives him a crazed appearance. His shadow is tremendous. Then all is sconce light and normalcy. Ian is watching me.

"Goddamn but it's strange," he says.

"What is?"

"No sign of Keith or Jane. I've been here, I've been there, and I haven't seen anyone but you."

"Everyone's hunkered down."

"Ah."

"Big meeting coming."

"That's it." Now he is serious. He leans to the counter, temple propped on fingers, nodding. "Very big." No, this is a parodied seriousness.

"Something on your mind?"

Ian summons a refill. He holds up his glass to the light of the television. The sportscaster is a striking, doe-eyed girl with a headful of nascent dreadlocks. Glyphs pile furiously. "What's on my mind is . . ." His lips go on moving, but there is a flash and a clap like board on board.

"What?"

"Oh Jesus, spare me." He shakes his head, grinning. "Back when we first worked in the same place, he used to come down to our floor to review the troops. Sales had all these young assistants, Tri-Delts fresh out of Georgia, good Southern girls still with that Daddy thing, and he'd have these poor kids so wet they were practically sliding off the chairs!" He swallows whiskey matter-of-factly. "So don't tell me. That emperor's confidence or something. You carry yourself like you know your way around the bedposts and good things happen. And look, she's ambitious. Nothing wrong with that. I don't say it's the only reason, but it's a contributor, only natural. She's good-looking, smart. Not bookish—sharp. Lives and breathes in the world that matters to him, speaks his language. I run down the list and I say, All right. I can see where she'd run to his tastes. *Bit* unpredictable maybe, *bit* of a loose cannon. 'Loose' being the operative word! No, I shouldn't have said that. That's the drink talking. But all of which is fine and good. My only modest objection—" The thunder is a building coming down and words disappear. "—company and who am I to mother-hen?"

"Wait a minute—"

"Take a page from your book and just learn to zip it."

"Ian."

"Yessir?"

"What are we talking about."

"What do you think. Ze birds *und* ze bees."

"I didn't hear half of what you just said."

"Oh! I said he's fucking her."

"Who."

"Keith."

"Is fucking who."

He studies me.

"No. For a minute there—but you're serious."

"Jane?"

Ian takes a sip, brows raised. He whistles tunelessly.

"Baloney."

"Don't look so rattled. We're not pastors any of us."

"Totally ridiculous."

He nods vigorously. ". . . that you didn't know. Pardon me, I thought it was a fairly open secret."

"Be serious."

"Look, we're better off. Let him pump out some of that stress."

"Listen to me. She's a friend, and I can speak for her, and I say no way."

"Does her a world of good too, I imagine. Little pony ride to—"

"Careful."

"I'm sympathizing! That husband of hers, Jesus. I'm her, I'd settle for a breeze if it were stiff enough."

"I've never been more serious."

His hands are up. "OK. That settles it. My mistake." Ian notices his watch. "Time for bed." He makes to leave.

"Totally ridiculous."

"You said that."

"Where do you invent these things? What, her promotion? Him alone at her brunch?"

"Ah! You see? I'm not the only one. And you're right: him flying solo at a family-friendly thing like that? Keith's not one to socialize on weekends in any case."

"But you don't turn around and say, This can only mean they're—"

"Or were! Are or were . . ." Ian falls back on his stool, lock-kneed. "Hell, you know how it goes with these office romances. What gets them started? A, proximity. And B, frustration on the home front. You're feeling misunderstood or what have you, and here's this bright, smart coprofessional who treats you with respect, and you're thrust together in this tidy place away from whatever your personal mess, et cetera. But, but: it's a fragile thing. Why? Because you work to-gether. You have to keep pulling the mask on and off. So the romance is forever dying on the vine, only to spring back to life when one party or the other hits another little bump in the road."

Somewhere in this he's resettled himself at the counter. His wrist is curled over his glass, fingers at play on the rim. ". . . Or gets an itch that needs scratching. Look at it: She's just been promoted. He goes out of his way to come to her little brunch, alone, which by his protocol is a no-no. Past this there're all kinds of signs and signals that they're friendly: every meeting the man's practically falling over himself to reassure her that her ideas are good. Her ideas are fine, most of them. But I swear the woman could queef and he'd treat it like the gift of the Magi. As for her, I've seen his effect on the opposite sex, specially ones that work for him. He's a towering figure; her husband's a twat. And never, never discount raw ambition. Now here we all are together in this little hotel, far from hearth and home, with no sign of either of them?"

A soundless pulse lights the room. Not a corner is hidden. Moments later there is an approving murmur, very far off. Ian nips at his drink, a humble mouthful, taken in a shy motion that speaks compunction, repentance for what must be said.

"Upstairs, somewhere, right now, are two exhausted bodies wrapped up in wet sheets."

Again the lights fail. There are groans from the lobby, but we are silent. The lightning breaks, and breaks again, and Ian drinks, paying no mind. His couriering of glass to lip shows in bursts: hand on counter, glass to face, hand on counter. He pushes back his hair, and in the flashing it seems he is clawing at his skull. For my part I am aware of a contest. The pitting of brain against heart. Not much contest, to tell the truth. What a poor thing is the rational brain. What a sad shield it makes. You tote it along, warm in pride of its smart escutcheon, crossed rulers under open book. But come to battle, where are you? Only in the hoisting do you discover the truth of its materials: substance gone, heft evaporated, a thing not of iron and hide but glitter and papier-mâché. This is what you carry against folly and enormity. This has been your plan. A yarn-handled crafts project, clenched against the dragon rage.

"Tell you what." Ian's voice comes out of the darkness. "Never mind. I'm drunk and full of it and I say what you say: Monday's an important day and they've holed up separately to prepare. End of story."

MARCH

Seven

1

Jane is beautiful and speaks beautifully and today she knows it. She stands before the room with the light of thirtieth-story windows full upon her. The storms are gone; the day is blazing. Our audience, men all of them, is rapt. Occasionally one will come to his senses, remember he is being sold to, and raise a challenge. She meets all comers with ceramic poise: shoulders squared and feet at fourth position, hands locked in cradle. I watch her with a soreness in my heart.

Breakfast was nothing. Really, there was quite resolutely nothing in the air. Keith was clipped and direct and did not speak of his weekend and did not ask of ours, and Ian ready and raring, and Jane dark-eyed and watchful at first but never strange or faraway—no, we spoke politely to each other, and when I said I'd called her Saturday and again yesterday she said she was sorry "not to have had a chance to connect." Over the coffee and pastries and chilled butter pats molded into blossoms she smiled once or twice in my direction when not to would have meant too much; she gave not an inch but was pure cool centeredness and professional friendliness, engaged and full of intelligence and ready to do her part. It was hell.

"Excuse me: Could you go back a slide?"

"Here?"

"Yes." The man, a sandy-haired comptroller with an earnest face, studies the screen behind her. A scatter diagram plots Cyber's products against the competition. "Now, OK, the x axis is Value Potential, but I didn't follow—"

"Value Potential here is a measure of return on investment. The better your ROI, the further along the horizontal you go: y is Execution Capability. All the players sitting down here are really more talk than action. Great vision, but in the real world their products don't get the job done. Of course we like this evaluation because it ranks us way out here." Jane stands on toes, reaching to draw a circle around the upper right quadrant with her little finger. Doing so pulls her blouse taut under the raised arm, pushing a swell of breast full against pearl-colored silk.

"Yes, I see that, but . . ." The man seems to lose his train of thought. Is he blushing? Jane waits, the voltage of her eyes upon him. "Oh, OK, yes," he stammers. "Never mind."

It is a promising session. Keith and Ian in their turns speak convincingly and well. There do not seem to be any ill effects from Friday's meeting. Hope revives, hope for the business and even, strange as it may seem, hope for Jane and me together. If the corporate life counsels anything, it is that the past is always past. I mean that the past is without authority. Its dominion is consigned to ivied buildings and empty streets. In business, the past is but a serviceable yardstick for present value. Ask a company for its historical record, and there will come into your hands a slip of paper registering fiscal performance in bygone quarters: the slimmest possible accounting of lived hours, retained only as a benchmark to current performance, and to forecast future turnover. Our memory lane is narrow and short, and the view is of percentages. Already Ian's revelation, his rumor-mongering, has lost its sting. Barely two days old, yet it seems as unlikely, as inert and locked away, as one of those Paleolithic specimens found coffined in the permafrost.

Yes, hope revives, the lessons of the near past gathering in axis against the future, against the wrong future; there is only the right future, as airy and startling as the view from the windows. So when during a break Jane consults sotto voce with Keith at the table's end, her hair on her cheek and her eyes fine, following his hand as he makes some diagram on paper, it is like a blow to the stomach.

"Impressive," I tell Jane, catching up to her.

"Why thank you, Henry."

"You had me reaching for my checkbook."

"Thank you."

She holds to her grip, eyes dead ahead. The moving sidewalk hums along. An electronic voice speaks of cancellations. The voice is everywhere in the high-windowed canyon of the terminal.

"Really great work."

"How kind."

A quick rapping on her torso would confirm it: here stands not Jane but her chrysalis.

Keith and Ian wait in line at a coffee concession past the sidewalk's end. Keith yields his spot to Jane and comes back to stand with me. Ian catches my eye. His face is as inanimate as clay.

"What do you make of it all?" Keith wants to know. Now this is the question. But of course he means the session today.

"I thought it went well," say I crisply.

"Why."

"They asked the right questions, we had the answers, not much push on price."

"Could be a problem. Serious buyers push on price."

"You once told me if they'll take the meeting, they're serious enough."

He gives me a quick crediting look, then goes back to studying the menu board. "What else?"

"No hangover from Friday."

He nods. "Didn't seem to be."

"Lucky for me."

"Lucky for all of us, maybe. We'll know this week."

"They promised a decision so soon?"

"Ian mentioned the quotes were good only through quarter's end.

I expect we'll hear word in the next day or two. Otherwise we can forget it."

Keith loses interest in the menu. Crossing his arms and pressing thumb to lip, he falls to thinking.

"Friday wasn't entirely your fault. They caught us off guard. You were the one stranded."

"I appreciate it."

"You won't appreciate this next thing. But you need to hear it."

It is my turn to look at him. So here it is. He remains abstracted, eyeing the polish on his cap toes. One would think nothing more was at hand than a remark about the sensibleness of quality footwear. I have to admire his choice of setting. In line for coffee at Bush Intercontinental. It is a backdrop as neutered of spectacle, of consequence, as a dentist's lobby.

"I want you to get over it," he says.

The electricity moves up my neck.

"What is it I need to get over?"

"Doesn't need saying, does it."

"You tell me."

He is blinking irritably. "What's the matter with you? What've we been talking about? Never mind Friday. You nearly screwed us today."

"What?"

"Forget the engineers. Let them score their little points and feel like kings. But *today*: today the decision makers were in the room. And there you were, moping like a man at sea."

"I—oh." Braced for his disclosure of a double life, the wrenching reeling sordidness—but now only this. A reprimand, almost surely a pep talk.

"What's done is done. I need eyes forward now. These deals don't get locked down without you. Damn it, you're the product authority. We can't afford our authority looking like he's lost in the woods."

"No."

"Follow?"

"Yes." Not only braced for his disclosure but, it must be admitted, expectant too: for my elevation, however fleeting, to the privileged station of the affronted, the blameless.

"We've got one more crack at this thing Thursday. I need everyone on their A game."

"I am, I will be." (Can it be I am actually disappointed? It is perverse.)

"You're sure."

"I'm sure."

Keith is not convinced. He turns, feigning interest in something above and beyond my place. His face is blank, preserved in the anodyne for the sake of onlookers. Only if you knew him would you see the warning signs. He addresses the rafters in a normal speaking voice:

"Pull. It. Together."

A muscularity in his jaw bites off the words.

On to the plane and down the aisle, shuffling along in slow hope, half believing in symmetry, Fate, a seat next to Jane. But no: I can see my seatmates are to be a cheery blond girl with college hair and, between us, an older gentleman who looks brittle and put-upon. Jane is nowhere in sight. I arrive to take my place at the window. The coed vaults into the aisle like a majorette; the man shambles. His mouth is pinched in a sort of bitter embouchure, like a trumpeter. What a figure he is. Tragic in bearing, this grim mouth and sour face a portrait of the races of northern Europe, sun-starved and philosophical. German, I would bet my life on it.

Up we soar, northward over field and forest. I am pleased to report no dislocation. It has something to do with our entry into the Midwestern sky, sky of my childhood, an astounding basin of powder blue, upturned and emptied out. Or seemingly emptied—in fact the clouds are far below us, white helpings dolloped at intervals on an unseen surface. Their shadows make dark islands on the fields below.

Up and up we soar.

God, but there is beauty in the world. Beauty and space and majesty and—what? Sadness? My mother is dead and in the ground and never to be seen again. The fact is a lump in the throat of my soul. But I am alive and life goes on, life and love, love's promise at the least. What a monarch is the human heart—I see now! It abides, come what may, sanguine, defiant, fierce with the pulse of life.

But the sadness: how peculiar that joy should never be without it. I have only ever known the adulterated kind, the joy that tastes of the seeds of its passing. Even now the sky is reddening in the west. Ahead lies winter. I summon a vision of journey's end, a forgotten stretch of prairie middle country where the moon is everywhere and the snow crunches with native artifacts and pioneer bones. I have never been to Kansas, yet its territories are as half remembered to me, as spirit-haunted, as a place of birth. It is mystifying, how a person can step onto new soil only to stumble upon familiar prints, the very weather of a place, its smells and skies, charged with private messages. Such places have all of the ghosts and none of the comforts of home. They sponsor a strange quality of remembrance, deeper than homesickness, a sort of muscle memory of that ancient instant when first the body was awakened to its predicament, pinned down in time, the spirit cupboarded, the clock started—terrible but for an attendant longing, a saving grace: the awareness that only by this dire ticking did one's inklings of possibility begin.

Two flight attendants wrestle a drink cart down the aisle. They make an elaborate show of careful steerage. (Really they are deadeyes for every ankle and elbow in their path.) I survey the world from my porthole window. A scale model of farms and fields scrolls mere yards beneath the wing. I can feel its miniature fragility through the soles of my feet. More uplift is needed. By pulling on the armrests and clenching my buttocks, I am persuaded the model gains another inch or two of clearance. When the drink cart arrives I order a double. Two tiny bottles of Gordon's, side by side on my food tray. Something faintly pitiable there. The boars peer out with their fiery yellow eyes: Save your pity! But even a double of Gordon's can't punch with this great Midwestern sky and its fitful ecstasies and fears. The twin airplane bottles and their piercing piney spirits only help to recall Friday night's catastrophe. The memory is like falling down a rabbit hole. When I have clambered back into the present, the cabin lights are dim. In my lap is a small dull dish of starlight. So long, old sky. The model earth is whitened now, a dim winter color like old tablets. All else is gone to darkness. Vast plats of subdivisions drift into view. Their streets burn brightly and make geometric markings in the plains. I draw the shade and think of other things. Parse trees. Linked data structures. Drink my drink. These raptures, these little junkets into beauty. They are never profitable. Always there is the same seizing in the throat. What would it be to live in one of these homes, one of ten thousand, especially at dusk, with the prairie howling at your back fence and the living room full of dying sun, the smell of pot roast and boiled potatoes on the curtains, carpet particles snowing in the red archaic light? I should ask the gloomy fellow next to me. His people would have a name for it, this variegation of joy and dread. Something trenchant and unpronounceable, seven centuries of mute human experience finally cooked down to a strong mash of gutturals—some mouthful for which my countrymen and I, yet in our infancy, don't have the stomachs.

The intercom chimes. Our captain is speaking, an oracular voice full of premonitions and advisements. We are starting our descent. Buckle up.

At my shoulder, the German sleeps the sleep of the ancients.

2

No sooner am I checked into my room than does my sister call. I know the reason for her call, but it is a relief to hear her voice. Kansas is more harrowing than imagined. Its colorless flatlands are the world all around, and the sky menaces from every side. Really it is total, this sky. Coming out of the shelter of baggage claim and staggered by the oceans above, I wanted to lie down against the sidewalk and hold on for dear life. It is we who hang over this sky, not the other way around. The others sense it too. Riding from the airport our van was silent. There was only the hoarse roaring of the vents, a smothering wood-warm engine heat, a wariness amid the sleepiness. To travel

I-635 S fifty miles from Kansas City International in winter is to pass through the last panels of color and form, to be magicked beyond the drawn frame. Approaching our exurban Radisson, the only three-dimensional structure for a thousand miles, a floodlit column of honeycombed concrete made to seem fledgling and ridiculous by the sky—approaching, even Ian showed signs of the malady.

"God Almighty," muttered he. "The hell we doing way out here in the Negev?"

Gretchen and I exchange pleasantries. There are several minutes of polite throat-clearing before she comes to her point.

"So . . . next week."

"Next week."

"Monday."

"Yes."

"You'll make it?" She endeavors to sound neither hardened nor hopeful, needing an answer but not putting much stock in it. Again her tone recalls our mother: practical, chin up, please just answer Yes or No and then let us Get On With It.

"I'll be there."

"I knew it!"

"I'm halfway home already." I explain to her the circumstances of our trip. "We'll be finished Thursday. After that there's not much to do but wait."

"Oh, that is just really, really great."

"How's Dad?"

"OK, really. But I feel so, so much better knowing you'll be here for it."

Something has happened to the country outside my window. An ice fog has materialized out of thin air. Seven stories down the parking lot's bright acre has begun to soften and steam. At the curbs the work of recent storms is piled up in filthy mountains. The window unit, wheezing like a bellows, pumps hot air onto my eyeballs. Its emanations smell of the floor spaces underneath beds. I do not tell my sister that after exposure to the gases here on the white planet, a quarantine among home and family is essential. The sooner, the better.

The line is quiet. A brief dread space. Together we think of it: she and I and our father shuffling around like ghosts, waiting in the wintry hours as the time approaches. The waiting will almost certainly be worse than the day itself. Rushing to fill the silence, we interrupt each other.

"Sorry!" she says. "You go."

"Go ahead."

"Oh, I was only going to say, you know. No *event* or anything. Just us together."

"No cake?" Jesus, what a terrible thing to say. I can hear the catch in her throat. "I'm sorry—"

"It's all right."

"This is going to be hell."

"Don't say that! Don't say that. I'm looking at it as a time for gratitude too. I'm grateful for you, I'm grateful for Dad. Just by coming back together I genuinely believe we honor her memory."

Now understand, I am glad my stupid goddamn despairing little crack did not push her over the edge. But when she talks like this my heart sinks. Tears would be better. Or if only she would say, *Yes, dear brother. This is going to be hell. Worse than hell, but there is no way around it and better we face it together, propping up Dad, propping up each other, failing at all of it, than trying to sneak past alone.* "Honor her memory." How mealy are these little pulpit catchphrases. My sister remains as I was for a time, poring over the grief literature, filling its margins with notes and "breakthroughs," drinking in the peculiar phrase and idiom, bewilderment and night terrors become "a process measured in stages."

"I hope so," I tell her.

"I am utterly convinced of it. Really."

She is utterly convinced of it. And I am utterly convinced this sonorous phrasemaking will rob you and leave you empty. On the subject of utter convictions, mine is: better mute fury or choking sadness than this silvery ventriloquism; better the dark mornings when there were no words for it and we did not try.

It is time for bed.

"Right. So. See you soon?"

"See you soon! And HH?"

"Yes?"

"Thank you. Truly."

"All right."

"Good luck with work."

"Thanks."

We fish around for a moment. This grocery list of good-lucks and see-you-soons. What is wanted is something essential.

She says, "You know I love you."

"Yes. I love you too."

But even this feels a little pat and by the book. Somewhere a celebrated author nods, jotting an approving note. If I had an ounce of courage and could remember anymore how to speak with my sister, what would I say? Nothing as reducible as an I-love-you, God help me. I would say: Gretchen, losing Mom I will manage because what choice is there. But to lose you too would be too much, that would be the bitter end, and if we keep on like this I don't know what to do, I make no warrants for my actions.

3

Tuesday and most of Wednesday we are left to our own devices. I winnow my email; I work on performance reviews owed next month; I speak with Cory and Rahim. (The team is fine but eager for news. I allow only that there is "room for cautious optimism." A handy managerial chestnut.) It is not so bad. With a full in-box and the curtains drawn, it becomes possible to forget the prairie proofs of one's displacement. Not that I am holed up. I know better. In my early years of travel I learned that holing up, or polishing off the minibar, or leering at cocktail waitresses—these are evasive maneuvers. They work only to credit the matter. As much as possible you must remain yourself. The trick is not to overact, overreact. It is like walking a forest path and feeling from the trees the eyes of some wild beast, and knowing that to run is to invite chase. Better to whistle along, in faith and courage of one's own no-accountedness.

Also I need to see Jane. Alone. It requires some chance encounter. Tuesday afternoon and again Wednesday morning, I lurk in the hotel's common areas. The fitness room seems a particularly good bet. For two days I am changed into a health fiend: forty pounding minutes on the treadmill, followed by light weights and stretching. In all of these exertions I am conscious of form—conscious, but not too conscious. If I am discovered, she must find me only abstractly focused, not as one of these weight room Narcissuses who gravely investigate their every nerve twitch. So it is that I will sit on the floor between exercises, forearms across knees just so, the right wet muscle thrust to prominence. Or I will stand with feet together and round over at the waist, shoulders loose and heavy in their sockets, taking calves in palm, a figure of seamless muscularity, elongate and gracefully asweat as old Achilles, all the while listening for my cue, an annunciatory shriek of hinges, and when finally it comes (!) raising a damp indifferent brow to the room's entrance, there to lock eyes with:

The cleaning woman.

Wednesday afternoon I pick up a voice message from Keith: "I've got us a conference room in the hotel's business center. We're going to meet up there at five thirty. I want to finalize any prep for tomorrow morning. Also: we got word from Houston today. They're in for the whole enchilada. You know what it means."

It means we are almost home free.

The business center is on the hotel's top floor. At twenty of six the room is still empty. I am beginning to wonder if I've mistaken the time when in walks Jane. She hesitates ever so slightly before proceeding to the far end of the table—a dead giveaway. Not a little wounding to discover her plan. A deliberately late arrival, the small talk dispensed with, meeting safely under way.

"Where is everyone?" she wants to know.

"I don't know. I thought maybe I'd gotten the time wrong."

Jane says nothing. She stands over her valise, rummaging inside, frowning and preoccupied.

"You haven't seen them?" I ask her.

She retrieves a pen and folder and sets them at her place. "Nope."
With a quick smoothing run of hands, she tucks her skirt and sits.

"Great news about Billico," I say. Christ. What cowardice.

"Mm-hm."

"A lot of credit to you."

She grants me a tight little smile, then busies herself with the folder.
I am stricken.

"Jane, please listen."

"I'm all ears," she sings, not looking up.

"All right. First off"—First off? Is this how I've rehearsed it?—"I
should apologize. I do apologize. I am not exactly sure—" But now
Keith does appear, goddamn him. He strides into the room and goes
straight to the whiteboard. "Ian's on his way."

There is nothing to do but wait.

On the board Keith writes:

$4.00M (OR WE'RE FINISHED)

And beneath, the tally:

-$0.25M
-$0.40M
-$1.50M
-$0.75M (Billico!)
$1.10M: TOMORROW

This last he circles in red. "That's the sum of things right there."

Jane meets his eye, nodding. She is a marvel of composure. I cannot tell what my expression is. Keith's eye only confirms I am not so
successfully poker-faced. As he looks at me, there is a flash of puzzlement.

Ian enters, phone to ear:

"I won't hold you to it, but give me your best guess . . . Really. Aha.
Of course not, of course not. I'm not an idiot. Listen—I appreciate
it. Yep." He claps the phone shut. For a moment he is away in his
thoughts. Finally he says:

"There's more money on the table here than we knew."

Keith has gone still.

"How much?"

Turning to the board, Ian rubs out the *1* after the sum's decimal place. He replaces it with a *5*. A hush falls over the room. Even as engineer, I know to freeze. We've stumbled upon a covey of rare birds—one false move and the money spooks.

Ian says, "Buddy of mine's been working Nexus as his main account for a couple years now. When I say I'm about to pitch 'em on security, he wants to know how much. I mention a roundabout figure—it gives him a good laugh. He says to me, 'Ian, yall're stepping over dollars to pick up nickels.'" Ian taps the new figure. "We're off by at least four hundred thousand. My guy says Ops have been getting crossed up enough by security bugs that they'd happily throw our guys some of their own money to get it fixed."

Keith has taken up position behind one of the swivel chairs. He works the padded shoulders with crushing squeezes. "Forget meeting our quarterly numbers. If we actually *beat* them—!" The chair is delivered a terrific thump. He throttles his excitement down to a kind of animated solemn seriousness:

"Corporate's expecting the numbers to be grim. In line with targets, but grim. So to come in over the top . . . Folks: this is how careers get made. And I'm talking all of us. These kinds of opportunities? In your working life, the stars might never line up like this again."

Thus are we spurred to a final dress rehearsal. It is not a drawn-out affair, thirty minutes at the most. By now we know the motions and can execute them with a mechanical fluidity that pleases me. Backdrop to our rehearsal is the whiteboard and its equation. I experience not a single stray thought or distraction, for money is a great clarifier. There is only my responsibility to a winning pitch. I am to be a font of technological data, to "challenge" my cohorts when a certain speaking point feels too easily glossed, when it has not done justice to the elegance of our product, and to remain humble before our questioners—above all to flatter their intelligence. In short, to comport myself as a modest figure of effortless engineering mastery.

Jane is distracted by a busyness in the windows.

"Oh, look—it's really snowing."

She is right. We line up along the glass like children. It comes down on a swift diagonal, undetectable in the high darkness, manifesting only once inside the bright skirt of rooftop lights, streams as thick and flurried as volcanic ash. Already parked cars far below have taken on the softened, slightly bloated aspect of parade floats. I measure four inches at the least.

For a few moments we are quiet.

"Looks fierce," says Ian.

"I didn't pack for this weather," says Jane.

"Might be half a foot out there," I say.

There is something awkward about standing with other people, transfixed by natural wonder. It is too much the bearing of public witness to some embarrassing atavistic yearning. Yet Keith is not touched by our same sense of nakedness. He raps the glass as though to acknowledge the storm's efforts, and to send it along. "I wouldn't sweat it," he says, returning to the room.

But for once his authority is misplaced. In the morning, and no matter the framing window, the picture is changed. A bright, clear sky. An obliterated landscape as far as the eye can see.

Lunch Thursday is a sullen affair. Keith and Ian have spent the morning in a series of calls of rising franticness, laboring to iron out a new schedule with the customer. For a bad hour this morning it seemed that Nexus would not reassemble its audience for Monday, the first working day the roads will be cleared. So that was that. It was over, our valiant striving cut short. Except that at the last Keith reached out to his executive counterpart at Nexus and pleaded with her for mercy. This alarming near miss, the storm and the subsequent bowing and scraping, have left Keith and Ian in foul moods. Jane's mood I cannot read. She does not grouse about our snowed-in circumstance as they do. She listens, or does not listen, elbows on the table, fingers laced as a hammock for her chin. She cocks her head. She tunes her watch. Where Jane is concerned, my radar is not much good.

When lunch is over we go our separate ways. After ten days traveling together and now marooned, the first signs of company fatigue are beginning to show. (At one point during the meal, Keith mistook Jane's water glass for his own. She went tight-lipped, and when he failed to notice his blunder signaled with broad irritation for a fresh glass. My heart leapt.) I retire to phone the airline. When my travel arrangements are settled there is nothing else to do. It is time to face the music. I must tell Gretchen.

This requires some summoning of courage. I wander the room, rehearsing possibilities. The sun has migrated far enough west that it is possible now to open the curtains without risk of blindness. Two pickups, affixed with snowplows, ply their masses in the white depths at the edges of the lot. The stranded cars are buried to their windows and will need to be shoveled out by hand. There is a hill behind the lot where must exist, in warmer weather, a small null space of grass. A lone bench sits on top, shrouded in humps. Toward this marker some brave soul of neuter gender is making his (her?) way with a Dalmatian in tow. The dog thrusts along like a porpoise, leaping and plunging in the mysterious accretion.

Gretchen answers on the third ring.

"So what does it mean?" she wonders, after I have explained myself. "Tomorrow night?"

"Well—"

"They'll have the airport and all the big roads by then."

"Yes. Probably. It's just that meeting-wise . . ."

"Meeting-wise. You don't mean—oh God."

"I'm afraid yes."

"Monday."

"Yes."

There comes over the line a low sibilance like a teakettle approaching steam. "How can this be happening."

"I'll be in by eight."

"Eight. PM."

"Yes."

Silence.

"It was the earliest."

"Sure, sure. I'm, ahm. I'm just thinking . . . Why bother?" Hearing the shrewishness in her tone, she softens. "I didn't mean that. You know I didn't." She waits, breathing hoarsely. Now she clears her throat, a little workaday noise for reassurance, no heavy emotions here, thank you. "Just really, truly . . . disappointing."

I am touched by her strength of effort. To receive such surprise bad news and then to pivot, in mature adult fashion, making of it no more than routine letdown.

But as she presses on, her voice breaks. There is a dampening of sounds, the receiver abandoned while she gathers herself.

"Ugh," she says upon return.

"Gretchen?"

"Yup."

"Let's make it a point to be in touch over the next few days."

"All right," she says dully. "I'm all right." Her caregiver pride is roused. "You don't need to worry."

"No, but it could be good for both of us."

"Oh. Of course, yes. God, listen to me. So hung up on myself."

"You're not."

"I am." She is quiet for a moment. "Lonely in that hotel."

"It's fine."

"Way down yonder in Kansas." A fondness has come into her voice. Commiseration, at the least. "Don't go crazy."

4

Somewhere during the night I wake in a fit of manic perception. Finally I am on to it. My first clue is the window unit hissing away behind the armchair. In the smell of its thiols, I detect the Thing's very life and breath. What a perfect disguise. Never in a million years. I have known certain places as incubators for it, yes. But always these were revealed as penny-ante plays, franchise operators.

The pall, specter of my livelong existence, enters consciousness by way of this room.

A short time later I am dressed and heaving through drifts with the padded stillness all around. No dream this, though there is a quality of dream silence, a vacuumed absence like a pressure in the ears. The cold is a relief. It is an ugly thing to come awake late in the night in a strange room far from home. The anxieties are no figments, and the longer you wait, the deeper their talons dig. But the cold is a relief. It fills up the chest cavity, freezing out the spirits of three AM. It restores the brain to noonday keenness.

Someone has shoveled out the bench on the small hill at the back of the lot. It now sits within its own little tidied crop circle, enclosed by clean white walls. When finally I have gained the hill and settled in, it is as though I am up to my neck in the surrounding bank. This is how the prairie dog must feel. Crouched in the shallows of its burrow, taking alert survey of the territory. Perceptibly warmer here. The insulation of the dugout walls. Quite peaceful in fact. The sky is quiet; the darkness is beginning to thin to grayness. There is even a view of sorts. Not an actual view, but elevation enough that the surrounding monotony is pushed down, pushed away. I had forgotten how constant are these white landscapes. There is the scooped-out quarry of the parking lot, yes. But everywhere else is remote and parameterless. Only the hotel, a leviathan concrete presence half a football field away, makes a case for the vertical.

I am startled by a burst of snow from the left bank. The beast comes plunging in, tracking and snuffling heavily—a dog, the Dalmatian. It works a furious scent trail along the bench, up the inside of my knee and straight on for the crotch. There it parks its muzzle. I am held with a soulful stare. Its powdered nostrils steam and twitch; the dog sneezes violently.

"Oh Lord," comes a woman's voice. "I do apologize! Ordinarily it's just us chickens." The Dalmatian canters over to receive her. She climbs down through the broken embankment, a figure in moon boots and a burgundy quilted parka. Her face is deep inside the fur-lined hood.

"May I?"

"Of course." I shift obligingly, though there is room enough. "I was on my way."

"No, no. Don't you do that. You'll make us feel like interlopers."

She sits forward with hands on knees and her boots crossed beneath her, alighted rather than settled in. Only the dog is introduced. "That's Rupert," she says. Rupert is standing with his backside to us, nose to the ground at the base of the shoveled wall. At his name, the head lifts and cranes around. He peers down his spine. "Hello, Rupert," I say, because the animal seems to be waiting for it. He returns to his snuffling investigations.

"He's a stubborn mongrel, but I love him. He's the right size. You see all these women my age with their little pocket dogs. Their little pocket dogs and their little pocket husbands! No thank you. I'll take this great galoot any day of the week."

"How old?"

"I am sixty-four."

"I'm sorry—I meant Rupert."

"Oh! He must be about five. I haven't had him his whole life. He's a shelter animal. Had some hard times I think, poor creature." She sighs, and I understand her meaning. I've never met an owner of a shelter animal who didn't suspect abuse on the part of some former warden. My mother, a great harborer of dogs herself, was forever finding in ours behavioral evidence—the need to chew the baseboards, a dislike of cheese—that testified to criminal prior treatment.

"You're here at the hotel?" she wonders.

"Yes."

"What brings you to town?"

"Business."

"Well, sure, *business*." She makes a little mocking cluck—self-mocking as it turns out. "Nobody comes to darkest Kansas for pleasure! What is it you do?"

"I'm in software."

"Software. Now I don't know a thing about software. Except that it's important." If she is being ironic, it is gentle enough. "What do you make of our little perch here?"

"It's nice."

"It is, isn't it? This must be the only rise for a hundred miles. It's like being on a throne. Rupert and I come here all the time. He does his business and I survey the kingdom. It's still a little early but—"

She turns, holding back the hood's cuff so to gain an untrammeled view of the country behind. It is the first I've seen of her face, this cheek with its familiar complexity of lines and the sharp gray eye. A whitened brush of hair covers the ear, cut and combed just as my mother's was cut and combed before it was gone. "Yes, it's just beginning. Do you see? That milky quality above the horizon? Of course the first blaze of sun is nice too. But this quieter sort of light . . ." She glances at me, then turns back around, her face again going behind the hood. "It's the most hopeful time of day, I find."

After a moment's silence, she snorts. "Such mindlessness. You have to indulge us older folk."

"Not at all." Indeed she is the age my mother would have been.

"Anything not to go back to that hotel, I imagine. I had brunch in there once. It struck me as a horrid place. Very remote-feeling. Maybe you're used to it, traveling to all these strange places. Do you travel a great deal?"

"Lately, yes."

"I marvel at it. All this getting on planes and flying thousands of miles and stepping off in some far-flung locale as though it were nothing. When I was a girl . . . No, I won't bore you. But it's foreign to me, I'll say that."

The cold has begun to seep under my collar. I turn up the heavy wool lapels and shrug down between them. Fixed in its place ahead and above is the glass eye of my room. There are sixty facing windows at least, but not for an instant have I mistaken any other for the one.

My neighbor inclines ever so modestly, a slight theatricalism of confiding.

"Tell me. These dark mornings in a place you don't recognize. Does it ever bother you?"

Her forwardness is not so strange. I recognize it as a privilege of time and place: under confessional darkness, our little hill excepted from the rules and regulations of the country below. What is unnerving is her intuition.

"Sometimes."

"So you take a walk."

"Today, yes."

"And that helps."

"Sometimes."

"Today?"

"Yes."

She moves a little at the waist so that I understand she is nodding away inside the hood. "Maybe it wouldn't be so foreign to me after all, your kind of travel."

I wait. Watching her, I can see only the hood's obscuring cuff. Her breath erupts in billows and disappears.

"To think of it, I'm more a visitor here now than I was when I was forty. How odd that is."

Not understanding, I ask her politely how long she has lived here. She is away in her thoughts and pays no attention.

"We arrive, and everything's so wonderful and new. Then, gradually, it isn't anymore. You're home, so to speak. For better and worse. A few days ago I was eating in a restaurant, and I happened to eavesdrop on the table next to mine. A boy was eating a piece of cake with his mother. I don't know children's ages; I would suppose about four. And this boy, he had dug out his first bite of this lovely thick chocolate cake, and he said to his mother: 'It's like a chocolate cliff.' And I had the most vivid sort of—that *memory*, of how you used to perceive things. You're much closer to everything, and see it in such magnified detail, and scale is still rather rubbery in any case. Nothing is actual size. I knew exactly what he meant, about the broken-off place in his cake looking like a cliff. I hadn't seen the world that way in sixty years!

"That newness never comes back. When it's gone, it's gone for good. Gone: you're darn right it's gone! You've worked hard yourself to see it off. No self-respecting adult walks around that dewy-eyed. But it's the strangest thing. After enough time, all the familiarity with the world that you've worked to hoard . . . Poof! It goes too. Well, no. Not poof. It dribbles away. It's like having a hole in your pocket. Everything is right where you need it to be, just as it always was, until one day you reach in—there's that horrible feeling of carelessness. You find yourself looking back the way you've come, sick to your stomach at your own stupidity. Because nothing—and mister, I mean *nothing*— is the same. It's all . . . foreign. Foreign."

Vapor spills from behind the cuff. When she speaks again it is with a brisk, never-you-mind air:

"Now don't think I'm just some befuddled old Mr. Magoo! I'm not talking about VCRs and whatnot. I mean something else entirely. I mean being bolt upright in the middle of the night, thinking: Here I am with the party over and my ride gone home!" Her briskness dies. Rupert has gone stock-still. His nose is in the air, testing.

"Who said, 'Old age isn't a battle, it's a massacre'?" she wonders.

"I don't know."

"Not someone who got to duck out early, I can tell you."

It is hard to know what to make of this. "Duck out early"? She is no sentimentalist, I give her that. Not even my father, clear-eyed thinker that he is (was?), ever put it like this.

"You read about these poor people stuffed full of tubes in hospital rooms, with their families only wanting them to be left alone to die. But oh no! Here come the politicians, hopping up and down and turning red in the face about life this and life that." She speaks now in a kind of probing half-mutter. I am reminded of the etiquette of dinner guests who begin by hinting their indignation at some political matter, sounding for kindred ears. "And do you know the thing I notice? These speechifiers? Never a gray head among them."

"Is that right."

Something fishy is going on. It is enough that this likeness should arrive out of the clear blue. But that her mission should be to argue the hell of old age—

"I mean, there are worse things than death. That shouldn't be so shocking, should it? Why is that so shocking?" Abruptly, she springs away into levity. "Heavens, Rupert! Do you think this poor man knew what he was getting into when we joined him? Do you think he raced out here hoping to find us going on like this?" Rupert is a cooperative foil. He spins around, setting a chin on his master's knee. "Hum? What do you say, you miserable creature? Is your half-wit master going to make friends that way?" She grips him by the jowls, shaking his head for him. "Telling the world about all her little creaks and confusions? But it's no picnic, is it? Is it?"

Not since I was fifteen has someone affected to speak to me via the dog. This was my mother's way, in those sullen teen years, an effort to preserve our old bestest-buddies standing while still getting in some sermon time.

". . . It is no-ho picnic! No, *sir*. No, *sir*."

Just as then, I can feel impatience rising. Very well. It is no picnic. I believe you. Except do not think hearing of the difficulties of the long haul is a comfort. Do not try to convince me we were spared. It is absurd. Better you were alive, whatever the troubles down the road, whatever the fear and trembling to come.

She carries on with the dog until he too has had enough. He pulls away and bounds to the farthest edge of shoveled wall. There he is possessed by a hunkering seizure, haunch tucked and straining commenced. My neighbor is instantly embarrassed.

"Oh! All right. You go right ahead. Never mind us." The dog glances around nervously. His eyebrows shift one way and the other. Here is the very face of grimacing apology: molars bared, a pained begging of pardon. "I mean honestly, Rupert." She is shaking a plastic bag from her coat pocket. "Your timing. How marvelous."

I excuse myself and head for the hotel. Not that I'm so eager to go back. But I am glad to leave her with her crap.

5

By evening our little company is cheery. The cold fact of the storm has settled in. We are liberated, knowing there is nothing to be done. What remains is an improvisatory spirit of doing the best one can. Jane, with her keen nose for the exalted place, has somehow unearthed a fondue restaurant not far from the hotel. The outside is nothing to speak of, but inside it is all tapestries and trembling gaslights and brass-nailed leather booths, snug and redly warm. We huddle over burbling earthenware pots, stabbing in long steel forks with cut bread or cubed potatoes and washing down the molten lumps with sweet burning kirsch. The room is jammed to the gills. There is a kind of fever of shared merriment, the esprit de corps of perfect strangers who have come out of the cold and into the same place of warmth and drink and shelter. Jane herself is enlivened beyond recognition. Moments ago she leaned to me and half shouted (though privately; in the noise of the place even half shouts are private) that she felt she was in a nursery rhyme. "Ha," I allowed, not sure I'd heard her. "This place!" she cried. "All cozy with the little potbellied stove glowing away, it reminds me of the fox's den? In a nursery rhyme?" "Oh, right. Right! Yes, you're right." She waved me off, but good-humoredly. This was the kirsch speaking, I know. Yet there are unmistakable beginnings of a détente. Earlier while waiting to board the van, she approached directly and addressed me by name—not as an arm's-length stand-offishness, but in the way you might make a notifying little rap on an office door before proceeding in: brisk, cordial, forward-looking. Did I think open source software was a workable standard only for smaller enterprises? I did. She nodded. Then: "We've absolutely got to nail this one." There followed a nice beat or two of silence as together we licked our chops over the unsuspecting future. It dawned on me how much Jane has come into her own. The concentrated performance of the road show suits her. Now when she speaks as the tough-minded business moll, she is convincing.

Ian rings his glass and announces in a crocked, seriocomic way that whoever's bread falls off the fork while dipping must confess something embarrassing. Jane likes the idea but not the penalty. She thinks the loser should have to sing.

"Long as the stakes are humiliation!" Ian crows.

He is first to lose. Swearing bitterly, he extracts himself from our half circle of booth. I see he is rising for a proper serenade.

When the world goes wrong, as it's bound to do
And you've broken Dan Cupid's bow
And you long for the girl you used to love
The maid of the long ago

Why light your pipe! Bid sorrow avaunt!
Blow the smoke from your altar of dreams

A turkey-necked old man in the next booth has turned around in his seat. He watches Ian. In his face is the light of recognition.

And wreathe the face of your dream girl there
The love that is just what it seems

The girl of my dreams is the sweetest girl
Of all the girls I know
Each sweet coed, like a rainbow trail

It is too much. The man frees himself of his booth and pads over, a frail, stoop-shouldered being in cinched corduroys. There he stands: eager, spellbound, a little unsure of himself. Ian folds the man under his arm.

. . . The blue of her eyes and the gold of her hair
Are a blend of the western sky
And the moonlight beams on the girl of my dreams
She's the Sweetheart of Sigma Chi . . . !

Together they carry the final note. The man's eyes are squeezed shut. On his face is that sort of flatness of flesh, the rigor mortis of purpose that comes over tenors in the throes of the big finish. I recognize it from weddings and class reunions, a kind of death mask of sentimentality worn by old soaks moonstruck for fraternal order and football drums and the grassy darknesses of yore. The man rounds off the note. There is some sympathetic applause; the diners return to their table spaces. He stands blinking and lost. Just as quickly as it has come, it is gone. There is nothing left but to go back to his seat. An unsteady business. So besieged is he by yearning that he must actually brace himself, holding to the seat backs as he goes.

Ian sits at ease, calibrating the lay of his drink napkin. His eyes are hooded but gleaming. He is still a little in orbit himself. Jane watches him coolly.

"You were a Sigma Chi."

He looks up. "I was. Boy, you don't miss much!"

"Ugh."

"Ugh yourself."

She jabs me. "You. You were no frat guy." I confess I was. Jane is aghast. "Kappa *Alpha*? No. Not really."

"Good man," says Ian.

Jane is struggling for purchase. "But they were the *worst*. Just absolute *pigs*. Do you know what they did on our campus? They would hire kids from the local junior high—*black* kids, only black—and dress them up as footmen for their big formal ball, that idiotic sabers-and-hoopskirts thing. Those are your 'brothers'?"

"We never—"

"How do you know they had to be black?" Ian wants to know. "Those kids maybe're the hungriest and hardest-working. First to grab the job." He is not really paying attention. Of greater interest is his fork's action in the pot, the safe evacuation of his bread. Jane doesn't credit him a response. She's not through with her census taking.

"Keith?"

"Yes?"

"Fraternity: yes or no."

Keith replies no; he has never been much for bathhouses. Peace is restored. Jane tips into herself, squeezing her nose so not to lose her drink through it. Ian holds his head. "*Now* I learn this?"

Again and in harmony we fall to eating, a good meal in a warm place on a cold night. The sauce is a rich liquid heat. Its sharpness raises a granulation on the tongue. The kirsch is sweet and fiery and brings halos to the gaslights. Next to me Jane touches her chin to her shoulder. She occupies this posture for several moments. I think of a wren with its head tucked for the night. In a humoring whisper she says:

"That's all right, Henry. I forgive you."

She means only my fraternity sins. But for an instant I imagine we are starting over.

Later Jane goes to dip and sees her fork come back empty. Ian pounces. "Oh, are we still playing?" she wonders, with not much hope of sale. Already we have given her our undivided attention. Jane groans in despair.

She sings well. Quietly and half in apology, but sing she does. She doesn't bray or shirk or clown. Her song is a radio staple of some twenty years ago. I don't recall the name. You would know it perhaps, one of those effective tearjerkers played at organ tempo, a crane shot of the songstress adrift on an empty boulevard, neon quivering in the street puddles. More than anything Jane is embarrassed. By holding her arms in her hands and looking nowhere but the little tooth of kerosene flame, she works to make herself as small as possible. Really her voice is very good. Her eyes are gone glassy and staring. The truth is I am a bit destroyed. In the low cast light with the heat on her cheekbones and the soft melody in her throat, there is about her a kind of human plausibility. When you see it you remember. There is a shock of recognition.

We are spearing fat hothouse strawberries when a chanting starts up by the kitchen. Instantly it overtakes the neighboring tables. Everyone picks up the chant readily and happily:

WHO IS THE something something *SOUND THE* something!
WHO IS THE ONE something *SOUND THE* something!
WHO IS THE ONE WHO'LL SOUND THE something!

Sound the what? Horn? Yes: I see now. A man in a white apron is circulating among the tables, holding aloft a round brass instrument. It is old and battered. A simple coil of tubing ending in a flared bell, the kind made to emit a single-note blast like a clarion. The man (surely the proprietor) threads among the tables, shaking the horn like a tambourine. With the other hand he conducts the chant: raising it, lowering it, now shutting it off.

"Folks!" he cries. "Folks!" Talking and laughter; one table works to restart the chant. "Folks, please . . ." The room quiets.

"Thank you. Much better than last night's savages. Now let me ask: Are any here for the first time?" A smattering of hands. "All right then. Because the one rule of the horn is, no do-overs. Now"—he tucks the horn under an arm and fixes the carpet with a faraway look—"the legend is that many, many years ago . . ." There erupts a chorus of boos. The man looks up, wounded. "You don't want to hear my story?" Loud nays. He has a broad mustache and pug's chin and these he works to farcical, trembly effect. "I see. No one wants to hear the ramblings of an old man, an immigrant to this country whose family for genera- tions struggled—" Now the noise is of sarcastic pity. He cracks up and sheds the act. "All right. For you newcomers, this is the arrangement. One person is given one chance to blow. If you sound the horn? A round of drinks for everyone. But if you fail to sound the horn . . ." A little shudder. "Terrible, eternal shame is yours, and those kind of things. The catch is, it is a very old horn and very difficult to blow. True lung power is required and most don't got it. OK? So. Who is the—"

"Right here!" Ian is boosted on one knee, arm high. "This guy!" He means Keith. The room bursts into applause and more chanting. Keith's objections are swallowed up by the noise. Before he can delegate, the proprietor has brought him the horn and presented it with some ceremony. I see the instrument is designed for ridiculous effect. The bell curls up and around and back upon itself so that it faces the player, enough that as Keith positions his lips on the mouth- piece there is some negotiation between his forehead and the bell's rim. "How loud is this thing?" he wants to know. "We've never heard it!" someone answers to laughter. Now Keith lowers the horn and per- forms some calisthenics with his mouth. Everyone gets a kick out of it, though I detect he is ill at ease. The frivolous spotlight doesn't suit him. He has no special need for these people; their audience holds no business purpose; they are not even comrades-in-arms. To play monkey for them is not his idea of fun. "I'll remember this come bonus time," he mutters to Ian. Ian is only eager for victory. He tells Keith to hit it; he is ready for his gaddamn drinky-ink. Jane watches in the slack, self-forgotten way of an onlooker. For the last time I am glad of her company, of our company—last time because of the misery to come.

The room takes up a straightforward cry . . .

BLOW!
BLOW!
BLOW!

. . . and Keith, with a dramatic heave, obliges. There is a muffling of air, and a *ppft*, and an explosion from the bell's mouth. His head disappears. For a moment it is difficult to process. A great cheering laugh comes up from the room. Clapping, banging of tables, hooting. Ian looks on in astonishment before he too is carried away. Jane is speechless. She won't take her eyes from Keith—not Keith anymore but an extraterrestrial, a moon face, two blinking spots in a caking layer of flour.

It is an old game of course. The proprietor sprints over with a clean towel and a tray of drinks, all grinning accommodation. Keith is brushing off his head, raising clouds and more laughter. Seeing Ian's hilarity, he claps the flour from his hands directly over Ian's glass. The room makes known its appreciation and Keith, having repossessed himself, raises a hand and smiles assurances from his mask. *What fun we're having, folks, what a delight to play a part.* He is homicidal beyond any shadow of a doubt. Jane is transfixed. Even after Keith has tidied himself, even after he has contoured his indignity into a genial outrage and threatened Ian with all kinds of reprisal (Ha-ha! cries Ian, laughing, deflecting, growing more uneasy by the minute)—still she can't tear her eyes away. I think I understand her fascination. How exotic it is to see him like this, at the butt end of things. Jane stretches out an arm. She takes the lobe of his ear tenderly in thumb and finger. My poor old brain is late to the game. There is the barest latency: here is Perception, and here, where should be Explanation smack against it, this infinitesimal gap.

It is the abyss.

Arriving, my brain dashes around in circuits, patching and accounting for—some leftover fringe of dust, a drunken bit of mother-henning, *Yes of course* and *Of course yes*—and so on and so forth and et cetera but too late, too late. Already I have put a foot into empty space. Already I have experienced the calamity of it. The maroon of her nail on his ear. His *unflinching* ear.

Now understand, I don't pretend to any great detective work. It takes only a student of the particular to know. The merest gesture— two gestures, in fact: hers and, in the next instant, the way Ian holds my eye then goes away into his drink.

6

Grimmest of all is the plain squandering way she anointed him. And the ease, the yawning entitlement by which he received it! (This same entitlement convicts him. He showed no more awareness of her touch than would have a husband of twenty years.) Do I misremember, or did she not permit her hand a lingering moment on his arm?

O Christ.

I kick away the covers and sit up. The room is black and hot. Still the register hisses away. It is immune to temperature. The only relief is by the curtains. I push them aside to bathe in the wide coolness of the glass. The parking lot is green and spectral. There is a presence about it, the shade of castoff places. I know this spirit. It is the same one that occupies vacant lots and last bus stops. God, the sorrow of these threshold places where the scenery runs out, these gloaming margins where concrete turns to weeds.

A red gemstone gleam comes to life on the horizon. On-off, on-off, on-off it goes. The spirit is out of the bottle and now afflicts everything. How clearly I see the gemstone's source: a pinnacled tower, silver-boned under prairie moon. Blipping away from its remote planet sector, far-off mythical Nebraska, some way station for the melodies and bulletins and gregarious voices of our time and times before, a short history of confidence and merriment packed off for tenantless space.

And what a miracle of engineering this window unit is! On and on it goes! A perpetual machine! Whirring and knocking and pumping its mustard gas into the darkness . . .

When I was little and had come to my limit I would cry out for her and this was terrible because it gave final form to the dread.

Mom . . . !

The cry was the last straw. Its smallness pointed up the grotesque scale of things. The exploding sphere of the house and at bottom this fearful shrunken thing, a macabre little homunculus rigid upon his matchbox bed. Then it was a bad time waiting for her. All around and very high above was an illustrator's darkness. Yes: always it was brambly and crosshatched, a Victorian nightmare. By its jumping patterns, a kind of violent flashing of running black fabric, I knew it was exploding. This while I went scuttling toward the vanishing point. My hands were shriveled at my side. They were miniature claws and I would not look at them. Where was she! Never sooner than the nick of time—

Mom, I hear a booming in my ears. And she would wait, listening. There's no booming, darling. But there was no question of uncovering my head. Would you like me to sing to you? Yes. Sing me a song. "America the Beautiful," "Hush, Little Darling," "Day's Done."

It is bad. Even standing vigil the scene has changed. Out there is an uncanny atmosphere of the fabricated. Except for this glass partition, I might easily reach into the winter "landscape" and pluck out the red Christmas bulb blinking in the diorama wall. So was it one summer inside the natural history museum in Ottawa, where I stood riveted before a tableau of felt cattails and plastic lake ice, a wired string of geese rising into a painted V, and marveling at a curious awareness: the first I'd ever felt my young skin crawl. Now it is everywhere, this burden of verisimilitude. I myself am become but a unit of the terrible simulacrum, another among legions of puny figurines in the vast synthetic exhibit. Behold, ye tour groups of the future! Thus was it so for Third Millennium Man. Such was the poor, primitive state in which he lived and worked.

The bulb pulses.

Oh, it is bad. Very nearly the worst. Around the corner of the eye, sensed rather than seen, some rough beast is tramping down the ferns. I take a step closer to the window, never taking eyes from it. Do what you will. I have my escape.

And yet after some time there emerges the remarkable discovery that all is not lost. Even in the midst of the falseness and your manufactured grandiosity, there is a worm of hope.

Hatred.

Only with hatred am I able to return to the bed, there to lie and bask in fury. A great deal gets said on the side of love, but with the room coming down and your mother vanished and your father on his way and your sister as good as gone, and your latest diversion, your grand alleluia production of workplace amour, revealed as one more in a pitiable line of self-shams—in all of this love is not much use. It is too milquetoast a thing, forever being snatched away. But hatred, hatred perseveres. With hatred you are never truly bereft. It is a good bright hot principle, comfortably portable in the furnace of the heart. Even this mother of all palls must respect it. Yes, the worm is turning. The drone of the window unit falters. The beast is spooked and sent scampering into the underbrush. In the silence it is possible again to think.

HYPOTHESIS: There are no

The cursor waits, flashing at attention. The blaze of the monitor is fitting, fine and white.

facts, only interpretations.

Can I really mean this? No. The facts of the matter are clear. I strike the line and type instead:

You can be too cautious.

More to the point. It is all well and good to lead your life modestly, reconciled to your minor plot, forever on guard against grander narratives. But it can also hem you in. When the real thing arrives, you must be awake to it. Not to be

is to sacrifice worthy action on the altar of modesty.

God, that's the stuff. Now the words come flowing:

Once upon a time, worthy actions were the coin of the realm.
A person decided where he stood, and crossed swords with
anyone who aimed to move him. Once it was possible to
mark lines in the sand, not grandiosely or histrionically

("Historically," prompts the spell-checker, so that in the recorrecting I experience some diminishment of purpose . . . but hatred sees me through.)

> histrionically but with the simple aim of preserving what's right. Now to speak of what's "right," one must be six smirking planets removed. What disaster.

> But I am not fooled. You can be too careful. When crossed, either you curl up and go on your whimpering way, or

Or what?

Ah, for ancient possibilities, the old heroic phraseology, when men moved and spoke in unchecked purpose, and when impugned knew exactly how to restore themselves to the world.

Curl up and go on your whimpering way—or cry havoc, and let slip the dogs of war.

7

An expansive, smartingly bright window. Keith and Jane sit before it. They are constituent shapes in a dark mass. Owing to the dusk of the conference room (the lights have been dimmed for our presentation) and because I am directly opposite them, I cannot see their faces. Only Jane's hands are individuated from the mass. They are clasped starchily atop a notepad at the table's edge. From time to time one thumb will move to soothe the other.

An expectant silence has grown up around the table. I pop to: What was the question? Aho-ho! The room's laughter is forgiving, if a tad uneasy. Fine.

"I was just wondering if anything in your product can help with a DoS attack. We got hit about six months ago, order fulfillment on its knees for I don't know how long. Steve, what was it? Better than twelve hours? So you can imagine—"

"No."

"No" is verboten, of course. Never is the negative to be struck. It rings too loudly, echoes too long in the buyer's ear. Much better to read again into the record the product's catalogue of distinguished capabilities and only by some graceful elision convey the missing feature. A cramp of disappointment takes hold of the questioner's face. I am to understand a sore lacking in the Cyber product has just been uncovered.

Keith wades in.

"We might expand on that. A denial of service happens at the network level. What we're helping to seal off are problems in the application layer. Isn't that about the sum of it, Henry?" He is pointed, but not yet so pointed that he wants the customer to see it. I am still entitled to some liberties.

"Bingo."

Another helping of silence. Jane is quick into the breach.

"If you look at almost every survey out there you'll find that the number one security risk, bar none, is the application layer. Everyone spent years hardening the network, building up the castle walls. But now with applications we've opened all the windows!"

What a lovely pair they are.

Yesterday Gretchen read to me a think piece from the Sunday newspaper. It seems the writer, a well-regarded clinician, had set out to interrogate the old saw about time and wounds. His discovery centered on the idea that it was not "time qua time" that helped, but rather what a person did in the interval. Hearing this, I experienced the usual depression. How irksome that "qua" was. But more it was this maxim parsing, the guru's dialectical showmanship, which must always trump up some dunderheaded misinterpretation and then with wooden epiphanic flourish sweep it aside . . . I felt a hot pressure behind my eyes, my poor dear grief-struck sister with her diligent psychologism. Gather ye advice columns while ye may. I did not mention that it seemed as possible the opposite was true, that time was an accelerant for suffering, the wound beggared by the infection.

Ian is antsy. It shows in a choreography of veiled gestures, a recurrent fit of ear pulling and neck scratching: he might be an

obsessive-compulsive staving off the fantods. Only gradually do I recognize their purpose. These are batting signals. He means to direct
my engagement in a side discussion occurring on my left. It is something to do with Nexus's enterprise architecture, and the debatable fit
of Cyber therein. The sky is in the window. Today the clouds overlap
one another with space between. I perceive a gentle contest among
their ambling layers, the vying of carousel horses. ". . . pretty standard
three-tier architecture . . ." ". . . not agentless, so performance-
wise . . . ?" I gaze at the clouds and think of space travel.

Soon the room is called to order.

"Gang, these are important questions. Let's keep it to one conversation." The speaker is a woman of early middle age. She is healthily
fat, with good clear skin drawn taut over her broad face and forehead.
The tautness pulls at her eyes and gives her a shrewd, squinting
look. This is Keith's counterpart, the one he turned to when the
storm threatened our appointed meeting. Having granted him this
special audience, she has more than the usual advantage. Yet she is a
good negotiator who knows her leverage and holds it in reserve. With
her deft pen strokes and appraising eye, there is about her a serenity
of purpose. It happens her canniness suits my scheme. "Scheme" is
too strong a word. In the first instance, the idea occurred to me only
a few minutes ago. Also there is very little to it. Where a businessman
like Keith is concerned, there's not much in the way of worthy action
that can wound him. He takes what he wants when he wants, and who
are you to stop him.

But what about worthy *inaction*?

Our host is speaking. Nexus suffers from mismatched technologies.
Many of their purchased programs refuse to speak to others without
a translator; they are tired of paying for translators. "So one of the big
things we need to align on is how your product drops into the stack,
and what it'll mean for other technologies we use, now and in the
future." She runs an ample hand around her ear, clearing some dark
fallen strands. The little unveiling gesture achieves also a kind of en-
joinment: I am to speak candidly and clearly. "You understand this of
course."

"We're committed to supporting the widest possible range of en-

vironments." The voice is automatonic, faithful to its programming instructions.

"Ah yes," comes the reply. If she is impatient, it shows only in the
vigor by which she executes a scribble in the margin of her notepad.
"I've read the brochure. What I'm looking for is a little more color on
the subject. We've got a camp here"—she acknowledges the discus-
sants on my left—"who're convinced open source is the way to go. And
let me tell you, they're pretty darn persuasive."

I say nothing. Keith's shadow shifts impatiently, although it is Jane
who speaks first. "Oh, but with a company this size, I mean open
source . . ."

Our host brings her gaze to bear.

"Forgive me," she says evenly. "'A company this size'? Explain the
relevance." My heart goes out to Jane, unfailingly and despite everything. Sweet Jane, who in this matter is out of her depth and whose
natural charms here clonk like sparrows against pane glass. If there
were a way to rescue her while still shoving Keith into the briny
deep . . . But there is not.

Now His Lordship does speak. "It's a matter of accountability and
trust." (An ironic tingle goes up the back of my neck.) "With your market presence, the size of systems you're standing up, many of them
revenue generators, you need a reliable partner. One throat to choke
if anything goes wrong. It's different for smaller operations. There's
less on the line, they maybe can afford to roll the dice on communal
software." As he speaks I am reminded all over again how formidable
he is, how unlikely to be thwarted. Words are pawns. It is *communal*
software, not open source: the very adjective smells of tepee utopias
and shared toilets. ". . . exercise caution in trusting the shop to an
anonymous bunch programming in their spare time. Henry, anything
you'd add? You've studied this as much as anyone."

"No."

The presentation continues. Ian is explaining something about
something. His slide colors are mesmerizing. Moneyed grays and
greens, blues sharp against the white backdrop. I imagine glades of
ferns, open shocks of sky and sun encountered in a piney wood. Along
the bottom of the windowpanes where the ground is met, a thick

band of snow presses the glass. An exhibit, in neat cross section, of the strata of winter days and nights. But I don't see their folds and crumpled striations. Oh no: I see wet cotton sheets in a washer's porthole window. What relief it is to steal off into metaphor! Everything is like something else, when you're lucky. The commonplace can have a terrible weight, but at times it may be pried up, turned, enough that symmetry, even beauty, seeps into the depression. Take the old drabness and say it plainly and you make it bearable. But not her death. It is like nothing else and never greater than itself.

More questions, half heard and half replied to. Even when I agree, absently, that a design pattern like model-view-controller has seen its day, and their chief architect drops his hands with a slap and says it would be great, *great*, if they could hear something they didn't already know—even then I do not mind so much. No, I am at peace. Here at long last is the role I was born to. The inert machine. Plenty of computing power but, as the last few days have proved, no real awareness.

Presently our host lets fall upon me her shrewdest of looks. It is startlingly knowing, this look. Perhaps we really are in cahoots. What would I do, she wonders, were I in her shoes: stuck with a pile of technologies that do not play well together, and offered yet another solution (this she brackets with a tired flexion of fingers) whose vendor promises it won't add to the problem? The question is cynical, perhaps, but not entirely rhetorical. I consider my answer. The rest of the table, Cyber and Nexus alike, seem to lean forward. Keith himself emerges from darkness, into the cast-down yellowness of the lights overhead.

"Everything would depend on whether I trusted the people selling it," say I, shuffling folders into my bag. "You're buying them as much as anything."

Keith and I peer at each other across the table. Now the storm is in his eyes—ho-ho! How satisfying is his raging bafflement. I would stay and watch, but the wall clock says it is time to go.

Our host opens her mouth to reply, then switches course: "Are you leaving us?"

"Henry has a plane to catch." Having seized the truth, Keith would be rid of me as quickly as possible.

Blinks and frowns on all sides. I make for the door. Ian holds a thumb to lip, fascinated. His manner in the past hour has been as urgent, as respectful, as a majordomo's. But now he has forgotten himself and watches the proceedings with an emotion I can't guess. The thumb presses, lip going white. Beyond a doubt something is being suppressed. Is it outrage? An apology? A gassy lunch?

Is it laughter?

Impossible to say.

Gretchen is as good as her word. There is no liturgy, only hugs that last a beat or two longer than is customary, and the unfillable gap in the welcoming circle at the door. For his part, my father appears to soldier on with perfect awareness. At the table he raises a glass. He even stands. There is something defiant in his bearing. I can't look at him.

"To Margaret McCord Hurt, who lived all the days of her life . . ."

He makes it through; he is not tripped up. The words keep steady pace, remaining just ahead of their meaning. Only once ("and here her children") do sound and sense get their feet tangled, and he must pick himself up and begin again. The meal goes down with scarcely any taste.

But even in the dark sleeping house her spirit is nowhere to be found. Drifting off, I cannot be sure whether it is triumph or defeat. Perhaps recovery is not a far green shore gained by painstaking navigation. Perhaps it is only the shallows where, with true north lost and compass spinning, you one day scrape to rest.

Eight

"The important thing is that we walk away just a bit smarter." The precise degree smarter is measured between thumb and finger. "Mistakes—I'm using 'mistakes' as shorthand, I don't pretend to know the particulars—mistakes only remain so if we take nothing away from them. I can still remember the very first week of my very first job, answering my desk phone with a plain 'Hello?' and the caller—my boss's secretary—telling me it wasn't a home line, that in the office we answered phones by identifying ourselves. All right. Lesson learned. It wasn't in the manual, and so that little fumble became my first—and my first step toward full professionalism."

Keith stands at the window behind his desk, arms crossed. His face betrays nothing but cold fury. This is hardly the opening he would have chosen. But the speaker, settled comfortably at the desk, continues.

"My point is we build up these things, mistake and correction, all our professional lives. You think at my level you stop making mistakes? Ah, if only. But business is like life: there are only a handful of truly fatal blunders. You avoid those, you make sure correction always follows, well . . ."

Thomas M. Burges—Tom—is the president of our division. He is in from Dallas for the day. I know him only from the annual divisional meeting, a chief figure thundering over the dais floor to warm applause. Up close he is not quite so vigorous-seeming. His hair is of the same silvery material they stitch into the heads of CEOs, only too often now it falls from its brushed placements and into his eyes. When this happens he reminds me of leading men in old films whose scenes call for them to look sleepless or haunted. He has a leading man's easy good looks: trimly assembled, neck fastened to jaw with nary a sag in the fitting. Yet his eyelids are heavy. They have commenced their curtain fall, quitting on the labor of appearances even if the rest of him has not, quite.

I cannot be sure why the president of the division is addressing me this morning instead of Keith alone, although I have my theory. It isn't owing to any great grandiosity of crime, nor any real interest in the perpetrator. No, it happens that Tom is in the office today for reasons of close of quarter, and doubtless in the course of their conversation about likely final figures and the rationale for our failure—Nexus has decided against purchase—Keith explained what happened. Though Keith is not one for excuses. It may be that he spoke out of anger, or even pain (a prospect that doesn't fill me with half as much satisfaction as it did forty-eight hours ago—indeed I feel a little sick in the stomach). Whatever the reason, I do not think Keith bargained on our president's compulsion to give lessons.

So here we sit.

". . . That's not to say there aren't consequences. There are consequences. Exactly what, I leave to this guy." It is his first acknowledgment of Keith's presence (although in point of fact Keith's is the realer presence—it's Tom's I keep forgetting). "But now listen. You've heard the expression about what doesn't kill you making you stronger? Unless I'm severely mistaken, we're not talking the death penalty here. So the opportunity for you—big cliché euphemism, opportunity, I know, but I'm serious—the opportunity for you is to come away from this a better, stronger, more invested professional. I can't tell you how. But believe me when I say the opportunity is there. It'll be staring you square in the eye. Does that make sense?"

I am not at all sure that it does, but delivering these words he half turns to Keith, inviting his agreement. Keith doesn't budge. Their expressions make for interesting juxtaposition. Tom's is patient and seeking (if also habitual and a bit vacant); Keith is full of dead dark calm. He stands above and to the right, behind his superior and allied in body but nothing else. I am reminded of a certain kind of Japanese puppet theater, shrouded human forms working murkily at the backdrop, gestures shackled but utterly removed from the carryings-on of their wooden confederates.

I have a clearer idea of Tom's aim. An impulse to lesson giving is only the half of it. Already I am being converted into speaker's notes for a future keynote address.

```
Recently I spoke with a bright young man,
good at his job, but someone who'd recently
made what we call in the industry a CLM—a
career-limiting move. [pause for laughter]
This young man said to me an interesting
thing. "Tom," he said, "I don't really see
how I can recover from this." I told him
So I listened, heard him out. And when
he was finished, I said: "Look, one dumb
bad decision does not a career make. What
matters most now . . ."
```

It occurs to me that our president is a recognizable business type. He is one of those who have realized late that their gifts are too great for a single job to contain. I do not mean the sour dilettante who must condescend to a punch clock, hating every minute of it. The people I mean are executives: they have loved their jobs, excelled in their jobs, but having summited the org chart, they are left with the dizzy sense that real achievement is twelve planes up. Not that they are cowed by the view. On the contrary, these overlooks renew their far-seeing powers. They become as romantic and philosophical as old generals. On the formidable desks of their studies will appear pages of careful longhand: op-eds for the paper of record, or half an opening chapter in a study of the Napoleonic Wars, or the first lines of poems. Or they become builders of systems. They develop a love for textbooks and diagrams. It is nostalgia for studenthood, I think. Full of happy memories of their own promise, they reassume the habits of study. Later they emerge from their libraries, their garrets, waving schematics of such intricacy to account for everything under the sun—fantastic blueprint cathedrals that frame the career objectives of Man, complete with intersections to Maslow, Friedman, Drucker, Churchill, Welch, Kroc, Aurelius, Iacocca, Eisenhower, Buffett, Rand, Schwarzkopf, Branson, Feynman, Jobs, Solomon . . . However. I am sorry to report their capacity is only really for building systems around the facile or self-evident. Once years ago as part of a Cyber mentorship program, a retired company vice president drew for me a series of inverted, interlocking pyramids with annotated bands running across them, whose moral I at last gleaned to be: When Speaking to Your Superiors, Pay Attention to Body Language.

Tom is speaking again. He gives a shake of his handsome head. One hand is pressed humbly over the knot of his tie. The words I do not quite catch but the signs I know: I have used them myself. How bonded and hearty he seems! Only when I glimpse Keith above his shoulder is the effect ruined. Beneath that gaze the rest is just so much ceremonial benevolence. My old affections for him come racing back. And just as swiftly: the terror of what's at hand.

Good God. What have I done.

". . . anyway, all just one man's opinion. Henry? I've taken up enough of your morning." Tom stands, taking my hand in his good grip. After a briefly awkward moment it becomes apparent that he isn't going anywhere. He leaves it to us to move along.

Immediately outside the door, Keith turns. "You owe me a Why."

A cold drop descends from my armpit and goes running over my ribs on fly's legs.

"I made a mistake."

He explodes. "Bullshit! Passive bullshit! Have the guts to own it!" We are on the open floor: heads turn. Keith lowers his voice, but the violence remains. "You *sunk* us. And I want to know why. I spent the last two nights trying to figure out which of our competitors had turned you. Christ, I thought. What a bold money grab! Never in a million years thought you had it in you." He fixes me with an eye. "I still don't."

"No."

(It depresses me that the only reasonable explanation for my grand gesture is corporate skulduggery. And yet would that it were so. Better a rational traitor than this lunatic adventuring.)

"Then what? I'm at a loss here." He is not beseeching, yet I see how deeply I have wounded him. This is my victory.

"It's . . . hard to explain. I'm not sure I can explain it at all."

This is very nearly the complete truth. It speaks to a bafflement that is real enough.

Keith draws in deeply by his nostrils. "You can't explain it." He sets off down the floor, leaving me to follow. "Of course you can't! And why would you? You just got up on the wrong side of the bed, looked around, and said to yourself, Know what? Today is a good day to torpedo everything I've ever worked for. Makes perfect sense."

The complete truth, I fear, is this: there was never any affair.

Only this morning, returned to this practical place where I have spent all of my adult life, did the facts and interpretations begin to separate. It is as dull a truth as this: an affair would not make business sense. An affair would only throw open the door to contingency, a thing he abhors above all else. Keith is no great moralist, I make no claims for him, yet whatever his manipulations they have but one aim: to fatten the bottom line. In this he is as pure and single-minded as a monk. (Can the same be said of Ian? I am not so sure.)

"I was under the impression . . ." But the whole truth is too humiliating for words. If there was no affair, I must face it fully. What I can't face is my craving to believe there was. On the slimmest of evidence—on no evidence, in fact, but damned hearsay and my own imagination—I cast my mentor as the villain and Jane as the office whore.

Why?

". . . I was under strain. Not myself."

He does not look back. There is only the oblique line of his jaw, the angry coloring on his neck. "Temporary insanity. This is your plea."

We roam among desks and modular dividers, and spines bent to monitors. Not a single set of eyes marks our passage. The herd knows the cull animal.

"Fine." He is nodding at some aptness not apparent to me. "Great. You just hang on to it. I won't beg. It'll be one of life's little mysteries!" (In his mouth, this yielding to the unexplained is pure farce. Never was a turn of phrase less at home.) "I'll give you this, Henry. You know how to pull a guy's heart out. We were *this* close." He clucks his tongue, a terrible shaming sound. "Jesus, Jesus, Jesus . . ." But there is oddly little heat in this. Already his rage is washing into a kind of stoic objectivism. The present catastrophe will be past soon enough; what beckons is the future. "So that's that. Welp. Life's a bitch, then you die." He appears to take shelter in this long view.

"Keith: let me ask you something."

"Sure. Anything. Just you name it, guy." His acidity does not put me off my idea.

"It's twelve working days to quarter's end."

"You don't say."

"Is there a chance there's still time?"

"To find another lead, pitch them, and close them? No."

"But if I were to go back. To Nexus. Like Markitel. I could apologize personally, explain that I was under strain. They're not going to throw me out; they've already said no. Thirty minutes with their architects . . ." He is not the only one who can look to the future. And it is a good plan, I am sure of it. Even if I see it for what it is: the old lure of the liminal, past mistake transfigured by Prodigal hues, that sentimental American alchemy whose base metal is personal disgrace.

"'Under strain.'" Keith rolls the phrase around, savoring its play-acting echo. He stops, taking hold of a nearby divider wall as if for strength. "I don't know whether to laugh or cry. I mean that. Hand on heart."

We have reached an abandoned corner of the floor. The nearest desks are cluttered with ancient components. Pink tags affixed to the backs of chairs show the coordinates of their new intraoffice homes. Keith wanders inside one of the larger cubicles. A column of hard drives, memories degaussed, wait in blind-cut sunlight for the scrap heap. He strikes one with the flat of his hand, marking a pale, swash-like flourish in its fine powdering of dust.

"What goes on inside that head of yours? Honestly, I thought I knew. You seemed to me one of the cooler customers I'd encountered. I said to myself: Now here is one of my kind. Shows what I know. Two days ago you clam up in the most important meeting of your career, leaving the rest of us looking like idiots; this morning you're ready to fall on your sword." He shakes his head, parodying his own shell shock. "It's the craziest thing I've ever seen. You know who you remind me of? Barry. Same manic seesawing. This plan of yours—having ruined us, now he shall save us! Is that it?"

I am shamed into silence.

"What you're suggesting is insane. Markitel was just us smoothing out the ego of some asshole who got his feelings hurt over nothing. Nexus: you *shit* in their *laps*. That woman pulled her whole team to-gether after a major storm out of not much more than professional courtesy, which she was good enough to grant after I begged. And in the face of that courtesy? With our chances hanging by a thread?" He covers the space between us in three strides. I steel myself against the cubicle's half wall. "You. Shit. In. Their. Laps."

Noting his own looming closeness, the schoolyard menace of it, Keith stands down. He repairs to the desk behind him. There he props an elbow on the stacked drives, scrubbing his forehead wearily.

"Listen to me. It's a hopeless situation, but this is important. What-ever got into your head in the last seventy-two hours—I hope it's only that recent; it scares the hell out of me that I can't tell—whatever that grand scheme: ignore it, get rid of it, burn it out. If I haven't begged you to tell me your reasons, it's as a favor to *you*. Your reasons, I use the word loosely, aren't important. They're figments—and the last thing I'm going to do is credit someone's private little dramas. But you show up this morning with *another* fevered dream, us going rid-ing back down to Kansas City to save the world, and suddenly I'm not half as much angry as worried. It's just craziness piled on craziness." He presses his eyes with the heels of his palms. It is an effective way of making his point. I would give anything not to be a party to this despair.

"See, early in my career I learned something about people. People need a warp and woof for their lives. That's not what I learned; that much everyone knows. What I learned is how gladly, with what *relief*, they'll accept the boss's instructions as reason for their place on earth. *Oh, how terrible! What a cynical way to* et cetera, et cetera. My answer to that is Grow up. It's a big cold universe. People want a reason to get out bed—at least until the first mortgage payment. Then they do their own convincing. The only people who think it's sinister are the ones who live in a medieval fantasy. Because in medieval fantasy there's always some True Grail that needs questing after, and woe be upon anything that stands in the way." His mouth hitches in a kind of scornful moue. "Jesus, I remember my years as a first-line manager. When you oversee a bunch of twenty-somethings you get, every year, without fail, one savior or another coming in to tender his resignation. It's always the same audition. They close the door, flop down into the chair, rub their faces, 'Keith, listen. I've been thinking . . .' The earnestness of these people is enough to make your eyes water. And never, never were they leaving for a better role or more money. Oh no. Too mercenary, too boring. No, it was because they were needed for some world-historic undertaking: an internship on the Hill, curing malaria, film school . . . That's when I knew they were goners. They'd gotten themselves tanked up on Destiny, and that was that. Listening to those questers was some of the purest comedy of my life. There was no use saying anything. I just waited for them to finish, then took their badges."

There is nothing at all funny that I can see, but now his expression turns in an opaque little smile.

"Actually, I do wish I'd given them some advice. I wish I'd said, Look, friend, no matter what you do, the sands of Jupiter are going to keep right on blowing . . ." The smile moves on. Pressing his fists to the desktop, Keith powers himself upright. I understand we are at an end.

"In the spirit of showing you how little your grand designs matter, you should know we're going to meet our quarterly numbers just fine."

He is distracted by a smudge on the underside of his sleeve. I cannot locate the joke.

"How do you mean?"

"Four million was the reach target." Keith has turned his elbow over and is brushing at the smudge. "That's all I ever want Sales worrying about: the reach. As far as they're concerned, as far as *everyone* is concerned, that's the goal come hell or high water." Now he licks a thumb and rubs the fabric in more concentrated fashion. Satisfied the mark is not permanent, he inspects his other sleeve. As I watch him, it occurs to me he is somewhat bored having to explain it. "But I didn't stand up in front of the powers that be and swear to the reach. Heck no. When I step into the room and put my hand on that Bible, it's for a figure I'm ninety-nine point nine percent sure I can deliver. So I explained we were coming out of the holidays, first quarter is always soft, et cetera."

"What was the real number?" I am feeling at sea in my innocence.

"Two point nine."

It takes a moment to rerun the figures. "Houston . . ."

"Houston, Billico. Everything after was gravy. Don't think that excuses anything. Not on your life. If we'd gotten to four-plus, I might've leapfrogged ole Tom there by next quarter. That kind of performance has a way of standing out. As it is, it'll take at least the rest of the year to bury that carcass. And I meant what I said: when I jump, everyone's coming with me. Almost everyone. Did you give even two seconds' thought to what you might have done? What if four had been the real number? You think I was joking about the business unit being at risk? I was not. I don't joke about people's livelihood." His anger has returned. "So help me—if we'd cratered I would have sent you to the desk of every man and woman in the company to personally explain why they were out of a job."

It is true, and I am sickened to admit it, that in the grip of my adventure the wider damages were entirely forgotten.

"I'm sorry."

"You're sorry?"

"I am. Please let me keep my job. Demote me, dock my pay, but don't take away my job. I agree with you, destiny is a story for children. I agree with everything you've said. But destiny or no, this building is where I belong. You weren't wrong about me. It may be you know me better than I know myself. I can prove it to you again—" In the emotion of it I nearly say *if it takes me the rest of my career,* so sealing my fate as a caricature, but Keith saves me from myself.

"Nope."

His tone is not unkind. He approaches again, this time to take my shoulder in avuncular fashion. I am steered back onto the open floor. We continue our stroll.

"In fact, where this town is concerned, think of it as a salted well." A sighing, ruminative quality has come into his voice. "You want another job in the South, look west. Mississippi, Louisiana—I don't know many people in those places. But there's not a tech outfit within three hundred miles of this city that will touch you. You have my word on it."

He makes this pledge just as we are coming upon my own quadrant of floor. The team is hushed and circumspect, eyes locked to screens. With their busy snicking keystrokes, they devise for themselves a kind of audible mark of passover. Only Cory and Rahim brave death. As we pass their desks, Cory stands and steps into the aisle to grasp my hand, squeezing it firmly, wordlessly. Rahim is not quite so bold, but he does stand and nod to me as we pass, his face canted down and away, sidelong just enough to permit him deniability. I am having some trouble with my legs. It seems impossible this is the last I will ever see of this place, these people, this context. I cast a desperate eye in the direction of my office. My office! What will become of it? There arrives such a swell of proprietary tenderness that I am actually short of breath. In an instant my old workroom is metamorphosed into a place as storied and dear as an alma mater. Nothing must be touched. Its wastebasket and stapler, my air grid chair: these shall be as relics, the door permanently sealed. Dawdling, I explain to Keith that there are yet some personal effects . . . He jerks the leash—

"They'll be mailed."

We have come almost full circle. Here is the elevator bank, and just beyond: Ian and Jane in their adjacent work spaces. He is on the phone, a finger in his ear and eyes screwed shut. Pressing some point, nodding impatiently, now pressing again. I experience a pang of sympathy for the soul on the other end. Perhaps he or she is like me, eager to fashion an embellished refuge from plotless life, and with as little prudence for the meanness of the materials.

Jane is turned away from the floor. But the sun is on the window and her face is in the glass. She watches from among the city buildings. Inside that faded countenance stand two human forms in full, Keith's and my own. Her eyes, wary and disembodied, discover mine. There registers a fraction of uncertainty. What face to show? Sympathy? Regret? Disdain?

But no. This is ordinary social embarrassment. Our story is ended. With a small shake of her head, she reengages the papers on her desk.

At the elevator doors Keith holds out a hand. I do not mistake the gesture. Phone and parking badge, office key, and last my ID—these are dispensed into his outstretched palm. When the car arrives, Keith actually leans in after me to press for the lobby. He is leaving nothing to chance. I hardly blame him.

The doors hold themselves in check, waiting for it, his last advice. "Get a hold of yourself."

APRIL

Elsewhere I've made the claim that American businesspeople are unrivaled as self-improvers. Even ejected from their ranks, one feels strongly the old duty to parse and document, to bootstrap oneself with the findings. So in the days after my firing I withdrew to my home office, computer at hand, hell-bent on enlightenment. The lessons, said I to myself. What are the lessons.

It was not purely successful. My first breakthrough was this: in solitaire, do not clear a spot unless you have a king waiting for it.

More to the point, I've come to face the fact that one craves adventures. Even a modest adventure will do. At a minimum, it must persuade you that your deeds count, that something is at stake. And if you attempt to starve yourself, for even the most pure-minded reasons of modesty, logic, the sheer absurdity of the manic urge to grand doings, it doesn't work. Eventually the brain will churn out a substitute from whatever's at hand. In the end, Keith's intuition was right. I'd gotten myself tanked up on notions of worthy action, and I handpicked the facts to light my way (a business in which I had some help). Try to steer an adventureless course, and even the most rational soul will conjure up dragons.

What eludes me is Why.

As it happens, my analysis was cut short. On April Fool's, my father was hospitalized. A frigid day, yet a neighbor discovered him wandering the street at three in the afternoon wearing only his pajamas. She took him at once to the emergency room, leaving word on our home answering machine for my poor sister to find on her return from work. The sole physical consequence of the episode is second-degree frostbite on the toes of both feet. A relative mercy since the cognitive problem pointed up is of a different order. Yet in the hospital he was lucid and only irritated by the spectacle. Upon seeing me, his face fell: Surely I hadn't come for this? Nonetheless it was decided I would come home for a time, my father persuaded by his bandages and wheelchair and the need for Gretchen to have help.

His immobility has also given us cover to disappear the car keys.

To tell the truth, I am not sure his dementia is any worse than was mine. I still cannot quite digest what has come to pass in my life. It is like voyaging through a dream and, informed by a dim sense of dream impunity, indulging in a certain lunatic behavior—only to find in the morning that the consequences have stuck. Here I am wide-awake and out of work.

A few days after coming home, I gave in to the last urge of my old life. I called Madison. You may recognize this as a grasping at straws. Yet even as I dialed her number, there was a tingle of foreordination: *So in this circuitous way it was meant to be all along* . . . Waiting for her to answer, I experienced a great surge in the blood. It was a kind of euphoria. That white shock of possibility that comes when trauma has leveled the old-growth forests of your life.

"Hello?"

It was a man's voice. I made a quick check of the number. There was no mistake. Stumbling, I asked for Madison. "She's out." The voice admitted not the slightest possibility of rivalry. He practically yawned. I saw him: sprawled on the couch among the art books, a handsome catalogue fellow in his old jeans, all flaring hip bones and blue-eyed Weltschmerz. He hung up before I could.

After a week at home I confessed my firing to Gretchen. This was also a mistake. She has gotten it into her head that my joblessness is the result of some kind of personal awakening, that at last I marched in and said To Hell With This Place, etc. I explained to her that it is precisely the opposite, that owing to a very foolish mistake I was justifiably terminated. However, this is all I choose to say on the matter. As a result she has assigned to me some sort of cowboy reticence. The more irritably I decline to talk, the greater my modesty and lionheartedness.

I take refuge in television whenever possible.

My father has good days and bad, as they say on my hospital dramas, though the equivalence is not quite right. No day has been as bad as the crisis that led to his current condition, and his good days are as good as ever. He is the man he always was, even mocking his "sleepwalking episode." Yet the blank spaces persist. Some mornings he is hungry, sharp, prickling with opinions. On others, he picks at his bandages and looks around like an amnesiac. Yesterday he asked if my mother was awake yet. Despite this, it has been something of a relief to disappear my own injury inside the family's. For one thing there is a nice immediacy to the situation. My sister and I tend our father in shifts, organized according to her week's work schedule. He is not bedridden, but he needs help changing his bandages and getting into and out of his bunk, and on and off the toilet. (A word on this last chore. The physical embarrassment is surprisingly modest. After the first few times it becomes routine. It is the temporal displacement, this strangeness of helping one's father go potty, that is no picnic.) Because I find myself waking early these days, often I will take up station in the wing chair opposite the living room sofa where he sleeps—his bed until he can manage stairs again. This to provide him a familiar face by which, with luck, to regain the world.

There is no telling what comes next. Without work I have no triangulation point for the future. I can only watch television, help with my father, and do my best not to lose patience with Gretchen.

Today is Good Friday and the networks are rerunning religiously themed episodes wherever possible. A young man has arrived in the emergency room after a mysterious rail-yard accident, suffering from wounds that look suspiciously like stigmata. Gradually a whisper campaign among the nurses confirms he is no ordinary patient: his roommate is healed of bleeding ulcers overnight; a nurse's migraine evaporates as she is swabbing the man's arm. The doctors have scoffed of course, although here in the present scene one has just noticed that while the man's other wounds are healing in record time, a gash in his side looks as fresh as the day he arrived. Indeed, it bleeds anew each time the doctor comes to check on him. The camera pulls away to show the befuddled MD standing in rays of white light coming through the bed curtain; then it is off to a commercial for life insurance. I watch from the breakfast table, the small television perched on the counter divide between the kitchen and family room. My father is snoring away in the living room. Gretchen is puttering at the sink. She leans across the divide and snaps off the television.

"Mind?"

"Not really."

We peer out our respective windows in silence—not uneasily, although I sense a reproach in her killing of the television. The afternoon before us is gray and still. Three slender icicles droop from the eave above my window. I make a mental note to knock them down before my father wakes from his nap. I do not want him fretting over the insulation.

Gretchen says, "I'll make coffee."

Together at the table we sip from timeworn mugs. Hers reads SOUTHDALE PET CLINIC. Mine shows a crossword puzzle. She screws up one eye and makes a sour face. "When do you guess the filter was last cleaned?"

"It's fine."

She is having none of it. Both mugs are swept from the table and dumped. She sets about purifying the machine. A smell of percolating vinegar fills the kitchen space and brings old worlds with it, the PAAS dye kits and food coloring and this ancient acetic scent, eggs dunked in their pigmented baths at this very table, and cooled and dried and hidden in the nooks and crannies of this very yard. How loaded with aesthetic genius the whole thing was. I never realized.

That delight of pouring into the chill outdoors, the mind's eye quickened by image ideas of the hot pastel bulbs: knowing the landscape was burning with them but not yet seeing—then the little flash! The footrace! Eureka! Here in a pouch of quack grass, there in a birch's fork. An irradiated alien stone.

The coffee is better. We slurp noisily against the silence. I fight down an urge to turn on the television.

"Well?" she says. To my ear there is a flatness of expectancy—*Wull*—that makes me prickly.

"Well what."

"Have you thought any more on what you're going to do next?"

"No."

"One idea I had is People Serving People. I know a board member there, and she mentioned they've got all kinds of needs on staff. Homelessness is a growth industry. Her words. Even if I just connected you two for a sort of informational interview . . ."

"No thanks."

A fresh block of suet hangs in its cage at the window but goes ignored by the birds. Where are they? The yard is still and the snow balding and the trees austerely lovely. But the vacuum of winter afternoon feels absolute.

"Can I ask why not?"

Yes. It is because I did not lose my job, a good well-paying job, to fill its place with grander doings, the assorted monkeyings with the arc of the moral universe or whatever the phrase, I have always liked the ring of it, I do not know what it means. It is because some irritant persists, is growing worse, and it won't be gotten at by my donning a pith helmet and galloping around as a light to the nations. No more adventures just now, thank you.

"No references."

"Oh, boo. I know this gal."

I say nothing. Gretchen plunks down her mug; a shine of liquid seesaws at the rim. "I'm sorry, but I'm going to say it. You're free! I know you felt that job suited you, but there's just so much more, H. Honestly. So here you are, having at last left that place, but instead of being alive to the possibilities—"

"Please stop."

"I will *not* stop. Instead of being excited about what comes next, you're lurking around the house in this silent-sufferer mode. What gives?"

"First, I didn't 'free myself' from anything. I was fired. Put out on my ass. And I didn't go with head held high: I practically begged for my job. I'm still sorry it didn't work. Second, they were right to do it. I hardly left Keith a choice . . ." I consider the yard.

"Tell me."

"It's too humiliating."

"So summarize."

Summarize. "I convinced myself something was wrong, and took it upon myself to right it." She waits, not ill-humoredly. To hell with it. "The facts of the matter seemed very clear to me . . ."

"Did it involve Jane, can I ask?"

"Yes, but let's leave it at that. I took the facts as I understood them and then—here you would've been proud—I did something about it. I acted! It was a terrific feeling, to be convinced you were onto the right thing and doing what needed doing. I doubt we're ever more alive. Only I was dead wrong. I could hardly have been more wrong. It was like deciding to shout from the rooftops at precisely the moment you should keep quiet." Touching it all again, even in the abstract, sends a disagreeable heat over my neck. "I rationally pieced together the most irrational plan imaginable. But I don't think even that's the worst of it. The worst of it is the way, despite rational appearances, I've been cooking up one adventure after another. The hero lurching from romance to office derring-do—"

Gretchen takes hold of my wrist. She has been smiling, tolerantly and in my favor, and now for some reason she is laughing. "Henry, damn it, I want you in my life again. Or I want to be in yours. However you want to put it. It's good that you're here. It's good we're all together, whatever the reasons. Besides, you have a knack for helping Dad . . ." She peers at me. "You had the same knack with Mom. I remember. The rest of us were a mess but there you were, insisting on staying nights with her."

I hide away behind the mug's ceramic rim. It is green. What kind of green. Forest green. And whitely chipped. A plastered roughness on the lip. God in heaven, don't let me sob.

"It was hell."

"But you did it. Every night. Pillow under your arm, taking up your post."

I would dearly love not to disabuse her, now of all times. But there is no other way. "More playacting."

"Oh? Could've fooled me."

"I fooled myself. There's no end to the crap you're capable of when you think your name's been called. In Mom's case, my part had something to do with the gallantry of the eldest son. The firstborn protecting the matriarch. Protecting . . . I believe I actually thought so. Do you remember our neighborhood walks, and always at the Oakdale corner—"

"The Petersens' Doberman?"

"I would jump out of my skin, then remember the fence, and go and shake a mighty superhero's fist at the dog, showing her what a defender she had. Age seven. Take the ridiculousness of that times a thousand. I was frightened past all understanding."

"We all were."

"*Of* her: I was frightened *of* her. Of this thing that was coming for her. Her illness had given it a purchase. I'm sure I resented her for it too. But I was petrified above all else. Also the sleeping arrangements were terrible. There was an iron bar in the hospital couch. It was like a knuckle on the spine."

There was more, I'm afraid. There was the snap of nitrile gloves. There was the miasma of urine and rubber and ammonia, the sterile bulwarking the septic, just. There was her pained murmur when the bedclothes were changed, the cotton swabs of Vaseline touched endlessly to the corners of her mouth, the blotting of her raging head. When it was time to bathe her properly, I waited outside the door. It did not help. The bath blanket was heavy and warm and went on first. Her top covers were slipped out from beneath it. A towel was laid under the smoothness of her skull. The nurse wrapped the washcloth around her hand so that my mother's discomfort would not be made worse by stray scraping corners. Her eyes were done first, the water clear, the nurse's hand moving from nose to cheek, as a tear would run. Then her face, her swollen face. They dabbed from the midline out, one side, then the other, rigidly formulaic motions, nearly stylized, Christ, vary it please, she is still alive, these are the rote mechanisms of a sacrament.

My sister has commenced a soothing motion, her hand on mine. It makes no difference. Always the towel goes under my mother's arm, and another by her hand. Her hand is lowered into the basin to soak while the arm is washed. The skin between her fingers is closely dried. Then her neck and chest and abdomen, with a towel to cover what the bath blanket doesn't. Her feet are lowered one at a time into the basin to soak while each leg is washed. They dry carefully between her toes and clean under the nails and scrub her heel with pumice stone. When the legs are done, she is turned onto her side. A towel goes over her back and buttocks and is tucked there and beneath her shoulder. Her back and buttocks are washed and rinsed and dried. Then, with fresh water, her genitals and rectum. If you could find the mind's eye, you would gouge it out. Always the nurse holds up the deadweight of my mother's thigh with a butcher's dispassion, drawing the cloth gently from front to back.

"I hated her nurses. I hated their able-bodiedness, their wide shoulders, their sort of quick credentialed hands. Sailing around the room with their vigorous maternal competence, and her just lying there like so much wreckage."

"Henry—"

"No, I'll tell you what it was. It was how they washed her. There was a valedictory quality to it. They were preparing the body."

Now there is pressure from her hand. "All right."

"The worst of it is, my being there was no good for her either. She could never drag or weep: she had to spend her strength being someone else. There was the torture of waking, irritable and nauseated, and having to revert to a type: the Good Sufferer. And me, delirious with fatigue, my back on fire: the Good Son. The morning she died—"

"Don't tell me. You weren't there, leave it at that."

There is a pause while we consider this. I am tempted to take her up on it.

But fearing she has given the wrong impression, my sister keeps the subject alive. "I'm sorry. I wasn't accusing. Really I wasn't. I hadn't even remembered until you mentioned that morning. It just popped out. Please don't think I've resented it."

"You should. I wasn't there on purpose. Or somewhat purposefully. No, entirely purposefully. The truth is that morning I took one look at her and knew. There was a— There was no more performance. There was only . . . slackness.

"Don't, Gretchen. Bear it for another minute or I won't be able to get this out. This is important. I—'fled' is the word. I fled the room. Oh, there was some pretext, and I did this grotesque cheery thing—*Be right back!*—and I went out and got lost in traffic. There was genuine derangement because for almost an hour I convinced myself I really did have some urgent errand, only I couldn't remember what it was. And then outside the hospital, I froze again. I waited."

"This is *terrible*—" She takes away her hand.

"When I finally came upstairs and found you and saw the sheet drawn, I fell into mourning the same as anyone. And I forgot all about it. It just was a very bad time and one I didn't want to relive and so I didn't, I buried it in all kinds of urgencies and adventures, and the memory sort of atrophied."

My sister is away in her own agony for a period of time and there is nothing to be done. Only gradually, curiosity gets the better of her tears. She eyes me, blinking measuredly.

" 'It'—what 'it'? You forgot you weren't there when she died?" Her lashes are damp and spiny. She is *starry-eyed*.

"No. I've never forgotten."

"You forgot where you went?"

"In the particulars, I suppose. But I remember I'd fled to the car."

She draws a sleeve across her nose. "What then?"

Only when she asks do I remember. The fright is like a sprung thing. It drops out of the dark branches and onto my head.

"I forgot I don't know what it means to be born to die."

Here an interesting thing happens. Gretchen dries up. She goes to the kitchen and rummages in a drawer, returning with a traveler's package of Kleenex; she tends her sinuses noisily. This sudden composure is a deep mystery. There is a summary quality to her gestures that could speak of relief, forgiveness, as easily as dismissal and disgust. On tenterhooks, I wait.

At last she says:

"Is that what these adventures are? A way of avoiding the question?"

"Yes."

She nods. The thought is as new to her as to me, we are discovering it together, but my sister seems altogether unsurprised. "Yes. I think I've been doing the same thing." She dabs her nose, then stores the tissue away in the cuff of her pullover. It is a large loose thing, a figure skater's green overshirt. "I never told you this. In the days after Mom died, I felt I was onto a secret power. Anything seemed possible. I'd seen the worst, you see. But in certain manic instances it seemed manageable; it hadn't killed me, not yet. And with that knowledge in my pocket there was nothing I couldn't go out and do. I had the world at an advantage. Everyone out there was carrying on as though everything was normal, and someday they would be badly surprised. But I knew, and it gave me secret strength." Huddled in the depths of her overshirt, she has a quality I have observed in the very elderly. Not frailty, quite. A kind of comprehending humility, a parsimoniousness of self. It is somehow encapsulated by the little tuft of tissue conserved at her sleeve. "Except there was also the opposite. The terror of it was so wide and deep that it was all I could do not to fall into raving fits, pulling down pictures and tearing at the wallpaper." She peers out the window, dry-eyed. "I think the strangest thing I did—one of the stranger things—was to start wearing one of her blouses to bed. I've stopped. The scent wore off. But for months I did that."

"That's not so strange."

"No?"

"I don't think so."

"Oh. You were sleeping in her blouses too."

"Certainly, yes, and—"

"Her skirt."

"And heels, and a dab of lipstick. It's also how I grocery shopped." Too much, too far, but among these hairpin paths of grief the urge to hilarity is sometimes king. Perhaps it is a kind of mania, though I am not so sure. Whatever the case, it is some time before either of us can breathe again. The moment we do, the lull is punctured by a truly ob-scene snore from the living room—and back over the edge we go.

At last:

"What else?"

My sister thinks for a moment. "She used to wear a kind of fade cream. Esotérica fade cream. It's the most god-awful-smelling stuff. When I was a bitchy little thirteen-year-old and she would come down to breakfast wearing it, I would pick up my cereal bowl and go and sit in the living room. A few months ago I found a small jar of it on a shelf in her closet. I have it in my bedside table now. Sometimes when I wake up and it isn't morning yet, I hold the jar to my nose. It's enough."

"What were you doing in her closet?"

"You know perfectly well."

"Yes." I was in there at Christmas. I wanted to have a look at her bedroom slippers. The terry cloth inside is worn to a dark shine. They seemed among the most unlikely things in the world.

A jay pounces on the suet cage. His coloring is a shock, here in the gray country. What with the outlandish crest and vestments of impe-rial blue, he is like a medieval clergyman come to skim the tithes. He stabs and draws, sampling, a little lip smacking of the beak. Oh, the taste is to his liking. But already my sister is on her feet. Jays are bullies. She stands eye to eye with him. The jay peers back, yielding nothing. At last she raps the glass and sends him leaping.

I wish there were some sun. A little sun on the pinewood, the ad-vent of spring, etc. Gretchen sits and peers onto the yard and its balding cover. More bits of the past come present. My sister on her fourth birthday, goggle-eyed before the cake (a chocolate hedgehog with slivered almond quills, our mother's genius) and incredulous at the effect of time: "I'm *four*?" Thumping her chest, looking to our mother for proof. "Deep down *inside*?" By and by my hand rediscovers hers. The ridges of her nails feel as purposeful, as message-bearing, as the grooves on a record. So this is continuance, I think. I am not speaking of eschatology but simple biology, our mother's DNA alive and well. I never knew what a comfort it is, this matter of bloodlines, the human family's stubborn persistence.

Our father is stirring in the living room. Soon it will be supper time. Another jay (the same?) swoops to the cage and sets it spinning. He holds on for dear life. This time my sister leaves him be, leaves her hand, warm in mine in the dour spring light, she herself and I myself.